2/11

W9-AOE-843

Larkspur Cove

**Center Point
Large Print**

Also by Lisa Wingate
and available from Center Point Large Print:

Word Gets Around
Beyond Summer

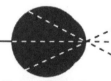

**This Large Print Book carries the
Seal of Approval of N.A.V.H.**

Larkspur
Cove

LISA WINGATE

CENTER POINT PUBLISHING
THORNDIKE, MAINE

This Center Point Large Print edition
is published in the year 2011 by arrangement with
Bethany House Publishers,
a division of Baker Publishing Group.

The text of this Large Print edition is unabridged.
In other aspects, this book may vary
from the original edition.
Printed in the United States of America
on permanent paper.
Set in 16-point Times New Roman type.

ISBN: 978-1-61173-002-9

Library of Congress Cataloging-in-Publication Data

Wingate, Lisa.
Larkspur Cove / Lisa Wingate.
p. cm.
ISBN 978-1-61173-002-9 (library binding : alk. paper)
1. Single mothers—Fiction. 2. Game wardens—Fiction. 3. Texas—Fiction.
   4. Large type books. I. Title.
PS3573.I53165L37 2011b
813′.54—dc22

2010046553

For Sydney and Ansley
And their awesome grandparents,
The Blues

Larkspur Cove

If you're lucky enough to be at the lake,
you're lucky enough.
—Welcome sign, Moses Lake

Chapter 1

Andrea Henderson

If you're lucky enough to be at the lake, you're lucky enough.

That motto is boldly emblazoned on signs at either end of the sleepy little shoreside burg of Moses Lake, Texas. The letters, carefully tinted with gold paint, shine in the sunlight like a heavenly promise.

Or a divine farce, depending on who you are.

If you're on your way to an appointment you can't afford to miss, and you find yourself lost on some back road, listening to the hiss of a tire going undeniably flat . . . well, then . . . proximity to water does not in any way alter your sense of misfortune. The only overriding feeling at a time like that, other than sheer terror, is an unhappy kinship with the road. A sense of being just like it—rutted, pitted, cracked, and scarred, wandering through the wilderness, headed in completely the wrong direction.

I'd always imagined, as I counted down the latter half of my thirties, that I'd be rolling through life like a family sedan on a superhighway—not in Moses Lake, certainly, but somewhere. It was a comfortable expectation. The problem is, however, that building a life is a little like planning a road trip. You travel mile by mile, each depending on the last. It's hard to end up where you planned to be when there are flaws in the map, and the more you look, the more you realize there have been gaps all along, and at this point you're hopelessly off course.

Now what? would be a logical question at such a time, but the problem with asking such questions—of God, or the universe, or whoever you believe might be listening—is that you already know the logical reply, and you're just voicing the query because you don't like your own answer. You want someone to tell you differently.

I pictured how I must have looked standing there on that middle-of-nowhere dirt road—an average brown-haired, brown-eyed woman in a new pantsuit and sensible shoes, shouting into the air, "Could this day possibly get any worse! Could this week, this year, this . . . *anything* possibly get any worse?"

Of course there *were* worse things than being stuck in the woods, thereby flubbing my first afternoon of field appointments. But considering my woeful lack of experience, I was fortunate to have gotten a counseling position at all, even if my duties did include driving the back roads to work with families who lived out in the sticks. It was a starting point, at least, and I couldn't afford to lose this job. One way or another, I had to get myself back on the road.

My cell phone let out a wobbly, in-and-out ring, and somehow I knew it wasn't one of the tow-truck drivers for whom I'd left messages with directions that included things like, *Turn by the forked tree, and go past the stinky hog farm with the fence made of contraband road signs, and keep going, keep going, keep going until you ford what looks like a bottomless mudhole, and at the top of the next hill, you'll see a blue car in the ditch on the right. . . .*

No telling whether those directions would lead anyone to me, but I had no choice but to leave them and to leave a message at my office, where no one had answered either. My cell phone was slowly losing battery strength atop a pile of CPS case files and maps, while tow-truck drivers everywhere took coffee breaks away from their phones. Thanks to my son, who at fourteen should have had no use for a cell phone car charger, I had no means of recharging my phone at the moment.

I could see the plan for the day rapidly disintegrating from *Attack first day of field work with passion, vigor, and determination,* to the old tried-and-true motto of the past year, *Get by somehow,* along with *Figure out how to change tire* (I'd seen this done on TV a time or two) or possibly *Hike to safety.*

Taking a hopeful breath, I tried to sound calm as I answered the phone, so as not to scare away whoever was on the other end.

My mother's static-laced voice sent a strange mixture of relief and queasy dread through me. Mom and Dad hadn't wanted me to take the counseling position, and this snafu in the woods would only help to prove their point. On the other hand, I was as good as rescued, and even having a parent lecture you at thirty-eight is better than being stranded in the middle of nowhere. "Mom? Mom, can you hear me? I need help."

She didn't answer. For a moment, I had the disheartening vision of my voice being lost between cell phone towers somewhere. Maybe I could hear my mother, but she couldn't hear me. Which also meant that all those calls to tow-truck drivers were a waste of what was left of the cell phone batteries. "Mom? I need help."

Mother was probably tired of those words, after a year in which so many of our interactions centered on my need for help. I couldn't blame her. *I* was tired of it. I was tired of myself, tired of not being self-sufficient, tired of this weird dynamic in which, after sixteen years of marriage, I was suddenly on my own again—destitute and back under my parents' thumb, living in their lake house. Hence, the job with Tazinski and Associates, which was at the low-paying end of the counseling spectrum but still a realistic means of rebuilding my life and supporting myself and my son. It was time to stop hanging on everyone else's apron strings, use the counseling degree I'd earned while my ex-husband was the vice-chancellor of a lovely Christian college in Houston, and make a life of my own.

"Andrea. Andrea?" Mother's voice crackled amid the static of a choppy connection. "Where . . . you? I . . . barely hear."

"Mom, you're not going to believe this, but I've got a flat. I need a wrecker. I'm out in the middle of no . . ."

"Andrea? I can't . . . ake out *one thing* you're saying. Pull to the top of a . . . and stop driving. . . . told you you'd have terrible reception out on the other side of the lake. What if your car breaks down, or you get . . . tuck in the mud? What then? It isn't safe . . . all kinds of riffraff live up there in the timber, and who knows . . . sort of people might be hanging around the public beaches. Honestly . . . drea! Most of those roads are so deserted, you could sit . . ."

"Wrrr-eck-er. I. Need. A. Wrrr-eck-er. Mom? Hello?" The line went dead, and when I tried to dial back, the phone just clicked, and clicked, and clicked, pinging towers in vain.

13

Thus, I had the answer to the hasty question I'd spit into the air moments before. What could be worse than having a flat tire in the middle of nowhere when you're supposed to be at an appointment?

Finding out that your cell calls aren't going through, and no wrecker is coming, and you really are all alone . . . and perhaps hearing the rumble of thunder somewhere in the distance on what had seemed to be a perfectly clear July afternoon.

"No, no, *no,*" I whispered, or perhaps by then I was begging. If a storm hit, the dirt road I was standing on would rapidly become a quagmire of chalky limestone-colored goo.

Shading my eyes, I looked up, but the narrow strip of sky visible above the thick canopy of live oaks seemed harmless enough. Just the gentle blue of central Texas summer. Not a cloud in sight.

The rumble grew, then waned, then grew again. A puff of breeze blew through, whipping a silty, white dust devil along the road. I turned my shoulder and squeezed my eyes shut, the force of the wind pushing dust through my clothing and into the pores of my skin. When the breeze died, the scent of dirt road and imminent storm remained, along with a faint noise I couldn't quite identify. Grit fell from my lashes as I blinked, straining toward the sound. A rumbling, but not the rise and fall of thunder.

A car. I heard a car.

Rescue! Oh, thank you! I moved closer to the road, but a hallelujah yell died on my lips as an old pickup, gray with spots of rust and a missing front fender, rattled into view amid the dust cloud. Squinting, I tried to make out the driver, but reflections on the dirty glass obscured the inside. The shadow of a pine tree, thick and murky, finally passed over the vehicle, yielding a fractional glimpse into the cab. The driver was tall, thin-shouldered, wearing a ball cap of some kind. He wasn't alone in the truck. Someone was in the passenger seat, the head rising just slightly above the dash. A child, perhaps. The idea was comforting, as if somehow the presence of a child indicated that I, too, would be safe.

On the other hand, my new career was all about the knowledge that children weren't always safe. I'd headed up here for a home visit with a woman who'd been reported to CPS by a summer-school bus driver who couldn't drop off the kids because a domestic dispute was ongoing in their front yard. Growing up, I'd heard the plethora of warnings about the riffraff living on the *other side* of the lake. There was no telling what kind of people resided in these hills, where patches of private land remained remote, surrounded by sprawling state park holdings and massive blocks of territory that had been timber tracts in days gone by.

Stepping back against my car, I held out an uncertain, one-handed stop sign, mentally weighing my options. I needed help, but I knew I was in a very vulnerable position. . . .

The truck drifted to the left, as if to go around me and pass by. Surely no one would simply drive on and leave a woman stranded alone on this remote road.

I moved forward a step, stuck my hand out farther.

Surely he'd stop.

"Hey!" I hollered. The truck was only a few feet away now, close enough that I could see a hand gripping the partially opened passenger window. A small hand. A child's hand, the fingers brown with dirt. "I need help!" I hollered above the engine's wheeze and chug. Something was squealing at an ear-piercing pitch, the sound bouncing off trees and cliffs. "I need help!"

As if in answer, a sudden gust of wind swirled up, caught the dust cloud rising behind the truck, whipped it in my direction. I threw my arm over my eyes, felt grains of sand and tiny bits of gravel pepper my cheeks.

Thunder rumbled somewhere nearby.

A dog barked and growled, the sound so close that I felt for the edge of my car, grabbed it and pulled myself back, prepared to climb in, if necessary. Squeezing my eyes open a pinch, I saw the dog, a pit bull with its ears flattened and teeth bared, poised to jump as the truck slowly circumvented my car. I watched in frozen fascination, the way voyeurs look into the eye of a tornado or ogle a traffic accident.

The truck cleared my vehicle, and behind the dog's frenetic barking, a tiny slice of movement snagged my attention. A little girl was watching me through the back window. She'd turned in her seat, climbed onto her knees, pressed a palm to the glass, her head tilted slightly to the side, as if she were curious about me, or confused by my presence on the road. Her dark hair floated in wispy, tangled curls around her face, her pale blue eyes regarding me with a concern that seemed out of place in the round orb of a child's face. She couldn't have been more than five, maybe six. Leaves were tangled in her hair, and her skin was brown from the sun, her cheeks a combination of pink sunburn and smudges of dirt.

She wasn't wearing a seatbelt. The mother in me protested, and the newly certified counselor made a mental note. It wasn't uncommon for people to skip the seatbelt while tooling around the lake on these back roads, but it wasn't legal, either.

The truck drifted to the shoulder ahead, the brakes squealing as it slowed. I caught a breath, relieved, and in the back of my mind, I turned over the seatbelt issue—looked at it from a few different angles. Was there a polite way to tell your rescuer that he needed to buckle up his little passenger? Judging by the stooped shoulders and shaggy strings of gray hair dripping from the edges of the ball cap, he was probably a grandfather who didn't know any better. Perhaps still living back-in-the-day when kids cavorted around car interiors unburdened by seatbelts, and the only safety restraint was a grown-up's hand shooting out at a sudden stop.

The truck rattled to a halt thirty feet past my car. I waited for it to shift into reverse and come back, but it only sat idling. The driver moved just enough to look in his rearview mirror as the dog ran to the tailgate to bark. The little girl continued eyeing me through the back window.

Walking to the center of the road, I motioned to my car. "Hey . . . hello? I have a flat tire. I . . ." In my head, a caution flag went up. This was not normal behavior. He was just watching me in the mirror. Something was wrong.

Overhead, a cloud blotted out the sun, and the wind caught the flat of my back, shoving like an invisible hand. Somewhere in the hills, thunder rumbled again, raising goose bumps on my arms and making me acutely aware of my desperate circumstances.

The dog clawed the tailgate, snarling and baring its teeth, its small, slanted eyes narrowing as if it were priming for attack. Inside the truck, the little girl turned her attention to the animal.

A child wasn't safe around a dog like that. That was the kind of dog that ended up on the news for mauling someone to death. What sort of a person kept a dog like that around a child?

I took a step backward, looking again at the driver. What was he doing? Why was he just watching me? Why would he stop but not get out?

Was he studying me, trying to decide if I would put up much of a fight?

*If you take your boat to the shallow waters,
you'd better know where the stumps are.*
—Anonymous
(Written on the wall of wisdom,
Waterbird Bait and Grocery)

Chapter 2

Mart McClendon

There was a summer storm popping up in the hills across the water—just a little thing, but if it kept coming this way, it'd drive the tourists off the water and put a damper on the day. One thing I'd learned in my short time here was that you couldn't predict the weather, or pretty much anything else. On Moses Lake, it was just about as likely the unexpected would show up as the expected. For folks who liked to plan, make schedules, and keep some form of electronic device strapped to the hip, Moses Lake was just a spot to pass by on a Sunday drive, maybe pull off at the scenic overlook above Eagle Eye Bridge and watch the weekenders tear up the water with their ski boats and pontoon rigs.

Those up for some adventure might cut off the highway near the dam, pick up a sandwich at the Waterbird Bait and Grocery, or rattle down through the trees and rent a cabin or book a canoe trip. Could be that half-day canoe trip or lakeside vacation wouldn't end up to be any more than a quiet, relaxing time-out from whatever they left behind. If they were lucky.

Moses Lake had a way of taking on a life of its own. You could ask twenty full-timers why that was, and you'd get twenty different answers— everything from Native American legends to ghost stories about the strange voice of the Wailing Woman coming off the cliffs at Eagle Eye. Some would say the lake was haunted by restless spirits from the farms and towns that were buried under twenty-five thousand acres of water when the Corps of Engineers seized the land in the fifties and built the dam. Others claimed it was the name—Moses Lake. Moses wandered in the wilderness for forty years before he found a resting-place, and even then he couldn't go in.

If I had to give an opinion, I'd say it's the water. There's something about water that attracts all sorts of folks and brings out impulses they didn't know they had.

There was never any telling, on any given day, who'd show up in Moses Lake and what would happen. After just under six months as game warden in the southern part of the county, I'd figured out that life in Moses Lake was as random as the weather. That must've been why, twenty-odd years ago, my folks didn't stay in the area any longer than they had to. Soon as my dad finished working construction on the hydro-electric plant, they'd loaded us four boys and beat it out of town. We'd ended up in southwest Texas, where you could figure on the weather, and the folks, and the rhythm of things. It was quiet down there in the Big Bend country—friendly, peaceful, and scenic, if you liked a long view and a big sky.

But for years all I could hear was the place that was special to me when I was a boy—Moses Lake—lapping at the shores of my mind and calling me home. When it came time for me to get out of the Big Bend country for good, I packed up my gear and headed for Moses Lake.

The place was just like I remembered it, which was exactly what I needed it to be. There wasn't a trace of what'd happened back in the Bend country. Here, there was just the water, the breeze shifting through live oaks, and the boats passing up and down the lake, leaving white-tipped trails that'd close up and go back to perfect inside of a minute. No sign that anything had passed by and disturbed the normal way of things. Moses Lake was a constant place, on the surface. But when I took the job as game warden, I should've known better than anybody that sometimes the surface is a pretty illusion. You can't always tell by looking, what might be brewing underneath.

If the undercurrents were a mystery in Moses

Lake, one constant was that old fishermen would be out in their johnboats before sunup and back at the Waterbird by the time the day turned too hot to fish. Today their favorite table was occupied by two of the regulars, Nester Grimland, who was all bones and skin and looked the part of a retired school-bus mechanic, and Burt Lacey, who'd been Nester's principal at tiny Moses Lake High until he quit education and took up full-time fishing.

"You think that's a doe or a loose calf?" Nester looked at me and pointed off the edge of the dock, a cup of Sheila's Waterbird coffee sloshing over his hand, soaking into his shirt cuff and the picnic table. Didn't matter, because the coffee was cold by then, the sleeve had fish guts on it, like usual, and the table was the same as everything else at the Waterbird Bait and Grocery—old and used to the weather.

Burt squinted through bottle-bottom glasses as thick and cloudy as something that'd been dredged up out of the lake. "Tough to tell from all the way across. It could be one of those emu birds again. Mart, you think that's a calf or emu over by the Big Boulders?" His leathery, sun-freckled mouth worked the end of that question like it had a nice aftertaste and he was ready for another bite.

"Or a doe," Nester added in, stroking the thick, gray moustache that gave him the look of an old

23

cowboy, fresh off the range. There wasn't really any need for me to answer the question. Nester and Burt could keep up their own conversation, like usual. They'd only brought me in because I'd happened to pull up to the dock to run into the Waterbird and get a refill on coffee.

"Reckon why a doe'd be wanderin' around in the open in broad daylight?"

"An emu would do it. They're not the most intelligent creatures, for the most part."

"How many emus you been around, Burt?" Nester winked out the side of his eye, while I finished tying up my boat. You know a place is home when you can be away twenty-five years, and it's like you never left. Nester and Burt didn't remember me from the old days—to them, I would've been just some scrawny dark-haired kid who came and went during a power plant refitting—but I remembered them like a photograph in my mind. They used to buy us kids cokes, if we could catch them in the store. Other than a few more wrinkles and a little less hair, not much had changed. Same old Nester, with the same old sweat-ringed straw cowboy hat; same old Burt, with the glasses a little thicker and fewer worry lines now that he wasn't running a school. Same old conversation, except for the bit about the emu. No telling what they were looking at. Most likely neither one of them could see all the way across to the undeveloped side of the lake.

Burt stroked a chin that'd probably get a shave sometime in the next day or two—for sure before Sunday at Lakeshore Community Church. "I had an emu show up in my yard last winter. Trying to get him out my gate was like dealing with the board of education." Burt leaned back and rubbed his stomach, the buttons over his gut gaping and pulling tight, like fish on a stringer, gasping for air.

Nester pointed toward the lake. " 'S comin' closer. Gonna get down to the water here in a minute'r two. Mart, what do you think that is? You're the fish-and-game expert. The one with the fan-nancy uniform and the badge. Ain't emus in the game warden handbook someplace?"

"Not unless you're in Australia." I looked out over the water. Fairly quiet in terms of traffic today, being Monday. Just the sun rippling on the currents, the little thundercloud rumbling in the distance, and a flock of cattle egrets flying by, like seagulls looking for a sea.

There *was* something moving over on the other shore, coming up one of the park roads, kind of weaving back and forth in the shadows, unsteady. It didn't walk like a deer, and it wasn't a calf, either. . . .

I watched it for a minute. Too big for a coyote, too clumsy to be a horse some camper had lost in the state park. Hard to tell, but it looked like it was walking on two legs, kind of stooped forward. Could be an emu, maybe injured or old. After the bottom fell out of the emu and ostrich breeders' market, ranchers had started turning their leftover birds loose. The economic climate being what it was, feral animals wandering the state park were a growing problem.

"Can't tell from here," I said finally and headed up the dock toward the store, where I could get a better view.

Sheila, the old hippie chick who ran the Waterbird now, had walked partway down the stairs that led up to the store. "You boys hush up and leave Mart alone," she hollered from halfway down. "Y'all are gonna drive him so crazy, he'll pack up and go back where he came from. Morning, Martin." She added a little smirk with *Martin*. The badge on my shirt had the real, full name, that'd only been used by schoolteachers or when I was in trouble with my mama. I'd been Mart ever since I graduated from high school. "C'mon up to the store. There's fresh coffee on— looks like you could use your thermos refilled." She motioned to the container under my arm. "Melicha just fixed some of her homemade gorditas. I had her make some with turkey burger and tofu instead of all that fatty stuff. They're good. Better get one before they all sell out."

"Yeah, that's all right. The coffee's enough." The way folks told it, the food at the Waterbird had always been good—man-food that was down-home, buttermilk battered, dripping in grease, sprinkled with salt, and doused in gravy. Back in the day, the old fella everyone called Pop Dorsey had a couple Mennonite ladies working in the kitchen, and they could cook up a double-meat cheeseburger basket that'd make a lumberjack blush.

Now Dorsey was in a wheelchair after a stroke, and his daughter, Sheila, had moved home to take over the store and poor old Dorsey's life. She'd just about ruined the eating at the Waterbird. Gorditas were supposed to be made with lard and filled with pan-fried potatoes and big chunks of meat with the fat still on. Stuff you could sink your teeth into, guaranteed to go right to your arteries and stay there. Now only the out-of-towners could buy the good chow, and Sheila pushed tofu on all the regulars.

"Don't do it, Mart," Burt called after me. "You'll have an aftertaste from now until midnight."

Sheila rammed her hands onto her hips. "For heaven's sake, Burt. You can't even tell it's soy. It's flavored up just like meat."

Burt tipped his head back and gave her a google-eyed squint through his glasses. "They had fishing flies like mine in *A River Runs Through It*. Doesn't make me Robert Redford."

Nester grunted. "This coffee's decaf, too, ain't it?"

Sheila tossed her salt-and-pepper ponytail with a look I remembered from our few months here when I was a kid. She hadn't changed all that much. I had, of course, which was why nobody in Moses Lake connected me with the band of dark-haired barefoot boys who'd hung around the Waterbird looking for free cokes. All four of us boys got my daddy's gift for blarney right along with his Irish green eyes, so we were pretty good at talking our way into things. Even back in the day, we couldn't pull the wool over Sheila's eyes, though. If she caught us hanging around hoping to talk her daddy into giving us penny candy, she chased us off. "Well, FYI, Nester, Maudie called and said not to give you any coffee. Said you just about sent the blood pressure monitor through the roof yesterday."

"Ffff!" Spit flew out in a cloud that glittered in the afternoon light. "I'm gonna take my business someplace else, and . . ."

The bell rang upstairs, cutting off the coffee war before I had to bring out the handcuffs to keep the peace. "Looks like you've got a customer, Sheila," Burt grabbed his cup and scooted to the end of the bench, craning to see up the hill.

Sheila started toward the store again. "C'mon upstairs, Mart. I'll fix your thermos with the real stuff."

"She ain't worried about *his* blood pressure,"

Nester grumbled, then surveyed the lake. "That emu still over there? Hey, look'a there. Ain't that old Len Barnes workin' trotlines over by the Big Boulders? Whatever that critter was, it probably got a whiff of Len and ran off. . . ."

We headed upstairs while the conversation turned to Len Barnes and trotlines. Sheila rubbed her eyebrows, the wind catching the sleeves of her shirt; a strange scarf-like thing that looked like a leftover from Woodstock. "Man, if I ever get to where I can't find anything better to do than sit around critiquing the coffee and talking about trotlines, just shoot me, all right?"

"This *is* what they do." Old fishermen were pretty much the same everywhere—they talked, they fished, and they talked about fish. It's one of those universal rules.

At the store, the door on the back porch was flapping in the breeze, in need of a few screws and a latch. I grabbed it, thinking that if I got a little time after work one day, I'd come fix the thing. In the little cabin I'd rented on Holly Hill, evenings set in too quiet and too soon. Staying busy helped. "Go on, look after your customer. I can take care of my own coffee."

"I've got it." Sheila grabbed the thermos, which was typical of her. She complained about having to take care of everybody, but then she took care of everybody.

By the time we crossed the screen porch and

went into the store, Pop Dorsey was halfway out of his wheelchair, trying to get chicken tenders from the hot case for a customer. Sheila set down my coffee thermos and took the tongs. "I got it, Pop."

The customer, a woman trailing two little kids in swimsuits, gave the warmer an embarrassed look and turned away, taking in the patchwork of stuffed wildlife, wood-burned plaques, and graffiti on the back wall, where anyone with words of wisdom and a Sharpie pen was welcome to leave behind a thought for future customers. Some people signed their quotes and told a little about themselves, and some didn't. Pop Dorsey kept an eye on the wall from his cash register, and for most of those sayings, he could tell you who wrote the words, and when, and why.

"Sorry for the bother," the woman said, turning back to the hot case as her kids headed over to check out the wall of wisdom.

Pop Dorsey snorted. "Ain't any bother." He started down the counter to the cash register. "Here, I'll ring you up."

"Don't worry, Pop. I'll do it as soon as I get the chicken boxed." Sheila rushed through closing the container, then wiped her fingers on a towel and skittered off to the cash register.

Dorsey threw his hands up and sank into his wheelchair. "Guess I'll just go count the minnows in the bait tank. Mart, you need somethin'?"

"Coffee," I said, and pointed at the thermos. I could've gotten the coffee myself, but that wasn't the point.

Dorsey gave the thermos a mouth-down look. "S'pose you can handle it yerself?" There was a cloud in his eye that put me in his chair for a minute. It wasn't right that a man who'd always helped the lakeside kids patch leaky inner tubes and untangle backlashed fishing reels should end up like this. But then, you could go crazy waiting for *right* to show up in the world. If there was logic in the way things worked, I hadn't found it. Lightning could strike anytime, and in the space of a heartbeat, your plans were gone in smoke. All you could do was try to make sense of the ashes, and sometimes you couldn't even do that.

I leaned over the counter, like I didn't want Sheila to hear. "Don't know which pot's the real stuff and which one's decaf, Pop. You better help me out. I want the real thing."

Dorsey brightened and reached for the thermos. "I'll get it. You don't want that stuff out there by the soda fountain. I know where the real coffee's hid."

"Sounds good." I followed him over to the warmers behind the café counter. Melicha was singing back in the kitchen, which probably meant that whatever she was cooking right now didn't have soy in it. "How come you're not down at the lake with the boys?" I glanced out

31

the picture window along the store's back wall. The docksiders had moved off to one of the boathouses, where they were checking out someone's catch and pointing at the storm across the hills.

Dorsey's mouth made a round line that matched his shoulders. "Too hard to get the chair down the hill, and Sheila's worried I'll roll off the edge of the dock into the water. I tried to tell her I'm not some helpless ol' cripple. Even if I did fall in, I can stand up in the water just fine— it floats me. But she's too hardheaded to hear anything."

"Water's good therapy." I took in the hill down to the lake, the stairs, the dock. With a little work and some ramps, the place could be fitted up to get a wheelchair down there. . . .

"Yeah, well, tell Sheila that. She won't let me anyplace near the shore. Fella can't fish, he might as well pull up the sod blanket, if you ask me." Pop balanced the thermos on the counter, worked to take off the lid, and lifted the coffeepot in a shaky arc. Good thing Sheila was busy at the cash register or she would've done that for him, too.

"Hey, Mart," she said when she finished with the customers. Dorsey jumped like he'd been caught at something. Coffee sloshed over the rim of the thermos and ran in streams onto the counter. "There isn't some new campground down below Eagle Eye Bridge . . . over by the Big Boulders, is there?"

Dorsey capped the thermos, slid it over the counter, and pulled out a hankie to sop up the mess. "There you go, son. Hot coffee. On the house." Cutting a glance over his shoulder, he frowned at Sheila, who was training binoculars out the window—the cheap kind of pocket glasses you'd pick up at the Moses Lake variety store in a blister pack. With so many bird watchers around the area, I would've thought she'd have a decent set.

I walked closer to the windows, and Dorsey scooted his wheelchair along behind me. "Over there by the Big Boulders? Nah, there's no way to get there, other than from the water—unless you know those old logging roads or you climb down the cliffs. Why?"

Sheila lowered the binoculars, shaking her head. "I just had the strangest feeling. Something caught the corner of my eye when I was counting out the change, so I grabbed the binoculars. For just a sec, I swear I saw a little girl over there. A little girl in a brown dress, running along the shore, but when I tried to focus in, she was gone. There's nobody in the area but old Len, checking his trotlines." She looked at me and rubbed her hands up and down her arms, like the room had a chill in it all of a sudden.

Dorsey lifted his baseball cap, scratching his

forehead with the knob of his wrist. "Not much chance Len'd have a little girl with him. Not much chance he'd have anybody, for that matter. Anybody within fifteen feet of Len wouldn't stay there long, I'll guar-own-tee. The smell would drive 'em off, for sure. Maybe it was the Wailing Woman you saw. Maybe she's out walkin' around in the daytime."

"Oh, Daddy, for heaven's sake, no ghost stories." Sheila scanned the southeast end of the lake, where the water circled a little island, narrowed under Eagle Eye Bridge and wound up the river channel. "Mart, I know I saw someone, though . . ."

Hooking his hands over the window ledge, Dorsey pulled himself to his feet. "I don't see anythin'."

"Len's already gone upriver. Careful, Daddy. You'll fall." She moved around the counter to slip a hand under Dorsey's elbow, and he shrugged it off, turning toward the deep water by the dam.

"Oh, hang, Mart. You better grab that thermos and go. Looks like you got a boatful of joyriders headin' for the Scissortail."

Snagging my thermos, I started out the back door. There was something about the Scissortail that brought in idiots like June bugs to a porch light. Hard to say what it was, but if there was a yay-hoo anywhere on the lake who was either too young or too sauced up to think his way out of a paper bag, he'd eventually get the idea to ignore the shallow-water signs, go around the warning buoys, and try to thread the needle between the two spikes of rock that rose out of the water like the feathers of a scissortail flycatcher. Couple that with the bird watchers looking for bald eagle nests, daredevils climbing the Scissortail to jump off into the water, and kids on party barges—and those two spikes of limestone amounted to a constant headache. I was out there at least six times a day, trying to keep some loser from ending up in a wheelchair or dead from pure stupidity.

I know every bird in the mountains,
and the creatures of the field are mine.
—Psalm 50:11
(Left on the wall of wisdom by a
missionary on a bicycle)

Chapter 3

Andrea Henderson

No determination exists under heaven like that of a woman afraid she'll be stranded in the woods when darkness comes. I was alone again, having successfully frightened away the creepy man in the pickup by pulling out my cell phone and pretending to talk to someone. After a few seconds of nodding and talking, I'd waved and yelled, "Never mind! A sheriff's car is coming. They'll be here any minute. Thanks, anyway!" But as more time passed, my sense of doom grew. I'd even tried walking to the top of the nearest hill to look for any hint of civilization. There was none.

I was having no luck with outgoing cell calls, and no more vehicles had passed. No one would come looking for me until this evening, when my son finally determined that something was wrong. If Dustin called my office at that point, the place would be closed, and no one would listen to phone messages until morning. Dustin wouldn't have a clue where my schedule had taken me today, or where to send the cavalry, in the form of my parents or my sister, Megan, and brother-in-law, Oswaldo. So, one way or another, I had to rescue myself.

A wave of willpower rose up in me, fanned by rumbles of thunder bouncing off the hills and bluffs of Chinquapin Peaks. If I had to pick the car up by hand and loosen those bolt-looking things with my teeth, I was changing the tire and getting out of there. By the time I managed to accomplish it, assuming I could, the workday would be pretty well shot, but at least I'd still be alive to tell about it. If I was lucky, I could call into the office before closing and explain what had happened or, best-case scenario, make it to my final client appointment before going home. I pictured myself—after delivering some stern parental admonitions about not taking the cell phone cord out of my car anymore—telling Dustin the story of my wild and harrowing afternoon, and I felt an odd prick of anticipation. Since our move to Moses Lake, all Dustin wanted was to be left alone, and all I wanted was to rebuild the bonds that had been twisted and crushed during a painful family disintegration.

Flooded with newfound resolve, I threw a packet of wrenches, a long, S-shaped piece of metal I couldn't identify, and what looked like a jack onto the gravel, then called up a valuable piece of information from some long-past e-mail forward for women—*if you're ever stranded with a flat tire, remember that the owner's manual in the glove box has instructions for using your jack.* That tidbit had been somewhere in the middle of a list of *Twenty-five Things That Might Save Your Life.* I couldn't remember any of the remaining twenty-five, but I did find my owner's manual in the glove box, and it did have instructions for using the jack, including the long S-shaped piece of metal, otherwise known as a *jack handle.* After spending some time reading the instructions, gathering materials, and wrestling the spare tire from the hidden compartment in the trunk, I began the process.

Unfortunately, someone with much more strength than I possessed had attached the enormous bolts, properly referred to as *lug nuts.* Try as I might, even after hooking the wrench onto the bolts and standing on the handle while clinging to the trunk lid, I couldn't loosen anything. Since step one was to *Slightly loosen the lug nuts,* the next step, *Placement of the jack,* seemed impossibly out of reach. So far, not one more vehicle had passed the entire time I'd been marooned. Somehow, I had to find another way out of my predicament.

I was gazing hopelessly up and down the road and trying to come up with a next course of action when the cell phone warbled. Scrambling to the driver's seat, I grabbed the phone and answered.

Megan was on the other end, her voice like angel song at the moment. If anyone could handle whatever arrangements were necessary to bring in the cavalry, it was my sweet sister, Megan, the queen-of-all-things-in-the-right-place.

I couldn't tell whether Megan heard me answer or not. ". . . ello? Andrea? . . . ere are you? Are you anywhere near home?"

"Megan? I'm here! I'm here! Can you hear me?"

Megan continued talking on the other end. ". . . isten, Andrea, hopefully you're getting this. You need to leave work, okay? Dustin just called. He's in some kind . . . trouble. Something about the lake patrol catching them climbing the Scissortail. They're taking the kids to the store there below the dam. The Waterbird. Dustin says they can't leave without an adult . . . pick them up. I'm headed in that direction, but I was all the way in Dallas, delivering some mortgage papers . . . be a while . . . fore I can get there. I'll call Mom and Dad, and see if . . . back from Round Rock yet. Dustin said he . . . get you on your cell. He . . ."

The phone beeped and went dead, and I stood by the car with my heart pounding and a lump swelling in my throat, the pressure growing and growing until I was breathless, the world turning impossibly fast. Bits of Megan's message swirled through my head like scraps of tissue paper caught in a tornado.

Dustin's in trouble . . .
They're at the store . . .
They can't leave without an adult . . .
I'll call Mom and Dad . . .
Mom and Dad . . .
Mom . . .
Dad . . .

Anxiety tightened my chest, gripping like a fist. *Run, just run,* a voice whispered in my ear. *Leave the car here and run.*

It was crazy. I was miles from the nearest house, and even farther from a main road. I could be walking for hours, and in the meantime, my son, my fourteen-year-old child, was in the hands of some stranger, in a place that, even though it was familiar to me from childhood days on the lake, was largely foreign to Dustin. Everything in Moses Lake was foreign to him. The lake house had been rented out for years. We hadn't vacationed at the lake since he was young.

Dustin didn't know anything about the lake patrol, or the rules of the water, or the fact that there was no telling what sort of people you could run into on the lake. Dustin only knew the life in our comfortable Houston neighborhood, his private school and our church just around the corner. All of that was a world away now. Houston, that neighborhood, the church, that life, the family we used to be, might as well have been the other side of the moon.

He wasn't prepared for this life any more than I was.

Mom and Dad. Megan called Mom and Dad. . . .

I felt sick. No matter how this played out, my parents would show up at the lake house, and Dustin's mishap, whatever it was, would become the springboard into a Pandora's box of all things left unsaid in the wake of the divorce. My parents didn't want Dustin and me living in their lake house any more than we wanted to be there. We were an embarrassment, an inconvenience, a burden, a mixed-up mess they couldn't sort out by putting the proper notations in their appointment books.

Whatever had happened today—nothing involving lake patrol and being detained at the local convenience store could be all that serious—my parents would make certain we talked it to death until we'd dipped our feet into all the ugly undertows. They'd mark this as a harbinger of things to come, proof that, in addition to letting my own life go down the tubes, I'd dragged my son along with me. Dustin was a hapless victim of a father with morals no deeper than topsoil and a mother who wasn't strong enough to keep a home together. What hope was there for him now?

I pictured him sitting in the little store by the bridge, apparently under supervision of the lake patrol, and another thought crossed my mind, sobering the whirl of family conflict.

What was Dustin doing out on the lake, and who was he with? With the lake house rented out for so many years, we no longer had friends in the neighborhood, and Dustin had a pile of summer reading and a workbook to do for the advanced-placement English class he'd be starting in school this fall. Moving to town less than six weeks before the beginning of the school year, he was behind the eight ball. He was supposed to be home reading, not running around with . . . I didn't even know who he was with . . . out on the lake.

Emotion swelled in my throat again—thick, painful—making the July afternoon even hotter and muggier than it already was. What if this *was* a harbinger of things to come? Only the beginning of a complete teenage meltdown? I couldn't be home policing Dustin, and at the same time out working to support the two of us, so that we could eventually afford a house. Our own house. Again.

What good was a job, or a house, or anything else if Dustin didn't come through this change in our lives intact?

The inside of my nose prickled and my eyes blurred as I hurried to the back of the car to search for something I could use to try to hammer the nuts loose. My head was far enough into the trunk that I didn't hear the rattle of an approaching vehicle until brakes squealed out a loud complaint. I jerked upright, my heart bounding into my throat as an advancing cloud of dust rose over the hill. Leaning down, I grabbed the lug wrench, thinking of my brief encounter with the creepy man in the gray Ford. The hood of a truck nosed into view, and I squinted to see who was inside. My hopes inched upward as I glimpsed a work vehicle with toolboxes built into the bed. A moment later, the big tow bar on the back end swung into view. A wrecker! I ran into the road and began waving wildly.

Thank you. The words in my mind, the feeling that a prayer had just been answered was a knee-jerk reflex, an old habit formed by repeat motion and muscle memory. Those words weren't aimed at anyone anymore. By luck, good fortune, a simple twist of cell phone signals, I'd been saved from what could have been a bad situation.

Letting out a gigantic sigh of relief, I slipped the tire iron behind my back as the Rowdy Ray's Tow and Tire Service vehicle squealed to a stop beside my car. "You call for Rowdy Ray?"

Rowdy asked, spitting a plug out his window before leaning across to talk to me from the passenger side. "You sure wasn't easy to find, I'll tell ya. What're you doin' way out here, anyway? You lost or somethin'?"

*Even a fish wouldn't get into trouble
if he kept his mouth shut.*
—Anonymous
(Left by Burt Lacey,
docksider and retired school principal)

Chapter 4

Mart McClendon

It wasn't any surprise that the bunch I'd rounded up at the Scissortail and towed back across the lake were teenage boys, mostly. Six boys and one girl who looked like she was sorry she'd gone along for the boat ride. I knew the girl, Cassandra. Her mom cleaned rooms in the lodge at the Eagle's Nest Resort, and her daddy did handyman work at the cabins and canoe rental just down from Lakeshore Community Church.

Cassandra's dad, Larry, was the last parent I called, but he was there quicker than a sneeze through a screen door when he heard his little girl was in trouble. Larry stood there turning fireplug red, listening to the story of how I'd rounded the bend to the Scissortail and found two boneheads in swim trunks climbing the rocks, while the group in the speedboat, including Cassandra, cheered from underneath.

"Everyone was having a real big time," I told

Larry. "And they would've, right up until someone landed in the hospital. When they saw me coming, they beat it out of there in a hurry. They made a run for it across the lake, but they skimmed a little nest of trotlines by the Big Boulders and sucked the rope into the engine. By the time I got over there, the kids were on shore. They tried to tell me the boat wasn't theirs—that two guys had just pulled up in it, jumped out, and made a run for the woods."

Larry's eyes went wide and shot fire at his daughter. At that point, I almost hated to tell him the rest of it, but I did. "There were a couple twelve-packs of Budweiser involved, and at first they didn't want to admit that was theirs, either." You had to laugh sometimes at what people came up with—especially kids. It was the kind of story my brothers and I would've tried back in the day. We probably would've done the same thing those kids did, and tried to look innocent while grocery sacks full of brewski sank slowly under the water.

My mama would've looked about like Larry did right now, and I probably would've been as dumbstruck as poor Cassandra. That face said she wanted to be anywhere but here.

In a booth by the wall, the ringleader—a tall, stringy kid—shook bleached blond hair out of his eyes and dropped his mouth open like he couldn't believe I'd told the parents there was alcohol at the scene. The other four boys ducked their heads, and Cassandra darted a wide-eyed look toward her father and me.

Cassandra's daddy didn't want to hear any more of the story. He let his little girl know she was grounded for the rest of her life, and then he followed her out the door, telling me he had to go pick up some canoers before the storm hit. He'd be back to talk to me later.

I helped myself to a cup of Sheila's coffee and watched puffy white thunderheads tower up in the east while we waited for the rest of the parents. The ringleader's dad showed up next. The man actually went down to look at the boat before coming into the store. By the time he made it up to the Waterbird, his kid was ready with some whipped-up tears and a string of excuses. Mostly, the boy wanted to make sure this wouldn't keep him from getting his driver's license the month after next. Seemed there was a new Beemer waiting for him. Dad was a lawyer, and right then, he seemed more interested in the legal end of things.

"Was there any property damage? Any injuries?" He asked, darting a quick glance around the room and checking the other kids lined up in the booths. No doubt he smelled a potential lawsuit.

"Nothing damaged but the boat," I told him. "Your son doesn't have his boater's education certificate, so he's not legal to operate the boat on his own. That thing isn't a kid's toy, and the Scissortail's not a playpen. We've had seven diving injuries, five wrecked watercraft, and two drowning deaths there this year alone."

I looked at the two who'd been climbing the rocks—a kid with some kind of symbol shaved into a buzz haircut, and a dark-headed boy who said he was fourteen but looked about twelve. Tyler and Dustin, in the order they were sitting. Tyler lounged back in his chair and shot me a glare like, *What're you lookin' at, dude?*

Back in the day, if I'd looked at a grown-up like that, my mama would've smacked that smirk off my face and used it to pepper my backside. When we got caught misbehaving, we at least knew enough to be scared of the consequences.

Mostly, the lawyer-dad couldn't believe his kid had the nerve to muck up his workday. He was more interested in telling the kid how much his time was worth per hour than in figuring out why his kid took the boat for a joyride, or where the two twelve-packs of Bud came from. The man nodded along to everything I said, like he was trying to wheel me forward and get this thing over with. "Well, I don't understand what those ropes . . . those—what did you call them . . . trotlines?—were doing out in the lake, where boats can run over them."

"Jug lines and trotlines aren't illegal on the

lake. They have to be tagged by the owner, and there's a limit on the number of hooks per line and total hooks per person, but the placement of the lines was legal enough. Part of the responsibly of operating a boat is being aware of potential obstacles."

I didn't bother telling him that the lines tangled in his motor weren't tagged. Later today I'd try to catch up with old Len Barnes and tell him one more time to properly tag his lines. The trouble was that, even when you tried to talk slow, Len only understood about half of what you said.

"So, nobody hurt?" Any minute now, the lawyer would whip out an affidavit and want me to sign it. "No injuries?"

"They're lucky," I said, and then I let him know that I was willing to cut a deal, of a sort. In general, my policy on juvenile offenders was that I'd rather work with the parents than ticket the kid. Once I wrote a citation for something like Minor In Possession of Alcohol, the whole thing moved into juvenile court.

"I've got Max, here, for unlawfully operating the boat, evading arrest, and minor in possession of alcohol. There's a Corps of Engineers water safety course starting two weeks from today. You sign him up, and I won't ticket him."

The kid's mouth dropped open like he couldn't believe what was happening to him. "Football camp starts next week." He gave me a look that said, *Whatever, dude. My daddy's here now. You can't do anything to me.*

I just handed Dad my card and a brochure for the course and said, "Think it over and let me know by five p.m. tomorrow."

"We didn't *do* anything," the kid whined. "I know how to drive the stupid boat. I'm less than two flippin' months away from getting my driver's license. Big flippin' deal that I didn't take the boater course yet."

Dad shot him a down-the-nose bewildered look that said he couldn't figure how this kid he'd bought all the nice toys for could go sour. "Get in the car."

While his dad was busy tucking away my card and the brochure, Max flashed a grin at his friends and headed for the door.

Pop Dorsey slapped a hand on the counter. "Son, you better show your daddy some more respect before you land in a heap of trouble." Until then, Pop had kept quiet and stayed out of things.

"Daddy . . ." Sheila gasped under her breath. She gave me an apologetic look.

I just shook my head and watched Max go. Kids like him made me glad I didn't have kids.

The rest of the parents showed up one by one, and we repeated the excuse-making and the begging and the smart-aleck looks and the thing about the water safety class. By the time I finally

50

got down to the last kid—Dustin, the scrawny one in the corner—I'd pretty much run dry on diplomacy. Dealing with the public was the worst part of my job. Out in the Big Bend country, you could drive all day and never see another human soul. If it was deer season, we had some hunters, and in the winter a few snowbirds or families on vacation, and some hikers in the mountains, but mostly the job was you, the wildlife, the ranchers, and a lot of wide-open space.

But there were worse things than having to deal with the public all day—like having to deal with your own demons. It's pretty much a given that it's easier to sort out other people's issues than your own.

In the far booth, Dustin looked like he didn't want anyone in his business. Pressed into the corner so tight there wasn't an inch between him and the wall, he sagged over the table like a potted plant left out in the sun too long. Pop Dorsey wheeled by and asked him if he wanted something to drink, and the kid just shook his head and drooped lower, picking at a crack in the Formica. Considering that he'd been sitting there for nearly two hours, waiting for a responsible adult to show up for him, he was probably thirsty.

"You sure someone's coming for you?" I asked. I'd stood over their shoulders while each of the kids called Mom or Dad for a ride. Dustin took two or three tries at it before he got hold of anybody. Then he had to beg the person to come after him. Looked like his mom and dad were too busy for him, too.

The kid nodded, mumbling, "My aunt Megan's coming." Looping his arms on the table, he slid lower and let his forehead rest on his fists. "I guess." The last words wallowed between his face and the Formica. Pop Dorsey gave a sympathetic look and shook his head, frowning.

"I'm not letting you go until somebody shows up for you." It crossed my mind to wonder whether Dustin had faked the phone call. Maybe he thought if he held out long enough, I'd just give up and let him walk out of here. He could waltz on home and act like it had been a normal day at the lake. *Hey, Mom, what's for dinner?*

"I know," he muttered.

I watched him a minute longer. Didn't look like he cared whether anyone came for him or not. "I've got your name and address." I took a step closer, figuring the easiest thing would be to take him on home and talk to the mom or dad. "Let's just head on over there and be done with it, son." The address he'd given me was in a gated community on Larkspur Cove that had been there since not long after the lake was opened to the public. Back in the day, Larkspur Estates was the place to be. The lots were old and large, and the houses sat up high, with a view of the whole county and long walkways down to private boathouses. When we were kids, we used to row over to the cove in our johnboat and drift along the shore looking at the rich girls and wishing they'd look back.

"Nobody's home." The kid lifted his head, then let it bounce off his fists like a tetherball, over, and over, and over. That had to hurt.

"We'll just wait here, then."

His shoulders inflated, then sank, and he shook his head, his face still buried in his arms. "I cannn-tell my mom-mat-hurfm-sahhh-bout-mrrff-class'n stuff'm." The tabletop probably heard him just fine, but all I could make out was a word or two. On my worst day as a potential juvenile delinquent, I wouldn't have sat there talking to an adult with my face in the table like a kindergartner at naptime. My mama taught me better than that. The problem was that these days too many kids hadn't been taught a thing—not even the simple stuff, like how to sit up, look somebody in the eye, and take your trouble like a man. *You're big enough to climb the rope; you're big enough to take the fall,* my daddy always said. Experimentation and hard knocks were the only two schools he had any faith in. *You hit the dirt a few times, you'll learn.*

Dustin looked like he didn't have a clue about hard knocks. He had arms about as big around as number-two pencils, and his skin had been sunburned raw-meat red where it stuck out of his

53

T-shirt. He had about as much business climbing the Scissortail as I did dancing the *Nutcracker* ballet. Playing Nintendo probably didn't teach you how far down a body goes when it hits the water with the kind of velocity you get from jumping off a tower like the Scissortail.

"Kid, you want to tell me something, you look me in the eye like a man. Otherwise, just sit there and be quiet." I flipped the page over in my notebook and started working on the day's log. No sense taking all the paperwork home. Then again, I probably wouldn't go home until I had to—too quiet there. I'd hang around the lake, see if I could catch Len running unmarked lines or popping some dove out of season.

It was always a game—finding the guys who thought that if you didn't get caught for something, it wasn't wrong. Up until now, I just hadn't had the heart to go after old Len too much. He'd be easy to catch. You didn't have to cross paths with Len more than once to know he was a brick or two short of a load. If he had a hunting license, he probably couldn't read the book that came with it. You had to feel a little sorry for the guys who were poaching so they could eat, though. Catching Len wouldn't really be any fun. . . .

Maybe I'd settle for sliding Pop Dorsey's screen door off the hinges, then hauling it home, putting some braces on the corners, and fixing a new latch. The thing was out there flapping in the breeze again, bouncing back and forth between the doorframe and the wall, making a steady rhythm that'd drive me buggy after a while. Sheila and Dorsey didn't even seem to notice.

The kid kept lifting his head up and letting it bounce against his hand, making the table rattle between two legs that were missing the metal caps, and about a half inch shorter than the other two. Noisy half inch.

Sheila glanced up from cleaning the warmer in the café area and noticed me checking the lake. "Mart, you see anything unusual over there by the Big Boulders—any strange tracks or anything? Burt and Nester will want to know when they show up to play dominoes. They're still arguing about what was over there earlier."

"Didn't get a chance to look. Busy bringing in this bunch of man-eaters." I thumbed toward the kid. His leg was jitterbugging against the seat now, making the vinyl squeak along with the table rattling. If somebody didn't come pick up Dustin soon, I'd have to go after some duct tape.

A sheriff's department call came in before the kid drove me all the way crazy. During a traffic stop, a deputy had nailed two guys transporting live alligators in a stock trailer. All four guys had different stories about where the gators came from, and the whole thing sounded like one of those redneck-brilliant ideas that seem good after a few days in the woods and one too many six-packs.

I asked how big the gators were, and the deputy said, "Heck if I know. Big. I'm not getting in there and measuring 'em. Big enough. These fellas are lucky they've still got all their hands and feet. They sober up a little, they'll probably realize that." As usual, the deputy only wanted to turn the whole thing over, which was typical of the sheriff's deputies in this particular county. Looked like my day was about to get a lot more interesting.

I hung up and thought, *Now what am I gonna do with this kid?* He'd sat himself up and perked an ear my way, listening in on the call about the gators. For about a half a second, he seemed interested, then as soon as I turned toward him, he slouched in his seat, remembering the two of us weren't friends.

"Son, I'm leaving you here with Pop Dorsey and Sheila until your aunt shows up for you. You don't move out of this bench until then. You understand?"

"Yes, sir," he muttered, looking down at the table again. Now that his friends were gone, he'd lost some of the teenage attitude. Most of them do. You take their buddies away, they're just scared little kids in bodies they still need to grow into.

"Look at me when I'm talking to you, son."

He fluttered bloodshot brown eyes my way and fidgeted his hands around.

"I'm telling you the same thing I told the rest of your buddies. I don't know what the bunch of you had in mind for later, but you're lucky I caught you before y'all dipped into the beer and did something real stupid."

He nodded but didn't answer. Hard to say if he was scared or not. Really, the kid looked like he didn't care if I threw him under the truck and ran over him on my way out.

"You can go on home when your aunt gets here." No choice about that. By the time I made it to the other end of the county, went through the paperwork to press charges, and figured out what to do with the contraband gators, it'd be the middle of the night. "Your mom or dad home in the mornings?"

"My mom. They're divorced."

"You let her know I'll be by at seven fifteen a.m. to talk to her. You make sure she's there." I couldn't wait to see what kind of mom went with this kid.

"Okay." He slumped over the table, folding his arms and sliding slowly forward again. I felt a pinch of pity for the kid, but pity wouldn't do him any good. What he needed was a lesson—the kind that keeps you from doing something stupid, twice.

The rainbows of life come after the storms.
—Anonymous
(via Pop Dorsey, proprietor,
Waterbird Bait and Grocery)

Chapter 5

Andrea Henderson

By the time I made it home to Larkspur Estates, limping along on the spare tire that Rowdy Ray had installed in a torrential downpour, I was damp, dirty, and emotionally numb. Rowdy Ray had been kind enough to send a text to Megan, letting her know I was all right, but as I entered the neighborhood, my mind spun ahead. My thoughts raced beyond the park and the tennis courts, past the private boat ramp, to the back of Sunrise Loop, where Highline Way jutted over the water on a finger of land surrounded by lake homes aging gracefully beneath cedars, live oaks, and crepe myrtles established long enough to have thick, knobby trunks.

In my childhood, a trip to the lake house had always meant freedom from an overly demanding private school in Dallas, a packed schedule of church activities, social engagements, piano lessons, ballet recitals, mother-daughter luncheons at the Lady's Club, book reviews, and other activities Megan and I dreaded. The lake house had always been a place to get away from those things, to shuck off the straitjacket.

When Dustin was little, we'd enjoyed family vacations here, but after Karl and I moved to Houston, the lake house was relinquished to the capable hands of a rental agency until Megan's twins came along and my parents regained their vacation home. Dustin and I were fortunate that it was there when we needed it. The lake house was a quiet place, a good place to heal, except for the pressure of being constantly under my parents' scrutiny.

As I neared the driveway, anticipating their comments on today's fiasco, I felt the air going out of me. Next door, two little blond-haired girls—the neighbor's grandchildren, I presumed—had set up a lemonade stand, the way Megan and I might have in the past. Their sign read, *Ansley and Sydney's Lemonade Copany*, sans *M*. They waved hopefully at me as I approached, then frowned and backed off when they saw where I was turning in. Shortly after Mr. and Mrs. Blue had bought the place last year, my mother had started a dispute regarding property lines and hedges. The Blues now steered clear of us, like all the rest of the neighbors. Sydney and Ansley watched like voyeurs at an alien landing as I parked behind my father's vehicle, gathered my things, and made my way into the house.

Inside, my parents and Megan were lined up on one side of the kitchen table. They registered surprise at my muddy, waterlogged state and dirty clothes. After apologizing, then trying to make the flat tire sound like a minor hiccup in the day—no sense giving them more ammunition than they already had—I ducked into the utility room to tug on some sweats and pull myself together before returning to the dining area.

The discussion there followed our usual family dynamic—Dad stoic, Mom fretful (dressed for some sort of ladies' event, judging by the carefully pressed aqua blazer and pants that nicely offset her blue eyes and auburn hair), and Megan, a younger, kinder, gentler image of Mom, trying to mollify, determined that no one should remain unhappy for long. Meanwhile, Dustin sat on a barstool in the corner, his head and shoulders resting against the wall, a glazed-over sheen giving his brown eyes the glassy coolness of denial.

As the discussion of the day's events oozed forth like meat through a sausage grinder, Dustin focused mostly on the window, then finally mumbled an apology for screwing up everyone's evening. "It was just, like, a mistake. They came by and asked if I wanted to go out on the boat. I didn't know they weren't supposed to have it— the boat, I mean." His eyes flicked toward me, then held fast, as if he'd remembered that an averted gaze made a story less credible. He'd probably learned that from listening to his father and me.

I can tell you're lying, Karl. You aren't even looking at me. Why don't you look me in the eye and try to tell me this only happened one time— that you haven't been seeing her for months, maybe even years? Tell me you had nothing at all to do with her divorce. Why don't you tell me that? See if you can make me believe it?

For heaven's sake, Karl. You knew she and Charles were having trouble. How could you do this? Have you been letting her buy things for her apartment on the college's dime? Is that how she's affording that place . . . all the nice furniture?

Dustin should never have overheard that conversation. He shouldn't have witnessed his father trying to lie his way out, begging me not to go public with the truth, warning me that life as we knew it would be over. There was already an ongoing financial inquiry at the college. . . .

Lately, Dustin seemed to be trying to perfect his father's art of false honesty. The change was heartbreaking, coming from a fourteen-year-old who'd always been the perfect kid, his days filled with places he was supposed to be—soccer practice, guitar lessons, youth group on Wednesdays, worship band rehearsals, a few volunteer projects through the school or the church. "I tried to call you on your cell before I left, but it wouldn't go through," he said.

Mother rolled her chin my way, frowning at me from beneath lowered brows, an expression that laid the blame for Dustin's mishap squarely on me. "I *told* you this . . . this traveling sort of job wasn't the right thing. For heaven's sake, Andrea, what is Dustin supposed to do when issues arise, and you're who knows where, going to some . . . some *appointment?* Half of these lake houses are empty during the week. Dustin doesn't even have anyone to call if there is an emergency." Mother failed to mention that the lack of neighborly support was her fault. Filing homeowner's association complaints about trash cans by the curb, bushes not trimmed at least six inches below windows, noisy lake parties, and boats coming up the cove too fast does not a good neighbor make.

I wanted to counter Mother's question with, *Tell me what else I should do, then? I have to work. I have to make a living.* Instead, I stuck to the subject at hand. Dustin. "Dustin knew he wasn't supposed to go anywhere, and certainly not out in a boat with kids I've never even met." I turned my attention back to Dustin, wishing everyone would leave, so I could get to the bottom of this.

"It's no big deal," Dustin offered. "I thought

it'd be okay." He glazed over again, as if he knew how the conversation was going to proceed. Next, we would move to a discussion of my reasons for taking the counseling job instead of going to work at my brother-in-law's bank. Somehow in our family, we couldn't seem to do anything but repeat familiar patterns, go over the same talking points until they were like overused chewing gum—tasteless and bland.

As usual, the family meeting ended after we'd rehashed all the normal issues.

From the foyer, Dad surveyed the cars in the drive and pointed out that he'd have to take my vehicle and leave his for me. "You can't be driving around the hills with no spare. I'll have all the tires looked at while I've got it." He offered his keys, and I gave him mine. No point being stubbornly independent. I had to be at work tomorrow, and I didn't have a clue where to get a tire fixed.

As Mom and Dad disappeared down the drive, Megan stood with me in the entryway. She apologized for having brought the folks in on Dustin's mishap. "It just scared me to death when Dustin called. I knew it'd take me forever to get here from Dallas." She leaned close to me, keeping the conversation between us. In the kitchen, Dustin was sliding wearily off his barstool, investigating the sunburn on his shoulder, sucking air through his teeth when he touched it. "I thought Mom and Dad could get here sooner than I could. If I'd known they were still on the way back from Round Rock, I never would have called them. I tried to head them off after I made it here, but, of course, they came on. I didn't mean to cause another big, hairy family meeting."

"I know," I said, but Meg looked worried, as if she was afraid I didn't believe her. A past history of intense sibling competitiveness never goes away completely. "Thanks for picking him up, Meg. I'm sorry for the hassle. I really don't understand what Dustin was thinking." After nearly an hour of family conversation, I was still confused. "Did you find out what, exactly, he was in trouble for?"

Meg's slim shoulders lifted, then dropped. "Well, from what Dustin said, one of the kids took the family boat for a spin without permission, and they got nabbed for climbing the Scissortail. When I made it to the Waterbird, the clerk was busy with a tour bus and Dustin was sitting over in one of the booths. He just told them he was leaving and walked out with me. He said the whole thing had been blown out of proportion by some game warden guy on a power trip."

She punctuated the sentence with a helpless look. Meg had no experience with teenagers. Her twins, still too little to converse, were no doubt

64

safely home in Cleburne with Meg's mother-in-law, who not only adored Meg but also provided grandkid daycare two days a week while Meg worked at Oswaldo's bank. Just like everything else about my little sister, her in-law relationships were perfect.

I gave her a hug and thanked her, trying to absolve the guilt I felt for harboring secret resentments. Misery loves company, and my little sister wasn't very good company. She never had been. She was too good at everything. She was the blue-eyed, petite golden child, and I, by contrast, was the one with my father's kinky brown hair, brown eyes, and square chin. Growing up, Meg turned heads with her bright smile and auburn locks. She led cheers at the football games, wore the cute little pleated-skirt uniform, and turned all the boys' heads. Boys aren't too interested in gangly, flat-chested, clarinet players, no matter how good the band sounds in the stands.

I walked her out and then stood on the path among Mother's collection of bird-friendly plants and seed feeders. One of the best things about our summers at the lake had always been the birds. Mother adored them. She knew all about them, and being something of an amateur photographer, she loved to photograph them. The interior of the lake house was decorated in bird-related paraphernalia—Mother's photographs;

empty bird's nests she'd spirited from trees; delicate, colorful feathers carefully pressed into shadowbox frames; tiny eggs no bigger than the tip of a finger, rescued from the grass, painstakingly dried and shellacked for preservation.

The birds were proof in some way that Mother did have a tender side. Beyond that, her study of them gave us something to talk about. Mother could identify each and every type of the enormous variety of fowl that migrated through Moses Lake. Most of our good moments together were spent taking long walks through the woods with binoculars and field manuals. Mother preferred me to Megan for this endeavor. I was quieter, she said.

As Megan climbed into her Lexus and drove away, her Junior League decal glinting in the sun, a lonely, miserable, helpless sensation swelled inside me. I knew better than to stay out there on the sidewalk alone with it. Now was no time for an emotional crash. I still needed to talk with Dustin, find out what really happened, and try to get a handle on what was going through his mind when he decided to leave without permission, in the company of a bunch of kids he'd apparently just met.

But in truth, I didn't want to be counselor, or Mom, or single parent right now. I felt bone-tired and weary, exhausted in body and spirit. I wanted to turn the problem over to someone else—say, *I handled it last time. It's your turn,* the way I could have in the past.

But now there was only half. Half a parental team. Half a family, trying to re-form into a new whole.

In the house, the living room was empty, and I could hear the shower running in the hallway bathroom. I knocked, but Dustin either couldn't hear or wasn't answering. The door was locked, of course. Short of breaking it down, I didn't have much choice but to keep an eye on the hallway and wait. I passed the time by e-mailing the office to let the secretary, Bonnie, know that I'd need to reschedule my missed afternoon appointments. Sending the e-mail off into cyberspace, I dreaded its arrival at the office. I'd look completely incompetent.

My stomach tightened and started churning, and I laid my head back against the chair, watching the birds enjoy bits of bread Mother had scattered on the deck. A misty rain started falling, and the weight of the day overtook me. I let my eyes close.

Just for a minute, I thought. *Just for a minute. . . .*

When I awoke, the birds were gone, and the house was dark. In the room with the bunk beds—the room that was still decorated in the soft rose and pale green hues of my childhood—Dustin was curled up, softly snoring with his face mashed sideways against the pillow. One long, sinewy leg hung off the mattress, a foot twitching just slightly, as if he were a napping hound dreaming about chasing squirrels.

He knew I wouldn't have the heart to wake him from a sound sleep. He knew I'd stand over his bed, think about how peaceful he looked, how young, so much like my baby boy. So smart. So handsome. So perfect. An incredible kid who'd always been honest, and tenderhearted, and smart, and faithful, and bold . . .

And now . . . damaged?

Broken? Fearful? Angry? Bitter? Closed off?

Tears welled in my eyes, and before I sensed it coming, a gush of emotion wrenched from my stomach and pressed out a sob. The sound split the silence, causing Dustin to jerk in his sleep, blink and rise in a clumsy push-up.

"Mom?" he whispered, his eyes narrow slits in the stream of light from the hallway.

"Shhh . . ." The sound shuddered, my lips trembling as it passed. I swallowed hard, trying to force the emotion down my throat, tuck it away where it wouldn't hurt anyone. "Everything's all right." I wished that were true. More than anything else about our old life, I missed the feeling of security, the confidence that everything was fine, that tomorrow would be the same as today. The same routine, the same people. Nothing out of the ordinary. Nothing to worry about.

Dustin collapsed onto the pillow again, exhaling a long sigh. I pulled the sheet over his shoulders, touched his hair, remembered the days when I'd fretted over homework he didn't do exactly right, or a friend who'd turned against him in school, or soccer games in which he didn't make the starting lineup. How many times had I knelt by his bed and prayed that the world would be easy on him, that everything would go his way?

How could I not have seen that the biggest danger wasn't outside our house—it was inside?

I went to bed and lay awake, my mind doing what it usually did—sifting through the past, rehashing history, trying to understand it, until finally I fell asleep. In my dreams I was sailing on the lake, the boat, a catamaran, skimming over the water on a clear day, the sails popping, stretching in a stiff wind. The freedom was golden. Closing my eyes, I let a cool breeze stroke my hair. I felt larger than life. Indestructible. Unbroken.

In the shelter of the Big Boulders, the wind died, and the boat floated along on the current, traveling under Eagle Eye Bridge, into the river channel. I felt no need to adjust the sails. The current knew where it was going. It was taking me someplace I was meant to be.

Overhead on the bridge, a rust-spotted pickup rattled by. In the passenger-side window, a little girl turned my way, her blue eyes curious, her dark hair swirling in the breeze. When the truck stopped, the little girl slipped out the passenger door and skipped across the deck of the bridge. She was too young to be up there alone. It wasn't safe.

Laughing, she climbed onto the railing, moved along it with her arms outstretched like a tightrope walker's.

I screamed for her to stop, but she couldn't hear me. The truck was backing up now, rattling toward her. If it shook the railing, she might fall. . . .

I adjusted the sails, tried to move the boat underneath her, but the current was pulling me the other way.

The truck rolled closer and closer to the girl, the railing vibrating, humming like a tuning fork.

"Stop!" I screamed. "Be careful!"

I jerked awake, looked around the room, struggled for a minute to sort out dreams and reality, to remember where I was. Thoughts raced through my mind in rapid-fire bits, ricocheting and repeating. Work. Dustin. Divorce. Lake house. Family meeting. Scissortail.

The little girl in the truck.

A glance at the clock whisked the dream into the dustpan of things to be considered later. It was after six thirty. If I didn't get moving, I'd be late checking in at the office. Dale Tazinski had been, so far, an extremely understanding boss, but one more slipup like yesterday's, and he'd wonder if his newly hired Licensed Professional Counselor was in need of counseling herself.

Whipping around the room, I grabbed one of the summer dress suits I'd purchased three weeks ago before starting my new job. Then I showered, toweled my hair, and slipped a ponytail holder over my wrist for later. By seven fifteen, I was dressed, had everything in a pile by the door, and was ready to head for the Tazinski and Associates office, forty minutes down the road in Cleburne. I hurried to the kitchen to pop some waffles into the toaster so that Dustin and I could sit down to breakfast together, talk about what had happened yesterday, and discuss the fact that he was grounded as a result. His parameters for today in no way included leaving the property. In fact, I'd be preparing a chore list, which I would text to him when I arrived at work.

Something caught my eye as I crossed the living room—a movement down the hill where the backyard sloped steeply toward the lake. There was a boat by our boathouse. A man was on our dock. . . .

I moved toward the bay window to get a better look. In the hallway, Dustin's bedroom door opened.

"Dustin," I called, a note of disquiet raising prickles on the back of my neck. All the docks in

Larkspur Cove were private. No one should have been there. "Dustin . . . there's someone down by the boathouse." Maybe one of Dustin's newfound friends was paying an early visit.

But the stranger on the dock didn't look like a teenager. He was tall and broad-shouldered . . . and coming up the hill.

A wise old owl sat on an oak;
The more he saw, the less he spoke;
The less he spoke, the more he heard.
Why aren't we like that wise old bird?
—Anonymous
(Left by a mother of six on a family vacation)

Chapter 6

Mart McClendon

The mom came down the hill with the kid rushing behind her, trying to talk his way out of trouble. I didn't have to hear what they were saying to figure out that Dustin hadn't bothered to tell his mama that I'd be showing up this morning. You work in this business awhile, you learn to read body language. Dustin was trying to do damage control, and it wasn't working. Judging from the way his mom was dressed, she'd been headed out the door to work. Right now she was moving at a pretty good clip, even with her high heels sinking into the sod. Her arms swung at her sides, stiff as baseball bats.

She looked like the type who would be living in a high-dollar waterfront place like this—kind of buttoned-down and uptight, all business. While she was walking down the hill, she pulled her hair up and stuck it in a ponytail, like we were about to have a wrestling match, and she didn't want the hair getting in the way.

This won't take long, I thought. *She'll ask where she can pay the citation, make a few excuses for the kid, and we'll be done.* I'd already had a call from the lawyer-dad this morning. He'd talked to some buddies who worked juvenile court cases, and he'd figured out that the kid wouldn't get any more than a slap on the wrist. He was going to pay Max's way out, so the kid wouldn't miss football camp next week. Probably wasn't the first time Max's dad had bought Max's way out of trouble. Probably wouldn't be the last. You had to wonder sometimes why people who couldn't be bothered to raise their kids got to keep doing a lousy job of it, when someone like my little brother, Aaron, never had the chance to see his kids grow up, and my little nephew, Mica, never got to grow up at all.

If these parents could've stood by those side-by-side graves, they wouldn't be in such a hurry to get to work.

Dustin and his mom met me halfway across the yard, Dustin babbling that he'd forgotten to tell her I was coming, and someone was asleep, and something about being in the shower. Considering that the kid hadn't had much to say for himself yesterday, he was spitting out rope like a twine baler today. Pretty soon, his mama was gonna hang him with it. She finally told him to hush up, and he snapped his mouth shut. I couldn't blame him. If my mama'd given me that look, I would've zipped it, too.

"We'll talk about this later," she growled, then turned from him to me and introduced herself.

Something strange happened, and her name flew right past my ear without going in. I lost focus for a minute. She had the prettiest eyes—big and brown, kind of nervous, the way a doe looks when she's deciding whether to bolt for the woods or stand her ground. She reminded me of someone, but I couldn't place the resemblance. Someone on TV, maybe. She was that kind of pretty, and tall enough to look me in the eye, standing uphill like she was.

"But Maa-om . . ." Dustin whined, and my mind snapped into forward gear. Somebody needed to tell him to square his shoulders and act like a man.

"Just a minute, Dustin!" She held a hand up, her fingers shaking. Moisture was gathering in her eyes, and all I could think was, *Man, I'm not in the mood for a crying jag this morning.* There was nothing here that was worth a big emotional display. All I wanted was to take the short road through the usual conversation, get this over with, and go home to bed. It'd been one long night with the contraband alligators.

After explaining yesterday's details to the other

parents, I had the routine down pat. The conversation was already rolling in my head. She'd have the same excuses as the rest of them—the boy hadn't ever done something like that before, he didn't mean to do anything wrong. He wouldn't do something like that on purpose. And there was no way he would be out *drinking beer*. He was a good kid, after all. An angel, really. Never been in any trouble. Why was I harassing teenagers on the lake, anyway? Didn't I have any better ways to spend my time? The county had a drug problem, for heaven's sake. Law enforcement should be focusing on the real issues, not harassing kids who made one little mistake. . . .

I pulled off my hat and rubbed my eyes, felt my head start to pound. I was beat and I stunk like swamp water and gator slime. If I was lucky, I wouldn't end up with amoebic dysentery from going with my partner from the north end of the county, Jake Moskaluk, to haul those gators back to where they belonged. On the way home, we'd stopped at one of Jake's favorite little Mennonite bakeries, and right now all that food had me ready to lay out under a shade tree somewhere.

I introduced myself, but I did her the favor of not offering a handshake. The lady didn't look like she wanted one, anyway. She could probably smell the swamp water from over there. "Look, I'll give you the short version," I said. "I'm guessing that Dustin, here, didn't exactly fill you in on how he ended up in trouble yesterday."

She cut a sideways look at the kid, and he backed away a step, holding up his hands. "Mom, I tried. . . . I mean, I was going to, but everybody was here and then you were outside with Aunt Megan, and well . . . then you were asleep and stuff. I was gonna get up and tell you this morning, but my alarm didn't go off."

"Tell me *what,* exactly?" She shot him a glare that could've poached an egg.

The kid fidgeted from one foot to the other, hiking his shoulders up close to his ears. "I just forgot, okay? It's not . . . like it's a big deal. I . . ."

Mom blinked at him, eyes ending up wide open with whites circling the top.

The kid had the good sense to backpedal. "I screwed up, all right?" He put a pretty convincing tremble in the words—a little staccato to let Mom know he was so sorry he was about to cry. If she could've seen him in the Waterbird yesterday, she wouldn't be buying it.

I held off from saying anything, figuring the kid was about to get a shucking. But Mama took one look at him, standing there all round-shouldered and sad, and she melted like butter. She blinked several times and swallowed hard, like she didn't know what to do next. After a minute, she seemed to remember they weren't alone. She turned back to me, wrapping her arms around herself and pulling one high heel, then the other out of the dirt. "I'm sorry. We had a very busy evening yesterday. I don't think Dustin meant to get himself in any further trouble."

Yeah, he didn't mean to climb those rocks or tool around the lake in the beer boat, either. "How much did your boy tell you about what happened yesterday?"

She chewed her bottom lip, and for just a second, I was thinking about her lips.

"We didn't . . . exactly . . ." Two pink fingernails pinched the bridge of her nose, her shoulders moving up and down with a breath. "We didn't have time to talk. It's really my fault as much as Dustin's. Yesterday was . . . chaotic. I should have followed up with him, and I didn't."

Followed up? She made it sound like she had to get out the Rolodex and call a business meeting with her kid.

"Ma'am, you need to know what your boy was into yesterday, and he was left with instructions to tell you about that and to let you know I'd come by here in the morning." She gave the kid another bewildered look, and I went on to explain what had happened on the lake and what Dustin was told while he was sitting in the Waterbird, waiting for her to clear her busy schedule and come after him.

She took a glance at her watch, and that pretty well drilled me.

"Listen, if all this is too much trouble for you, lady, just let me know." On a normal day, I wouldn't have popped off like that, but at the moment, I felt rough, dry, and impatient.

She jerked back, her mouth falling open. "I'm late for work," she said, like that explained everything.

I should've just let it go—spelled out Dustin's options, and left. I didn't need the hassle, but something about the way the kid was looking off toward the lake just burned me up. I had a feeling he'd be on the Scissortail again, the first chance he got. "Ma'am, are you aware that we've had seven drowning deaths on the lake this year alone? Over half of those were teenagers. Most involved alcohol and at least one stupid decision. I don't think your boy here has a full appreciation of that, but for his own good, you ought to drill it into him. He also needs to understand that underage kids and boats and beer aren't a good mix . . . before he ends up in court, or worse."

She jerked back, wide-eyed again. "Dustin would never . . ."

"Ma'am, you don't know how many times I've heard that—usually right after I find kids out in the woods partying, or wrapped around a telephone pole in a car, or upside down in a ditch, or in trouble on the lake."

She coughed like I'd offended her, and her cheeks went red and hot. Her gaze met mine with a smack, and if she'd seemed lost and confused before, she didn't look that way now. That was the look of a mama bear coming out to defend her cub. "Now, wait a minute." Hiking one hand on her hip, she pointed the other at her boy. "Dustin has never, *ever* been in trouble for anything involving . . . alcohol. He's a good kid, and maybe he didn't think things through well enough yesterday, but I can assure you that you won't be finding him out in the woods at some sort of . . . of . . . underage drinking party. He's new here, and he doesn't know those kids. I'm sure he had no idea they were carrying beer."

The boy stood a little straighter, like he figured his mama believing him would carry some weight with me. He didn't know how many times I'd picked up kids whose parents didn't have a clue what they were doing when they left the house.

"Well, I guess he oughta be more careful about who he goes out on a boat with, then, shouldn't he?" I aimed the question at him, not her, but she was the one who fielded it.

"I'm not saying that he shouldn't have. What he did was wrong, and he'll be in trouble for it." She sounded like she meant that, but Dustin looked like he was already relaxing and figuring he had this little spark of trouble tamped down. A boat passed by on the lake, and he watched it, not having much to worry about, I guessed.

"Is there anything else you need from me?" Mom asked, the words clipped short, letting me know I was sure enough harassing the two of them beyond what was right and proper.

All of a sudden, I was full-on annoyed. Some uppity rich lady trying to pave the easy road for her kid was a bad way to finish a long night. My people skills went out the window, which wasn't a long toss. Diplomacy, the lack of it, really, was the reason I'd stayed down in the dry country with the roadrunners and the coyotes for so long. "Well, as a matter of fact, there is, ma'am, and Dustin knows what it is. I'll let him tell you."

I rested my hands on my belt and watched the kid's Adam's apple bob up and down. He wasn't feeling like such a super stud now.

His mom turned to him, and he stuck his hands in the pockets of his sweats, looking at the ground while he talked to her. "Ummm . . . I've gotta . . . ummm . . ." His voice was high as a little girl's. He stopped and cleared his throat, and for just a second, I felt sorry for him. I remembered how it was to be a teenage boy with no idea whose voice would come out when I opened my mouth. Every guy remembers that. "Ummm . . . I've gotta either . . . ummm . . . get a ticket and go to juvenile court, or go to some . . . ummm . . . water safety thing . . . class the week after next."

The lady's mouth dropped open, and she

blinked at him, then at me. "You have *got* to be kidding." It was hard to tell whether she was talking to him or to me. "I understand that the alcohol is a big deal, but it wasn't Dustin's, and as for climbing the Scissortail, people have been doing that for years. *I* even climbed the Scissortail when I was young. No one ever made a federal case of it." She straightened her back, her chin jerking up, like I was some kind of lunatic. Nothing new there. You usually don't get thanks for trying to protect folks from their own stupidity.

"You been out there recently? To the Scissortail?"

"Well, no, but . . ."

"There's a big set of buoys that says to *Keep off the rocks.*"

"Well, I understand that, but . . ."

"It's a protected nesting site, for one thing."

"I understand, but Dustin didn't know that . . ."

"He can read, can't he?"

"Well, yes, of course he can." She checked her watch again, and I felt heat boiling under my collar. If she was in such an all-fired hurry, why didn't she just admit that her kid did something wrong and move on? Judging by this house, she could bail him out easy enough.

"Then he knew he wasn't supposed to be up there." I turned to the boy. He'd gone red and backed away a couple steps, trying to move himself out of the conversation. "Dustin, did you know you weren't supposed to be up there?"

He fidgeted from one foot to the other. "Well, yeah . . . yes, sir . . . but the other kids said it was okay. They said they do it, like, all the time."

"Well, maybe you oughta look into the company you keep, then, son."

He straightened back and got narrow in the eye, like all at once he'd gone mad to the bone. "I'm not your *son,* all right?"

His mom sucked in a breath. "Dustin!"

He swiveled her way with a snotty sneer. "Well, what am I supposed to do, huh? Huh? Just sit here all day by myself? This place is like a prison. There's nothing to do. I should've stayed back in Houston and lived with Dad and Delayne."

Mom caught a breath again, her hand flying toward her face like the words were a hard right cross. "Dustin!"

He looked satisfied, having landed a blow. "I don't need the stupid class, either. I'll take the ticket. Max already Facebooked me. He's taking the ticket. It's no big deal."

"You're on Facebook with those kids?"

"Yeah, so what." All of a sudden, Dustin was all attitude. The crying act was gone, and you could tell what was really going on inside. This kid was set to blow.

She pointed a finger in his face. "You know, *so*

what. You know what the rules are. You're not supposed to be adding anybody to your account without asking me."

"Oh, big deal." He bowed up his skinny chest, daring her to do anything about it. "I'm not just gonna sit here all day and do nothing. And I'm not wasting my time in some stupid class, either."

Now Mom had fire in her eye, and the thing with the live gators in the stock trailer seemed easy by comparison. All this teenage stuff was way too domestic for me.

"You are, if I say you are." She turned a shoulder my way. "You listen to me, Dustin James—"

"I'm not going! None of the other kids are going. Nobody's going!" The boy didn't wait for an answer. He just turned around and ran for the house, leaving his mama there in the yard, her hands in tight fists at her sides. When she turned around, her eyes were welling up again. I knew I needed to close this thing and head out of there before I got dragged into something that was out of my line of work. Wildlife was one thing, but crying women and family issues were another kind of mess altogether.

"Listen," I said, and handed her my business card and a brochure. "Figure out what you want to do and let me know by the end of the day. The class starts a week from Monday. Deadline to sign up is noon today, but I'll give him until five o'clock."

Her hand shook as she tucked the card in her pocket and the brochure under her arm without looking at it. "I don't have any way to get him to a class. I'm tied up with work all day." A glance fluttered my way, looking for sympathy, I guessed.

"Ma'am, all I can tell you is, between you and him, you'll have to figure that out. He needs to understand that the lake isn't a play toy. Used the wrong way, it's dangerous."

She bristled again. "He knows that. He's just . . . It's just . . ." She pressed a hand to her forehead, squeezed her eyes shut. "He's had a tough . . . year. He's not normally like this."

"I'm sure he isn't."

A crow flew into the tree nearby and let out a loud *caw*. She jumped and glanced at it, then checked her watch again.

"Let me know by the end of the day what you want to do." I figured it was time for me to leave. "It's your choice." I watched a flock of cattle egrets swirl above the lake. One more thing I was already behind on in my job—I was supposed to help with a list of invasive species for some database. The egrets were an invasive species, technically. I could add Burt and Nester's emu to the list, if I could ever find it. Pretty soon we'd end up counting those, too. "The Corps of Engineers doesn't keep the lake levels where they used to. A boy died there a couple months ago. Diving accident. Seventeen years old. Jumped off the rocks and never came up." I turned to head out. "Keep your boy off the Scissortail. For his own good."

Have patience with all things,
but first of all with yourself.
—St. Frances de Sales
(via Reverend Hay)

Chapter 7

Andrea Henderson

By the time I talked to Dustin and finally headed off to work, I was boiling in my own stew. Dustin didn't want to accept responsibility for having made a bad situation worse by not filling me in about the water safety class. All we'd done was talk in circles again. It didn't help that I was late leaving for work, and frustrated, and once again feeling like a complete failure as a parent.

Why was it so hard to find the dividing line between acknowledging Dustin's pain and allowing him to act out in ways that were inappropriate and disrespectful, even potentially dangerous? I wanted to be his confidant, his comforter, his soft place to fall, but at the same time, he needed a parent, a regulator, an enforcer of the rules. I couldn't seem to balance both roles, yet I couldn't afford to fail at either one. No matter what it took, I had to bring my little boy through this transition in life, and judging by the fact that his father hadn't even returned my calls about the late child-support check and the visitation that was supposed to take place in August, help wouldn't be coming anytime soon.

If I failed, Dustin would fail. The thought was terrifying. The fact that his father was busy building a new life with a new wife and two young stepdaughters was enough to send me over the brink. Mentally replaying the incident with the game warden didn't help, either. How dare he. He didn't know a thing about what Dustin was going through.

Keep your boy off the Scissortail . . . for his own good.

He can read, can't he?

Maybe you oughta look into the company you keep, then, son.

The more I recycled the conversation as I commuted to work, the more irritated I got. Maybe the game ranger . . . warden . . . whatever, was just doing his job, but he had some nerve acting like he knew Dustin, acting like Dustin was a teenage delinquent, looking for a beer bash on the lake. Dustin had never been to a beer bash in his life. He didn't even know those kinds of kids, much less hang out with them. He'd just . . . made an impulsive decision yesterday and landed himself in a situation he didn't know how to handle.

Hadn't he?

What had possessed him to climb the Scissortail? He was afraid of heights. He wouldn't even do the high dive at the pool in Houston. I should've told the game warden that. There was no way Dustin would have jumped off those rocks. He was probably scared to death the minute he started climbing.

Right now, I could come up with a million intelligent things I should have said to Mr. Mart McClendon, water cop, but when someone is attacking your child, it's impossible to keep cool. One of these days, I was going to mature into a fully developed adult woman who didn't react to conflict by getting in a mind frizz. After a master's degree in counseling, you'd think I would be making progress, but this morning when the game warden had shown up on our dock, I was as unprepared as ever. I was unprepared for Dustin to pick that moment to melt down, too.

I'm not your son, all right?

This place is like a prison. I should've stayed back in Houston . . . with Dad and Delayne.

What a mess. What an incredible mess. Did I have any business counseling families on how to raise their kids, when I couldn't even guide my own son smoothly through the transition from intact family to shared-custody household?

Was there a smooth transition for that?

Intact family. How many times had I heard that term thrown around in counseling classes—

blithely written it in research papers and in my master's thesis? Purely an analytical term, meaning nothing. I'd never imagined that term entering the bubble of our lives, crashing into it and leaving a jagged hole, like a bullet penetrating sheet metal, creating sharp shreds that pointed inward. Leaving Dustin and me *detached*. Separated. Not *intact*.

Other than Dustin's pain and his yearning for the way things used to be, it was the terminology, the labels I hated most, if I really let myself admit the truth, if I really got down to the core. It wasn't life within our old house or being with Karl I missed. I missed being married in front of the rest of the world. Being *intact*.

I pushed the thoughts away as I drove. One benefit to the flextime arrangement that allowed me to come in at eight thirty, rather than eight, was that I missed some of the morning tangle of commuters heading for jobs in the Dallas Metroplex.

My boss, Dr. Dale Tazinski, fondly known to personnel in our small office as Taz, was in the front hall by the coffee machine when I came in. "Nice of you to join us, Henderson. Hear you had some adventures yesterday." Fortunately, he was smiling when he said it. Remarkable, considering that I'd already called in this morning to tell Bonnie there had been a problem with Dustin, and I would be a little late. After yesterday's debacle, if I were the boss, I probably wouldn't have been as cheerful as Taz. In my two weeks of shadowing him while doing my in-office training, I'd learned that he was amazingly tolerant.

"You missed the morning meeting. It was a quick one, though." Taz's belly lopped over the table as he upturned a second coffee cup and saluted my arrival with the pot. "Coffee?"

"Please," I said, making my way into the entry while juggling my briefcase, my purse, Dad's car keys, and a cart full of counseling materials and CPS referrals I hadn't read last night. The door hung open behind me, and since my hands were full, I hooked the toe of my shoe over the edge and pulled it shut. Taz's secretary had promised me you got good at that maneuver after a while— a necessity, as Taz's plan to move out of the strip mall that housed his practice was temporarily on hold. The fact that decent real estate cost money had kept him in the decaying building, sharing space with a hair salon, a doughnut shop, and a secondhand furniture store.

Right now he was eyeing a box of chocolate twists the Cambodian lady next door had undoubtedly brought over. My boss was her favorite customer, and every time he got in the mood to actually follow his heart doctor's advice and lose weight, Mai plied him with freebies. In my weeks of following him around while learning the business, I'd quickly discerned that flattery and food were the ways to his heart. Once you got there, it was a pretty big place, fortunately.

The last thing I wanted to do was take advantage of that kindness. I wanted to prove myself by doing good work. Post-divorce adjustment or not, I needed to be competent and fully put together. Taz had hired me because the load of contract cases referred to his practice by CPS had grown beyond the scope that even a workaholic psychologist and his small staff could handle. He was so desperate that he'd given me the job, even though my only experience was the counseling time I'd racked up at a church-sponsored family crisis center in downtown Houston.

"Tough morning?" Taz asked, tucking away the coffeepot while eyeing the doughnuts. He licked his lips, salivating like one of Pavlov's dogs.

"Not so bad." I was afraid to tell the truth and expose instability at home. *No problems here. Nothing I can't control.*

He raised a skeptical brow, studying me with one dull hazel eye wider than the other. One should always be careful when lying to a trained psychologist.

Sighing, I snagged my cup of coffee from the table. "Just a little issue with Dustin. He and some friends had a minor run-in with the lake patrol yesterday. The kids were climbing on the rocks where they shouldn't have been."

Taz's gaze gravitated toward the doughnuts again, following the magnetic pull of carbohydrates and saturated fat. "That doesn't sound so bad."

"Well, I didn't think so, either." I relaxed and took a sip of my coffee, then leaned against the table. Taz's counseling powers were working. I was already feeling better about the morning. Maybe the scene wasn't as traumatic as it had seemed in the moment. Most things aren't. "The game warden was a real jerk about it, though. He came by to tell me what a delinquent my son was."

My boss's lips curved upward. "Sounding a little parentally defensive, there, are we?"

I shrugged grudgingly. I couldn't help being protective of Dustin. "Well, you know, the whole macho power trip thing was just a little hard to take first thing in the morning."

Taz fished a chocolate twist from the box, checking the hallway to make sure the secretary, Bonnie, wasn't within line of sight. Bonnie was the most maternal twenty-something I'd ever met. She wanted a husband and kids but hadn't found Mr. Right, so she'd taken up raising dogs and mothering everyone in the office, including the boss.

Shifting his coffee cup so that it dangled next to

the doughnut, Taz snatched up a coffee-spattered file folder and tucked it under his arm. "I'm an adult. I can have a doughnut if I want, can't I?" The question had a touch of the rhetorical to it, as if it begged an answer, but he already knew what the answer would be.

I shrugged, wisely remaining mum as he turned to leave.

Passing by the copier, he took a bite of the doughnut, then glanced back at me, dropped the remainder in the trash, and offered a little closed-lipped smirk with chocolate frosting on top. "Sometimes, it's the principle of the thing, Henderson. Even when someone is looking after our welfare, we don't like being told what to do."

Leaning over to check the trash can, he seemed pleased with himself. "A high school football player from Fort Worth broke his back jumping off the Scissortail last fall. Had a fundraiser for him on Channel 9. Nice-looking kid." Taz's gaze slid slowly from the trash can to me, his eyes suddenly seeming steady and wise. "It's all in your perspective."

He walked away without further conversation, and I stood there with my coffee cup suspended halfway to my mouth, thinking, *Andrea Henderson, you have just been counseled.* The primary reason I was still mentally rehashing this morning's conversation with the game warden was that I didn't want someone else telling me what my son needed.

Pride goeth before the fall. One of those inconvenient proverbs that lurks in the back of your head once you've heard it a few thousand times from your mother. Megan was always the pliable one in the family, and I the notoriously determined child who seemed to find trouble without even looking for it. My mother always complained that I took after my grandmother's sister, Lucy, the black sheep who lived an odd life hip-hopping around the world with the Peace Corps, until finally she took a medical ship bound for Africa, where she contracted anthrax and died.

In our family, Lucy had always been held up as an example of pride, stubbornness, and getting too big for your britches, but I admired her. I wanted to be like her, even though I'd never had the courage to step that far outside the lines. I was a frustrated crusader, afraid to leave my own backyard because my mother would make a federal case of it. Taking this job was the first out-of-the-box thing I'd ever done. Insecurity, in this situation, was defeat. I had to find ways to remain certain of myself, of my own plans, to provide Dustin with a sense of security and a vision of the future. I had to show him that we could create something good from pieces of our old life and pieces of the new.

Bonnie came out of the supply closet and passed by with an armload of printer paper. She was cheery, as usual, bouncing up the hall with a ponytail of slick-as-glass blond hair sweeping the back of her neck like a windshield wiper. "Hey! Mornin'!" she chirped, stopping a few steps up the hall. "Everything okay at home?"

"Sure," I said. "Fine."

"How's your son?" Nothing happened in the office without Bonnie getting in the middle of it. She already talked about Dustin as if he were her little brother or her nephew.

"Oh, well, you know. He's just becoming a teenager. Having a few growing pains."

Bonnie stood watching me with curious, empathic blue eyes, as if she knew there was more to tell. Drifting a few steps closer, she hugged the paper to her chest.

"He's never had to move before," I added.

She sucked in her cheeks, the action making her narrow face seem even thinner and more angular. "Oh, sure," she breathed, one side of her mouth pulling downward in a sympathetic frown. "It's rough, moving at that age. We relocated from Texas to upstate New York when I was in the eighth grade, and I just about went suicidal. The kids there thought I was some kind of alien from Howdy-Doodyville. Of course, it didn't help that I was already five foot eight, skinny as a rail, and had a flatter chest than most of the boys. If the basketball coach up there hadn't taken me under wing, I don't know what I would've done. She saved my life, I think."

I felt the inconvenient tug of shared emotion. I could relate to being the gawky, skinny, tall girl, and aside from that, I wanted to believe that someone here in Moses Lake would spot Dustin's talents and take an interest in him. "I'm hoping it will work out that way for Dustin—that he'll find some people at school he can relate to, I mean."

Bonnie squinted toward the ceiling, seeming to comb her memory banks. "I think there's a guy in my apartment complex who's, like, a coach out there at Moses Lake. I'll see if I can catch him and tell him about Dustin. It never hurts for someone to be on the lookout for you your first day, right?"

I had the urge to break all the rules of professional decorum and give Bonnie a great, big hug right there in the office hallway. "Thanks."

"Oh, sure." She batted a hand as if to say, *What's a little favor between girlfriends, hon?* Then she fished a few printed papers off her stack and handed them to me. "Here. Notes from the morning meeting. I'm working on contacting the appointments you missed yesterday and doing reschedules. A lot of these CPS families don't have phones, so all I can do is leave a message with a neighbor, or a relative, or whatever. I'll try to get them—especially the family that got reported by the bus driver—scheduled as soon as I can. You never know from one day to the next who'll be in the household and what the mood's gonna be. I guess Taz told you that. They just change when the wind blows. If you give them too much time, they'll come right back around to deciding they don't need family counseling, and then their CPS caseworker has to start all over again, trying to get them to cooperate with us."

"Thanks," I said, taking the morning meeting notes. "And thanks for offering to make a contact for Dustin."

Bonnie smiled brightly. "Oh, it's no big deal. The teenagers from the little church out at Moses Lake come over and do stuff with the youth group at my church, sometimes. I'll find out when they've got something planned, and you could bring Dustin. He can get acquainted, and you and me can go . . . have a latte in the coffee shop. I'll tell you all Taz's secrets."

My mind did a rapid rewind, racing backward. I hadn't meant to get sucked into an invitation to Bonnie's church. After having been ditched and gossiped about by so many friends and fellow church members during the divorce, I wasn't ready to build any social networks. I just wanted to live a quiet life, find purpose in my work, make a difference to kids who needed help, and take care of my son. "I think we'll be pretty busy until school starts. Thanks, though. Really."

I continued on down the corridor to my windowless office in the back of the building. Taz had been apologetic when he'd shown it to me. My accommodations didn't really matter, anyway. With so much fieldwork, I wouldn't be spending much time in the office.

After I'd glanced over the morning meeting notes from Bonnie and gathered yet another load of CPS referrals via e-mail, I headed off for my first appointment, and the day limped by in a strange mishmash of trying to locate homes and apartments that even my Garmin couldn't find, trips through creepy neighborhoods in various economically deprived little towns in the area, and awkward first meetings with families on my list of referrals. Compared to the two weeks of training, the actual job was a shock.

What Taz had referred to as *A position contracting with Social Services,* was really me driving around in my car, seeking out people whose reasons for being referred for counseling services were generally described to me in short, hurried descriptions dashed off by overburdened caseworkers. Complete addresses were a plus, but not a requirement. Names added another level of challenge. When faced with questions such as, "Was you lookin' for Big Bo or Little Bo?" I had no choice but to admit that I had no idea. At one household, I spoke to four different generations of a family, and not one person admitted to being the individual whose name was on the referral form. When you don't know whether you're looking for a client who's eight or forty-eight, it's anybody's guess. The referral e-mail simply read, *Bo Brown: family issues, depression. Please counsel for anger management.*

Late in the day, I finally visited with the family who'd been referred for fighting in the yard while the bus driver was running the summer-school route. We held a family counseling session on the front porch. The boyfriend who'd caused the commotion wasn't present, but I talked with the children and then with the mother, Lonnie. Lonnie had a black eye that had turned yellow and brown. Her boyfriend hadn't caused it, she insisted. The kids' horse had butted her in the face while she was feeding it. In the muddy lot beside the house, the old, rawboned horse looked like it hadn't seen oats in quite some time.

After getting Lonnie's side of the story, I asked to talk to the children alone. Lonnie shrugged and said, "Suit yerself. They don't got nothin' to say, except that the bus driver scared them the other day when he wouldn't let them off the bus. The kids on the school bus pick on my kids all the time, too. I want you to talk to the school about that. Tell them those kids're pickin' on my kids." She stood up and went in the house.

The little boy, John, and his older sister,

Audrey, shared the horse's tired, dull-eyed look. While we talked, they sat on the porch floor, pressed against the railing, eyeballing me as if I were an alien invader. A half-grown cat wandered by, and the little boy, John, picked it up and began searching through its fur.

"That's a nice kitten," I said, scooting forward on the old sofa that served as porch furniture. Dampness from the cushions had soaked into my pants, and I was quickly realizing that I wasn't properly attired for this job. My father's car wasn't the right vehicle for it, either. Right now it was parked out front, covered in mud and road goo.

"It's my favorite," John answered, then pinched something off the kitten's skin and dropped it into the weeds below. "He gots ticks."

A crawly feeling slid over my skin, and I wanted to get up and stand in one small spot, not touching anything. "Well, it's a good thing he has you to look after him, then, huh?"

John peeked up at me with a sliver of interest. "Tamp says if the little turd gets ticks in the house, he's gonna take 'im down and drown 'im in the lake. Tamp don't like cats."

From the corner of my eye, I saw Lonnie stiffen behind the screen door and shake her head at the unflattering mention of the man of the house. "Tamp never said he was gonna drown no kitten, John. Don't be makin' up stories."

I ignored her input and remained focused on John. "He's a beautiful kitten. He's your favorite?"

"Yup." John brightened again. His sister reached across the space between them and scratched the kitten's head. "Sissy had one, too, but Tamp run over hers with the truck."

"Tamp didn't run over no kitten," Lonnie corrected from behind the screen door. "I told you, that was my fault. I forgot to look before we got in the truck."

John slanted a sideways look at the door, then shrugged and began searching for ticks again. The timer on my cell phone vibrated in my pocket, which meant I was due to leave. I didn't feel that I'd accomplished anything beyond, perhaps, the building of a smidge of rapport.

"I'll bet that was sad," I said. "Losing your kitten."

Audrey nodded. "The coyotes or the bobcats got two. Or maybe a mountain lion. A mountain lion jumped on one of them hikers in the park a couple months ago." She looked up, her eyes a soft, golden brown in a frame of red hair. I wanted to lead her off the porch, put her in my car, and take her home.

"I hadn't heard that. I'm sorry about your kittens, though. Losing a pet is like losing a person in your family, huh?" The cell phone vibrated again. Time to go.

"My daddy died," John offered. "He liked cats."

102

A lump rose in my throat. "That's good. I like cats, too."

The next thing I knew, the cat was in my lap, and John was sitting beside me on the sofa. I stroked the kitten, and it purred.

My cell phone vibrated again.

"How come your pocket's buzzin'?" John asked.

I chuckled. "It's time for me to go."

"You gonna come back?" He tilted his chin up, his eyes meeting mine.

"Next week."

For a moment, he studied me, seeming to wonder if I really meant it. Then he took the cat from my lap, tucked it under his chin, and returned to the other side of the porch.

I confirmed next week's appointment with Lonnie, then left feeling useless and defeated. On the porch, the kids stood watching, their gazes tracking my movements, as if they were afraid for me to go, yet afraid for me to ask any more questions. Clearly, they knew what not to say. They'd already been in foster care five times in their short lives. All they really wanted to know from me was whether I was going to send them back.

I can't help these people, I thought as I walked away. *I don't even know where to start.* Counseling here was a world away from seeing clients at a church counseling center in Houston.

Even at the crisis center, people had come in because they knew they were in desperate need, but here . . . How could you help someone who didn't want help? Who only wanted to convince you to sign off on some form, so they could keep doing what they'd always been doing?

The sad thing was that my parents were right. This job was unpredictable, potentially dangerous, and I didn't belong in it. If Tamp didn't mind threatening school bus drivers, beating up his girlfriend, and drowning kittens, how safe was I? If I were working at the bank, short of a bank robbery, I'd be safe, but I'd never make enough money to provide a good life for Dustin and myself. We'd always be scraping by, taking help-money from my parents.

Aside from that, there was a nagging voice deep within me, warning that if I quit this job now, I'd never have the courage to do something like this again. My life in the future would be what my life had always been—a repetitive pattern of concentric circles, safely inside the box. I'd never become what I'd always dreamed of being—a woman like Aunt Lucy, who wasn't afraid to take on the world and do the good that would have gone undone without her.

On the other hand, if I continued in this position, I'd have to figure out how to actually do the job.

Hard to say which option was more frightening.

I contemplated my dilemma while seeing to my last visit of the day, a young mother who was struggling to care for a son with autism and three other kids, while her husband was deployed with the military. Her preteen daughter had run away from home, twice. They recognized the need for help, and even though lines of family communication were slow in forming, we did make progress. I gave them some family projects to complete before our next visit, and they sounded like they'd try. I left the session and headed home with a renewed sense of energy about the day. Maybe I really could do this job. I just had to be bold and keep learning. A lot and quickly.

It wasn't until I passed the Waterbird and spotted a game warden's truck in front that I remembered I was supposed to answer the question of Dustin's punishment before five o'clock today.

It was already five forty-five.

The bigger the fisherman, the bigger the tale.
—Anonymous
(Left by five old friends on
an annual fishing trip)

Chapter 8

Mart McClendon

I'm telling you, Mart, there's something going on. Daddy saw it. . . . Didn't you, Daddy?" Sheila had been on a tear since the minute I strolled into the Waterbird to pick up a deli sandwich for supper. It was hard to figure why she was so hung up on poor old Len Barnes and the little girl she thought she'd spotted by the Big Boulders yesterday. It seemed to me like poor old Len had enough trouble already. Other than fish-and-game violations, he seemed harmless enough, but Shelia was on this like a dog on a bone.

She was shaking a finger toward the Big Boulders while she talked. "Len was over there running trotlines again this morning, and there was someone moving around in the bushes. Whoever it was didn't come all the way to the shore this time, so I couldn't get a good look, but someone was there. Someone small, like a child."

"He's got all those mutt dogs. That could've been what you saw in the brush," Burt suggested.

He and Nester were holed up at the corner table, nursing coffee and having a domino game because it was too hot to fish. "I saw him out at the Crossroads selling tomatoes, as usual, and he was all by himself, except he had a great big dog with him—pit bull, I'd say. Kind of whitish-colored with a brown snout. He'd tied it to his bumper and parked the truck up the ditch a ways, then brought all his vegetable crates down to the shoulder. Guess he figured he better keep that dog away from the customers. I was glad of it. That mutt flashed a little tooth when I stopped. I bought my tomatoes and got out of there. I didn't want to trust my life to Len's knot-tying skills."

Nester glanced at me and winked to let me know he was about to put one over on Burt. "Mart, did you know I had a dog like that once? Big ol' pit bull, but then I found him out in the yard one day, deader'n a post."

"I didn't know that, Nester," I said, playing along with the joke, whatever it'd be. I leaned up against the counter, getting comfortable.

Burt hooked an elbow over the back of the booth. "Nester, what are you talking about? You didn't have any pit bull dog."

"You never saw 'im," Nester insisted. "Thing died two days after I bought it. Was a high-dollar animal, too. Paid two hundred bucks for him, over to the swap meet. Once he died, I called that dog breeder over in Gun Barrel City, and I said,

'Mister, you sold me a defective dog. He up and died.'

"Well, then that fella, he tried to tell me I was mistaken. 'Ain't no way that dog's dead,' he says to me. 'You get me some proof he's dead, well, I'll give your money back.'"

Shaking her head, Sheila leaned across the counter and muttered, "Mart, you better run while you can. They'll go on like this all night." She poured a cup of coffee for me, and I picked it up and took a sip. Decaf, no doubt. I should've had Pop get my coffee.

Nester launched into the rest of a story that promised to be entertaining, if not strictly factual. "So I load that dog up in the truck, and I take him to the vet. Old Doc Brown, he thinks I'm a little crazy, but he says okay, he'll check the dog over. So here in a minute, he brings in a little gray house cat. He puts that cat on the table, and the cat walks around my dog once, twice, three times, then he sits down on the floor and shakes its head, real solemnlike.

"The vet says to me, he says, 'Yes, sir, yer dog's dead.'

"So I tell him, 'Doc, I gotta have more proof than the say-so of a house cat. There's two hundred dollars on the line here.'

"The vet says to me, 'All right, then.' He goes out the door with the cat and comes back with a brown Labrador. The lab, he takes one look at the

108

examination table, then sits down and shakes his head. Doc says, 'Yep, your dog's dead all right.'

" 'Listen, Doc,' I say. 'I got to have some real proof other than the say-so of a house cat and a Labrador.'

"Ol' Doc, he just smiles and scribbles somethin' on a piece of paper and hands it to me and says, 'Fella, you just call up that man and tell him this dog's sure enough dead, and you got the cat scan and the lab report to prove it!' "

Nester reared back and slapped his knee, impressed that he'd sucked Burt into his joke. Burt pulled his hat down over his eyes and shook his head, Pop Dorsey hee-hawed so hard he knocked his wheelchair into the coffee counter, and Sheila groaned and rolled her eyes. I had to give Nester credit. I hadn't heard that one before.

"That's a good'un," Pop said finally.

Nester grinned. "It's all true." He pointed to a fish-shaped sign on Pop's wall of wisdom. "Just like that sign says, *The bigger the fisherman, the bigger the tale.*"

Sheila stepped out from behind the counter. "Well, you boys can swap jokes all you want, but I'm telling you, Len's got a child with him. I'm not imagining things."

"Nobody's seen her but you," Nester pointed out.

Sheila gave him a frustrated look. "Mart, didn't you see *anything* over there on shore by the Big

Boulders? Footprints or anything? That little girl must've left footprints when she came down to the shore yesterday, and she must've been with that old man. He was the only one around there, and then today, someone's prowling around in the bushes near where he's fishing? That doesn't seem weird to you?"

The door chimed, but none of us turned to look right away. Everyone's attention was fastened on me.

I took off my hat and scratched my head, sorry that the all-nighter with the gators had kept me from checking out the Big Boulders yesterday and settling the latest argument at the Waterbird. "By the time I went by there today, it'd rained. There weren't any tracks. I didn't come across Len, and I didn't see any sign of a little girl. My guess is Burt's right. What you saw was probably one of those mutts Len's always carting around in that old truck of his."

Sheila gave me a disgusted look. "I did *not* see a dog. There was *somebody* on that shore yesterday. A little dark-haired girl in a brown dress." The look in Sheila's eyes dared anybody to offer up the dog theory again. "You know, it's up to citizens to keep an eye out, and law enforcement"—she gave me a pointed stare—"ought to respect that. What about that case that was on TV, where that man kidnapped a little girl and held her prisoner in his backyard for almost twenty years? Concerned citizens saw things going on at that house, but none of it was ever investigated. It's just the kind of thing that happens."

"You oughta help Reverend Hay with his next theater production, down at the Tin Building, Sheila." Nester turned back to the domino game. "You got a flare for the dramatic."

Snorting, Sheila smacked a hand on the counter and turned away, quitting the conversation.

"I saw a truck . . . a gray Ford with a dog in the back and a little dark-haired girl in the passenger seat," someone offered from over by the door.

All three of us swiveled around, and there was Dustin's mom. I'd forgotten all about her, which was good, since this morning's meeting hadn't come out too shiny.

Sheila jumped on the new information. "You did? Where? When?"

Dustin's mom took a few more steps across the room, a little wrinkle in her nose as she eyeballed Dorsey's collection of wall-mounted fish and stuffed wildlife. "Yesterday. Somewhere up in Chinquapin Peaks." Motioning vaguely toward the hills, she walked past me like I wasn't there, on her way to talk to Sheila.

I watched her pass by. Nester caught my eye and pointed behind her back, his mouth circling in a silent whistle and his eyes wide, like, *Look 'a-there, Mart, a real, live g-i-r-l.*

I made out like I didn't notice—Nester or the girl.

"I was out on the other side of the lake yesterday afternoon, and my car broke down," she told Sheila. "The truck went by, and it was all just very . . . odd." She introduced herself to Sheila, and the name clicked in my memory. Andrea. Andrea Henderson.

Sheila shook her hand. "Oh, so you're Dustin's mom. Sorry we were in such a rush when you picked him up. One minute I heard someone coming in the door, and by the time I finished with the bus customers, Dustin was gone."

"My sister came to get him, actually," Andrea said. A flash of emotion crossed her face, but she smoothed it away, just as quick. This woman was cool as an icehouse latch, when she wanted to be. "I hated that I couldn't be here to help sort things out. Yesterday was pretty crazy. About the time Dustin was . . . AWOL on the lake, I was trying to get myself out of the backwoods with a flat tire. While I was stuck there, a gray truck came by with a seriously nasty dog chained in the back. There was an old man behind the wheel, and a little girl in the passenger seat. She turned around and looked at me when they passed. The driver stopped, and I thought he was going to get out and help me, but he didn't. He just drove away."

Sheila flashed a sneer my way, as in, *Mart, I told you that old man was up to something.*

112

In the booth, Nester perked up, sensing a topic that'd be even more interesting than the day's fishing report. "Was the truck all rusted up? Did it have a old greasy-haired man in a blue ball cap drivin' it?"

Andrea described Len and his truck to a T—right down to Len's dry-rotted ball cap and the way his truck wheezed and belched like a chain smoker gasping for air. Tired or not, my interest level went up.

"The whole thing gave me goose bumps at the time. I didn't quite . . ." She paused, her gaze taking in a stuffed bobcat with a quail in its mouth, her lip curling on one side. "I didn't quite know what to make of it, but I was busy trying to figure out how to change a tire." Her mouth twitched at the corners, like the memory was funny now. Guess she did have a sense of humor, after all. "But sometimes you get just a base-level reaction, and you don't pay too much attention right then, but it bothers you later, you know? It bothered me that the little girl was a mess, dirty and unkempt, and that she wasn't wearing a seatbelt. I just brushed it off as a grandparent who didn't know the laws, or didn't take time to buckle her in."

Nester rolled a narrow look at me, then turned back to Andrea. "That'd be Len, all right. But he ain't nobody's grandpa. Len's never had a family. He went off to Vietnam right after high school.

Got shrapnel in his head. He wasn't no Rhodes Scholar before that, but after, he come home and lived with his mama and daddy, and they took care of him. But they been dead quite a while, I reckon. Nobody's seen either one of them in years. Len probably dug a hole and buried them up there in the hills. That man's simple as a mudbug and smells twice as bad. Mart, there's no way some woman would be getting with him and makin' babies." Nester leaned back and frowned at me, concerned.

A question came to my mind, and I just went ahead and asked Andrea. "What were you doing up on the other side of the lake? That's pretty remote territory." It wasn't like me to be interested in other people's business. Normally, I was happy to let them keep theirs and I'd keep mine. Simpler that way. But I had to admit that all of a sudden, I was curious about Dustin's mom. I couldn't quite put a finger on why that was. In some way or other, Andrea Henderson just didn't add up.

Andrea seemed to think about that for a minute—like she wasn't sure whether she should tell. "I had an appointment up that way."

Appointment had a funny ring to it. "An appointment?" What kind of business would someone like her have on the other side of the lake? The land was worthless, half of it only accessible by logging roads the county didn't even maintain. Back in the day, the area suited rumrunners and mash brewers. Now it attracted pot growers, meth boilers, and folks like Len, who had to live anyplace they could.

The outgoing game warden had warned me to watch myself over there. *Stumble off into some redneck's marijuana patch, you'll wake up dead,* he said. *Don't try to be a hero out there. You spot something like that, you back off and call the boys from Drug Enforcement. That's their problem. You can notify the county sheriff, but you won't get him to go up there, either. He ain't an idiot.* He finished the conversation with stories about hikers, tourists in canoes, and hapless sheriff's deputies who'd stumbled into the wrong field and were never heard from again.

"You a real estate agent, or somethin'?" Nester asked, trying to answer the same question I was pondering.

"I'm a counselor working on contract with the Department of Family and Protective Services." Andrea flicked a glance my way. Maybe she knew what I was thinking. *The lady whose kid's been running loose on the lake tells other people what they're doing wrong?*

Nester seemed surprised, and Burt blinked and sat back. He probably knew what it took to deal with some of those families in Chinquapin Peaks. "I thought Tazinski did the CPS work up there.

We had some dealings, back when I was principal at the school."

Andrea stood a little taller, like she was trying to convince us that she was up to the job. "Dr. Tazinski hired me to assist in his practice. All the fieldwork for CPS is too much for him. He's had some health issues."

Burt's look turned serious. "You ought to be careful out in that area. Tazinski tell you that? Be sure you know exactly where you're going. Some of those folks don't cotton to strangers driving up. Isn't that right, Mart?"

Everyone but Andrea turned my way. "Some of them," I said.

Pop wheeled his chair from behind the counter. "Well, I been knowin' Len Barnes all his life, and I just can't feature that he'd hurt anybody. I've bought vegetables and jerky from him for years. Never known him to cause any trouble."

Sheila frowned sideways at him. "Daddy, you don't *know* Len at all, really. That's the truth of it. Just because he comes here with tomatoes and jerky, that doesn't mean you know what he's doing the rest of the time. He poaches in the park and lays out catfish lines when he isn't supposed to. Maybe he does other things, too. Look at that case that was just in the news. That man had neighbors, for heaven's sake, and a criminal history, and everybody just told themselves he was a little odd, or whatever. Now they think he may have been involved in the disappearances of other children over the years—three at least."

Nester nodded, stroking his chin. "There's been four kids go missin' around the lake and never been heard from again in the last . . . what . . . twenty years or so? First one was that little Sanford child. Disappeared from the fourth-grade field trip and they never found him. They dragged the lake and searched the woods for weeks, remember? In ninety-one, that was."

Burt cast a concerned look my way. "That'd be about the time we stopped seein' Len's folks, Mart."

I figured it was time to tone down the speculation, but Pop beat me to it. "All right, now, y'all. You're gonna have the man tried and convicted, and there ain't one shred of proof he done anything. Maybe that little girl belongs to one of his neighbors, or a relative, or somethin'."

"What neighbors and what relatives?" Sheila shot a worried look my way. "We need to call somebody. Mart, you're law enforcement. Get the sheriff to go up there. If you tell him to do it, maybe he'll actually get off his duff and go."

"I think Len's place might be over the county line," Burt put in.

Nester snatched a napkin from the basket and slid a pen out of his shirt pocket, like he was ready to take notes. "Somebody oughta check with the FBI and see if there's been any little girls of that description reported missin', or . . ."

"All right, now, hold on a minute," I said loud enough to get everyone's attention before we spun off into an episode of redneck CSI. "Everybody just calm down before we run Len up the flagpole. We don't even know . . ."

The door opened and Reverend Hay stepped in, carrying a nice rod-and-reel combo. Looked like he'd been on the lake, or else was headed that way. He had on all the official gear, straight out of a Field and Stream catalog. Being only a little over thirty and a big-city transplant to the Lakeshore Community Church, Hay had to work hard to fit in. He'd bought himself a used two-man bass rig, but he couldn't keep it running half the time.

He crossed the room and handed his rod to Burt. The thing was bird-nested so badly, he'd probably never get the line untangled.

"Well, Reverend Hay, you've got a mess here," Burt observed. "It'll need new line again."

Hay nodded. "I was afraid of that." He sauntered over to the drink machines, his long legs sagging and straightening like the pants on a scarecrow. Nester examined the reel while Reverend Hay whipped himself up an Icee. "Hey, Mart, you give any thought to what I asked you the other day?"

"Yeah, not really." Hay'd caught me at the gas station last Saturday and hit me up about helping with one of his productions at the Tin Building Theater. That was about as far from my kind of thing as it could get.

"We're doing *The Waltons' Christmas* as our production this fall. You'd be perfect for the sheriff."

Andrea gave me a surprised look, and Nester chuckled.

"You going to put Mart in the play?" Burt asked. He was chugging like a steam engine when he said it.

I could feel Andrea watching, and all of a sudden, I remembered the public humiliation that'd ended my acting career in the eighth grade. A guy doesn't recover easily from a blow like that. "Think I'm gonna have to pass on that for now, Reverend Hay," I said.

Hay shrugged, good-natured as usual. "Give it some thought. I'll be casting for a week or two." He filled his cup in different-colored layers, like a kid turned loose at the ice cream counter. "Hey, anybody know if old Len's got a family?"

All of a sudden, he had the eyes of everybody in the room. He was busy making Icee art, so he didn't notice the rest of the crowd hanging in air.

"What?" Nester scooted to the end of the booth. "You see Len with somebody?"

Hay finished drawing his Icee and noticed everyone's attention trained on him. His eyelids lifted on the top and stretched on the bottom, so that he looked like Wile E. Coyote, right about the time he realizes he's stepped off a cliff. "Well, yeah. I ran across him at the Crossroads earlier, and there was a little girl playing around in the cedars, up by his truck. I stopped to pick up some vegetables, and he seemed kind of flustered. It was a bit hard to understand what he was trying to tell me, but I think he said she was his daughter. I didn't know Len had anybody. Anyway, I thought I might go up to his place tomorrow and try to make a vis—" He stopped midsentence and set the Icee on the counter. "What am I missing, here?"

Sheila plunked down a roll of quarters she was about to unwrap. "That does it. I'm calling Social Services."

Every fishing water has its secrets. . . .
And to yield up these mysteries,
it must be fished with more than hooks.
—Zane Gray
(Left by an Irish poet riding out a
thunderstorm at the Waterbird)

Chapter 9

Andrea Henderson

My mother always warned that, sooner or later, I'd stick my nose into something that would be the death of me. Perhaps her fear hailed from the fact that I'd come into the world early, in fragile health, or perhaps it was just her nature, but she felt the need to convince me that I was created only to aspire to small, manageable, predictable things. Were I to attempt something grander, I would be going beyond my abilities and inviting disaster. Any path other than the one she'd laid out for me was the road to ruin. *Leave other people to their own affairs until you have your own house in order. God did not appoint you the keeper of the world, Andrea Jane.*

Maybe those very warnings were the reason I felt the need to step into the middle of the developing situation at the Waterbird. When the game warden told the woman behind the cash register to hold off calling Social Services until he could go across the lake and take a look, the first words out of my mouth were, "I'm coming with you."

He gaped at me, his face slowly turning stern under the brim of his straw cowboy hat. "Listen, this isn't some field trip. Once we get across the lake, we'll be going the rest of the way on foot, and I don't know how far that'll be. I'm not exactly sure where Len's place is, but I've got an idea where he puts his boat in and out of the river. You don't look like you're dressed for a hike in the woods." He motioned to my pantsuit and pumps, which I'd already decided were headed for the closet, only to come out on non-field days. When you're rummaging around low-rent apartment complexes and slogging through horse pastures and chicken yards to get to houses, casual attire is a must.

The game warden was probably right, but I couldn't help feeling that he was questioning my credentials rather than my clothes. "I can handle it. I've been through worse to get to CPS cases." *In my one and a half actual days in the field.*

He quirked a brow. His eyes were bloodshot and red-rimmed underneath. His hand rested on his belt, like he was going to draw down on me. I wondered if that was a habit, or if he meant something by it. Arrogant jerk. No wonder the incident with the kids had turned into such a mess yesterday. "Listen, lady, I'm not a baby-sitter. When we show up sniffing around Len's place, he's as liable to take potshots at us as to roll out the welcome mat. People up there don't appreciate visitors."

"Yes, I know. I work up there, remember? I'm aware of the risks." Inside me, the still, small voice of caution was whispering, *Are you out of your head? What do you think you're doing? You're not the keeper of the world, Andrea Jane. Mind your own affairs and let other people mind theirs.* In spite of the fact that I wanted to rail against my mother's admonitions, I knew she was probably right. I'd called Dustin to tell him I was stopping at the store and would be a little late getting home. He wasn't expecting me to be gone for another hour, or however long this would take.

On the other hand, Dustin was safe, warm, and dry. That little girl might not be. In the corner of my mind, the rusty gray pickup was passing by, a snarling dog in the back, the little girl pressing her hand to the window glass, her blue eyes watching me, curious, intent, needy in some way that touched a place deep within me. "Listen, if you send this over to CPS, there's no telling when, or if, it will be investigated. All you have right now are a few vague suspicions. Nobody's seen anything happen to this child. CPS has to focus on the most critical incidents—cases in which a risk to the child has been identified.

"If you go up there, if you do find that this . . . Len has a little girl with him, the situation becomes even more complex. You won't be able to count on the little girl to tell you the truth. Kids are very coachable. They quickly attach to their caretakers, even ones who hurt them. There are certain questions to ask, certain red flags to look for."

Before the words were even out of my mouth, I'd made up my mind. Every once in a while, you just feel a tug on your soul and know there's something you're supposed to do. If the game warden was going up there, one way or another, I was going along. With no real evidence and no complaint, CPS here could take weeks to look into it, if ever. In the meantime, anything could be happening to that little girl. It wasn't accidental that I'd been there when that truck passed by yesterday. I was meant to see.

"I think she should go with you, Mart," the pastor, Reverend Hay, interjected. "In general, children are more comfortable with a woman. I'd be willing to ride along, as well."

The clerk behind the counter nodded. "I agree; you need someone along who's trained in dealing with children in crisis situations."

The game warden, Mart, lifted a hand, palm-out like a stop sign. "Hold on a minute. Nobody knows there's a *situation* happening here. I'm just going to take a look around—figure out exactly where Len's place is, and see what I can see. Could be you've all got yourselves in a tangle over nothing."

"You *know* there's more to it, or you wouldn't be going," I insisted.

Mart drew back, blinked, and rubbed one eye with the pads of his fingers. "Listen, if there is a . . . something criminal involving this little girl, it falls under the penal code, not parks-and-wildlife code. It's the county sheriff's jurisdiction."

"Pppfff!" The clerk rolled her eyes, bracing her hands on the counter and leaning forward. "Come on, unless it affects the home-owners with money or the tourists at the state park, they don't care."

"I'm going with you," I said again.

Mart drummed his fingertips against his belt and squinted speculatively toward the opposite shore, as if he were trying to imagine what he would find. "Suit yourself," he answered finally, then started toward the back door. Holding it open, he waved toward the fly-infested porch. "Reverend Hay, you coming along on this tour, too?"

The pastor nodded, topping off his Icee. "Suppose I ought to." He started across the room, and I followed.

"You need any more help, Mart?" one of the

coffee-drinking customers asked, grinning at the game warden. "Want me to call SWAT?"

Mart slid his sunglasses into place, then grabbed the brim of his hat and pulled it low over his eyes. "Yeah, we might need it."

Before following him down the hill, I texted Dustin, letting him know I would be a while. According to his reply, he was outside working on the list of chores I'd given him that morning—his consequence for the Scissortail incident—and Megan had shown up with the twins for a swim. I was comforted by the fact that he wasn't home alone this evening.

It wasn't until I was bouncing across the lake in the game warden's boat that it occurred to me to tell Dustin we had lunchmeat, hot dogs, and a roasted chicken in the refrigerator, if Meg and the kids wanted something to eat. Pulling out my cell phone, I checked to see if I could get a signal. There was none, of course. Just before I folded the phone, we hit a wake, the boat jumped, I bounced out of my seat, and spray doused my phone. I caught the dashboard to keep from landing in Mart's lap. My feet slid in opposite directions, and I plopped back in my seat with an unceremonious "Oof!"

"Better hang on," Mart yelled, giving me an annoyingly snarky look as I was furiously drying my cell phone on my shirt.

In the back, the good reverend turned his

attention our way. "Choppy water today. More storms coming."

"Looks like it," I called over the noise.

The darkening sky reflected off Mart's sunglasses as he checked the clouds and shook his head, as if he were in control of the weather, too. He pointed a finger at a passing watercraft, telling the driver to slow down, I guessed.

Reverend Hay tipped his head back to study the patch of blue overhead. The wind caught his fisherman's hat and sent it spiraling into the air. It spun and fluttered behind the boat momentarily, then landed in the foam of our wake and floated there, while the pastor looked longingly over his shoulder.

Mart glanced in the rearview, then cast an exasperated frown over his shoulder. "Hang on," he yelled, and the boat whipped around so suddenly that my pumps slid across the floor like ice skates. The world was one giant, spinning blur, centrifugal force pulling me out of my seat as I clutched the seat back, my body swinging like a pendulum. Beside me, Mart stood up, leaned over the low side rail, and in one casual movement, dipped an arm toward the water and scooped up the hat.

Shaking drops off the rescued topper, Mart righted the boat, and I landed firmly back in my seat just in time to catch another spray of water—in the face this time. I tasted fish and algae, and saw something sliding across the floor. My cell phone. Ducking under the dashboard, I tried to grab it as the boat bounced along. When I sat up again, my head was whirling and rocking, and my stomach rose to meet it. Slapping a hand over my middle, I clenched my jaw and swallowed hard, rubbing my stomach as our ride finally slowed to a gentle wobble and the engine hushed to a dull hum.

"Tell me you're not about to get sick in my boat." Mart eyed me while tossing the hat back to Reverend Hay.

"I'm not getting sick in your boat," I bit out. *I will not get sick in the boat. I will not get sick in the boat. I will not . . .*

The next thing I knew, I was gagging over the side rail. Fortunately, it was just a case of the dry heaves. I slid back into my seat with the good reverend making his way up front to check on me, saying, "Put your head between your knees. You're white as a sheet."

"I'm fine. I'm fine." Putting my head between my knees was what had gotten me in trouble in the first place. I waved him off, closing my eyes and taking deep breaths. "I just haven't been out on the water in a long time. Lost my sea legs, I guess." Even though the boat had slowed, the waves continued rocking underneath, sloshing my stomach side to side.

Reverend Hay chuckled indulgently. "Kind of

strange to live on a lake and not go out on the water."

"We've been busy unpacking." Grabbing the hem of my new silk shirt as we idled quietly between an island and the Big Boulders, I dabbed the water from my face. If the cleaners could salvage this outfit, it would be a miracle. Right now, I would have gladly traded it for hiking boots and combat gear.

"Here," Mart said, and something landed in my lap. A towel. "Sorry about the splash." He didn't look sorry. He looked like he was laughing on the inside—enjoying the chance to prove that his big, bad game warden boat was no place for sissies.

"My fault, really," Reverend Hay interjected, wringing out his fishing hat. "You'd think I'd know to hang on to my hat when Mart's driving."

Mart's lips spread into a grin beneath the brim of his straw cowboy hat. For a minute, I caught myself just . . . watching him smile. He had a really nice smile, actually—like something from a cologne ad, but a little impish, too. The expression seemed kind of mischievous, as if he and the reverend had a private joke between them, and Mart was enjoying it. I never would have imagined that side to Mart McClendon. He wasn't all law and order, after all. . . .

"You're new to the area, then?" the pastor observed. "You and your husband?" Perhaps he

129

was looking at the ring on my left hand. It wasn't my wedding band, but an antique anniversary ring passed down to me by my grandmother. It *could* have been a wedding band, though, which was why I was wearing it. The first time a seemingly friendly stranger in the grocery line had asked me if I was single, I'd been completely flustered. After that, I'd dug out my grandmother's anniversary ring, so that question wouldn't come up again.

Single didn't seem like the right word for where I was right now. I wasn't sure that word would ever fit. I'd seen friends go through the process of a divorce and handle it smoothly, but even after a year, I couldn't help feeling that sooner or later I'd wake up in my old shoes—be the comfortably married mom again. I'd volunteer at school, work one day a week at the food pantry, head up the church prayer group, do some volunteer counseling at the church and crisis center downtown, so that someday when my mommy years were over, I could move smoothly into a career and fulfill the dream of doing the kinds of things Aunt Lucy did. *Someday* wasn't supposed to have arrived yet.

Reverend Hay looked as if he sensed that he'd hit on a touchy subject. He had the perceptive gaze of a man who'd seen it all before.

"Just my son and me," I said, leaning over the backrest in an effort to shut Mart out of the conversation. Even with the boat running at low speed, though, there was enough engine hum to prevent any quiet conversation. "We moved to the house in Larkspur after I took the new job. Our office is in Cleburne."

He raised a brow. "You've got a pretty decent commute, then. How old is your boy?"

Despite the fact that Mart was there, I found myself being drawn in. Reverend Hay was charismatic, in a gentle, unassuming sort of way. "Fourteen," I answered.

"Ohhh, a teenager." His sympathy was obvious. In the past, I would have quickly remarked that teenagerhood had been a breeze. Dustin was naturally upbeat and agreeable. He enjoyed being a people-pleaser. I could hardly say those things with Mart nearby. He'd never met the real Dustin.

I nodded, staring across the lake toward Larkspur Cove. I could make out the Scissortail, but nothing beyond.

After we passed the Big Boulders and coasted under Eagle Eye Bridge into the river channel, I lost sight of home altogether. The water stilled and the boat quieted even more, the motor almost soundless now. Looking back at the bridge, I thought about my dream—the little dark-haired girl balancing on the railing. Was the dream a warning? A sign?

"Guess your son must get bored, being out here

at the lake by himself," Reverend Hay observed. "Not much to do but watch the birds go by."

I couldn't help flicking a glance at Mart. Clearly, word of Dustin's status as a delinquent hadn't spread to the local pastor yet. Mart's smile faded into a sardonic smirk, and the protective, motherly part of me wanted to throw something at him. The anchor, maybe.

"Dustin is busy with chores today," I bit out. "I left him with a list."

Reverend Hay, completely unaware that there was an undercurrent inside the boat, not just beneath it, laughed cheerfully. "Oh, the dreaded chore list. He must be a good kid, if you can leave him home alone with one of those."

"He *is* a good kid." If Mart said a word, I was going to take him out with the nearest solid object. I really was. "The move, and it being just the two of us now, has been an adjustment for him, but he's a good kid. His father still lives in Houston, so it's all a little . . . hard for him to get used to."

The reverend nodded. "Well, transition is a struggle when you're young. Isn't that so, Mart? You moved around a lot when you were growing up, right?"

"Hadn't thought much about it," Mart replied blandly, then stood behind the steering wheel and scouted the river ahead, letting us know he wasn't interested in relating his past to Dustin's current struggles.

For some reason, I found myself cataloging that bit of information about him—*moved frequently as a child.* Maybe that was why he was so . . . maladjusted.

"We have some great summer activities through the church," Hay suggested. "It's just a small group of kids, but we try to keep them active. I'd be happy to stop by and pick your son up anytime."

The invitation came loaded with an obvious scattershot of expectation. I knew the pastoral drill. As the wife of former pastor, and then a college vice-chancellor, I'd performed the drill many times on visitors to our various churches. *Find out something about the person, make a connection, learn a little background, suggest ways that he or she might plug into activities.* "Does he have any interest in theater?"

"Theater?" I repeated, doing a mental rewind.

"I have parts for teenage boys in our fall production at the Tin Building."

I tried to imagine what Dustin would say if I suggested it. In the past, he'd enjoyed performing in vacation Bible school skits, and he'd even taken on a few bit parts when the college theater needed a child actor. Now . . . ? Who could say?

"I'll talk to him about it." Beneath the question of Dustin's reaction, there was another concern. If we got involved in the community, everyone would eventually know our history. It was so much easier to be anonymous. "Right now he should be busy with the chore list and his summer reading for advanced English next year." At least, I hoped he was. I cast another worried look toward our wake, where the last views of the cliffs over Eagle Eye Bridge were disappearing behind a bend in the river.

"He is." The answer, and the fact that it came from Mart, took me by surprise. "I passed by your place earlier. He was out there, pushing a lawnmower back and forth across that big ol' yard."

A tender feeling warmed inside me, followed by a sense of relief. Dustin really had been doing what he was told. He'd given me the truth in his text message. He was right where he was supposed to be today, at home, accepting the consequences for his poor decision-making. Maybe the worst was over with him.

On the heels of that thought came another. *The sour-faced game warden took time to look in on my son.*

As we wound our way upriver, I pretended to survey the overhanging trees on the opposite shore, but really, I was watching Mart, studying him, trying to put together the pieces. There was more to Mart McClendon than what showed on the surface. He wasn't the iceman he pretended to be. . . .

Ten minutes later, when he cut the engine and

steered us toward shore between two over-hanging willow trees, I realized I'd been idly analyzing him, watching the way he moved, listening as he and Reverend Hay talked about the migration patterns of waterfowl along the river. As we drew near the shore, Mart cut the engine, climbed onto the front of the boat, grabbed the rope, and waded through the mud to shore. Tugging the rope, he pulled the boat forward, so that the front of it was beached in the muck. I had the sudden realization that there was no dock here, and getting out of the boat in heels was going to be . . . well . . . undignified at best.

If Mart was concerned, it didn't show. He tied the rope to a tree, said, "If I had my regular boat, this'd be easier. This one's a loaner. Wait here a minute." And then he disappeared into the underbrush.

In the rear seat, Hay was rolling up his pant legs. Since exiting the boat with no one watching seemed preferable to exiting with an audience, I staggered to the front, searched out the most solid-looking spot, and swung my legs over the edge. I landed in the mud, heard a flatulent sound and felt something cool and slimy oozing into my pumps. A visceral shudder ran over my shoulders—pathetic for a girl whose favorite childhood place had been the lake-shore, where I could run barefoot all day, dig in the dirt, and let the wind and the water turn my hair into a giant knot, which my mother would spend hours combing out later. What had happened to that girl, anyway?

"Hang on a minute," Mart called from somewhere in the trees. "I'll bring over a . . ." The brush rustled, and I shuffle-slogged in a semicircle just in time to see Mart emerging from the brush, dragging a fairly large log. Judging from the way he was looking at my mud-covered feet, the log was intended to provide a bridge of sorts, to transport me over the mire. "Guess we don't need this anymore." Mart tossed the log aside.

"I'm fine," I said, indicating that I did this kind of thing every day.

Behind me, Reverend Hay called out, "Banzaiii!" then jumped off the boat and landed past the muck line. Mart started toward the trees, and I squished my way to dry land. The pastor fell into step behind me.

"How far is it to the house?" I ventured, even though I was partially afraid of the answer. In contrast to our side of the lakeshore, the riverbanks here were wild and undeveloped, lonely and far from welcoming, framed by tall trees and thick tangles of underbrush, which, now that I looked closely, harbored copious amounts of poison ivy and probably snakes. As far as I could see in either direction, there was no sign of a house or a road, or human habitation of any kind.

Tipping his head back, Mart studied a tree ahead. "Well, we must be in the wrong spot. These trees've got too much bark on the north side."

Three thoughts crossed my mind. *You mean I climbed out of the boat and slogged through the mud for nothing? How am I going to get back into the boat?* And then, a final, random thought, *He can tell where we are by the bark on the trees?* "You're kidding, right?"

Mart turned just far enough that I caught a glint in the corner of his eye, then he grinned, shook his head, and walked on.

Behind me, Hay chuckled. "Game wardens are full of hooey. It comes with the job."

Ahead, Mart held aside a curtain of wild grapevines, waving a hand to usher us through. I glanced up to see if the smile was still there and caught the last bit of it fading. Somewhere under the uniform and the straight face, there was an actual personality. Go figure.

Once we'd made it through the underbrush, Mart quickly located a road that was little more than twin ruts winding off into the forest. Whether the trail was still in use seemed debatable, but Mart nodded like he'd dis-covered what he was looking for. "It shouldn't be far from here," he said. "I figured Len was using one of these old logging trails to cart his stuff down to the water. He probably has his boat hidden in the brush near here. He puts it in the water right past those cedar trees."

A creepy feeling crawled up my spine, and goose bumps prickled my skin. All of a sudden, I felt like we were being watched.

Perhaps coming here wasn't a good idea.

God gave men one mouth and two ears,
so they can listen twice as much as they talk.
—Anonymous
(via Mart McClendon, state game warden)

Chapter 10

Mart McClendon

On the way up the hill, I started thinking maybe it wasn't the brightest thing, bringing along Hay and Andrea. I wasn't really worried about Len deciding to take a shot at us—after ten years of dealing with poachers, game thieves, and gun-toting rednecks of all kinds, you get a sense about people—but between Andrea asking questions and Hay jumping out of the boat yelling *Banzai!*, we'd given Len plenty of warning. Usually, if I was making an unannounced visit, I didn't want my suspects to hear me from a mile away. That's what makes the visit unannounced.

I had a feeling Len could see us, but we weren't likely to be seeing him. Folks who lived in these kinds of places had their reasons for avoiding people, but as we clattered up the ridge, I fanned a hope that having Hay and Andrea along would convince Len I wasn't there to pin him down for having too many lines in the lake. Maybe seeing them would pique his curiosity a little bit, make him think we were there handing out free food baskets from the church or something. Folks up in these hills would put up with some interloping if there was charity involved. In general, they knew that strangers dressed too nice for the territory and church pastors tended to come bearing gifts. Game wardens came bearing citations and warnings, mostly.

"How much farther?" Andrea asked as we topped the hill. I could see a clearing ahead and a four-wheeler trail that somebody'd been using quite a bit. With the bridge washed out on County Road 47, it was a long drive down some pretty rough back roads to get into town from here, but going upriver and across the lake, Len could make the Waterbird in twenty-five minutes or less, which was probably why he'd been showing up there quite a bit this summer with vegetables and mushrooms to sell in the parking lot. The fact that he'd changed his pattern these last couple weeks and started selling at the Crossroads again could definitely mean he was trying to keep from being seen by too many people.

"Are we close yet?" Behind me, Andrea had stalled out. Her pants were caught on a bramble, and she'd stopped to pull it off.

"Could be another mile or two—just guessing." I looked at the clearing ahead. Back when Len's parents were alive, that'd probably been a farm field, but now it was overgrown with shoulder-high Johnson grass and scrappy cedars. Across the way, I could see what was left of an old slabwood fence and the carcasses of a couple junk cars. Len's house was most likely behind the cedar hedge at the other end of the field.

"Another *mile* or two?" Andrea repeated. I had to give her credit for determination. Even in dress shoes, she was keeping up pretty well. Hay'd started to lag behind after stopping to dump a rock out of his high-dollar rubber fishing treads. "You've got to be kid—" Andrea's heel hung on a root, and she stumbled, leaving the shoe behind. Her bare foot came down in the moss, mud, and nameless squishy stuff typical of a forest floor after a rain. Letting out something between a squeal and a growl, she hopped to the side of the trail and started wiping off her toes on a little fern plant.

"Better look out for poison ivy," I said, and she shot a sneer my way.

"I *know* what poison ivy looks like." Her hair had fallen out of the clip, so that it hung in long curls around her face. Her cheeks were red, and she had fire in her eyes. She looked good that way. Not so . . . stiff. "I'm not a complete idiot."

Slipping around behind her, I grabbed the shoe, then set it on the ground by her foot. "There you go, Cinderella."

She gave the shoe a shocked look, like she really couldn't believe I'd bother. Guess I hadn't made too good an impression so far. I wasn't really trying to, but my mama did raise me to be a gentleman. I wouldn't walk off and leave a lady stranded on one shoe. Not even this lady. I would've put that log down to help her off the boat, too, but she didn't stay put when I told her to. The muddy shoes were her fault, mostly. Bet those were starting to chafe about now.

Hay caught up, and he was so busy looking for birds with his fold-up binoculars, he almost ran Cinderella off the path and toppled her into the ooze.

"Better put down those field glasses, Hay," I said. "We're here." As usual, Hay was as out to lunch as anybody could be. Had his head in a sermon or in a book most of the time, and now he was an amateur bird watcher, too. One of these days, he was gonna step on a copperhead snake while he was busy watching clouds pass over.

Last year's dead leaves crunched and squished as Andrea hurried to catch up. "I thought you said it was another *mile* or *two*."

Pushing some brambles aside, I gave a shrug toward the clearing, where the logging-road-turned-ATV-trail wound its way through overgrowth toward the old fence. "You shouldn't believe everything you hear in the woods."

Andrea's mouth dropped open, then snapped shut. "You're . . . just . . ." She trailed off, seeming like she couldn't find the word for it. It wasn't the first time I'd had that effect on a woman. When you're in the field all the time, you get in the habit of treating everybody the way you'd treat your work partner or law enforcement personnel in other departments. Guys joke around. It keeps you on your toes. And when you're in the field, you need to be on your toes.

It's all fine, until you're dealing with women and children. They don't always see humor where you do. More than once, I'd ended up with my nephews or my sisters-in-law crying at the annual McClendon campout in Big Bend, and I didn't have the first idea what I'd said or done to cause it. My mama's opinion was that the game warden school needed to add sensitivity training.

Andrea finally finished with, ". . . not . . . *nice.*" She turned up her nose and followed Hay through the opening.

"I try." I ducked down to slip through behind her. A branch sprung back and whacked me in the head so quick I didn't have time to catch it. Lucky for me, it was pretty pliable, so it just ripped half my ear off, sent my hat flying like a Frisbee, and took out a chunk of hair. I said something I probably shouldn't have. When I grabbed my hat and looked up, Andrea was watching me with her hand over her mouth, and I knew right away that branch hadn't come my way by accident.

"Oops," she muttered and bit her lip, but she

wasn't very convincing. For one thing, she was kind of smiling when she said it.

"Good trick," I told her, pushing the dent out of my hat.

"I try." She tipped her chin up, then headed off across the field with Hay trailing along behind, looking for bluebirds.

Halfway through the Johnson grass patch, we cleared the end of the cedars, and I saw Len's estate ahead. It was pretty typical of the area—a patchwork barn, piles of junk here and there, a couple rusted-out tractors floating like flotsam in a sea of broomweed. Beside the house, a dilapidated school bus had been sitting in one place so long the wheels were buried up to the axles. No telling how they'd gotten that thing up here. The house itself was old, gaps in the siding covered with bits of secondhand lumber and scavenged road signs, the knobby cedar porch poles pushing outward like buckteeth. The whole place listed to one side, so that it seemed like it might just fold up if a good enough wind moved through.

I stopped near the edge of the yard, if you could call it that, and hollered Len's name, then identified myself and told him we wanted to talk to him. Near the barn, a mule brayed, a rangy old milk cow climbed to her feet, a pig squealed, and in a ragtag pen built from shipping pallets and hog wire, two grown dogs and a batch of pups went wild, barking. I hoped those dogs were locked up. They didn't sound friendly. Andrea and Hay slipped around behind me, like they were thinking the same thing.

I identified myself again and called out Len's name over the barking. No answer. Hay tried raising Len, next. During his time in Moses Lake, he'd learned that, out in the hills, even a pastor ought to hail the house before walking up to it. "I don't think anyone's here," he said finally.

"Doesn't look like it," Andrea agreed. Both of them turned toward me.

"Won't hurt to go on up and check," I said. "Could be he's out in the barn." Occupied or not, I wanted to get a look at the place while I was there. Besides, if Len was hiding in the woods and saw us sniffing around his farmyard, he might flush out. "You two stay put a minute. I'll be right back."

Andrea and Hay stood side by side, watching me head off to the house. When I rounded the cedar break and started across the yard, the dogs took a run at the rickety fence behind the house. In the dry-dirt corral next door, the mule ran around bucking and kicking. Even with the noise, the farm had an eerie feel to it, a little like a graveyard when you're all alone, and you can feel the people there, even though they're gone.

The dogs ramped up the threat level when I stepped onto the porch and leaned close to the two wood-paned windows on either side of the weathered door. Between the layer of dirt on the glass and a set of dry-rotted curtains hanging inside, I couldn't see anything.

Leaving the porch, I walked across to look in the barn. Inside, the light was dim, the shadows of the hills and trees falling long now, but I could make out Len's collection of live traps, deer feeders, and a harness for the mule.

Along one wall, a stack of homemade cages of various sizes looked to be ready for use. They were empty at the moment, but I wondered what normally lived in them. There were bowls with mold-covered food, and bug-infested water dishes, and the whole place smelled like scat. Several cages had been recently emptied, the ground still wet from tipped-over water bowls. If nothing else, the cages were grounds for me to come back. Keeping wildlife without a permit— either for sale or for skins—was illegal.

I wasn't surprised to find the cages, considering Len's history in terms of fish-and-game regulations. What I didn't see here was any sign of a little girl. . . .

"Did you find anything?" Hay's voice made me jump and grab for my belt. I turned and had a Barney Fife moment, tripping over some boards hidden underneath the loose layer of straw.

"Dadgummit, Hay. You trying to give me a heart attack? Don't sneak up on me like that."

Andrea was standing beside him. She gave my hand on the gun a concerned look, like she was wondering if I could be trusted with the thing.

Hay surveyed the inside of the barn, then wrinkled his long, narrow nose and sneezed. "What do you think he keeps in here?" He pointed at the cages, and beside him, Andrea's brown eyes got wide. She looked like she was picturing something out of a horror movie. Shivering, she took a step backward, and headed out of the barn.

"A little bit of everything, it looks like," I said, taking my flashlight and shining it into a dark corner, where more live traps and cages were stacked up. There was a long, gray feather in one of them—probably off a turkey or a hawk, but if that came off an eagle, Len could be in serious trouble. Eagles were federally protected. Stepping over to the cage, I pulled out my pocket camera and snapped a picture. Hay moved into the barn and looked over my shoulder.

It crossed my mind that, if there was going to be an investigation later, I didn't want Hay mucking up the evidence now. "Let's go. There's no one here." By the house, the dogs were raising Cain again, and I had a feeling Andrea was over there sniffing around. I had to give her credit for guts, but if those dogs found a way through the fence, it wouldn't be pretty.

I walked out of the barn with Hay behind.

Andrea was on the other side of the house with her nose poked into the old school bus and one foot on the step. Glancing back, she motioned us to her, then put her hand over her mouth and backed out of the bus. The horrified look on her face flashed a picture in my mind. Maybe old Len had tipped back one too many pints of sour mash, crawled in there, and expired in the heat . . . or something worse.

Jogging around the front porch, I met Andrea at the bus. "It looks like someone's been living in there," she said, and I relaxed a little.

"Wouldn't surprise me." Up here, you were likely to find a dozen or more different family members and hangers-on, all squatting on one place, employing any sort of imaginable human habitation.

That did bring up the question of what use Len would have for guest quarters, since everyone agreed he didn't have any family and didn't socialize. If he was living in the house, then who'd been staying out here, and where were they now?

Taking a step into the bus, I identified myself and called out Len's name. I didn't expect anyone to answer, but procedure is procedure for a reason. You don't follow the rules, you might muck up a case that needs to be turned over to state troopers, or the county sheriff, or the feds. "Anybody in here?"

Climbing a couple more steps, I took a quick glance around the interior. The seats had been cleared out, and there was a mattress wedged against the back doors. A wood stove squatted near the front, and a lopsided plywood table lounged in the window light along one side. Two Styrofoam bowls and a set of china teacups sat on top of it. Leaning over the handrail, I looked inside the cups. Empty. They were just sitting there, like someone'd planned to sit down to dinner, then decided against it. I couldn't blame them. You took your dinner in a spot like this, you were liable to end up with *E. coli*. The whole bus was strewn from one end to the other with towels, blankets, and clothes. It smelled of mold, and little piles of dried feces dotted contents here and there, as if coons had moved in, or someone had been keeping puppies in here, or both. A mud-covered set of women's clothes lay piled near the door—jeans and a faded T-shirt. Modern-day stuff, not old enough to have belonged to Len's mama, back when. Whose were those? Did Len have himself a woman no one knew about?

The question turned over in my mind as I headed down the stairs. "Reverend Hay, you got any idea whether Len might have a girlfriend?"

"A girlfriend?" Hay coughed. "You're joking, right?"

"Well, I don't see any sign of a little girl, but

there's a mud-covered set of women's clothing piled by the door in there. They look fairly recent. I'd say someone's been here besides Len." I stepped off the bus, and one of the dogs stood on its hind legs and tried to crawl over the shipping-pallet fence. Andrea backed away and retreated to the front porch.

"We better let things alone here before that mutt decides to chew his way out," I told Hay, and we followed Andrea's lead back toward the porch. "You see anybody else with Len when you ran across him this afternoon?"

Hay shook his head. "Not a soul. Just him and the little girl. Like I said, she was playing up in the cedar brush off the road a ways. I just happened to catch sight of her because she wandered out in the field for a minute. I asked Len who that was, and he said it was his daughter, or daughter-girl. Something like that. He was a little flustered, but you know that's how Len is when he has to talk to somebody. I don't imagine he could think on his feet quickly enough to lie, even if he wanted to. I'm still learning who's related to whom around here, so I just figured he had family I didn't know about." Hay pulled off his fishing hat and scratched his head, concern sketching a wrinkle between his eyebrows. "None of this makes sense, Mart."

"Doesn't seem to," I agreed. "But right now, it's pretty clear he's either not here, or not

150

coming out." The best thing to do when you knew something was wrong but couldn't find the evidence you needed was to get out quietly, then show up unannounced another time or two—see if you couldn't catch your culprits in the act. I wasn't sure what I was trying to catch Len at. In my career, I'd assisted in a few kidnapping cases—adults, mostly—and worked with FBI and state troopers in hunts for missing kids, but my mind really didn't want to go there. After the past few years, I wasn't ready for any more tragedy. Hopefully, Hay was right about Len, but one thing was for sure: Len knew these woods better than I did. If he got worried and decided to go underground for a while, he could do it.

Hay nodded. "Well, it could be I misunderstood him. Len's done some work for me down at the church a time or two, weeding and cleaning the flower beds. He gets his words fouled up. Could be he meant to say she was a neighbor girl, or something. There are people up here who would drop their kids off with almost anybody, just to get them off their hands for a little while."

"True enough." Hay was right. Chinquapin Peaks was like a trip to a whole other world. On the south side of the lake, kids had all the finest things money could buy. On this side, there was no telling. "I'll pay another visit up here tomorrow and see if I can catch up with Len. If he's got something going with a neighbor, or has a girlfriend with a kid, maybe I can pass the information along—get someone to come by and do a welfare check. Anyone who'd be using Len as a baby-sitter probably needs a little monitoring."

Rubbing her hands up and down her arms, Andrea stepped off the corner of the porch into the scrappy grass below. "There *has* been a child here." She pointed to the ground, and we crossed the porch to see. Not far from her feet, a patch of bare earth by the downspout was decorated with measuring cups, a broken plate, a few odd pieces of silverware, a margarine tub, and a rust-covered coffee can. The margarine tub had been used to produce a mud cake, complete with dry leaves and pebbles for frosting, and feathery shoots of field grass for candles. No chance Len had made that.

"Adults don't play in the dirt," Andrea observed.

I took a look around the woods, wondering if Len had been watching us this whole time. The more we snooped, the less likely he'd be to follow his normal routines tomorrow. "Let's go for now."

"We're just leaving?" Andrea's eyes flashed wide, her lips hanging open a bit.

I nodded and started walking.

She trotted to catch up with me while Hay lagged behind, listening to an owl hoot in a dead

live oak. "We can't just *leave*. We should wait."
Even as she said it, she glanced at the sun,
hovering low over the hills.

"There's no evidence a crime has been
committed here," I pointed out. Other than the
jug lines and possibly the feather in the barn, I
didn't even have a legal reason to come back.

Andrea looked over her shoulder, her lip
curling a bit. "But this place . . ." Her eyes, full
of worry, begged me to do something—solve the
mystery, fix the problem, be a hero. I wanted to
tell her she was looking at the wrong guy. I
wasn't anybody's hero. I didn't deserve to be.

"You keep working on this side of the lake,
you'll see a lot of places like this," I said, and she
stiffened like I'd insulted her. "The rules are
different in Chinquapin Peaks."

*I firmly believe that nature brings solace
in all troubles.*
—Anne Frank
(Left by a visiting philosophy student
who read the whole wall)

Chapter 11

Andrea Henderson

As we crossed the lake, my stomach was churning, but not because of motion sickness this time. I couldn't stop picturing the little girl in the pickup truck, and trying to decide what emotions I'd seen on her face.

Closing my eyes as the boat cut cleanly through the swells, I imagined the scene again. In my mind, her expression was one of fear and need. But was I only imagining what I thought should be there—what a trip through Len Barnes's camp made me expect to see? The place was like something out of a mission video from the Third World—unfit, unclean, filled with cages and traps, animal skins hanging everywhere, catfish heads strung up to rot in a tree, snarling dogs breeding indiscriminately in a yard filled with junk. Mart hadn't even given those things a second look, but when I'd noticed the toys in the dirt next to the porch, my emotions had skidded into a tailspin. No child should have to play there. I wanted to find the little girl right then, to confront whoever was responsible for her, to remove her from the environment immediately.

But now, a part of me was questioning the impulse—drawing back to my original gut reaction when I'd seen her in the truck. The truth was that she hadn't seemed nervous or fearful, only curious as to why I was on the side of the road. The presence of the snarling dog and the looks of the vehicle had worried me, but my first impression of the girl was that she wasn't afraid. In actuality, I'd had a much more visceral reaction to John and Audrey talking about their kittens and their mother's boyfriend. When those children looked at me, their trepidation was evident. They wanted to tell me things, but they knew they'd better not. They wanted help, but they were afraid of what it might lead to. I didn't gather the same feeling from the little girl in the truck.

Then again, how would I know? There were no reference points in my life for places like this, for people like this. As a child, I'd seen the other side of the lake from a distance. We used the swimming beaches on our side, came and went from private boat docks, caught a few rays on sun decks only we had access to. Occasionally, my mother cautioned us to keep away from the public beaches when we were out on the jet skis, because those places *gathered riffraff*. We'd vacationed in the bubble of Larkspur Estates during its glory years and never looked far beyond.

I'd married in the bubble, raised Dustin in it and lived comfortably there, only venturing out for a mission trip with a group of Karl's university students now and then. It was good public relations for us to go along. We'd taught English for two weeks in China and built houses in Mexico. The poverty there was stark and startling, but it was on the other side of the world, where you expected it to be.

As Mart pulled in to drop Reverend Hay at the dock behind tiny Lakeshore Community Church, I caught myself gazing up the hill at the unimposing brownstone building, watching its white wooden steeple glimmer in filtered pink light. I realized I was talking in my head. *I need to know if I can handle this before I get in any deeper. I need to know if I'm on the right path. . . .*

It was a prayer, I guessed. Nothing so formal as I would have offered in the past—no *Father God* or *Amen*. But even though I didn't want to admit it, I knew whom those words were addressed to. Perhaps it was the presence of the church nearby, or the monumental challenges of my new job, but I felt the need to tap into something larger than myself. I felt the tug of that cross, silhouetted in the fading daylight.

"Come on up and see the place. I could run you back to your car in a bit." Reverend Hay's voice pulled at my thoughts. "We've got our greeting card–makers' meeting tonight." Checking his watch, he cast a concerned glance toward the parking lot. "Hope they're not out front beating down the doors already."

"That's all right, thanks. I'd better be getting home to my son." On the far horizon, the sun was a crimson orb, sinking into the treetops. By now, Meg and the twins would be gone and Dustin would be back in the house. Maybe Dustin and I could do something tonight—watch a movie or sit on the screened porch as the lightning bugs came out, the way we used to. I missed those times. I missed him, the way he used to be.

Reverend Hay nodded amiably, then reached down to give us a shove away from the dock. "Ask your boy about the production at the Tin Building. Hard to fill all the roles for this one. We'd love to have him." He waved as Mart turned the steering wheel, and the boat drifted in a semicircle. "You too, Mart."

Shaking his head, Mart kicked up the motor without answering, and we sped away. As we zipped across the corner of the lake, the last bands of sunlit water bending around us, I tried to imagine Mart as a budding actor.

"What?" he asked, catching me studying him as we idled down at the *No Wake* sign near the

Waterbird, just letting the boat drift in. "Don't worry about Len, all right? I'll pay him a surprise visit in the morning and sort this thing out."

"I wasn't thinking about that," I admitted. "I was thinking that you don't look like a thespian." An awkward feeling slid over me. I hadn't meant to indicate that I'd been pondering him. My mind should have been on the little girl.

Cutting the engine, he slid the boat up to the dock and looped the rope over a post. He stopped and looked at me, then leaned on the seat back, one long leg draped casually over it. "You stay here awhile, you'll learn to watch out for Hay. That bumbling, clueless act is all a facade. The Rev could sell ice to Eskimos. He'll talk you into things, especially where that theater is concerned. It's his passion—other than the church." His lips quirked to one side as the late-day sun slid under his hat, catching his eyes and turning them a soft, earthy green.

I had the weird thought that I'd never seen eyes quite that color. "Everybody needs one—a passion, I mean." What a stupid comment, especially coming from me. Did I really think the game warden wanted to talk about life's passions? He was a man's man. An alpha type. Not the sort to consider life in the ethereal sense. I was only making myself look like more of a foreigner and an oddball.

Mart gazed down the lakeshore, where the

church steeple and the buildings along the main drag of Moses Lake were barely visible above the treetops. "Guess everybody does."

"So, I take it that yours isn't acting." It was meant to sound like a joke, but it came out sounding like a probe—one of those hypothetical-yet-pointed questions a psychologist might ask in a personality profile interview.

His lips pursed slightly, then parted into a grin, and he ducked his head so that the hat brim hid his eyes. "Gave it up twenty-five years ago, after doing Robin Hood in the eighth grade."

"Robin Hood?" I felt a smile pulling at me. "So you do have a history in theater." I did a little mental addition . . . *twenty-five years ago, eighth grade. . . .* Mart was around my age.

The official emblems on his shirt rose and fell with a soft laugh. "There was a cute student teacher directing the school play that year. She charmed me into it. Not just me, come to think of it. Half of the football team showed up for auditions."

"But you got the part?"

I couldn't tell for sure with the hat in the way, but I could have sworn he was blushing.

He scooted a stray bit of rope out of the way with the toe of his boot. "Seemed like the thing to do at the time. Guess it never crossed my mind that the rest of the football boys might back out and leave me there twisting in the wind. You put on green tights and prance around the stage, you're never gonna hear the end of it in the locker room. Amazing what a boy'll get himself into when there's a cute girl involved."

I chuckled at the image of him in the Robin Hood suit, trying to impress the student teacher. He must have been about Dustin's age then. Dustin was about to be a freshman in high school. Unfortunately, he hadn't hit his growth spurt yet. He was small for his grade, still physically immature compared to the other boys. "To tell you the truth, I think that's how Dustin ended up on the Scissortail—trying to impress someone."

Mart glanced up. Perhaps he wondered if I was using the conversation to try to get Dustin off the hook. "Well, I could sure tell him it's not worth it. That student teacher took off with the football coach and left me sitting outside the auditorium in my green tights."

The image formed in my mind, and being the mother of a fourteen-year-old boy, I couldn't help it, I sympathy-laughed. There was a whole side to Mart McClendon that I'd never even imagined. "Oh, that's so . . . wrong. You poor thing."

"I know," he agreed, and I tried to imagine the vulnerable eighth-grade boy inside the man. It was difficult. Mart seemed like the type who'd never been vulnerable—the kind who'd been a star in every sport, a golden boy with the world by the tail and a big ego. "And that was after the whole dadgum team showed up to watch dress rehearsal. I was already a scrawny little runt, and then . . . well, you get stuck with a goofy family name like *Martin*, then put on green tights and prance around saying things like, 'Forsooth,' and 'Hark, Maid Marian,' you're really setting yourself up for a beating. I pretty well figured it'd be better to jump a train out of state than go home and have my brothers triple-timing me about it."

The image in my mind shifted, like a reflection in the water turning wavy after a rock ripples it. When the ripples stilled, the picture was different. Mart McClendon, scrawny kid, insecure, nervous. Like Dustin. "So, what happened? I'm assuming you and your broken heart didn't hit the road in the eighth grade."

He shook his head. "Nah, my mama figured it out. She showed up behind the auditorium, and we went for ice cream. Just the two of us."

"Oh, good for your mom."

"Yeah. She knew." Mart's gaze met mine and held it. "Don't let your boy fool you when he acts like he doesn't need his mama. He does."

A lump rose in my throat, and emotion welled behind my eyes. Mart couldn't have imagined how much I needed to hear that right now. "Thanks." I swallowed hard, trying to get myself under control. An emotional moment with the game warden wasn't anywhere in my plans for the day, and such a moment with me was undoubtedly not in Mart's, either.

"I want him to take the water safety course, by the way. I'll have to figure out how to get him there, though. It's too far for him to walk from Larkspur, all the way to the community center. Maybe I can get my parents to come out and drive him." *You'll never hear the end of that,* a voice inside me was saying, but what choice did I have? The community center was almost halfway around the lake, in a little strip of historic buildings that had been part of the Mennonite village of Gnadenfeld, most of which ended up underwater when the lake was built. Even if I let Dustin ride his bike, it was still too far for him to travel, especially by himself, and in the summer heat. I couldn't ask Megan to pack up the twins or take time off from the bank during her work days so she could drive out here to shuttle Dustin around.

Mart chewed the side of his lip, pushing off the seat back and standing up. "I'll come by and get him. I'm out on the lake anyway. You give me his cell phone number, and I'll call him about it."

For a moment, all I could do was stare at him, stunned. Mart McClendon was *nothing* like I'd thought. He was actually . . . well . . . a nice guy. "Oh, well . . . well . . . all right. I . . . Thanks," I stammered. Mart grabbed a clipboard with wavy wet-and-dried paper, handed it to me, then added a pen from his shirt pocket. I wrote down Dustin's number and mine, as well. "I put my cell on here, too. In case you can't get in touch with Dustin." Dustin was going to have a fit when he found out I'd signed him up for the class *and* agreed to allow the game warden to transport him there. What if he decided to go completely oppositional and refuse?

Then again, maybe just the fact that the alternative was for us to drag Grandpa and Grandma into the situation would be enough to convince him. After the family breach with Karl's father, Dustin had grown closer to my parents, but he still realized that their visits came with lectures and demands. Love, in our family, had always come with strings. It was a reward for perfect behavior. It wasn't handed out for free.

I'd never wanted Dustin to learn that form of exchange, but here, he would.

"Thank you for trying to help him . . . us . . . out," I added, embarrassment warming my neck and cheeks. I was used to being the one offering help, not the one needing it. It was so much easier to be the vice-chancellor's wife, magnanimously handing out my time and talents—a ride to a doctor's appointment here, a casserole for a funeral there, a sympathetic ear for a friend going through a family crisis. I was good at rescuing other people, at swooshing in and playing savior. I'd never once considered what it cost the people on the other end to accept my help, to admit they needed it.

"Sure. No problem," Mart answered, like he didn't want to make a big deal of it. "I'm on the lake anyway." He'd already said that once. Maybe he felt the need to reassure me that it really wasn't any trouble.

He swung a foot over the edge of the boat, then stood there with one boot on the seat and one on the dock. I realized he was waiting to help me out of the boat.

The conversation between us felt unfinished, and for reasons I couldn't explain, I was disappointed that he'd stepped onto the dock. As I slipped my feet back into the muddy pumps that had rubbed a hatch pattern of blisters, Mart lifted a hand and yawned behind it. I remembered that, when I'd first come into the Waterbird, he'd looked like he was almost asleep on his feet. He was probably exhausted by now.

As I stood up, the wake from a passing watercraft caused me to stagger across the floor in three unsteady steps, leaving behind a slug trail of mud. Mart caught my arm, his grip warm and firm. "Easy there, Cap'n," he said, a laugh in the words. "Better work on those sea legs, if you're gonna live by the water."

"I'll take that under advisement." I stepped

from the boat, his grip half-steadying, half-lifting me onto the dock. He let go of me then and braced an elbow on his knee, his stride still bridging the gap between the boat and the dock in a pose not unlike Robin Hood surveying Sherwood Forest.

I pictured him in the school play, and a laugh tickled my throat. Mart squinted at me, as if he wondered what was going on in my head. No surprise there. Lately, I wondered what was going on in my head most of the time. My thoughts and emotions were all over the map, like they didn't know where to be.

Robin Hood, I thought. Not just every grown man would tell that story about himself— especially the part about the crush on the student teacher. Back in high school, Karl had been a band nerd with glasses, the smart guy who always set the curve. I was four years younger than him, but he lived just down the block from my parents' house in Dallas, so I'd known him most of my life. He hated the fact that I knew the nerdy high school part of him. In Houston, all anyone saw was the guy who'd grown his hair long in seminary school and joined a Christian rock band. When he'd come back to play for a youth weekend at our church, I'd barely recognized him. We'd kept in touch after that, and one thing led to another. The one time I mentioned his band-nerd days to table guests during a university dinner, he'd laughed it off uncomfortably, then reprimanded me in private, later. He'd said I was *undermining him.*

I found myself hesitating on the dock, contrasting that with Mart and his story. Why, I couldn't say. "So, will you let me know what happens, when you go up to Len's cabin in the morning? I really just . . . I keep thinking about seeing that little girl in the truck. I need to know she's all right. That place up there . . . That house was awful."

Mart pulled off his hat, set it on his knee, and scratched the thick, dark curls near his ear. I noticed he had a pretty decent welt where I'd snapped the branch back, sort of accidentally on purpose. It had been a spur-of-the-moment impulse that was way outside my usual behavior. "You know, that's pretty typical in Chinquapin Peaks." His look was reserved, as if he were wondering whether I really understood what I was getting myself into.

"I know." I tried to keep the statement flat, to mask the swells of uncertainty inside me. *God doesn't give us a desire without a means,* Aunt Lucy would have said. I had the desire for this job, and one way or another, I would find the means.

Mart nodded, dropping the hat back on his head, as in, *suit yourself.* Even that seemed like a compliment, a silent endorsement of my ability to handle the challenges ahead. "I'm usually patrolling somewhere in the district." Slipping a hand into his shirt pocket, he grabbed a business card, then extended it to me between two fingers. "If you have trouble, or you need to know more about a place you're going, call me. For obvious reasons, I've met a lot of people up there. I get most of my tips from friends, neighbors, and family members of the guilty parties. You'd be surprised how quick they'll rat each other out when they're either in trouble themselves or mad at someone else."

"Thanks." I hadn't really thought about what a game warden did all day, aside from keeping kids out of mischief on the lake. "I'll remember that." I reached for the card, and my fingers brushed Mart's.

The Waterbird's back door slammed overhead, and I jerked upright, pulling the card away. Tipping his head, he studied me, his lips a speculative twist. "That'll be the news crew. Figures they'd still be waiting around the Waterbird. Anything that happens on Moses Lake, they've gotta know about it."

I heard the domino-playing crowd talking as they came down the stairs. "You find something over there? Mart? You see any clues at Len's place?"

Mart sighed and pretended he didn't hear the questions. Remembering the conversation that had sent us on this spur-of-the-moment reconnaissance mission, I slipped my hand into the pocket of my bedraggled, mud-spattered jacket and pulled out the keys to my father's car. "I think I'll let you hold the press conference." Even as I said it, I felt a little guilty. Mart would probably end up stuck here another hour, explaining where we'd been, but I needed to get home to Dustin.

"Not a chance." With a wink and a grin, Mart unhooked the rope, kicked off the dock and slid into the driver's seat. "Make sure you fill them in on all the details. They'll need something to talk about at the coffee club tomorrow." A moment later he was revving the motor, leaving me at the mercy of his public.

"Hey!" I called, but he just waved over his shoulder and kicked up the throttle. I imagined that I could hear laughter drifting behind him as he glided off, disappearing into a trail of glistening water that led to the setting sun.

I turned and started toward my car. The crew from the Waterbird headed me off at the pass, of course. They invited me in for coffee, so that I could fully share the details. I declined the invitation as politely as possible and gave them the short version. Clearly our mission to Len's had been the talk of the neighborhood. Somehow, by having gone along, I had been elevated from stranger to one-of-the-bunch. It felt good, in a way. The locals even wanted to know if I'd seen any bass jumping on the other side of the lake—as if I'd know a jumping bass from a goldfish in a bowl.

As I was finishing the abbreviated version of the story, one of the men frowned toward the dock. "What'd y'all do with Reverend Hay?"

"We dropped him off at the church. He said something about having a card-making class tonight."

The tall, thin man who looked like a cartoon cowboy widened his eyes. "It's card-making evenin', fellas. You know what that means."

"Night fishin'," one of his companions surmised. "Those women'll be at the church clippin' and pastin' and hen talkin' 'til after the late evenin' news. Maybe later."

"Boys, let's hit the lake."

Our conversation ended abruptly. I took the opportunity to hurry to my vehicle and head home.

Ansley and Sydney were cleaning up their lemonade stand for the night as I pulled in. Business hadn't been too brisk, judging by the look of things. The lemonade pitcher was three-quarters full. The girls paused, tracking me with curious looks. One of them turned a few cartwheels in the dusky light, blond hair tumbling over her face as she checked to see if I was watching.

"Nice cartwheel," I said as I gathered my things from the backseat. That was all it took to bring Sydney and Ansley across the property line to introduce themselves—Sydney, who was twelve, and Ansley, who was ten.

"You need any help with your stuff?" Ansley inquired, leaning around me to check out the house.

"No. I've got it. But thanks." Juggling my briefcase, laptop, and purse into one hand, I slipped my key ring off my finger, in case Dustin had the front door locked.

Sydney grabbed a pencil that was about to slide off my clipboard. "I can open the door for you." She, too, peered toward the entry, clearly seeking an invitation to follow me. As cute as they were, I was too tired for company tonight.

"I'm fine, but it's nice to meet both of you."

"Want some lemonade?" Ansley rushed out. "We've got cookies, too. They kind of melted together, but they taste good."

I declined again, and then promised to buy lemonade tomorrow when I came home.

"Your shoes are muddy," Ansley observed. "They're, like, ruined."

"I know," I lamented. "I got in kind of a mess at work."

When I turned toward the house, Sydney had moved in front of me, forming a blockade, so to speak. She handed my pencil back. "Can he play?" She thumbed toward the house, and all of a sudden, I understood. It wasn't me they were interested in. It was Dustin, which made sense, considering that he was the only other person under sixty living in close proximity.

"Who? Dustin?" I asked, as if I didn't know.

Sydney's eyes narrowed, as in, *So that's his name* . . . "Mmm-hmm. He said he couldn't. He said his mom just makes him work all the time. And then his aunt came, and she said he can play, but then we had to go to Catfish Charley's for dinner, and then when we got back, he went in the house."

I imagined the conversation that had probably taken place sometime earlier, when Dustin was out in the yard. "Well, he is grounded," I admitted. "But just from leaving the property. He doesn't have to spend every minute working."

The answer seemed to satisfy Sydney and Ansley. "Cool!" Sydney said, and the two of them scampered away, whispering and giggling amongst themselves, making plans for tomorrow, I suspected. Maybe I'd suggest to Dustin that he see if they were interested in kicking the soccer ball around or doing a little fishing off the dock. Younger girls probably weren't his first choice for someone to hang out with, but at least they wouldn't be showing up with beer and speedboats.

The lights and the television were on inside the

house when I started up the walkway. Dustin must have heard me coming. By the time I'd unlocked the door, the living room had been abandoned, a sweating glass of iced tea still on the end table, Dustin's sneakers underneath, the television playing some overly comedic show about teenagers in a high school.

I hit the Mute button and went to find him. He was in his bedroom, of course, strung across his bed with his laptop computer, trying to look like he'd been there all along.

"Hey," I said, leaning on the doorway, emotion thick and doughy in my chest. I'd never get used to having the person I loved the most not even look at me when I came into the room. There was a time when he lit up whenever he saw me. "Did you have a good day?"

"I did the stupid chores." It was neither a yes, nor a no. Just a statement of fact with no warmth in it. A passive-aggressive complaint.

"That's good." I swallowed hard. *Don't break down. Don't.* Just because I was feeling needy, just because it had been a long afternoon didn't mean I could allow teenage emotional blackmail to work. "Anything else happen today?" *Like a group of hooligans stopping by in a boat? Unauthorized rock climbing? Anything like that?*

His lips pursed and his eyes narrowed. "I'm doing my summer reading for the stupid English class, okay?" He snorted at the end of the words to let me know what he thought of summer reading.

The muscles in my back tightened, and in the space of an instant, I went from depressed to irritated. "I asked you a question, Dustin. I know you were just in the living room watching TV, so I doubt that you're too engrossed in your studies. When I ask you a question, I expect a civil answer. I haven't seen you all day, and it isn't too much to expect you to fill me in on what you've been doing, especially after what happened yesterday."

Pushing the computer out of the way, he swung his legs around and sat up, the slouched posture intended to let me know that I was bothering him. "Well, let's see. My awesome, exciting, wonderful day. I did the stupid chore list. It was, like, a hundred and ten flippin' degrees out there. The little girls from next door followed me around the stupid yard all afternoon. The weed eater jammed up about eight times. Grandma and Grandpa came by and griped about the weed eating—by the way, Grandpa's keeping our car until he can get some new tires put on it. Then, Grandma found out her . . . some stupid . . . something-or-other plants were all broken off and stuff. First, she said I did it with the weed eater that doesn't even *work,* and then she decided the kids next door did it—like Ansley and Sydney just ripped up her plants. Grandma went over there and got in a fight with the neighbors. Aunt Megan came for a while, and just now the game warden dude called about the water safety course. It was a really *great* day. That what you wanted to hear? Thanks a lot for getting me hauled to the stupid safety course by the water cop. Like you can't just trust me to go on my own?" Capping the sentence with a wounded, narrow-eyed look, he ricocheted from angry, to hurt and insulted.

Take a deep breath. Take a deep breath before you say anything. He's just trying to push your buttons. "In the first place, you don't have any other way to get to the class, and by the way, make sure you read the brochure so you'll know if there's anything you need to take with you. In the second place, it's only for a week, and in the third place, you're in no position to be giving attitude. It's just fortunate that nothing worse happened yesterday. Do you know that two different people today have told me about recent accidents at the Scissortail? One boy died and one is in a wheelchair for life. Both teenagers."

Dustin scoffed, sagging over his knees and picking bits of grass off his foot. "Who told you that?"

"The game warden, for one, and my boss at work, Mr. Tazinski, for another."

Dustin stopped picking grass, seeming to briefly consider that yesterday's reality could have been terribly different.

"We're just lucky you're all right. Very lucky."

Stiffening, he sat up and looked toward the window, as if he were seeing the lake through the mini blinds he kept closed, giving his room a cave-like pallor. "Yeah, we're *lucky*." The last word was laced with hidden meanings I could only guess at.

Momentarily, I considered telling him about the places I'd been today, describing the tumbledown home in which Audrey and John lived or the little patch of dirt at Len's, where a child had been playing. Lucky was all in your perspective. There were people with problems worse than a painful divorce, a broken weed eater, and a mandatory water safety course.

If he could see some of the things I'd seen . . .

But did I really want him to? Those realities were hard for adult eyes, and he was still a child, working through his own difficulties with only adolescent coping mechanisms to rely upon.

"Did Dad call about me going to Houston for August?" His gaze fluttered my way, a bit hopeful, a bit guarded, a bit belligerent—as if to point out that, if I made him too angry, he'd pack his bags and go live with his dad and Delayne. The truth was that he hadn't been invited there. Karl was busy settling into a new life with Delayne and her two little girls. He didn't seem to have much interest in the ties to his old used-up life.

Dustin didn't need to hear that, although to some degree, he already knew. Karl had been missing weekend visitations even before we'd left Houston. Dustin's acting as if, any minute, the *good* parent would swoop in and save him from Mean Mom was just another way of lashing out at whomever was near. Right now, I was the only one near.

"Your dad hasn't called. He just started that new job, though. That could be keeping him pretty tied up." After months of unemployment and searching, Karl had finally settled for a teaching position at a rehab center for teenage boys.

"Yeah." Dustin stared a hole in the blinds, his chin trembling almost imperceptibly, until he swallowed hard and wiped the expression away, hardening himself against it.

My heart split open. I wanted to do something to take away the pain and disappointment, to make everything better. To fix things. There was no *right thing* to say, no verbal magic bullet. If I shared my opinions of Karl, I would hurt Dustin. If I made excuses for Karl, I would be silently saying that I supported Karl's moving on and leaving his son behind.

Finally, I settled for changing the subject altogether. "Tell you what. Why don't we run to town? We'll pick up some line for the weed eater, and then we can grab some cheese fries and an ice cream at Catfish Charley's out on the lake."

"I ate already. And the hardware store's closed."

I should have thought of that. Everything in Moses Lake was closed by this time of the evening. Catfish Charley's was only open because it served the tourist crowd, who didn't come in to eat until the day on the lake was over. "We can still go get an ice cream. We haven't been to Catfish Charley's in forever." When Dustin was small, lake house visits had included frequent stops at Catfish Charley's to enjoy a hand-dipped ice cream and toss food off the dock to waiting ducks, or visit with Charley, the primordial giant who lived in a huge fish tank in the back of the restaurant. "I'll bet Charley is over a hundred pounds, by now."

Dustin seemed to considerer it briefly. I took another step into the room, dangling the olive branch, in the form of ice cream and a hundred-pound catfish. I waited, ready for a little time that wasn't spent struggling, or fighting, or butting heads.

"I've gotta do my stupid summer reading for the AP English class." Dustin was already sinking back onto the bed, slowly, like a wrinkled piece of paper unfolding. "It's not like I'll get anything done while I'm sitting in some stupid class with the water cop."

Disappointment and a sense of hopelessness

fell over me like a wet, heavy tarp, making it hard to breathe. Were Dustin and I ever going to find a new kind of normal? Were we doomed to wallow in this mire of guilt, conflict, and emotional blackmail forever?

I steeled myself against letting the wound show. First and foremost, I had to be the parent, the adult. "All right," I said, and feeling the need to leave behind a droplet of hope, I added, "Maybe tomorrow, then."

Knowledge comes, but wisdom lingers.
—Alfred Lord Tennyson
(Left by an anonymous fly fisherman)

Chapter 12

Mart McClendon

After another day of passing by Andrea's lake house and watching the kid out there mowing, cleaning flower beds, and trimming trees, I was actually starting to feel sorry for him. His mom ran a tough ship. I doubted he'd be climbing any more rocks anytime soon. He had a little company now, at least. Whenever I drifted by, the neighbor's little blond-haired granddaughters were tailing after him. When I called to give Andrea an update on Len, she told me that Dustin had an admiration society forming next door. We laughed about it. "Well, there are worse things than having girls follow you around with lemonade and cookies," I said.

Andrea chuckled. "I told him that."

When we got done talking about Dustin, I didn't have much to report about Len and the little girl. "Haven't caught up with them yet, but it's not for lack of trying. He's laying low. And for a simple-minded fellow, he's good at it. I figure he's hiding out at one of his deer camps during the day, then coming back to his place at night to feed his livestock and look after his garden."

The more time went by, the more I worried that I might be wrong about old Len, and Andrea might be right. I didn't want to believe the worst, but why would a man go to so much work to hide out, unless he was doing something he shouldn't be?

Finally, after two days with no luck, I settled on a plan with my partner, Jake Moskaluk. He'd meet me on the lake tomorrow morning, and we'd catch Len when he hit his trotlines at first light. Jake would hang back in the brush while I talked to Len, so as not to scare Len any more than necessary.

I called Andrea as I was leaving the Waterbird with my supper sandwich in hand, and I told her that by tomorrow I'd have Len tracked down. We talked for a while after that—not about anything special, just little stuff. I'd met her little neighbors that day—Sydney and Ansley—at Catfish Charley's, and they really could talk the bark off a tree.

Andrea laughed and said, "Maybe all their chatter will help get Dustin in the mood for water safety class." The laugh in her voice faded into a sigh. I wondered if she was upset about the lack of progress with Len, or if she was having trouble with her boy again. I didn't ask. It wasn't my business.

I caught myself looking up toward her house after I hung up and headed home across the lake. Maybe it was the phone call, or the sad sound in her voice, but she was on my mind. Maybe it was just the fact that I was going back to my rented place on Holly Hill, and I knew it would be the same as always when I pulled up to the dock. No lights on. No signs of life. No real reason to want to go in.

Tonight there was a message on my answering machine when I walked inside. I knew who it'd be, even before I hit the button. Nobody called the cabin number, except the family back home.

The phone call was from my sister-in-law, Laurie. She was hoping I'd come home for Levi's sixth birthday party later in the month.

I called her back and told her I couldn't. If she'd had any sense, she would've known it was better that way. But Laurie couldn't quite let go of the way things'd been for the past three years. I guess in some ways, she felt like it was her fault I'd left Alpine behind. It wasn't her fault, really. It was just how things had to be. Laurie and the boys needed to move on, and now that she'd found a good man, it was time. If she could just make up her mind to turn loose of the past, she could start a new life and give Levi, Hayden, and Samuel a family again. A new family. Maybe

Laurie and Chris would even have more kids. She was young yet. The best thing I could do was get out of the way, so life could move on.

Laurie wasn't really my sister-in-law anymore, because my brother was dead. All Laurie and I were to each other was a constant reminder of what'd happened. Even if she couldn't see that, I finally had. Every time I looked at Laurie and the boys, I thought of Aaron, my little brother, and Mica, the gap-toothed carrottop who was Aaron's spitting image, except for the red hair. It's a hard thing to have a little boy frozen in your mind at seven years old, to know he isn't going to grow into the baseball glove you bought him for Christmas, or fix up an old truck someday, or go on a date, or take a girl to the prom. That's how my nephew would always be for me—seven years old, with a smile that stretched ear to ear and a spray of freckles over a sunburned nose.

"Come on, Mart," Laurie begged. "The boys want you to come. I mean, for the past three years, they've been with you almost every day, and now you're just . . . gone? They miss you."

Something painful twisted under my ribs. I missed those boys in a way there wasn't words for, but as long as I was right down the street from Laurie all the time, they were never going to start taking baby steps toward a new place. We'd always be stuck where we'd been— dredging up photo albums and videos, reliving past vacations, old fishing trips, the last Christmas we were all together. Clinging to the past so hard it was like leaving an arrow embedded instead of pulling it out and letting the wound bleed clean, then heal.

There was a difference between keeping memories alive and using them as an excuse not to start living again.

"I miss them, too, but I can't get off." It was easier to make an excuse than to explain things to Laurie. I'd tried a hundred times before. *I know you're not Aaron,* she'd say. *I know you're not him, Mart.*

But before Mama had passed eight months ago, she'd told me that I didn't need to worry about Aaron and Mica anymore. She was going to be with them, and with my older brother, Shawn, who'd been killed in Afghanistan. I needed to move on with my life, be happy. If she couldn't have all her boys together in one place, she wanted to know everyone was okay, at least.

I told her I'd work on it, and then we'd talked awhile longer before she relaxed in the bed. The next morning when the hospice nurse came, Mama didn't wake up. The nurse said that sometimes people needed to feel like they'd finished their business on this earth before they could let go. Mama'd finished her business. She'd said good-bye to all the grandbabies. My middle brother, Jay, had spent some time alone with her, and she'd done her best to make sure we were all taken care of. Now I was doing my best to keep the promise I'd made to her.

"Mart, please," Laurie whispered, her voice shaking. "Chris and I want you to come."

"Laurie, it's better this way." Chris didn't want me to come. Chris was a nice guy, but having to share space with a third wheel and a dead guy was more than any man could do forever. If Laurie didn't wake up, Chris would pack his bags and head out the door. "Y'all just go on and have a good day with Levi—just the five of you. Do something . . . different than usual." Something that didn't end in sitting around a half-lit room, sipping wine and drowning in memories.

"It's not right without you here," Laurie whispered.

"It can be. You've just got to make up your mind to it." I loved Laurie like a sister, and I always would. She loved me because I was the closest link she had to my brother and Mica. I was the last one to see them alive.

I was the one who should've looked after them that day.

Laurie didn't see it that way, though. She'd never blamed anyone for it—except maybe Aaron for not being more careful, especially when he was taking Mica out in the boat with him. Aaron should've scanned the storm reports. He should've checked over our little bay boat

184

before he took it out—made sure that, if the weather changed, he and Mica wouldn't end up trapped out on the water when the bay turned rough and dangerous. The fuel filter had been clogging up and killing the engine. I had a new filter waiting in the back of my truck—a little ten-dollar part. I should've been there to put it in the boat, but I wasn't. I was at work, clearing up one last case, when I should've been at our little man-shack on the beach, getting the boat ready for a weekend of bay fishing with my brother and his boy. An extra hour at work and a ten-dollar part had cost Aaron and Mica their lives.

Laurie pulled in a trembling breath. She was probably off in a room by herself, trying not to let anyone know the past was wrapped around her so tight she couldn't breathe. "I was just . . . looking at the pictures from that trip to Taos. Remember? Aaron and me, and you and Melanie." She laughed softly, and I could see her sliding a hand over the pages, her fingertip caressing the faces. "Mica was just little. Remember, you got him all dressed up and stood him in your ski boots? He looks so funny in those huge skis."

"I remember." The good times slid around me with the softness of freshly combed fleece. The past turned in my head like a spinning wheel, slowly twisting fleece into thread, and then into rope. Melanie was Laurie's best friend, the maid of honor at their wedding. The four of us did everything together—trips to the beach, campouts in Big Bend, weekends in the mountains. The ski trip. None of us had any idea that we were living on borrowed time. Just a few years later, Aaron and Mica were gone, and Melanie was packing her bags to move back home to Kansas, saying she couldn't take all the grief anymore. *I feel like I'm choking on it,* she'd said. *You're all choking on it. You just don't see it. Sometimes things aren't anybody's fault, Mart. Sometimes bad things just happen. They got caught in a storm. The boat capsized. That's it.*

"I'll try to get home for Christmas," I told Laurie. "Tell Levi there'll be something coming from Uncle Mart in the mail for his birthday."

"He can call you when he opens it." Laurie's answer was flat, and she followed it with a quick good-bye. I sat staring at the phone after I hung it up. I wanted to call back and tell Levi I'd be there for his birthday, but I knew it would be ten steps backward.

All of a sudden, being dog-tired seemed like a stroke of luck. I took a shower, ate my sandwich, and sacked out instead of wandering around the little lake house, bouncing off the walls and trying to find something to do with myself.

In the morning, I was up before first light and ready for work. While I was pouring coffee into my thermos, Jake called to let me know he was down with food poisoning from some roadside taco stand, and wouldn't be able to come for an assist this morning.

"Should've stuck with the Mennonite bakeries," I told him, and he let out a weak laugh that actually made me feel a little sorry for him. Jake would eat just about anything that didn't crawl away first. "Don't worry about it. I'll go ahead and sidle on up Len's way—see if I can catch him heading out to check his trotlines at sunup. I don't think it'll be a problem. If anything looks dicey, I'll call the boys from the sheriff's department." Jake and I traded a snipe or two about the sheriff's boys, and then he warned me to be careful, before he hung up the phone in a hurry, on his way to the bathroom again. I got the rest of my stuff together and headed out the door.

A low fog clung over the grass, cutting my legs at the knees as I walked down to the lake. In the glow of the dock lights, the water was silver and still, like a pool of mercury poured between the hills. A lazy crescent moon rested on its back just above the ridges to the west; and to the east, the first gray light of dawn challenged the pinpoints of a million stars.

I took a deep breath, and a handful of memories were tied to the scent of water, damp grass, and mist. Good memories. The kind that run through your mind barefoot and laughing and kicking up dust. I remembered the way the grass felt that summer at Moses Lake when we were kids—slick, wet, and cool with the dew still on it. I could hear the four of us laughing. I saw Shawn running ahead, heard Aaron lagging back, whining because it was dark, and he was scared. I told him to shut up—if Mom heard us sneaking out, we'd be dead. *Crybaby,* I said. *Quit whining or go away.* Aaron was always the crybaby, the mama's boy. The little freckle-faced whiner who that summer had the nerve to shoot up like a weed and get taller than me. All I wanted was for him to buzz off.

Be careful what you wish for. The voice in my head was older and wiser now. Now I would've given anything to head down to the lake with my brothers, all four of us together again. That summer was the last of it. The end of the four of us. This place would always be special to me because of that summer. When we left Moses Lake, Shawn turned eighteen and joined the army. Now he was gone, and Aaron was gone, and there were just two—just Jay and me, the two who would've been in the middle on that race down to the shore.

Here at the lake it felt like they were still with me, tramping through the fog, headed out to see what the day had to offer before it'd even begun. Here, I didn't drive by the church where we'd held Shawn's funeral, or the cemetery where we'd laid Aaron and his little boy side by side.

Here, they were all still alive, frozen in time. No reminders of how it'd ended, except the ones you carried with you.

The lake felt good this morning—quiet and calm, the air just cool enough to pull steam off the water. There was the faintest scent of fall in it, a whisper promising that soon enough the weather would change, the tourists would go home, and the shores would be left to the locals.

Heading across-water, I passed by Larkspur Cove, looked up the hill at the houses there, and my thoughts took a sharp right turn. There was a light on in one of Andrea's windows. I wondered if she was up this early, and what she was doing if she was. For a half a second, I was tempted to grab my field glasses and look over that way. The impulse was a stealth attack, and as quick as it came, I tossed it over the side of the boat and let it float away in the wake. Peeping into houses with binoculars was wrong in a half dozen ways, and besides that, I was on duty.

The idea followed me across the lake, trailing behind the boat like moss that wouldn't quite shake loose. I realized there was a strange fantasy circling in my head, the kind you have early in the morning before your mind wakes up all the way. I'd drift by Andrea's house, and she'd just happen to be out on the dock, getting a little fresh air . . .

Before sunup. *Yeah, right.*

I throttled the motor down, passing the Big Boulders, then slid under Eagle Eye Bridge. Overhead, a breeze blew through the cliffs, and I heard the Wailing Woman's voice. She was moaning low, mourning a child who'd disappeared from the wagon train as they forded the river, or so the story went. In the day-use picnic area across the way, the mockingbirds echoed her voice along with a medley of mimicked birdcalls.

The Wailing Woman's moans and the mockingbirds' answers faded as I started up the channel, and there was nothing but predawn stillness and the soft song of mourning doves. When the water was dark and quiet like this, the rumble of the motor floated like smoke, traveling for miles, winding into the trees.

I hoped I'd started out early enough to get to a resting spot and cut the motor before Len made it down to the water. My plan was to pull up in the cedar overhang just past the place where Len had been putting his rig in the water. I could wait there for him to come down for his morning spin on the lake. That'd be a pretty good place to catch him for a friendly little chat. He wouldn't be able to avoid me at that point, unless he wanted to up and make a run for it, in which case, I'd have to start the day by detaining a suspect.

I hoped it didn't come to that. Innocent men don't run, for one thing. I didn't want to be wrong about Len, and it seemed a shame to muck up such a nice morning by having to haul someone to the county lockup. Aside from that, there was the fact that I wasn't hoping to find out anything bad had been happening to that little girl. I wanted to finally be able to tell Andrea I'd sorted out the situation—that some neighbors had been at Len's place, and the little girl belonged to them.

It crossed my mind that I was thinking about Andrea again—imagining her catching a breath and looking relieved when I told her the little girl was fine. Andrea smiled, in my mind, laughed about the big adventure up to Len's cabin, and said she'd ruined her dress shoes for nothing. I told her if she was going to be working with Texas Parks and Wildlife, she'd better get some more practical footwear.

I shut down the conversation in my head as I pulled the boat up into the cedar overhang and waited. It wasn't like me to have my mind on anything other than work. Normally, even with seeing the sleazy and sometimes downright stupid human behavior that went along with this job, I was happy to stay focused on the task. While I was at work, I didn't wonder how Laurie's boys were getting through the baseball season without Uncle Mart there to have a catch with them. I didn't wonder if the new stepdad was arranging his day so that he could go by the ball field and help Levi learn to hit off the tee.

Maybe that was why I was thinking about Andrea now—maybe I was trying to fill the gap in my life. Another single mom, another boy who needed a man around. Maybe I was working to cap the black hole now that Aaron's family had a new man in it.

Pulling the plug on the chatter in my brain, I sat back in the seat and watched the last of the stars fade overhead as the day crept in, light gray at first, then misty and pink. The lake yawned and stretched and came to life, little perch and bass popping the top of the water, doves calling in the trees, their wings beating the air as they flitted from branch to branch, a mockingbird imitating the calls of the doves. The dove cooed in reply, and I figured the mockingbird had a laugh over it. He'd fooled someone.

I waited, sort of drifting in and out of a doze, longer than I thought I'd have to before I heard movement in the brush. My pulse jumped. I sat up and listened, but it was just a rabbit or squirrel, maybe a little bobcat or a fox. Nothing to get excited about yet, but anytime now, Len would come tromping down the hill. In the morning quiet, and with the blanket of dead leaves underfoot, he wouldn't be hard to hear. I'd be able to tell from the sound whether he was alone or had someone with him.

A hawk left its nest and circled overhead. I

watched it gliding on the warming air currents, stretching its wings in the mist. Passing over me, it cried out a complaint, letting me know I was horning in on its territory. I thought of my grandpa, a one-quarter Chickasaw who lived in the hills of northeastern Oklahoma when I was a kid. He talked to wild things like he expected them to answer. Looking back, I guessed he was the one who'd given me a love for the woods. The summers we went to visit at his farm were some of the best I remembered. A trip to town in his old pickup was always an adventure for us boys. We'd go in the five-and-dime and pick out penny candy, or pinwheels, or kites we could fly in Granddad's hayfield.

There was a game warden who hung around the old feed mill. I'd sit on the porch and listen to his tales while Granddad jawboned with the men inside. It was that game warden who gave me the idea that maybe I'd like to do his job one day— have all those adventures like he did, not be tied to an office or a desk. Guess, even though my daddy left when I was fourteen and I didn't see my granddad much after that, a little of Granddad and that game warden stayed with me.

A twig snapped on the hillside while my mind was in Oklahoma. I sat up and listened. Footsteps for sure this time. Just one person coming—a long, loose, easy gait, dragging one foot a little. That'd be Len. He was pretty late getting down to the lake this morning. By the sound of things, he was carrying something fairly heavy—fishing equipment, cast nets, and jug lines wrapped in a tarp, maybe. Hopefully not some kind of trap I'd have to cite him for.

I moved to the side of my boat and slipped off into the mud where I wouldn't make any noise, then worked my way along the shore and stopped at the edge of the cedars, waiting for Len to make it down the hill. Once he'd uncovered his boat and started wrestling it down to the water, I would let him know I was here. By then his hands would be busy. He was probably carrying a gun, and I didn't want him to get surprised and decide to use it.

He was about twenty feet away—just on the other side of the cedar brush—when I heard him set down whatever he was carrying, then work his boat out from under a tangle of branches, turn it over, and push it toward the water. The swish of the hull over the leaves moved away, but then there was another noise. Something closer— where Len had set down whatever he was packing. A dog, maybe? I should've thought about the fact that he could have one of his dogs along. If that was the case, the whole picture changed. A protective pit bull goes a long way toward making the odds uneven. Surprising Len was one thing, but surprising one of those dogs was another.

If it was a dog, why hadn't it sniffed me out yet?

Nearby, Len grunted and struggled, the boat hanging up on something. My ear strained into the brush, tried to pick up what was out there, to figure out whether it was a threat or not. My heart pumped. I settled my fingers over my gun, broke it loose in the holster.

The carpet of leaves shifted and rustled, and then there was the faintest sound. It seemed out of place at first—soft and peaceful. An exhale of breath, like a child sighing in its sleep. The leaves shifted and crinkled again, and all at once I knew. Len wasn't alone. The little girl, whoever she might be, was right there on the other side of the cedars, not more than eight or ten feet from me.

My thoughts whirled like fish schooling up. What would Len be doing at the shore with a child first thing in the morning? Nothing good. Nothing normal. He probably hadn't picked her up at some neighbor's house before seven. Whoever she was, he'd had her with him overnight, and now he was . . . was . . . what? Where was he headed?

Stories from the evening news and missing persons cases pushed into my mind. Maybe I'd been wrong about Len. Maybe everyone had. Maybe his mild manner and his slow, stuttering speech was all an act. Maybe he wasn't mentally handicapped at all. Maybe he was some kind of a long-term perp, a fox hiding right here in the chicken house. The lake and the parks were full of kids, all summer long. . . .

I shook off the idea. No point in speculation. Right now the only thing certain was that I couldn't let Len leave here with the little girl. I should've arranged some other form of backup when Jake called in sick. Coming alone had been a bad choice. I'd been at this job long enough to know that a situation could seem safe enough one minute, then blow up in your face the next.

Crouched there in the cedars, I thought through the scenarios. If I went after the child, Len would perceive me as a threat immediately. If he was armed or chose to fight, I'd be weighted down, trying to protect and contain the child while Len was free to come after me in whatever way he wanted. . . .

He'd worked the boat loose and was pushing it toward the lake again now. I heard the aluminum hull grind over the rocks at the edge of the brush cover. *A better chance isn't coming along anytime soon,* I thought, and made sure my gun was ready, but I didn't draw it. Better to make this look casual, try not to set him off.

While the boat was scraping along, I slipped back the other direction a bit, got to the shoreline where I could see clearly, and started Len's way, just moving at a casual pace, so as not to come up on him too quickly. Rounding the last of the cedar brush, I could see him pulling his rig through the shore muck. I checked him over as I moved in. No visible weapons, except a hunting knife on his belt. I doubted I was in too much danger from that.

He hadn't seen me coming yet. He was turned toward the lake, pulling the boat along with a piece of frayed rope wrapped over his shoulder. He slid a hand up the line, and I could see that he had on bulky work gloves. That was a point in my favor. Gloves like that make it pretty hard to use a weapon of any kind.

"Mornin', Len," I said, and he jumped about three feet, dropping his draw line. His eyes flew open wide, and his gaze darted around. For about a second and a half, I got the strong feeling he was thinking about running. If he did, I'd have to stop him before he made it back to that brush. Len wasn't a big man. He might've been at one time, but at this point, he was shrunken up and stooped over, old looking. The skin on his neck moved up and down like a turkey wattle as he swallowed hard, his eyes tracking from my badge to my gun and back.

I held my hands away from the holster a bit. "Don't panic on me now. I just want to talk to you a minute. You know who I am, right?"

Of course Len knew who I was. He and I'd had too many conversations about jug lines for him not to know. The real question was why he was looking at me like he was scared to death. Usually, when I confronted Len about fishing violations, he just came across as confused by the fact that the lake and land around it had actual rules he was supposed to follow. When I explained that fact to him, he just hung his head, slurred out, "Yyyes-ir," in his strange garbled way, and then he went on and complied with whatever I'd asked him to do. I'd cited him once for shooting a couple wild turkeys out of season, and he'd even taken that pretty calmly. Len didn't know much, but apparently, he had some experience with paying fines for wildlife violations.

Today he looked panicked enough to bolt into the lake. Darting a glance toward the cedar brush where I'd heard the child, he took a step sideways.

I held up my hands, palms out, to calm him. "Len, I don't want any trouble, all right. I have to ask you not to go any closer to the brush, though. I need to talk to you for a minute, and we'll stand right here where I can see what's around us. You understand?"

I waited for his next move. There was a pretty decent chance he had a rifle up there in the woods with the rest of his stuff. If there was a child there, the rifle and the child might be in the brush together.

The situation was getting more complicated by the minute. Some way or other, I had to hurry things along before Len's mind could cycle around and come up with a plan. Fortunately, Len wasn't a quick thinker.

"All right, now, listen," I said. "First thing, I need to know what you've got stashed up there in the brush."

Len swallowed hard again, his lips tightening. His tongue kneaded around his teeth as he worked up some words. "I ain't . . . s-s-shot unn-no utt-turkeys." *Turkeys* came out in a hail of spit I could feel from four feet away. The wind shifted then, and I could smell him, too. Len stunk worse than something that'd been dead on the side of the road for three days. Hard to say whether that shack of his had indoor plumbing or not, but it must not've had a bathtub.

"I didn't say you shot any turkeys. I asked what you've got up in the cedar brush. There someone out here with you this morning?"

He darted a look toward the brush again, rubbing his hands over his grease-coated jeans, like he was trying to dry his palms even though he had gloves on.

"I need you to keep your hands where I can see them," I said. The hands stayed where they were, his gloved fingers tightening over baggy folds in his clothes, pulling and tugging nervously. I couldn't help feeling a little sorry for him. Most of the suspects I dealt with were scum with long legal histories of petty crime, drug violations, DUIs, and domestic incidents. I usually found them driving around in cars registered to wives, girlfriends, mamas, or grandmas, because they couldn't keep up the payments on a vehicle themselves. But Len, even with his limitations, was trying to scratch out his own living on the little bare-dirt farm left behind by his folks. "You got somebody with you this morning?"

"Unn-nobody," he answered, working hard to get the word out, a bead of tobacco dribbling from the corner of his mouth and hanging in the gray stubble on his chin. "Unn-nobody th-th-thar." He glanced toward the cedar brush again, his hands worrying the tails of a denim shirt that'd probably been scooped from the trash barrel behind some gas station.

I looked him in the eye, and he ducked his head like he was hunting a hole to jump into. "Len, we're walking up to that cedar brush now, and I don't want you to cause any trouble. I need you to show me what you've got hidden there."

*I will charge thee nothing but the promise
that thee will help the next man
thee finds in trouble.*
—Mennonite proverb
(Left by Mennonite fishermen
with a load of blue catfish)

Chapter 13

Andrea Henderson

My first appointment of the day was a session with a grandmother who was trying to raise three grandkids after the death of her son. Taz had been working with the eldest of the boys, Daniel, since before Daniel was removed from his mother's care and given to his grandmother. Now Daniel had begun to realize that his grandmother couldn't physically control him. He harbored an underlying fear that she, too, might abandon him, and that fear had begun manifesting itself in destructive ways. He'd been kicked out of the school's summer enrichment program for showing up with a mini baseball bat and threatening another kid with it. Now Daniel had no friends and wanted to drop out before beginning the fifth grade.

I suggested that we look for some positive activities for Daniel—something that would not only occupy him, but also give him a boost in self-esteem, teach him relationship-building skills, and bring him in contact with good male role models. Mart's water safety class came to mind. I made a mental note to check into the possibility.

"Well, I guess it'd be all right," the grandmother, Mrs. Crandall, said wearily. "If you can find someplace that'll have him. But we can't pay for anything. His mom doesn't even bother to send child support for him." She said it in front of Daniel, and the boy just looked at the carpet, trying to hide the tremor in his bottom lip. These adult issues were too much for a ten-year-old to deal with.

"We'll work that out," I told her, and patted Daniel on the shoulder. "Do you think some new activities sound like a good idea, Daniel? Some things to get you out of the house?"

Daniel shrugged.

I put on a happy face meant to convince myself, or Daniel, or both. "I'll get back to you with some ideas and information." After setting up our next appointment and leaving the family with a workbook about grief in children, I proceeded to my car and sat jotting down notes and thinking that I should have brought some food along with me. It was only nine thirty in the morning, and I was already hearing whispers from the granola bar that had been knocking around my father's car with me ever since we'd traded vehicles. My next appointment was at least a half hour's drive away, even deeper into the hills of Chinquapin Peaks. Once that was over, I had an hour and a half before my afternoon appointments, but it would be a long way to anyplace where I could buy lunch.

Starting the car, I gazed across the lake. The shimmering view seemed an odd contrast to the Crandall home, a crumbling three-bedroom brick structure that must have been nice when it was built, but now lacked for maintenance. Backing out of the driveway onto the county road, I considered my location, the route to my next appointment, and the problem of finding some lunch after that. As the crow flies, I could run home in fifteen minutes, grab lunch, and spend a little time with Dustin. Unfortunately, I wasn't a crow.

The phone vibrated in my jeans pocket as I topped a hill and stopped at a crossroads. Scooting forward in the seat, I slipped out the phone and put it on speaker.

"Hey." Bonnie, the world's most cheerful office secretary, was upbeat as always. "Got a couple messages for you. Your ten o'clock canceled, so we moved it to Monday morning at ten. Taz wants to remind you that group meeting next Wednesday should be on your schedule, and someone named Mart McClendon called. He says he's the . . . game warden? He wanted you to call him ASAP." The last letter ended on a high note, floating through the phone with an obvious underlay of curiosity. "I hope everything's okay." She waited for me to grab a pencil, then she read off Mart's contact information.

My mind raced ahead as I jotted the number on my clipboard. Mart's call could be good, or it could be bad. Either Dustin was in trouble again, or Mart finally had news about the little girl at Len's house. "Okay, Bonnie. Listen, can you tell Taz I won't be back into the office until the end of the day? I have afternoon appointments out here in Chinquapin Peaks. There's a little picnic area upriver from here. I think I'll just use the extra time to pull in there and eat my granola bar while I work on reports. I have my laptop with me."

Bonnie clicked her tongue playfully. "Sounds like tough duty. Don't get a sunburn."

"I'll try not to make it obvious," I joked, then told her good-bye and made a couple notes about the Crandall family while I had the pen in my hand. Cases were starting to run together in my head—a blur of names, faces, and furniture that smelled like something other than foam rubber and fabric.

As I dialed Mart's number, a strange sensation twittered inside my chest—an almost buoyant anticipation—and before I was even aware of it,

I was smiling at the empty crossroads and smoothing stray hairs into my clip, as if someone were there. Over the past couple days, our calls about the situation at Len's house had seemed to linger beyond business. We'd found other things to talk about—Dustin's progress on the yard work, the way Sydney and Ansley seemed to have adopted Dustin, the horrendously poor condition of roads out in Chinquapin Peaks, even the fact that my father had insisted on ordering some sort of special extra-ply tires for my car, so that I'd be less likely to get another flat. "Good idea," Mart had said. "Gotta tell you, though. A car isn't the right vehicle for Chinquapin Peaks."

"I think I need a tank." I'd already figured out that my vehicle was going to be a problem on these rural roads, but replacing it was pretty much an impossibility right now.

Mart had chuckled, sending a warm, snuggly feeling through my middle. "Well, now, there's a picture. . . ."

A moment later the conversation had turned back to business, Mart telling me about his plans to lay in wait for Len this morning and promising to finally get to the bottom of the situation with the little girl.

Now I tried to tamp down the flutter of anticipation as I listened to the cell signal clicking along. What was I anticipating, exactly? Why was I preening my hair and smiling at the stop sign? I contemplated answers to that question while the call ping-ponged off towers.

The phone rang three times, and then Mart's voice mail picked up. On the recording, he sounded businesslike, slightly stiff. The fluttery feeling inside me evaporated, and I responded in my own business voice. "This is Andrea Henderson, returning your call. Sorry I wasn't able to reach you. Please feel free to contact me on my cell phone . . ."

The call waiting beeped as I was leaving the message, and I rushed to answer, "Andrea Henderson."

The call was faint, the voice difficult to hear, "Andrea, this is Mart McClendon. Sorry I missed your call, I . . . " His voice faded into a haze, and I switched off speaker, pushing the receiver close to my ear.

"Mart? Hello? I can barely hear you. Are you there?" Pulling the phone away from my ear, I checked the screen to see if the call was still connected, then I listened again.

"That better?" Mart's voice was still faint but clearer. "Can you hear me now?" There was an underlying urgency in his voice that made me straighten in my seat and look around the crossroads. Had something happened with Dustin, or was this call about the little girl?

"Yes, I can hear you. What's going on? Did you go to Len's this morning? Did you find anything?"

"I'm . . . there now." He hesitated, as if he were carefully choosing his words or deciding how much to tell me. The anticipation inside me darkened into dread. Mart was calling with bad news.

"Is Len there? Did you find the little girl?"

"Len's here." The response seemed measured, cautious. I wondered if Len was listening in on the call.

"Did you learn anything about the little girl?"

"She's . . . here, too."

My head spun. My surroundings fell out of focus, and momentarily I was at Len's cabin, peering into the school bus, my nose filled with the scent of mold, animal feces, stale bedding and clothes. "She's there? Who is she? Is she all right?"

Silence answered, and for a horrifying minute, I wondered if the call had broken up, or if something else had happened. "Mart? Mart, can you hear me?" Grabbing the county road atlas, I tried to guess the approximate location of Len's house and which roads might lead me there.

"I'm here," Mart's voice seemed calmer. I swallowed the pulsating mass in my throat. "I'm just at a loss as to how to . . . proceed at this point. It's a little hard to say what the . . . protocol would be for this . . . situation." Mart was couching words, trying to make me understand something without coming right out and saying it.

"Mart, are you all right?"

"Yes, I'm fine."

"Are you in any danger?"

"No. None."

"Is Len listening?"

"Yes."

"And the girl's there with him?"

"Yes. We've been talking about her for quite a while, as a matter of fact. I told Len that, since she misses her mama, she might like to spend a little time with a woman. He wasn't too crazy about the idea, but I told him I had a friend . . . a lady . . . and he said it'd be all right if my *friend* came by to talk for a little bit. When I called your office, they said you were out on this side of the lake, and I just thought you might take a ride up here, see if she wants to visit with you at all. She's not too interested in talking with me, but you know how little girls are."

"Yes . . . I do, but . . . you mean now?"

Mart went on talking as if he hadn't heard the question. "So far, Len's been a real good host. Real cooperative. I'd like to keep it that way, if you know what I mean. We've looked around his barn and checked a few things out. He's got a baby raccoon in the house we're going to have to talk about, but mostly, it'd be good if you could come by and have a chat with this little girl while everyone's in the mood—just to see where we need to go from here."

I heard someone speaking in the background, a man's voice, and then dogs barking. Mart answered, and I realized he wasn't talking to me. "Yeah, I know you need to head down to the lake, but we have to talk about that raccoon kit in the house and the feather in that cage out in the barn, so you can't go anyplace right now, Len. You understand? I need you and your granddaughter to stay right here with me. You understand that? You understand what I'm telling you?"

Len's answer was a muffled slur in the background.

"His granddaughter? She's his granddaughter?"

"That's what he says . . . his *daughter's girl,* and that the mother left her here willingly," Mart answered. Len was still talking in the background, the cadence of the words speeding up, growing agitated.

"Does he have any proof of that?" How could the little girl be Len's granddaughter? More than one person in town had confirmed that Len didn't have a family.

"Well, he told me that she was sick with an earache when her mother brought her here a couple weeks ago, and they took her to the doc at the rural clinic in Moses Lake—the one in the building across from the church. After Len and I talked awhile this morning, we called the clinic. I talked to a friend there, and she did confirm that Len had been in there with the little girl *and* the mom, and that nothing seemed to be out of the ordinary."

Mart paused again, as the voice in the background increased in volume, and a second barking dog joined in. "Now, Len, just calm down. We'll get out there and look over those cages in a minute. If that feather is really from a wild turkey, and you didn't shoot it out of season, you haven't got anything to worry about there. Just give me a minute to talk on the phone, and then we'll go look."

"Mart, you need an investigator from CPS," I said. "They're the ones who do the initial case assessments. After they assess the case, then they can draw up a service plan, and if needed, we get a referral, and I can—"

"Yeah, I don't think that'll fly too well." Mart's answer was cryptic, a message in code. "*Those people* were mentioned early in our conversation, and that drew a pretty emotional response here— if you know what I mean. I think there'd been some warning from the mom, before she took off, not to talk to any of *those* people . . . from *that* place . . . Okay? That make sense?"

The tumblers clicked in my brain, clarifying the picture. In my short training stint with Taz I'd learned that clients often viewed Social Services personnel as the enemy. Parents with issues saw them as a danger—authority figures intent on taking their children away, and children saw

210

them as the vehicle through which they were removed from all that was familiar and placed in foster homes or emergency shelters. No matter how bad family life was, kids tended to opt for what they knew, to cling to biological bonds, even when those bonds were painful and destructive.

"Yes, that makes sense. I understand."

"Where are you?"

I checked the map again, then looked at the single, leaning road sign marking the intersection. "Not very far away, I think. I'm at the crossroads of CR 4120 and . . . something. The other road sign is missing. Just judging by the map, I think I might be at the junction of 4120 and 3013. There's an actual stop sign here, but not much else in the way of landmarks."

Mart made a contemplative sound. "Stop sign on 4120 . . . Can you see the river?"

"I could a minute ago, but not now. I was headed to the little picnic area just below Eagle Eye Bridge and the Wailing Woman cliffs. I know it's down this way somewhere. I passed it the other day." I looked around for more landmarks. "There's nothing here but trees."

"Any driveways close by?"

"No. None." Strike two.

"A big oak tree that's been struck by lightning?"

"Nope. Sorry." If the underlying situation

211

hadn't been so dire, our conversation would have been funny.

"Bullet holes in the stop sign?"

I looked up, checked the sign. "Yes . . . actually, there are." That wasn't much of a landmark, really. Half of the signs around had been the victims of drive-by target practice.

"How many?"

"How many bullet holes?" He could tell where I was by the number of bullet holes in the stop sign? This guy was good. "Three. Right in the P. Actually, the sign says STO."

Mart made a perceptive sound, honing in. "Is there a new culvert under the road?"

I leaned out the window, taking in the mound of fresh gravel beneath my car. "Well, yes, actually, there is. I'm sitting right on top of it."

"You pointed east or west?"

"West."

"All righty, then," Mart's voice faded as he talked to Len. "Len, can you tell me how to get here from where they just put in that new culvert at the crossroads down from Eagle Eye?"

I proceeded to get directions to Len's place. The strangeness of that struck me, as I was jotting down turns and landmarks. Len was afraid of Social Services, and he wanted Mart to go away, yet he was helping to give me directions. Very odd.

"It's about six or seven miles, judging by the

map," I said when we finished. "I'll be there in a few minutes."

"As quick as possible would be good," Mart replied. "I really only have jurisdiction here over the baby raccoon and the feather, if you know what I mean."

"I understand. I'll hurry."

Len spoke to Mart again, and Mart added one last thing as I pulled away from the intersection. "Len says to stay over to the left when you get to the low-water crossing. It's boggy on the right side. You'll get stuck." That final bit of advice left me not knowing what to think. On the one hand, Len was worried about anyone checking up on the situation with the little girl. On the other hand, he wanted to make sure I didn't get stuck in the mudhole.

As I followed Mart's directions through a maze of county byways, logging roads, and finally down a rutted set of tracks that had last been maintained sometime after Conestoga wagons traveled over it, I tried to imagine what I would find at Len's house. If Len was as people described him, how could he possibly be caring for a child? What sort of life was she living? Why had she been left in such a dismal place?

After the past few days, the third question wasn't so hard to sort out. There were any number of possible answers. Because the mother had a drug problem, because she was occupied with a new boyfriend, because she didn't have the mental capacity to understand what she was doing, because she was tired of being tied down with a child and wanted the freedom to do her own thing, because she was out of money or patience, or both. Between my travels and the stories I'd heard at the office, many scenarios made sense.

I turned off the rutted path onto an even narrower trail and found myself bumping through a scrappy cornfield, then past a hedge of cedars that shielded an enormous vegetable garden. The garden was surprisingly lush and well kept, the dirt freshly tilled, all the weeds pulled, the tomato plants carefully tied up in wire cages, protected by crudely built arbors of cedar branches.

The garden faded into long scrappy grass, dirt, and weeds as I drew closer to the house. Mart jogged out and met my car in the driveway. When I rolled down the window, he leaned in, glancing back toward the house, where Len was waiting at the bottom of the steps, eyeing me suspiciously. "Act like we're friends. He's pretty nervous. So far, he's been cooperative, but I don't have a warrant, and there's really no evidence that he's not telling the truth about the little girl or that she's in any obvious danger. For now, we're just here on a friendly visit, as long as he's willing. Once he turns over that baby raccoon and the feather from the live trap, he's free to ask me to leave anytime. He's skittish about anything having to do with Social Services, and it's pretty hard to make him understand things. It sounds like this little girl has been here since the medical clinic visit the week before last. Apparently, the mom was around for the first few days, and then once Len got her car in working order and put gas in it for her, she left."

"Okay," I answered, trying to think through the situation. "Is the little girl all right? How old is she? Where did you find her? What else did he say about her?"

Mart held a hand up to quiet me. "I can't really get a bead on whether he expects the mom to show back up anytime soon. Just guessing by looks, I'd say the girl is about five, maybe six years old. She seems fine, physically. The rest, I can't tell too much about. It doesn't look like she's afraid of Len, but she doesn't want anything to do with me. I found them this morning by the lakeshore. She was still half asleep. I guess he'd taken her from bed and carried her down the hill. He probably wanted to run his trotlines before the lake got too populated."

I turned off the engine and grabbed the keys. "He was going to put a child in the boat asleep? With no life vest on?" That, in itself, was endangerment of a child.

Mart opened the door and waited for me to slip from the seat. "I don't know, exactly. I caught up with him before he got to that point. He did have a couple old vests in his boat—probably found them washed up on the lakeshore somewhere. He's been ticketed enough times, no doubt he knows enough to keep vests in the boat. He may not understand everything, but he knows that citations cost money."

Closing the door, Mart walked with me toward the porch, where Len continued eyeing us suspiciously. Repositioning his baseball cap nervously, he spat a plug of tobacco, then crossed his arms over a long-sleeved shirt that was too thick for the day. As we came closer, I could see that he was sweating, beads of moisture drawing narrow trails down the gristly coating of dirt and stubble on his neck. He didn't come out to meet us, but he didn't back away, either. When we cleared the corner of the porch, I realized that the little girl was nearby, playing in the shady patch of dirt where I'd seen the dishes and mud pie before. She'd turned her back toward the adults, her long, dark hair falling in uncombed tangles adorned with bits of grass and leaves.

Mart and I halted, and Mart made introductions. "Len, this is Andrea. I thought maybe Birdie might like to talk to her for a minute while we take another look at the things you've got in the barn."

Tipping his head to one side, Len squinted at me, and then glanced at Mart. "Dis y-y-you gul-friend?" He didn't wait for an answer. "What h-h-her unn-name?"

"This is Andrea," Mart offered, and Len turned an ear toward him. Old burn scars pockmarked his other cheek, and his earlobe had healed with a crescent-shaped piece missing.

Len regarded me again. "She a p-p-purdy ulll-lady." He smiled at Mart, revealing a row of stained and partially missing teeth, dotted with bits of tobacco. The scent of foul breath and body odor wound up my nostrils, and I swallowed a swell of stomach acid.

"Yes, she is." Mart slipped an arm around my shoulders and pulled me close. "But you remember she's my lady friend, so don't be flirting with her, now."

Ducking his head, Len laughed bashfully, then spit another plug of tobacco. "She unnn-nice?" He looked at me again.

"Sometimes." Mart caught my eye and winked, and for a moment, I forgot where we were and why. "How about we let her talk to Birdie while we go look around the barn some more? Now, you know that trapping or keeping nongame birds is illegal, right? An eagle is a federally protected nongame bird. You can't just catch coons out of the wild and keep them, either."

Len shifted uncomfortably, stuffing his hands

into the pockets of jeans that hung shapeless on his stooped-over frame. "I ain't uhhh . . . uddd-d-did . . . unnn-nothin' bad. Ugg-got them f-feathers ulll-last year. Off a turkey. The c-c-coon mama ugg-got dead . . ." He paused, clearly struggling for words. "Ull-lightnin' ugg-got her."

Mart pushed up the back of his cowboy hat and scratched underneath. "Len, the thing is, you can't be keeping a wild animal, even if you did just find it wandering. You understand? It's against the law. Raccoons carry rabies, for one thing. You understand what that is—rabies? You've got that little coon in the house with Birdie. It could make her sick. You understand that?"

Squirming, Len nodded. "Lil' c-c-coon, him just a ubb-baby. S-s-somebody ugg-gotta feed-um."

Mart cast a sympathetic look toward the house, where a masked face peered through the corner of the screen. "You can't keep a wild animal for a pet, Len. You find something like that, you have to bring it to me, and then I'll take it to somebody who can feed it. I won't let it die, I promise, but you can't keep it."

Len's lips pushed together and pursed outward, and he scratched the dirt-etched wrinkles on his chin. "I c-can uff-feed it. Umm-my mama udd-done it."

Rubbing the back of his neck, Mart sighed. "I'm sure your mama did, but this isn't the old

218

days. There're laws against keeping wild animals. It's against the rules. You understand? You'll get a ticket for that. And besides, you've got Birdie in the house. It could bite her."

"He uddd-don't bite unn-nobody. Him's all urrr-right. Bbb-Birdie likes um."

When Len said her name, the little girl stopped playing for a moment and turned her head the slightest bit, as if she were trying to catch a glimpse of us without being noticed.

"Let's go look in the barn." Mart's voice held a patient tolerance I hadn't imagined he would possess. I'd guessed him to be hard-nosed, in terms of law enforcement—the unforgiving sort he'd been when he showed up on my dock to talk about Dustin. "You're going to have to give me the raccoon, Len," he added as he started toward the barn. Hands pushed into his pockets, Len followed, darting apprehensive glances over his shoulder toward Birdie and then toward me.

I waited until they'd disappeared before I moved to the corner of the house, where the little girl was playing. In the backyard, a white dog flattened its ears and charged the fence. I recognized it as the one that had wanted to eat me alive the day Len and Birdie passed by in the truck. This little girl was in more danger from that dog than she was from the baby raccoon chattering behind the screen.

"Hi, Birdie," I said, squatting down, so as to be

eye level with her. "Remember me? I saw you the other day when my car broke on the side of the road. You and your grandfather went by in your truck."

Birdie continued playing, cocking her head to one side as she scooped dampened dirt into a dented measuring cup. Her eyes narrowed in rapt concentration as her fingers, stubby and round like a toddler's, packed the soil carefully into the container.

"What are you making?"

No acknowledgment. I knew she could hear me, because I'd seen her react when Len said her name. She'd been listening to our conversation even though she didn't want to participate.

"It looks like a cupcake." I duck-walked a little closer, out of sight of the dog. Birdie seemed oblivious to the barking and growling, but it had me on edge. In the back of my mind, I was planning escape routes, in case the dog got out. "A chocolate cupcake," I added.

Birdie swallowed, then licked her lips, as if she were thinking of chocolate.

"I wonder if we could find some frosting for that cupcake?" I took note of her clothing, which would have played well in a production of *The Grapes of Wrath*. Her oversized brown cotton dress still had the plastic string from a store tag hanging off the collar, but it was so soiled that the tiny blue flowers were almost invisible in places.

The dress had been paired with incongruous red cowboy boots. A blue knee sock rose from the top of one boot, but there was no evidence of a sock on the other foot.

The boots looked to be at least three sizes too big, more suitable for a ten- or eleven-year-old. Someone had wrapped a piece of twine around the ankles and tied it tightly in an attempt to snug up the fit. Birdie's legs protruded from the jury-rigged footwear, thin, sun-browned, and dotted with bug bites. Altogether, she looked like a little girl playing an odd game of *let's pretend* in someone else's clothes. Her hands and knees were soiled from digging in the dirt, and she had leaves and grass in her hair, but I'd seen more unkempt kids in my travels thus far. She also appeared to be well fed and comfortable with her surroundings, with the exception of my presence there.

"You have very pretty boots," I said and touched the toe of one. "I think I'd like to have a pair like that. Do you know where I can get some?"

Pausing in her dirt-packing operation, Birdie cocked her head to one side and observed my finger touching her toe. Sliding the boot away, she pressed her feet together and wrapped an arm around her legs, then looked toward the barn, hoping to find Len, I guessed.

"Oh, I didn't mean that I wanted to take *your* boots. I don't think they'd fit. Do you?"

Birdie studied her boots, then the sensible loafers I'd put on for the day's fieldwork. Lifting a hand, she swiped wisps of dark hair from her face, her gaze moving back and forth between her shoes and mine, as if she were making an acute study of both. Whether or not she was willing to fully engage in our communication, she seemed to have no problem with cognition. She understood exactly what I was asking.

Sliding my foot across the space between us, I matched it to Birdie's. "I think mine are bigger, don't you?" Actually, there wasn't a huge difference between my shoes and hers. There should have been, but there wasn't. "You'd look pretty funny in mine, don't you think? You'd be like a clown at the circus, with big, big feet." I forced a laugh to see if she would react, but she only studied the shoes a moment more, then went back to packing dirt into the cup.

I returned to discussion of the mud cake. "I know how to make a castle in the dirt—like a princess would live in. Do you know how to make a castle?"

Her shoulders moved up and down the slightest bit, an answer . . . or perhaps she was only shrugging away the hair that had bunched in the neckline of her dress. Resting her chin on her knee, she packed the last bit of dirt into the cup, then slid it across the space between us, folded her hands over the top of her boot, and waited for me to build a castle.

I grabbed the next smaller-sized measuring cup and set it by her foot. "Here, you fill that one, all right? We're going to need it next, and I'll fill the smallest one. It takes at least three sizes to make a castle tower. Have you ever made a tower before?"

She didn't reply but filled the half-cup measure while I filled the smallest one. When all three were stuffed and compacted, she sat back on her heels, watching with anticipation.

"Now, we need a small stick. An itty-bitty one about as long as . . . Oh, let me see. . . . How long are your fingers?"

She spread her fingers in the dirt, and I pretended to survey them with much thought. "Well, yes, those are the perfect-sized fingers. We'll need a stick about as long as your little pinkie finger, and then a leaf from that big, tall grass—the grass with the red edges on the leaves. Red, like your boots. We need the red grass to make a flag for the castle. Do you know where the flag goes on the castle?"

Again, no reply, but she held her hand in the air, her fingers splayed. Slowly, she folded each and pointed her index finger.

"Oh, no, not that one." Carefully, I touched her hand, taking the pinkie between my fingers, extending it and shaking it gently. "This one.

This is your little pinkie finger. Can you find a stick this long?"

Brushing her hands on her dress, Birdie stood up, her tongue protruding from the corner of her mouth as she studied her finger and surveyed the yard. A moment later, she clumped off in her oversized boots. To my complete horror, she went around the corner toward the corral of vicious dogs. A gaggle of puppies scampered to the fence when they saw her, and a brown-and-white half-grown dog cavorted back and forth along the wire, yapping and wiggling as if it wanted to come out and play. Birdie stuck a hand through the fence and let the dog lick her palm, and my heart climbed into my throat. A moment later, the man-eater I'd seen in the back of the truck came around the corner, stopped a few feet from the fence, planted its feet and growled. I realized it wasn't growling at Birdie, it was growling at me—protecting her. Stepping back around the corner, I waited until she returned with a stick and a stalk of tall grass. The grass wasn't red, but as we squatted in the dirt again, she held it against her boot, as if she were realizing the difference.

While I prepared to build our castle, I took my keys from my pocket, handed them to her, and asked if she could show me the blue one. The question appeared to confuse her completely, and after looking at the keys, she set them gently in the dirt by my feet. Apparently, she didn't know her colors, which most likely meant that she hadn't been to preschool or Head Start. She was about kindergarten age, probably not old enough for first grade.

As we continued building our tower, first dumping out the largest cup, then building upward by carefully adding blocks from the smaller two, I noted that Birdie did know how to play cooperatively. She could remember and follow more than one instruction given in sequence, and she did seem to experience delight as we carefully poked our field-grass flag into the top of the tower. Sitting back on her heels, she looked at me and smiled. Her teeth were brown and rotten around the edges—a condition known in the Medicaid world as *bottle mouth,* because it typically came from baby bottles of sugary, corrosive drinks, used to keep babies quiet or put them to sleep.

Her eyes were beautiful—a deep, clear blue with impossibly thick lashes fanning outward.

I heard Len and Mart coming out of the barn as we sat admiring our tower. Mart was carrying a cage in one hand and a feather in the other. "Len, it doesn't matter if you let it go once it got healed up. Keeping a bald eagle in captivity is illegal. Only people with a certain license can do that. You understand? If you find something hurt—a wild animal—you've got to bring it to me, or send me a message to come get it. We both know this feather came off an eagle, not a wild turkey. There's a big fine for that. A bad ticket. Understand? You understand what I'm saying? I'm trying to help you here, all right? Now, go ahead and get me that raccoon kit, and I'll take him with me."

Birdie stood up as Len started into the house. Dashing up the steps in her clumpy boots, she caught Len at the door and grabbed the hem of his shirt, her gaze turning upward, pleading. He leaned down, and she whispered something in his ear. Laying a hand gently on her hair, he shook his head, and they disappeared into the house.

A forest bird never wants a cage.
—Henrik Ibsen
(Left by a backpacker
who stayed overnight on the dock)

Chapter 14

Mart McClendon

The little girl was upset that I was taking her pet away, and she hung on the screen door, her cheeks wet and red as Len carried the coon kit out by the scruff of its neck. Birdie didn't argue or yell or whine. She just watched with big tears rolling down her cheeks, like she'd learned not to raise a fuss. The raccoon was making more noise than she was, chattering and growling with all four paws stiff in the air as Len stuffed it in the cage, smacked the door shut, and shoved the cage at me.

Between Len looking at me like I just stole his best dog, and Birdie turning on the waterworks, I felt like a heel. But a wild-caught coon and a little girl don't belong in the same house. We'd had a couple of confirmed rabies cases in the county this year.

Birdie sank down to her knees behind the screen door, her eyes as big and blue as robin's eggs. One thing was for sure—she didn't want me for a friend anymore. Right now, Len didn't want me there, either. Birdie's crying had him stirred up, and he was antsy for us to leave. Even the dogs in the backyard were growling, and the whole situation had the feel of a powder keg, about to blow.

Andrea took a step toward the house, like she was going to head inside and try to comfort Birdie. I caught her hand before she could pass by. "Well, we're gonna leave you alone now, like I promised, Len. I want to thank you for doing everything I asked you to. I'm sure you'll be headed out on the lake as soon as I'm gone. You can't have Birdie near the water without a life vest on her. Not at all, you understand? Not even if she's around shore while you're working. A little child can drown quicker than you can let out a sneeze."

Len lifted his chin, shifting a wad of tobacco in his lip. "Sss-she sw-swimmed ugg-good."

I pointed a finger at him to make sure I was getting my point across. "It's against the law to have a child on a boat without a proper life vest on. I've got a couple kids' vests some campers left behind in the state park. I'll set one there by your boat, and I want you to make sure she has it on and it's buckled up tight. And don't be letting her out in the yard with those dogs, either. I know they're friendly to you, but you can't ever tell when a dog might get upset or confused and jump

228

on a child. I've seen some kids get pretty torn up by dogs that aren't used to having kids around."

Len seemed mighty confused now. He moved a step toward the yard, like he thought I was about to take his dogs away, too. Behind the screen, the little girl sniffled, her fingertips drawing wet trails in the grime-covered mesh. She looked like the most miserable little person in the world. I made up my mind that, after I'd delivered the coon to my volunteer wildlife rehabilitator, I'd take a picture, so I could come back and show her he was safe in a new place. Maybe when I got a chance, I'd stop by the souvenir shop at the state park and pick up a toy raccoon or a teddy bear— something a little girl could play with that wouldn't bite. When Birdie's mama, whoever she really was, had dropped her off, she hadn't left playthings or supplies of any kind, as far as I could tell.

In the cage, the little coon was going crazy, sticking his paws through the wire, fishing in air, trying to grab on to something to keep me from taking him anywhere. He chattered out a high-pitched distress sound, crying for his mama, and every dog, puppy, mule, milk cow, and loose rooster on the place started making noise. I had to yell to be heard. "Some people might want to come back here and talk to Birdie." As soon as the words were out, I knew I should've kept that piece of information for later. Bad timing.

Len went stiff as a rail fence, and his eyes turned hard and gray. "Unnn-nope. Unnn-no. Unnn-no. I ugg-got no trrr-red-pass." He pointed to an old *No Trespassing* sign that had long since turned to rust. How in the world was I supposed to make Len understand the law, as it applied to child welfare? *Listen, Len, there are people who are like . . . game wardens for kids. They come onto your place to look in after little girls, the same way I look after animals. They're not here to hurt anybody. . . .* That whole speech would probably go over about as well as moonshine at a tent preaching, considering that I was taking off with his pet raccoon right now. "Well, I'll let you know."

Len chopped a hand in the air, like he might decide to really get difficult. When I left, I'd have to watch my back. Right now he was pretty emotional, and so were the dogs and the little girl. "Unnn . . . unnn-no! No-buddy! Birdie's umm-mama say unn-no no-buddy."

Andrea laid a hand on my shoulder, stepped forward and smiled at Len. "Thanks for letting me meet Birdie." Her voice was soft and calm, the tone a mother uses when she's quieting a baby. "We had fun building a little castle over there in the dirt." She pointed, and Len sidestepped to see around the corner of the porch. "Would it be all right if I came back to play with her again? I don't get to play with any little girls.

I only have a boy. He's a big boy, though. Fourteen." She held up a hand, like she was measuring Dustin's height against hers.

Len answered with a slow nod. "I ugg-guess . . . ugg-guess ohh-kay." Looking befuddled, he turned around and headed for the house. When he got to the porch, Birdie ran out the door and clung to his pants leg. He laid a hand protectively on her shoulder, and she leaned her head against his hip.

I turned around and started for Andrea's car, the raccoon kit running circles in the cage.

"Do you think it's okay to leave her here?" Andrea muttered under her breath. "Is she safe?"

"Look over your shoulder and smile and wave," I told her under my breath. "The best thing we can do right now is keep it friendly. If Len wants to disappear off into the woods with that little girl again, he sure could. For that matter, we don't know where Birdie's mama is, or whether Len could send Birdie back wherever she came from. I'm just going on a hunch here, but I've got a feeling that little girl was worse off before she got here. That dress and those boots she's wearing—Len bought for her. That's why they're too big.

"When I first found him this morning, we sat down at the lakeshore and talked for a long while until he'd calmed down. Then we talked some more up here, after we made phone calls about the medical clinic visit and such. It isn't easy, getting the full story out of Len. I asked him what shape Birdie was in when she got here, and near as I can gather, she was barefoot in a nightgown. Her mother showed up without anything, toting a kid with a fever and an earache, and driving a car that was on its last legs. Once she got what she needed—gas, money, and car repairs—she left Birdie here. You gotta wonder what kind of situation causes a mother to do that to a little child."

"Or what kind of mother," Andrea added, emotion making her voice catch. She hesitated, like she was thinking of going back to Len's cabin. I pressed a hand against the small of her back and moved her toward her vehicle. We needed to head out before Len got any more shook up.

When we made it to the car, I opened the door for her. "Just circle around right here and drive on out, okay? It's not like you'll ruin the lawn. I'll meet you at that picnic grounds you were talking about earlier—the one just down from Eagle Eye Bridge. Len doesn't need to see us standing here talking about him, okay? If he thinks we're planning something . . . well, that might not be so good. Just smile at me and say good-bye like everything's fine, and I'll catch up with you at the park."

She checked her watch, then nodded. "All right. I'll see you there."

I could feel a steady gaze watching me from the cabin. "What's Len doing back there?" I didn't turn around—just let Andrea sneak a glance.

"He's looking at us. He's holding on to that little girl like he thinks we might try to snatch her." Andrea's eyes were round and unsure, a pulse fluttering under the smooth skin at the base of her neck. "Are you going to be all right when I leave? What if he changes his mind about the raccoon?"

"I'll be all right," I said. It wasn't the first time I'd left a place carrying someone's contraband and keeping one eye over my shoulder.

Catching a breath, she nodded. "Okay, well . . . good-bye, then." She pasted on a tense smile that I guessed was meant to convince Len everything was fine. Even Len could probably see through the act.

"Good thing you're not trying out for the theater," I said. "He has it in his mind that you're my *lady friend,* remember? Act like you like me. You could give me a hug. It'll make this look more convincing."

Her eyes met mine, and for just a heartbeat, I forgot I had a coon kit in a cage hanging from one arm.

"Are you serious?"

"Sometimes, you know, in the line of duty, we've got to make sacrifices." I shrugged, like it was a tough thing to ask, but for the sake of the job, I was willing to do it.

Andrea's pretty brown eyes rolled a half circle. Stretching onto her toes, she pinched the brim of my hat between two fingers, pulled it to one side a little, and kissed me on the cheek. "There. That good enough?" She slipped her arms around my shoulders and smacked me so hard on the back that Len probably heard it.

"Guess it'll have to be," I coughed out, and set my hat to rights again as she stepped back. She was smiling, and for just a moment, all I could think was that those were the kind of eyes a brown-eyed girl oughta have.

The coon rocking his cage jarred my brain back to life, and I stepped away. Man, I'd been out on the lake too long. "See you at the park."

"It'll take me a while to get there." She slipped her keys out of her pocket, and suddenly we were all business again.

We parted ways, and I headed around through the broomweed and the tall grass back to the woods. I made the walk at a good pace, just in case Len changed his mind, but I was also getting my head clear. It wasn't like me to get distracted by a pretty girl when I was working. Actually, it wasn't like me to get distracted at all, not in the past few years, anyway. I didn't need the complication. Getting involved with somebody only meant bringing up the past, eventually— talking about Aaron and Mica, and trying to explain why Laurie kept calling. For the last few years, it'd seemed like there was too much muck in my life to drag someone else into it. It was easier just to work, and not think about it, and not have to talk about it.

Especially not to someone who did therapy for a living. Somebody like that would have a field day with me. She'd want to dig down to the core of everything—figure out the *meaning* of it, decode it and decide how to cure it. I wasn't interested in ending up as an emotional ball of goo on someone's couch. I'd been through enough mental warfare in the past three years to last me a lifetime. Coming to Moses Lake was all about moving on, letting that go, leaving it behind. I shouldn't have told Andrea the Robin Hood story, either. Not only did it make me look like a sap, but also it pointed out that I was one of four back then. I didn't want anyone here bringing up the kinds of questions you answered at class reunions, or when you ran into a high school girlfriend at the Dairy Queen—*where've you been, how's life been treating you, how's your family?*

I was upriver long before Andrea rolled into the little picnic area across from the cliffs at Eagle Eye. The park was usually empty during the heat of the day. Toward evening, a few fishermen and maybe a picnicking family or two would show up, but for now, we had the place all to ourselves. Andrea looked down the row of stone tables as she got out of her car, seeming surprised there was no one else around.

"Guess I should find a little more populated place to stop off and do my paperwork in the future," she said. "The last time I passed by here, half of the spots were full."

"Depends on the time of day and the day of the week." I slid off the picnic table where I'd been waiting. "When it's this hot, you won't find many people at a day-use area like this, especially since there's no real swimming beach here. The park headquarters has a nice picnic grounds by the gift shop and the caverns, if you're looking for someplace where there's a little population. That might be a better choice. You've also got a church camp a few miles upriver in that direction, and then a few miles farther upriver, in my partner's end of the county, there are a couple bakeries and a café in the little Mennonite settlement. Good eatin' there. There's the artist colony about six miles south of here, down on 2300. The artist colony has a decent little coffee shop—never know what you'll see hanging around there—artists, weavers, quilters, hippies, beetle-bug cars and all manner of exotic pets. It's interesting, anyway."

Her forehead narrowed, like she was trying to picture those places. Then she seemed to leave off the idea. "Thanks for the tip. I'll watch for those spots while I'm making my rounds. To tell

236

you the truth, right now I'm lucky just to find my way to appointments. Even with the county road map and the GPS, I'd be completely lost if I didn't have directions from my boss with valuable tips like, *turn by the tree with the big knothole that looks like a face,* and *go until you see the orange fence post."* Walking closer to the picnic table, she rolled her eyes. "You know how many orange fence posts there are around here? That is *not* a landmark."

"That's the way navigation's done in the hills, cowgirl," I said, just playing with her a little. "Knotholes and fence posts. It's a different kind of work environment."

"Truly." She stopped by the picnic table and braced her fingers on the small of her back, looking over the four-foot drop to the riverbank. "By the way, I almost got stuck in the mudhole coming back. I forgot to stay to the side."

"Bet you won't forget again."

She answered with a smart-aleck twist of her lips, and I decided that even if we had gotten off on the wrong foot to begin with, she was okay. "I'll mark the artist colony and the church camp on your map for you, if you want. The state park HQ's probably already on there." I sat down on the edge of the table again and rested my feet on the bench.

"That would be helpful. Thanks." Squinting against the reflection from the river, she took in a long breath and let it out, her mouth straightening like she was thinking about something—getting down to business, I figured. All of a sudden, she looked like a woman with something on her mind. "What's that sound?" she asked absently.

I listened for minute. There was a mockingbird overhead going through a couple dozen birdcalls, one right after the other. "Mockingbird. They're always nested here at the picnic grounds where they can scavenge people's leftovers. You come here night or day in the summer, you'll hear mockingbirds. Earlier in the spring, there was a pair nested in a branch right by the restroom. It was pretty good entertainment, watching them take strafing runs at the tourists. They're gutsy little birds. Pushy."

She glanced toward the squatty limestone restroom. "Actually, I meant the other sound—that moaning sound. What is that?"

"That's the mockingbirds, too. They're copying the Wailing Woman." I pointed to a sign down the hill by the water—one of those points-of-interest markers that told the legend of the Wailing Woman. "Not too much wind in the cliffs right now, so she's kind of quiet, but those mockingbirds have heard her enough that they do a pretty good imitation. They're probably the only mockingbirds in the world that know how to cry."

Andrea cocked her head to one side, listening.

"That's the strangest thing. You know, in a million years, I wouldn't have known what that was."

"Oh, sure you would, if you'd been here a few times," I told her. "Every place in the woods has its own sound, if you stop and listen. The river has a sound, and the hills have a sound, and the rocky draws have a sound, and the cliffs have a sound. Folks wouldn't get themselves so lost in these hills, if they'd stop and listen."

Andrea smirked at me. "Easy for you Daniel Boone types to say. Some of us feel like we're wandering blind up here. It all looks the same. It's no wonder hikers get turned around."

I couldn't help it; I laughed. "Well, here's a free tip—if you're ever lost, head for the water. In the summer, there's plenty of traffic on the lake, and if we're hunting someone in the cold weather, we'll have boats and a helicopter out."

"I don't think I'll be doing much hiking." She moved to the edge of the drop-off, where she could take in the historical marker. I waited while she read the legend of the pioneer woman whose baby daughter had disappeared from the wagon train. Even after days of searching, the woman wouldn't leave her daughter behind and travel on with the wagons. Legend had it that she wandered those cliffs and the river basin still, trying to find her baby. According to Burt and Nester, that tale had scared many a Boy Scout and kid camper, and kept them from roaming into the woods at night.

"That's really sad." Andrea came back to the picnic table. "My dad told us about the Wailing Woman, but he never brought us to see the sign. My parents didn't like to come to this side of the lake."

"Most people from Larkspur stay around Larkspur." I probably could've skipped saying that. It sounded like criticism. "Thanks for showing up today," I added. "I had myself in something of a bind, there. I figured it'd really send Len into a panic if I got the sheriff's department involved, and you were the next person I thought of, since you already knew what was going on. I didn't want to leave Len there with that little girl until someone looked things over. I've got to admit, I haven't come upon anything quite like that before."

"Me neither." She slid in on the other side of the picnic table, so that there was just a little space between us. "The question is, what happens now?" She seemed to expect me to come up with an answer.

"Shoot if I know," I admitted. "I deal in displaced animals, like that fella down there in the crate." I motioned to my boat, which was tied up in the shade, with the little bandito finally all worn out and asleep.

Andrea braced her elbows on her knees,

pressed her hands together like she was praying, and blew a long breath through her fingers. "If you had to guess—you know more about Len than I do—do you really think she's safe with him?"

I stopped to consider that a minute. The protocol was to report it to the appropriate agencies and let them investigate, but what I wanted to say about the cooperation I'd had out of the county sheriff probably wasn't proper to say in front of a lady, and in the professional sense, it wasn't the right thing to speak ill of another branch of law enforcement. If you did, you'd likely find yourself twisting in the wind when you needed backup. Most places, the folks from the county sheriff's office are good as gold, but in this county, they only provided services where they felt like it.

Andrea tapped her thumbs together, impatient for an answer. Considering everything I'd seen that morning, I gave the best one I could. "It's just a hunch, a gut feeling based on what I could gather from watching Len with Birdie. I think he really does care about the little girl, and he's doing his best to look after her, but I also know that we've got to find out who she really is. The mother did leave her there on purpose, apparently. So did the mom mean to abandon her, or is the mom coming back? Len's had Birdie for a couple weeks, and he's given her whatever medicine the clinic sent home and changed his normal routine so that he could take care of her—even to the point of carrying her down to the lake in the morning when she's still asleep."

I tipped my hat back and stretched the knots from my neck, trying to make sense of it all. "Let me just put it like this—I don't think the situation would be high on the sheriff department's list. There isn't any evidence of a crime, for one thing. We're in Chinquapin Peaks, for another, and having a dirty kid isn't a crime. Leaving your kid in the care of a friend or relative isn't, either. If it were, there'd be a lot of kids in this county taken away from their parents."

Andrea nodded, seeming to understand. "Is it likely she is Len's granddaughter—might he have a legitimate claim to her?" She rested her chin on the tips of her fingers and cut a sideways glance at me, her eyes catching the river's reflected light. "I mean, what if he's not even supposed to have her? Maybe the mother brought her up here and dropped her off during some kind of custody dispute, and she's trying to hide Birdie here. Len could be involved in something he's not even aware of."

"Definitely possible," I admitted. "If somebody told Len that child was his granddaughter, he'd probably believe it. He just keeps insisting she's his daughter's girl. When I asked him how that could be, being as he never had a family, he got flustered and said his daughter lives with his wife, somewhere a long ways away. The name they used at the clinic wasn't Barnes. It was Marsh. The little girl's name is Lillian Marsh. I'm guessing *Birdie* is a nickname, and Marsh is her daddy's name. I took a look at Len's record over the weekend, and other than fish-and-game violations and an outstanding ticket for the license plate light on his truck, he's clean. There's no evidence that he's ever been tangled up with anything involving women, minors, or sex offenses. I don't think he's got the mental capacity to be— not on purpose, anyway."

Andrea's shoulders rose and lowered with a breath. Her stomach rumbled, and she looked at her watch. "I don't think we're much better off on my end. I'm professionally obligated to report any suspicions of child neglect or endangerment, and abandonment falls under that spectrum. But it's not considered abandonment unless the child is left for three months or more. I'll make CPS aware of Birdie's situation, but I don't know if anything further will happen right now. Like you said, Len seems to be taking care of her. If CPS were to investigate, I might get a referral for family counseling. They would want to find the mother, of course, and see what her situation is." Her stomach growled again, and I realized I had a hollow spot inside, too.

"You saw how Len feels about Social Services," I pointed out.

"He let *me* talk to Birdie. Maybe you could get a CPS investigator in there the same way you got me in."

"What, tell him I've got another girlfriend who wants to drop by?" I asked, wondering if even Len would fall for that one again.

She pulled her bottom lip between her teeth. For a second, I was just looking at her lips. "Guess nobody would be stupid enough to believe that."

I leaned away, surprised. "Well, dadgum. I think my pride's hurt."

She blinked three times fast, then the corners of her eyes crinkled. "All of the CPS investigators in this county happen to be *men*." Her mouth hung open on the last word, while she waited for me to catch a clue.

"Oh, yeah . . . hey . . . Well, forget that idea. Looks like we need a plan B."

She cracked a wide smile and laughed a little, then got back to thinking. "Considering the backlog of CPS cases, we probably have time to think about it. Surely we can come up with something, if need be." Her stomach growled so loud that if there'd been any black bear left in these woods, she would've attracted one. The problem was contagious, because my stomach rumbled, too.

"How about we talk it through over lunch?"

She frowned at the deserted picnic grounds. "Did I miss the drive-through window?"

I chuckled. She could be funny, whcn she wanted to be. "I've got a sandwich from the Waterbird and some canned drinks in the boat. I'll go halves."

She looked temped at first, then shook her head. "I can't take your lunch." But her gaze drifted toward the boat, and she had hunger in her eyes.

"Got a date somewhere else?"

She turned away from the lake, and we were close together. Close enough that I saw a question in her eyes, but I didn't know what the question was.

"No. I don't." The words were soft, like she was breathing them out without meaning to.

"Good," I heard myself say. "I hate to eat alone." *What a joke, Mart. All you do is eat alone. She can probably tell that, just by looking.* The talking in my head stopped then, and out of the blue, I had the thought that it seemed like the natural thing would be to kiss her.

I had the feeling she was thinking that, too.

A Sea-Doo raced by on the river, the noise echoing against the cliffs, and we jerked apart. My brain sputtered like an engine with water in the gas line. "I'll go . . . uhhh . . . grab the . . ." *The what . . . the what . . .* Clearing my throat, I slid off the table. "The lunch," I said, and headed off to the boat.

Never give up listening to the sounds of birds.
—John James Audubon
(Left by a J. O., birdwatcher on a
pilgrimage to the eagles' nests)

Chapter 15

Andrea Henderson

The picnic with Mart was surprisingly nice—an oasis in the middle of an otherwise disjointed and confusing Friday. Alone in the park, with the river passing lazily and the mockingbirds singing an endless repertoire of songs, it was easy to forget the appointments ahead, the reports that remained unwritten, the uncertainty about Birdie, the way she looked at me, her face filled with questions she couldn't or wouldn't voice. That was the hardest thing about children. So often, you had to learn their stories from the things that weren't said—piecing together their lives like puzzles, so that you could figure out what was missing.

"I'll do some more checking on Len's background," Mart offered as we ate our sandwich halves and cookies. "It may take me through the weekend, but I'll let you know what I find out. I've got a friend in Ft. Worth who does investigations for a credit agency. She's good.

She digs up more than the usual information."

"All right." I noted that this friend and the friend who'd given him the information about Birdie's medical clinic visit were both female. That caused a nagging curiosity. I popped out another question without really stopping to consider why I was asking. "Do you think she'll be able to find Birdie's mother?" In reality, I was fishing for the *she* connection, wondering why *shes* everywhere were willing to do favors for Mart—wondering if he was . . . was . . . involved?

The realization hit me like one of those Gatorade baths that coaches get after winning a big game—cold and sticky. An unpleasant shock in the middle of a perfectly wonderful picnic lunch. I was enjoying being here with him, listening to the river, watching the shade filter through the trees and dapple the grass underneath. It was surprisingly cool under the thick canopy of branches, considering that August was right around the corner. I'd let my mind go adrift, felt myself relaxing and enjoying the moment. I'd relaxed too much, apparently. I'd forgotten that we were working together, not . . . not . . . What? Having a date?

The idea compressed my stomach tightly around my ham sandwich and pecan cookie from the Waterbird. One of the things I couldn't even begin to envision when divorce became my reality, was ever cycling around to the idea of dating again. I'd never really even dated in high school, and then Karl and I got together the summer after I graduated. The rest seemed to follow a natural progression. By the time college graduation drew near and the wide world loomed large, I was watching my friends get engaged and plan weddings. I wanted that for myself. Karl did, too. Life seemed to be falling into place. I was happy to be settled down, to have someone.

Even back then, I'd felt sorry for friends who were floundering in the dating pool. But now, with the baggage of an entire life dragging behind you? What would you talk about that wasn't tied to that other life, that other person?

I hoped Mart knew that we were only professional acquaintances. Perhaps even friends, but nothing more. Why would he want anything more? A guy like Mart—an alpha type with a uniform and an impish grin—undoubtedly had women throwing themselves at him everywhere he went. All those *she* friends, who did favors for him. He wouldn't have any reason to be interested in a frumpy, thirty-eight-year-old single mom.

"She should be able to dig up some things, but I have a feeling that Birdie's mother doesn't want to be found. I already tried the phone number she put on the form at the medical clinic, and they've never heard of her." He watched me curiously, his eyes narrowing, as if he'd sensed my change in posture and wondered what was behind it. "You going to be home later? I'll stop by and let you know what I find out."

A thrill of anticipation bounced around my chest, a racquetball shot, hard off the back wall. I hunted it down and swatted it out of the air. "I'm not sure, but you have my cell number, right? Dustin and I might need to . . . There might be something . . . " I was, indeed, the world's worst liar. I never could think on my feet, which had gotten me in trouble with my mother more than once. Megan could make invented reality sound so convincing that even she believed it sometimes. "Something at the school. Tonight. An open house . . . for new students." Then I wondered if he was aware of the school schedule. For all I knew, he might even have kids and an ex-wife living right here in Moses Lake. He'd never mentioned anyone, but perhaps leaving behind the old life was part of the divorce code. Karl had done it. . . .

"I'd better go." I slid to the edge of the bench, and Mart drew back, undoubtedly surprised by the abrupt shift. I probably seemed strangely schizophrenic to him—borderline flirtatious one minute, one foot out the door the next. The people-pleaser in me couldn't just thank him for the sandwich and head to the car without cracking open the door I'd just slammed. "I'll be anxious to hear what you find out about Birdie. Thanks for keeping me in the loop." *Keeping me in the loop* . . . Good grief, how stupid. I sounded like I was talking to Taz.

But wasn't that what I was trying to do—keep this on a business level?

Mart snagged his hat from the bench and dropped it onto his head. The shadow shielded his eyes, so that I couldn't see the expression in them. "I'll let you know when I hear something," he said, then waited for me to get in my car before he headed for the river. As I started the engine and backed away, I watched his boat slip into the current and disappear along a diamond-dust path of sunlit ripples. A part of me wanted to be beside him in the boat, surrounded by miles of open water, experiencing whatever the day had to offer. Not a care in the world.

Cares crept in as soon as I began contemplating my afternoon schedule, of course. But as the day wore on, I found myself thinking about lunch, and then about Mart and the raccoon. I wondered where they were and what they were doing.

Driving back to the office after my last appointment, I wondered again about the *she* Mart was contacting to dig into Len's background. Who was she? Was he talking to her now?

I did my best to exit that train of thought in the office parking lot, leaving it outside the door as I went in. Taz's door was already closed and locked for the weekend when I passed by. Either the family trainer or the substance abuse counselor was having a session in the counseling room, and Bonnie was wrestling with a spreadsheet on her computer.

"So did you talk to the game warden guy?" she asked, watching me from the corner of her eye, with more than idle curiosity.

"I did." It occurred to me that I could end up in trouble for going off on my own while I was technically on Taz's clock. I could have classified the visit to Len's and the subsequent river picnic as my lunch hour, but it was way more than an hour. I'd taken up almost all the time yielded by the cancelled morning appointment, and my reports still weren't done. "I'll finish my session log tonight and turn it in on Monday."

"Oh, whenever." Bonnie moved a folder on her desk, looked under it, and moved it back. "The game warden guy has a nice voice." The eyebrow quirked upward, followed by a look. Clearly, she wondered what was going on.

Drawing a drink from the water cooler, I attempted to appear nonchalant. "I hadn't noticed."

She focused both eyes my way. "Really?"

Shrugging, I sipped my little cone-shaped cup of water. The giant bottle burbled, then whined as the air pressure adjusted. The sound made me think of the river and the Wailing Woman.

"So what's he look like?" Bonnie wanted to know.

"Who?"

"The guy on the phone."

I tossed the cup in the trash and watched it settle. "Like a game warden, I guess."

"Ooohhhh," Bonnie purred, leaning over her desk, suddenly rapt with interest. "Really? Like all woodsy and everything? Is he single?"

"Bonnie!" Her name came out in an undisciplined squeal, and suddenly I felt like a high-school girl. I cleared my throat before continuing. "How would I know?"

Bonnie huffed a breath. "Well, you've met him in person. You've got to learn to read the signs—like, does he wear a ring? Does he drive a family car? That kind of thing. It's important information."

"He's giving Dustin a ride to the water safety class the week after next. That's it." I was talking to myself as much as to Bonnie.

Her answer was an interested hum and a fanning of eyebrows. "Mmmm, so you'll be seeing him again."

"You have such a one-track mind."

She actually looked shocked and mildly offended. "You are absolutely no fun." Giving me a snide look, she went back to work.

I took my no-fun self back to my office to wrap things up, check the upcoming appointment schedule, and look at the most recent referrals. While I had the CPS e-mail addresses in front of me, I sent a message, apprising them of Birdie's situation and my concerns about it.

While I worked, Bonnie's assessment, *You are absolutely no fun,* played a repeating loop in my head, even though I was trying to ignore it. There was a time when I *was* fun . . . wasn't there? When I was a little less like me and a little more like Bonnie—impulsive, free-spirited, a little fanciful?

The answer to that question was, quite frankly, a bummer. I'd scorned impulsivity for as long as I could remember. My parents had thoroughly convinced me that the way to peace, prosperity, and the blessings of a work-for-reward God was to live up to expectations in both word and deed. I focused on being competent, measured, controlled, an intelligent decision maker and dependable daughter worthy of love and praise.

When I married Karl, those skills came in handy. Even though Karl's eventual goal was a professorship and then university management, we both knew that, at least while he was working his way through his doctoral degree, he'd be serving on the pastoral staff at a church. Ministers' wives need to be perfect. When you have a whole congregation eyeballing your life, you can't afford to leave the house without your lipstick on.

During the divorce, Karl told me that was part of the problem—he was tired of trying to live up to everyone's standards. Especially mine. *You can't ever just . . . let go a little,* he said. *I'm suffocating.* Suddenly, it was my fault that he'd been an unfaithful husband and a dishonest employee. I'd driven him to it by being *no fun.*

Stop, I told myself as I closed my office and left for home. *Just stop.* Rehashing the past, analyzing it, trying to decide what had gone wrong was pointless. Maybe Karl had changed. Maybe I'd changed. Maybe once he'd made his climb up the life ladder and secured his dream job, it wasn't all he'd thought it would be. Maybe he'd needed another challenge.

I reminded myself again that I wasn't to blame for his decisions. He was. I'd held up my end of the bargain. Done everything that was expected of me, even when I was lonely, when I sat in Bible study groups pretending our lives were perfect, when I tried to talk to Karl and he acted like nothing was wrong, when I felt hollow inside and it seemed that Dustin's little-boy love for me was the only true thing in my day.

I'd done what I thought was right for our marriage, for Dustin, for the commitment I'd made before God and everyone. I'd held up, even when Karl gave speeches, and sermons, and wrote thesis papers about healthy relationships and faithful marriages, and then came home and passed by me without so much as a word on his way to the TV room to decompress.

Bonnie was right. I was no fun. I was like a spool of thread wound so tightly that even I couldn't find the end of the string.

The unproductive mental dialog haunted me all the way home, nipping at my heels like one of Len's guard dogs, taking painful little bites of skin and bone. When I reached the lake house, my car was in the driveway, which meant that my mother and father were there. My stomach clenched immediately, and it occurred to me that I should have driven by the car wash on the way home. Len's mudhole was all over my father's car.

Inside, my parents were serving up chicken nuggets from the Waterbird—a nice gesture, really. They and Dustin were gathered around the table eating when I walked in. Dustin looked like he was strapped to the dentist's chair having a cavity drilled.

"I can't see why he should have to attend some . . . water safety course." Mother started in before I'd even set down my purse. "We don't own a boat anymore." She pointed toward the empty boathouse, as if to support her argument.

"It's the arrangement we made with the game warden," I said flatly. I really didn't need this, but the chicken nuggets did smell good. I helped myself to a plate. "Thanks for bringing supper."

Mother nodded. "When we called about returning the car, Dustin said we shouldn't come. He said he didn't know when you'd be here—that you've been late getting home at night. We thought we'd at *least* drive over and bring him some supper." Which meant, of course, that I'd left my son alone and starving, night after night, and I should be ashamed of myself.

The truth was that I'd only come in after six thirty the one evening that I'd gone to Len's cabin with Mart and Reverend Hay. When I'd arrived home that night, I'd found Dustin in a foul mood because his grandparents had stopped by and criticized his yard work, then embarrassed him by starting yet another argument with the neighbors. No wonder he'd tried to stave them off tonight by telling them I might not be here.

Patience. Patience. We are living in their house, and they did bring fried chicken. Undoubtedly, this was only the beginning of many drop-by visits. At thirty-eight, I was moving backward in life, once again being raised by my parents. But pride goes down like milk of magnesia when you have to build a new future using your half of the bank account that has been run dry by divorce lawyers, legal fees, and a husband who was carrying on a double life.

"I only worked late one night." For a half a second, I had the crazy impulse to tell them about my trip to Len's place and the situation with

Birdie. Maybe they'd be . . . interested, even impressed, that I was doing something important—protecting a child who couldn't protect herself. The thought flitted away like a sparrow hopping from tree to tree. Actually, I'd be opening myself up for a grilling. They'd point out that the situation could have been dangerous, and I had no real idea what I was doing.

The phone rang, and I was relieved to have the distraction. Megan was on the other end. "Hey, Sis. You had enough of Mom and Dad yet?"

Bless her, Meg was the best person I knew. She was adorable, kind, beautiful, and she could read minds. "Yes, thank you."

She laughed softly into the phone, and my mother's head whipped toward the sound. "Is that Megan?" She scooted to the edge of her chair. "Ask her if the twins are home yet."

Meg could read Mom's mind, too. "Tell them Gloria just dropped off the twins. They can come by and bring the balloons from the bank now, if they want to. The twins are pretty tired after the zoo trip. I think it'll be an early-to-bed night." The sentence ended in a sigh. Lately, Meg had been the wishbone in a silent granny tug-of-war between Oswaldo's parents and ours.

"Super," I said, which was code for, *You are the best sister in the world.* "I'll let them know." Meg and I exchanged *I love you*s, and then I hung up and told the folks that Meg wanted them to head on over before the twins fell asleep. Mother popped up like she'd been shot from an ejector seat, and my father was close behind. On the way out the door, I thanked Dad for helping me with the tire problem, argued with him about letting me pay the bill, and apologized for having left his car in such a mess. Fortunately, they were in too much of a hurry to be worried about any of it. I helped them transfer the freebie one-hundred-year-anniversary bank balloons from my car to theirs, and they climbed in with little commentary. Rolling down her window, Mother pointed out that she had replaced the blocks in the suet feeders, and there were more in the garden shed. Then she rolled up her window, and they left to win the twins' hearts with helium-filled Mylar.

When I came back inside, the chicken nuggets remained, but Dustin was gone. He'd moved to his room. I went in to try to lure him into going for a walk down the shore with me, but he wasn't having any of it. "I don't feel good."

"Did you hang out with the Blues' grand-daughters today?" I asked, noticing a lemonade cup and a half-eaten cookie on his desk and hoping to pull forth a reluctant confession that a little something good had happened while I was gone to work. On the way in, I'd spied a Frisbee lying in our front yard. Not much chance that he'd been playing Frisbee by himself.

Dustin didn't want to admit to any outdoor fun, of course. He wanted me to know that he'd been slaving away, as usual. In prison, in complete misery, a hostage of an unreasonable grounding and the evil chore list. "Pppfff! Yeah, right. I'm still only halfway down the chore list, I've got all the junk for English, and Grandma wanted the flower bed cleaned out, where the plants got smashed and stuff. I'm just everybody's *slave*. That's all I am." He delivered an icy stare over the top of the book, letting me know this wasn't a joke. "Did Dad call about August? I can't wait to get outta here. When's he coming to get me?"

I took a patience breath before answering. "I've e-mailed and called, but I haven't heard anything yet." It galled me to be making excuses for Karl day after day, but what else could I do? The alternative was for Dustin to feel completely unwanted. "Hey, but speaking of August, there's a new production starting up at the community playhouse—the Tin Building. The pastor from Lakeshore Community is in charge, and he asked if you might like to help—he has some parts for teenage boys, but you also know how to run sound and put together sets. You're good at all those things."

Dustin raised the book again, so that I couldn't see his face. "I won't be here in August. I'll be with Dad." He shot the words across the room like arrows, intended to wound. They hit the mark, and I had that prickly here-come-the-tears feeling. I hated Karl in a way I'd never hated anyone—in a way that most certainly wasn't healthy.

"All right. Well, I guess we'll just see what August brings," I managed to croak out, and then left the room. I headed outside on my own, needing fresh air, an escape . . . something. Standing under one of the pecan trees, I braced my hands on my hips, tried to catch my breath and swallow the urge to cry. Karl wasn't getting one more tear from me. He wasn't.

As I propped up my determination, Sydney and Ansley came trotting out Mrs. Blue's backdoor with sandbox pails and shovels. They were headed for my mother's conveniently empty flower bed. They stopped when they saw me and stood frozen, like deer in the headlights. "It's all right," I told them. "You can play in the flower bed while there aren't any plants in it. Just don't do it while Dustin's grandmother is here."

Smiling, they skipped on over to the freshly tilled bed at the edge of the pecan shade.

"We didn't dig up her flowers," Sydney offered, squatting over the dirt and filling a shiny green bucket. "The deer ate 'em."

"I guessed as much."

Ansley plunked down beside her sister and began pulling up earthworms and dropping them in her bucket. Their heads bent, blond hair falling over their suntanned shoulders, they looked perfectly content in the flower bed—a calendar-photo scene. I couldn't help contrasting it with the picture of Birdie scratching in the weed-filled dirt in front of Len's cabin. Sydney and Ansley were only a few years older, yet their lives were so different, their childhoods what childhood should be—new sand toys, days on the lake, summer fun at Grandma and Grandpa's house. Visits that didn't happen in the middle of the night. A suitcase and toys instead of a nightgown and bare feet.

"Deer like to eat roses," Ansley interjected. "Grandma says if the witch had half a brain, she'd plant lantanas out here."

"Ssshhh!" Sydney spat, and gave her little sister a mortified look.

"It's all right," I told her. "My mother thinks the deer ought to read the *No Trespassing* signs."

Both girls giggled. "Somebody oughta tell her deer can't read," Sydney interjected.

"Nobody tells my mother anything."

Ansley flashed a mischievous grin at me. "That's what my grandpa says."

Sydney swatted her in the arm, and they argued for a minute.

"Thanks for sharing your cookies and lemonade with Dustin," I offered, before the argument could go too far.

Both girls turned their attention to me, now that

Dustin was the topic. Ansley dusted off her hands and smiled. "We gave him s'mores, too. Grandpa helped us make some on the grill, down at our boathouse. Dustin ate *four,* and two root beers. It was hot out while we were swimming."

"I didn't know Dustin went swimming with you today." This was news, since Dustin had told me he'd been too busy working to have any fun.

"Kinda," Sydney took up the conversation. "He went on and jumped in, since he was down there hammering the nails in the dock anyhow."

"Oh, well, it was nice of you to share your s'mores." I felt the weight on my shoulders lift a little. It seemed that Dustin's miserable days weren't entirely miserable. He was beginning to participate in life here, at least a little bit.

Unfortunately, what he really wanted and needed was his father. He needed to know that even though his parents weren't together, he still had a father who loved him, cared about him, and would be there for him.

One way or another, I had to force Karl to live up to his responsibilities and make plans for August.

I spent the weekend leaving phone messages for Karl, and filled in the gaps on Monday by sending texts from hilltops while traveling to field appointments around the county. Karl finally got annoyed enough to respond in a text, but the answer wasn't helpful—*Job busy. Check sent 2 U today.*

He didn't answer my return message—*What about Dustin & August?* I knew he wouldn't. The check would probably come, though, as Karl's guilty attempt to end the conversation.

I went to lunch at the state park headquarters and sat outside on a picnic table, trying to decide whether I should tell Dustin the truth or keep leading him on in hopes that Karl would come through at the last minute. Mart pulled in as I was tossing my brown bag in the trash, and we stood by his truck, talking about the situation with Birdie. Mart was still digging into Len's background, trying to piece together the family history. Birdie's mother remained largely a mystery, and so far I hadn't had any response to the e-mail I'd sent to CPS.

"Reverend Hay gathered up some clothes and toys from the clothes closet at the church, and we took them up there yesterday," Mart informed me. "Len was working in his garden, and Birdie was sacked out right there in the dirt, under a shade tree. She seemed all right, though."

"Thanks for checking on her." I was reminded again that Mart was a nice guy. A softie, really. He was headed into the park gift shop to buy a stuffed raccoon to take to Birdie.

"She still doesn't like me too well. I took a picture of the little coon to her over the weekend, just to let her know he was all right, but that didn't fix things, I guess." He shook his head and smirked a little, his green eyes crinkling at the corners. "I should've left the coon with her, anyway. My wildlife rehabber is out for gall bladder surgery, so I'm stuck with the little chatterbox on my porch, for now. He keeps long hours." He rubbed his eyes and yawned, and I laughed.

For a moment, I forgot all about Karl, and how angry and hurt and worried I'd been. My concerns about the new job flew right out the window. Even though I needed to be leaving for my next appointment, I drew out the conversation a few more minutes. Being there with Mart felt comfortable. Safe. "Hey, listen, I've been meaning to ask you—can anyone sign up for the water safety course next week?"

Mart quirked a brow. "You been out climbing the Scissortail, too?"

I chuckled. "No." Although, considering the issues with Karl and Dustin, I might be looking for a high building pretty soon. "I have a client family—a grandmother raising several grandkids. There's a ten-year-old boy who just . . . needs something positive to do with his time. I thought an activity like the water safety course, where he'd largely be around people who are older than him, might be a good fit. He wouldn't have the opportunity to bully anyone or pick fights. He's not doing too well in his own age group right now. Is it too late for someone to sign up? Is he too young?"

"Not if you've got the right connections." A grasshopper buzzed by and landed on Mart's shirtsleeve. He glanced at it and then just left it there. "I'll drop a form by your house later. He can bring it with him next Monday. I'll let the Corps of Engineers boys know to expect him. They run the class. I just help out."

"Sounds good." I found myself hanging momentarily on the words *by your house later,* looking forward to it.

We parted ways after that, Mart heading into the park store to shop for stuffed raccoons, and me traveling to my next appointment. The afternoon clicked along on schedule for a change, and I was home by five thirty—in time, I hoped, to catch Mart when he dropped off the water safety form for my client.

Dustin had removed himself to his room when he heard me driving up, as usual. Standing in his doorway, I made the mistake of asking him if the game warden had been by. Maybe I said it with too much familiarity, or maybe, now that we were less than a week away from the water safety course, he had begun descending into panic mode, but suddenly, he had a renewed determination. "I'm not going to that stupid class. I've got stuff to do—the summer reading

265

and all the workbook junk. Grandpa said he'd pay the fine."

"No, Grandpa's *not* paying the fine." I felt my blood pressure rising. The situation with Dustin wasn't being helped by my parents butting in all the time. "Do you realize because you're a minor, that ticket starts a process in juvenile court?"

"Everyone else is doing it. They're not worried."

"Everyone, who?"

"Everyone else who was on the boat."

I was momentarily confused. "How do you know that? Have you been talking to those kids again?" He shrugged, remaining reclined on his bed, his gaze fixed on the top bunk. "Dustin, look at me. You've been talking with those kids after I told you not to?"

"Just Cassandra, mostly. Just texting." He rolled over with a huff.

"Cassandra, who?" I demanded. On top of everything else, there was a girl involved, and she was texting back and forth with my son? Dustin had no experience with girls, other than as friends. So far, he hadn't shown any interest in dating. *So far . . .*

"Her mom cleans cabins down from the Waterbird, and at the Eagle's Nest. It's no big deal, Mom." Dustin's cheek and ear turned red, conveying that *no big deal* wasn't an accurate description. "What? Now I'm not allowed to text, either?"

A dizzying swirl of teenage possibilities ran through my mind. The Eagle's Nest resort was within walking distance of Larkspur Estates—just past the public access area and boat ramp my mother had always warned us about.

"Has anyone been over here while I'm away at work?" *Please, please, please,* the voice in my head was saying. *I'm not ready for this issue.*

Dustin rolled his eyes, like I was an idiot for asking. "No. Cassandra's grounded, too."

Thank you, God. So Cassandra did have parents—real parents who grounded their child and stuck to it. "Maybe she'll end up going to the water safety class, then." I couldn't believe I was suggesting that, but right now, I just wanted the fight to be over.

"I doubt it," Dustin grumbled.

"Have you asked her?"

"Uhh . . . no. She'll think I'm a loser. Everyone's gonna see me getting hauled out of here by the lake cop, like a . . . a flippin' convict. When school starts, nobody's gonna want to get within ten feet of me. I'm not going there, either."

"To school?" Tension pinched the back of my neck, like a clothespin snapping over skin, hanging me out to dry.

Nodding, Dustin tunneled into the pillow and threw an arm over his face. Tears seeped from beneath, wetting his cheeks, slowly drawing a dark blot on the brown pillowcase.

"Dustin," I said softly, crossing the room and sitting on the edge of the bed. I laid a hand on his shoulder, and he immediately rolled away, a low sob escaping him. "I know you're nervous about school. That's natural. It's a lot of changes at once, but that doesn't mean it's going to be bad. You're such a great kid. There's no way this . . . Cassandra, or anyone else, could keep from seeing that. You just be yourself and you won't have any trouble making friends. And give the water safety class a chance. Maybe it won't be that bad, and when you finish, you'll know how to use a boat the right way."

"Pppfff!" he spat. "Like we'll ever be able to afford a boat."

Grief poured over me in wet, heavy shovelfuls. One of the things that hit Dustin the hardest about our new life was the change in finances. He'd always had everything he wanted. Now it was a struggle to manage the debts I'd assumed in the divorce, pay off lawyers, and provide necessities.

It's your father's fault! I wanted to scream. *He did this. Where is he now? Why isn't he here? He should have to see what he's done. He should be the one watching you cry.* I wanted to run from the room and call Karl again and again and again, until he answered. I wanted to tell him that our son was curled up in a ball on his bed, sobbing. Again.

Instead, I folded my hands in my lap, closed my eyes, tried to think of something comforting to say. "It'll be all right." The words fell flat, and tears stung my eyes in the silence afterward. I stood up and left the room, feeling like I'd never find my way across the chasm the divorce had left behind. *Please,* the word whispered in my mind. *Please bring Dustin what he needs. Please bring him someone he can depend on.* It wasn't much of a prayer—just a scrap of one, really—but it was something.

I went to my bedroom, changed into shorts and a T-shirt from some long-forgotten discipleship weekend, and splashed water on my face to tamp down the heat of emotion. Rather than breaking apart and spending another evening with my head buried under a blanket, I sat on the sofa, pulled out my briefcase and laptop, and spent the time catching up on case files.

While I was working, I started a file on Birdie. The more I thought about it, the more I knew that we had to get CPS involved, one way or another. There were so many risks in Birdie's situation— Len's mental capacity, the dogs and other animals she might come in contact with, water-related dangers, undoubtedly firearms in the home, the questions about Birdie's mother. What if this mother, whoever she was, simply came back and picked Birdie up? They could disappear without a trace. A child in Birdie's situation needed to be monitored by the legal system and assessed in terms of physical, emotional, and educational needs.

Setting the computer aside, I rested my head against the chair and let out a long sigh, trying to sort through all the potential problems. I wanted to talk it over with someone—with Mart. I wondered where he was, and why he hadn't come by with the form for Daniel, and what his thoughts about Birdie's situation were now. . . .

The cell phone ringing woke me, and I sat up, confused. I'd been asleep long enough to have lost track of where I was and what I'd been doing. Picking up the phone, I answered, blinking the fog from my eyes.

Mart was on the other end. "This is Mart McClendon." The greeting seemed strangely formal, as if my voice had caught him by surprise. "Sorry to be calling so late. I got tied up with a stolen-boat case. I figured I'd get your voice mail."

"No, you got the real thing." I glanced at the clock. Eleven thirty. Down the hall, Dustin's music was blaring, the bass rattling the walls, so that the house seemed to have a heartbeat. "I was up working."

"I didn't mean to catch you by surprise," Mart apologized again. "I just didn't want to head in for the night without letting you know I can bring the water safety form by tomorrow. I got a little more information about Len and Birdie this afternoon, though."

Head in for the night . . . I wondered where he was, and why he was working at almost midnight. I felt mildly guilty for the fact that he felt he had to call me. "We can wait until morning to talk, if that's better."

"Nah." I heard the rumble of an engine behind his voice. "I was just on my way home. Wanted to call while it was on my mind."

I was on his mind, fluttered through my head, bright and giddy like a bluebird. I quickly shooed the thought away. *It.* He'd said *it* was on his mind, as in the issue involving Len, and possibly the water safety form. "Where are you?" Blood prickled into my cheeks. That sounded like an invitation.

"Down here on the lake. I saw your light on."

He saw my light on? So he hadn't expected to get my voice mail, after all. . . . Something did a hitch kick inside me. I stood up and walked to the window, gazed down at the expanse of velvety blackness that was the water. Above the hills, the moon rocked on its back, a large, lazy half circle, casting a silvery trail across the water. I scanned the expanse for boats. Tonight the lake was as still and silent as ink in a well. "Where?" Standing on my toes, I gazed toward the Scissortail. Maybe he'd been flagging buoy-zone violators again.

Red and green navigation lights came on and glittered against the water below our dock. "Right here," he said. "See me now?"

I'm coming down there. The words were on the tip of my tongue, but I looked down at the old T-shirt and shorts, slid a hand over my lopsided ponytail, and thought, *I can't go out there like this . . . in the middle of the night.* "Oh, okay, I can see you now." What a completely bland, uninteresting thing to say. Backing away from the window, I had the unsettling thought that if I could see the boat, he could probably see me standing in the window. "What did you find out about Len?"

"I should probably just catch you tomorrow." His voice was flat, no longer throaty, warm, inviting. What was the undercurrent I heard in those words? Disappointment? "It's complicated."

You are absolutely no fun, Bonnie complained in my head.

I pictured myself slipping into the flip-flops from the back porch, running down the hill, the dewy grass cool and slippery underfoot. I tasted the night air, heard the water ripple softly, bending and changing the moon glow, making it dance.

You shouldn't. You have absolutely no business going down there. He'll think it's an invitation. Besides, you look terrible. What if the neighbors see . . .

"Hang on a minute, I'm coming down." My

heart zinged into my throat, and before I could do one more thing to talk myself out of it, I went silently through the back door and slid my feet into the flip-flops. At the Blues' house, a little dog barked warily. Pressing a hand over my mouth, I snickered, feeling like a schoolgirl sneaking out after curfew. Even as a schoolgirl, I would have been afraid to sneak out at night. I'd heard too many warnings about the reasons I shouldn't, couldn't, had better not.

Freedom, life, exhilaration swirled through me as I dashed down the hill in the moon shadow of pecan trees. An owl hooted, and I stopped short, then laughed silently at myself and continued toward the water, my feet landing in the wet grass, splashes of dew flicking upward, showering my skin with cool pinpoints. I felt alive for the first time in recent memory—as if in this moment, running alone through the night, I could leave behind everything I dragged with me during the day. Here, in the darkness, I was free of those burdens, free of myself.

When I neared the water, I could hear Mart's boat bumping the dock in the darkness. By reflex, I reached for the light switch as I passed the electrical box, but then I left it be. There was enough moonlight to see by. At the end of the dock, Mart was throwing his mooring line over a post. He stepped off the boat, a tall dark figure silhouetted against the moon.

My heart rose into my throat, and a rush of possibilities whirled through me—fast, wild, out of control. Stopping at the edge of the grass, I smoothed my clothes, tried to catch my breath. Mart waited, leaning against the railing near his boat, his long legs crossed comfortably, his head tilted as if he were watching me approach.

I wondered how much he could see. Maybe the faded T-shirt and oversized shorts didn't show in the moonlight. Maybe I looked like Julia Roberts, striding down the beach in a scene with warm, false lighting.

Not likely, but the fantasy was a confidence booster.

"Hey." Mart's greeting seemed quiet, intimate. "You get your feet wet?"

I realized that my flip-flops were making squishy, flatulent sounds as I walked. So much for the movie-scene image. Julia Roberts never made squishy sounds when she walked. "It felt good," I said, a giddy giggle in the words. "In all the years we came to the lake, my mother never let us walk down here at night. She was always afraid we'd step on a snake or catch some disease from a mosquito bite."

"Doesn't look like you're afraid." It was probably one of the nicest things he could have said to me. He had no way of knowing that, of course.

"I'm not." It was a lie, but I wanted it to be

true. Stopping beside him, I rested my palms on the railing and gazed at the water. "It's gorgeous out here." Mother didn't know what she was missing.

"It is," Mart agreed. "It's my favorite part of the job—being on the lake after dark."

"I can see why." Taking in a long draft of moist air, I tipped my head back. A million stars poured out across the sky, so bright and close it seemed as if I could feel their heat on my skin. How foolish I was to have wasted evening after evening curled up on the sofa crying, when something so incredible was right outside my door. Here, with soft currents strumming the shoreline and the black velvet sky stretching toward the horizon, it was hard to feel as if anything could be wrong in the entire world. "Guess I should get out more."

"Guess you should." From the corner of my eye, I saw him reach down and scoop a pebble off the dock, then skim it across the lake. "You really haven't seen it until you've seen it from the water. How about a ride?"

A tingle of expectation slid over my skin, featherlight—and for just a moment, I imagined speeding over the surface in the darkness. In the fantasy, Mart was at the wheel, his smile wide and white in the moonlight, a challenge of sorts.

I looked at him, caught his face in moonlight, and his smile was the one I'd imagined. "It's worth the trip," he said, his eyes dark, fathomless.

The breeze tickled loose hairs on the back of my neck. I wanted to say yes, to build a wall between myself and reality, and glide onto the lake with him. But even now, a dozen hesitations were pressing at the edges of my consciousness, like the sentries of an oncoming army. What if Dustin came looking for me? What if I couldn't think of a thing to say out there? What if, once we were in close proximity in the dark, it was uncomfortable and awkward? What if it gave Mart the impression that all of this was leading somewhere?

What if he meant for it to?

That last thought rushed through my mind like a vehicle hydroplaning out of control. A squeal of brakes quickly followed. "I really shouldn't. I have so much work to do."

Nodding, he rested one leg on the dock railing, so that he was half sitting on it. He crossed his arms over his chest, as if he were perfectly happy to hang out here on the dock with me. "Maybe another time."

"Maybe." I felt like such a loser. So much for fun and impulsive. I was back to my boring self. I rested my elbows on the railing, sighed, felt freedom just out of reach.

"Maybe tomorrow night." The invitation in his words was obvious. My body quickened in response, and loneliness pinched in some broken part of me. Did I really have it in me to . . . to . . . What? What was he was asking for?

He was leaning toward me, his head inclined slightly to one side, waiting for an answer. "No pressure or anything, just a ride on the lake," he said finally.

I chewed my lip, trying to come up with the right thing to say. For some reason, *no* didn't seem like the right thing. I wanted the invitation to remain open. "I'll have to see how Dustin's doing tomorrow. We didn't have the best night tonight." Most certainly I didn't want Dustin to see me jetting off in the company of his nemesis, the game warden. With all the problems between Dustin and me, and his latent resentment toward Mart, that would be a disaster.

"Fair enough," Mart agreed, as if I didn't need to explain further. Still, I felt I did, or maybe I just needed to talk to someone.

"Dustin is having such a hard time settling in. Everything here is different for him—the house, the neighborhood, the kids. It being just the two of us, instead of . . ." Without meaning to, I'd stepped onto the slippery slope of divorce history. This wasn't the time and place to get into it, but somehow, the truth came spilling out of me anyway. "Dustin misses his dad. They were close, but . . ." There was no way to put a good light on the past, no way to say it that wasn't humiliating. "His dad has . . . moved on to a whole new life, I guess you'd say. Dustin doesn't understand it. It's like he's lost everything at once—his friends, his house, his school, his dad, his church." *His faith. Our faith.*

My fingers gripped the rail, its texture rough and weathered, earthy and real. I shook my head, swallowing a rising lump in my throat, feeling as helpless and confused as the fourteen-year-old boy I'd just described.

"He hasn't lost his mom." Mart's voice was an island in the storm, something solid.

"Sometimes I think he'd like to."

"Well, you know, sometimes we're hardest on the people we know we can count on not to ditch us no matter how lousy we act."

I turned to look at him, wishing I could see this face. This wise, tender side of him was so out of keeping with the badge and the uniform and the gun. "Spoken like someone who has experience with kids." Suddenly I found myself on a fishing expedition—trolling for details again.

"Just nieces and nephews, and the kids I run into on the job," he admitted. "I tend to catch a lot of kids at the moment that they're about to realize they're not as big as they think they are. I can remember being in their shoes. My brothers and I got in more than our share of scrapes growing up. You put a kid in a tight spot, and the first thing he wants is his mama—believe me."

"Thanks." I felt a stone lifting from the pile weighing on my heart, shucking off into the lake. I heard it sinking to the bottom, disappearing. "I just hope things go well when school starts. I hope he's over the obsession with this . . . Cassandra girl before then."

Mart clicked his tongue against his teeth, producing a speculative sound. "Cassandra. We'll be seeing Cassandra in the water safety class, actually. Her folks don't come from big money like the other delinquents in the boat."

"Oh, great. I was hoping at least *that* complication would be gone before school started."

Mart chuckled. "Well, now, Mom. A cute girl's the best motivation I know of for regular school attendance."

I groaned inwardly at the idea of Dustin taking up an interest in girls when everything else was such a mess. He had enough issues to deal with right now. "He just doesn't need any more disappointments . . . temptations . . . whatever. I don't know what to do to make it better for him. I try to talk to him about things, but it's like he cringes every time I walk into the room."

Mart leaned closer, so close that the space between us felt intimate. "He's a fourteen-year-old boy, and you're his mom." His voice was low, as if he were divulging a secret. "There're things a fourteen-year-old boy can't tell his mama."

"He never used to be that way." The sentence trembled with a ridiculous amount of emotion. I pressed my fingertips to my forehead and closed my eyes, embarrassed. "Sorry. Some psychologist, huh?" I needed to steer this conversation back to the information Mart had learned about Birdie. We'd drifted way too far into personal issues, and I was making an idiot of myself.

"Could be there're some things they don't tell you in psychology school." Mart chuckled softly, an empathic sound. "He's in that rough period when everything changes with boys. One minute, you're a stringy little kid, chasing frogs, and your mama is your best girl. You go to sleep, and you wake up three inches taller, with a voice you don't even recognize. Next thing you know, there's a whole world of girls out there who look interesting. You can't exactly tell that to your *old* best girl, can you?"

I buried my face in my hands. "Ohhh, I'm not ready for this." Dustin's entire childhood flashed before my eyes. Why did he have to pick now to become a teenager?

Somewhere in the storm of mom emotions, there was a small island of comfort. Perhaps not all of Dustin's issues were related to the divorce. Perhaps some of this was normal—just growing pains.

"It'll sort itself out." Mart's voice was kind,

surprisingly close. I felt the nearness of him, and when I looked up, he was a tall shadow blocking the stars. "Be patient," he said quietly. Suddenly, his presence there felt so normal, so reassuring and right.

I butted him softly with my shoulder, the way a friend might after a joke. "That's not my strong suit, in case you haven't noticed."

"I've noticed." He chuckled again, and I knew I should move away, but I leaned into him instead. The palm of his hand slid over my cheek, brushed my hair, tilted my face upward. I didn't stop it.

His eyes met mine in the soft glow of the night, and I felt the dock shifting, breaking free of the land, drifting out onto the water. I raised a hand, braced it against his chest, felt the strong cords of muscle underneath. His fingers slid over mine, lifted them, and he pressed a kiss, featherlight against my skin. The sensation burned through me like a flash fire, and I caught a breath, then let it go, shivered with a strange expectation at the touch of his skin against mine, his arm slipping around me, strong, solid, unexpectedly natural. The pad of his thumb caressed my chin, tipped my head back. I closed my eyes, felt his breath, then his lips touching mine.

The night swirled like a vortex, a whirlpool of sound and sensation, desire and surprise. I abandoned myself to it, let myself be swept away on the water, the storm too powerful for the anchors of fear or hesitation. For now, there was only Mart and me, floating off into the night, free of all ties to shore.

All good things come to those who bait.
—Anonymous
(via Nester Grimland,
retired mechanic and regular customer)

Chapter 16

Mart McClendon

My mama had a theory that I'd never settled down and found the right woman because that first heartbreak with the pretty student teacher had left behind some sort of lasting damage. She was sorry she'd ever let me sign up for the play.

When I kissed Andrea, I sure wasn't thinking about that student teacher, but I did feel like Robin Hood. I felt like I'd slipped into the stronghold, stolen something valuable, and whisked it off into the night. Some sappy, poetic line from the play—stuff about the moon and the stars and Maid Marian's lips—dredged from my memory banks. Luckily I was kissing Andrea right then, so nothing stupid spilled out my mouth.

Everything about that moment, even the random lines in my head, seemed to suit, though. I didn't understand those lines as a fourteen-year-old lovesick boy, but now I could relate to Robin Hood's motivation.

Moments like that have to end, of course. The thing about borrowed time is that it always runs out quicker than you want it to. Andrea pulled away a little, and I let her go, and for a minute, we stood a few inches apart, her face turned upward, her eyes searching mine.

I probably should've said something, but I felt like one of Nester's tackle boxes after a fishing tournament—everything in a jumble.

She watched me like she wondered what I was thinking, or she was waiting for me to explain what'd just happened.

A whippoorwill called in the distance, and from the tangle of branches stretching over the boathouse, its mate trilled out a reply. Andrea's hand left my shirt, and she reached for the dock rail, leaving a cool spot on my skin. Instead of pointing out the whippoorwill's call, maybe saying something intelligent and romantic, I cleared my throat, straightened my hat, and said, "I guess you're wondering what I found out about Len today."

Man, what a hunyak I was. She probably didn't have Len on her mind right that minute, and I didn't, either. I really needed to get out around people more. You could sure tell I'd been spending most of my time alone in a boat or a truck.

Her eyelids fluttered, like she was trying to clear up her vision. Then she blinked hard and nodded. "Oh . . . umm-hmm . . . yes, I was wondering about that. That was what you came up here for."

Well, not exactly. I didn't admit that, of course. I had wanted to tell her what I'd found out about Len and what'd happened when I'd gone to his cabin with the stuffed raccoon for Birdie, but when I saw Andrea's light on, I wasn't thinking about a business meeting. The truth was that I was thinking of a pretty night and a pretty girl. It felt good to be focused on the here and now, or maybe even the future, instead of rehashing the past, for a change.

Andrea stiffened and moved away a step. "Guess we got off track a little, huh?"

"Maybe not," I said, and felt a little less like a hunyak. Not a bad answer, and it opened the door to . . . well, something anyway.

She looked down and smoothed the front of her T-shirt, then threaded her arms over her stomach, hugging tight.

"Cold? I've got a jacket in the boat." All of a sudden, I was John Wayne. My mama would've been proud. The spare jacket was mossy oak camo, and it probably smelled like carburetor cleaner, but it's the thought that counts. At least I'd thought of it.

"I'm fine." She checked the house, like she felt a tug. "What did you learn about Len and Birdie?" Now she was nothing but business.

Disappointment nipped me like a red ant, but even shoptalk was better than heading back home to the contraband raccoon on my screened porch.

"Well, after a few days and some favors, I think I've got it pieced together, pretty much. Looks like right before Len shipped off to Vietnam, he was married. They divorced even before he came back injured, but he did have a daughter, Norma Barnes. The name matches the information from the medical clinic in Moses Lake, except her last name is Marsh now, or at least that's the name she's using."

Andrea smoothed her hair from her face. "But where did she go when she left Len's house, and why did she leave? Is she gone permanently or temporarily?"

A muscle twitched in the back of my neck. Even with a few dozen phone calls, I hadn't been able to track down much about Len's daughter, Norma. There was no work history, and the information she'd given at the clinic—address, phone, Social Security number—looked to be fraudulent. Her driver's license hadn't been renewed in six years.

"As near as I can figure, Lillian Jane, the name she wrote on the clinic form, probably is Birdie's real name, but I checked the address Norma gave at the clinic, and it's actually for a hardware store in Buna, Texas. Nobody there knows anything about Lillian or Norma. Just from the paper trail, it's like they've been living under a rock. Usually in situations like that, what you eventually find is a string of aliases with rap sheets, but so far, nothing."

Andrea drummed the railing with her fingernails. "So do we know for sure that Birdie really is this Lillian Jane, Len's granddaughter?"

I looked out across the water, thought of my visit to the cabin. "Reverend Hay and I went up to Len's place again today. I brought the stuffed raccoon, and Hay brought more things for Birdie—clothes from the clothes closet at the church, a pair of shoes that are more the right size for her, shampoo, a toothbrush, and whatnot. I asked Len if Birdie had another name, and he knew enough to tell me it was Lillian. I tried the name out on Birdie, and she turned right around, like she'd known it all her life."

"Kids don't usually fake something like that." I could tell by Andrea's tone that she was thinking about what should happen next. "How did she act when you went up there?"

"A little more comfortable this time. She didn't seem quite so worried about us being around." I leaned over the railing next to Andrea. "She likes Hay, but then they all do. He's got a way with kids. He's about half kid himself. You know, if you can talk your boy into being in Hay's production of *The Waltons*, you should. Hay will introduce him around, help him get to know folks. Some of the times we moved as kids, I don't think we would've made it if Mama hadn't gotten us tied up with a church. Those men were like extra fathers and grandpas to us. Good examples. We needed that. Church gave us something constant, no matter where we were."

Ripples of light reflected off the water and slid over Andrea's skin. For a second, I forgot what we were talking about, and the kiss came to mind instead. I wondered how she felt about it. Too bad I hadn't waited a little longer to suggest a boat ride. Maybe she would've decided to go. Then again, maybe I was giving myself too much credit. Right now, she seemed to have her mind squarely on business.

"I think I'd have to drag him down there kicking and screaming."

"He's a little big for that." I couldn't help feeling sorry for Andrea. She had her hands full. I couldn't picture what kind of guy would leave someone like her, not to mention his own kid.

Her shoulders sank. "Yes, he is. Unfortunately."

Everything in me wanted to slip an arm around her, pull her close, promise to make her situation turn out all right. Not that I'd know how to do that, but maybe after I took Dustin to the water safety course one day next week, we'd just happen by the Tin Building Theater for a few minutes. I could come up with some excuse for needing to go there. It wasn't like the kid would have any choice about it—unless he wanted to swim home.

I thought about mentioning the idea to Andrea but then decided I was probably better off keeping it to myself. If it didn't work out, she wouldn't have to feel bad about it.

She shivered, and I knew I needed to let her go inside. The day was catching up with me anyway, and I was ready to head home and crash. Unfortunately, I still had the little bandito to take care of.

"I should go inside." Andrea eyeballed the house again. "Will you let me know what else you find out about Birdie? I'll talk to my boss when I get to work tomorrow—see what more we can do to get some help for Birdie. At the very least, the situation needs some oversight until we can figure out what's going on with the mom."

Even though in some ways I hated to agree, I knew that Andrea was right. Len obviously cared about Birdie, and she seemed attached to him, but he didn't have a clue about taking care of a little girl, and that place he lived in was a wreck. I just hoped that whoever came in on the case had some understanding of a man like Len. A lot of folks would take one glance at him and write him off. But if you really looked, you could see that Birdie needed Len. It was hard to picture him as a parent, but he was looking after that little girl the same way he cared for helpless animals, like that baby coon.

Andrea and I told each other good-night, then I left her with the water safety form and went on home. Neither of us had said anything more about the kiss, but it was on my mind as I crossed the lake and pulled up to the dock by my cabin. Across the way, high above everything else, I could see the lights of Larkspur Cove as I tied up my boat and headed into the cabin. It was late enough that I figured I could just shower, feed and water little Bandito, fall into bed, and be dead to the world. I didn't want to ponder anything tonight, or lay in bed staring at the log beams on the ceiling. I just wanted to close my eyes and believe that Moses Lake might be a new beginning, after all.

For a few minutes while I was there on the dock with Andrea, it was like all the painful stuff floated off into the lake and disappeared. I wanted to hang on to that feeling, to believe it was possible to build a life that looked forward instead of back. Letting go of the past is easier said than done, but right then I could see where it might be possible.

For the first time in a long time, I went to bed anticipating tomorrow. The last thought that crossed my mind, right before I drifted off, wasn't about Aaron and Mica and whether they were scared, or in pain, or suffering in those moments before the waves swamped the boat and swept them under. I didn't picture the scene in my brain—try to rewrite it to where I was there with them, to where I could pull them out of the water. Or better yet, tell Aaron not to get the boat out at all—there was a storm coming, and the motor needed work. Usually, before I went to sleep, I was back there on our little beach, warning Aaron to keep off the water.

But tonight, I was just across the lake, with a pretty girl on a pretty night.

In the early hours before sunrise, something soft and gentle stroked my hair. I was caught up in the middle of a good dream. In it, I was racing across the lake, the boat moving so fast the hull was high in the water, skimming it, smooth as glass. The night was clear and cool, a big orange moon hanging on the horizon. Strands of silver-edged clouds streaked the sky, hanging in patches over the stars. Andrea was beside me in the boat, her hair loose, streaming behind her like dark ribbons. Tipping her head back, she laughed into the wind, stretched her hand across, slipped it into mine, brought my fingers to her lips and . . . nibbled on my pinkie . . .

The moonlit night, the lake, the boat, and Andrea vanished like a mirage in the dry country, but the finger-nibbling kept on. I cracked an eye open, and in the dim, gray light from the dusty window over my bed, I watched a pair of tiny black hands pick up my ring finger. A little masked face looked it over to see if it was edible.

"Hey!" I croaked, and jerked my hand away. Bandito scampered to the edge of the bed, then stood up on his hind legs and chattered at me, his head bobbing back and forth like he was trying to make a point. From the looks of things, he thought I was late with breakfast.

"How'd you get out?" Sitting up, I yawned and combed back my hair. My ear was wet and slimy. All that good stuff in the lake dream was really just me getting a grooming from a raccoon. "You little rascal," I said, and he scampered to the hollow spot between my knees, then rolled over onto his back, laid there with all four feet in the air, and started purring like a cat. I grabbed a cell phone cord from the lamp table and dangled the end above him, and he batted at it. No wonder people tried to keep baby coons as pets. They were cute little things. Too smart for their own good and not much fun to share a house with when they got older, but you had to like the little ones.

I played with him a minute before I picked him up, got his breakfast from the kitchen, and then took him back to his cage on the porch. He'd opened the slide latch slick as a whistle. Guess he'd watched me do it enough times that he'd learned how. After he got out of the cage, it wasn't any problem for him to slip into the cabin through an old cat door. The only good thing was that he'd come looking for me instead of ransacking the place. I'd seen what could happen when raccoons found their way into houses. A gang of smash-and-grab burglars had nothing on a mob of raccoons. They were quick, smart, and could get into almost anything.

I put the little convict back in his cage with his vittles, which I figured would keep him occupied while I looked for some wire to keep him locked up while I was gone.

The phone rang, and when I answered, my nephew was on the other end. Levi's voice was still faint and squeaky this morning. I figured Laurie had rousted him early, so she could have him call before I headed off to work.

"Hey, buddy, what's up?" I said, and I was almost dreading the answer. I knew that Laurie was bringing in the big guns to try to get me to come home for the birthday party next weekend.

"I dunno," Levi yawned out a long, sleepy sound. "I just woke up."

"I can tell." I heard Laurie whispering something in the background. I could almost see her wheeling a hand in the air, trying to get Levi to move on to the point of the call. "How's your ball team doing, buddy?"

"Good." There was a long pause. Laurie

whispered again, then Levi came back. "I got a home run last night."

"A home run? Your first one?" I said, and felt the sting of not being there to see it. That was Laurie's point, of course. She knew I'd spent hours out in the yard with that kid, working on hitting Wiffle balls.

"Uh-huh. Coach Lee gived me some lessons."

"Coach Lee?" I asked. "The high school coach?" What in the world was Laurie thinking, getting private lessons for a kid in T-ball? She couldn't afford that, and Levi didn't need it. Right now he should just have fun and enjoy the game. Just because his daddy had gone to college on a football scholarship didn't mean Levi needed to start training in kindergarten.

"Uh-huh. Chris took me. He got me a bat for my birthday present, but it's not my birthday yet, but it's okay if I can use the bat, Chris said."

"That's good, buddy." Laurie knew it'd be hard for me to hear about Levi getting his first home run without me, and Chris setting up lessons. Since he was a school principal, he had pull. "That's real good. I knew you'd get a homer this year. You just keep working hard. That's how your daddy did it." That old, heavy feeling settled over me like outdoor gear too warm for the season. I remembered how it felt to be back in Alpine, stirring guilt like a boiling pot.

But the truth was that right now Levi sounded

as happy as I'd ever heard him. "Uh-huh. It was so cool! The ball . . ." He went on with a blow-by-blow description of his big moment, and I felt like I was living it right along with him.

"Awesome," I said when he was done, and this time I didn't cast his daddy's shadow over him. "You worked hard and it paid off, huh?"

"Yup."

I started telling him about the baby coon on the back porch. Laurie was talking in his other ear, though. He barely heard me.

"Uncle Mart, you comin' for my birf-day?" he repeated, like a robot.

"No, buddy. I can't make it this time, but next week, you watch for the UPS man to show up, all right. He's bringing you a big birthday present from Uncle Mart. You share it with your brothers, too, you hear?" When the boys got that blow-up waterslide I'd ordered, Laurie and Chris's yard would be a permanent mudhole, but man those kids were gonna have fun.

"Okay," Levi chirped, just as happy as could be. That probably vexed Laurie some.

"Say hi to everybody at the party for me, all right?"

" 'Kay," Levi answered, and hung up the way the kids usually did—without bothering to go through a long-winded good-bye.

I headed for the shower with Levi's birthday on my mind. Aaron's birthday was the same day as

Levi's, but this year Levi's birthday could just be Levi's birthday.

I climbed into the shower with the big homerun on my mind, but without even thinking about it, I switched tracks and started replaying the dream where I was gliding across the lake with Andrea. I thought about feeling her hand in mine, and then waking up and figuring out I wasn't sailing off into the wild blue with a pretty girl—I was being nibbled by a raccoon. Before I knew it, I was laughing to myself, my head falling back against the wall, the water streaming through my hair. I couldn't remember the last time I'd laughed like—

A squeal, then a flapping sound broke up the moment, and a blast of cold air hit me. I jerked my head up and blinked away the water just in time to see Bandito losing his balance on top of the shower rod. For a second, he stood on two feet, flailing his paws like a fat man on a high wire. The shower curtain swayed, the rod wobbled, the raccoon lost his balance, and the rest was a five-second disaster. Bandito tumbled forward, caught the top of the curtain with one paw, and then the next thing I knew, coon, curtain, curtain rod, and two towels were headed my way. I ended up pinned in the corner, water spraying all directions, and the coon squealing, spitting, snarling, and trying to claw his way through the curtain.

"Dadgummit!" I hollered. Most of the noise bounced off the curtain and came back at me while I was trying to get my feet untangled, catch the coon, and turn off the water. I had a hold on him through the curtain at one point, and was halfway on my feet before he wiggled loose.

While I was making another grab for him, I lost my balance, twirled like a ballerina, bounced off the sidewall, about knocked myself out on the faucet, and landed in the corner again. For a half second, I just sat there, watching little tweetie birds flutter around my head. Then I came to, heard the coon spitting and chattering as he scampered off, and realized the water was still spraying around the bathroom. Once I figured out which way was up, I unwound myself, found the water faucet, and got it turned off. When I finally made it to my feet, the bathroom was covered with water, the coon was gone, the curtain was in a wad on the floor, and the guy in the mirror had what looked like it might turn into a shiner in an hour or two.

When the phone rings at a time like that, you ought to know the smart thing would be just to let it go to voice mail. I must've been a little addle-brained from the coon-and-curtain assault, because I grabbed a towel, followed the trail of watery coon prints across the house to the living room, snatched up the phone, and spotted the coon rubbing off on the stack of laundry I'd just picked up from the Wash Barrel in Moses Lake the day before. What had been fresh uniforms were now wadded-up piles of pants and shirts covered with hair, water, and what looked like damp pieces of Oreo cookie. Apparently, Bandito'd been having a snack before he came to hunt me down in the shower.

My eyeball started pounding in its socket, and I had murder on the brain when I flipped open the phone and answered it.

A moment like that is the exact wrong time to find your sergeant on the other end, and the last thing you want him to do is give you orders to go pick up your partner and head to another part of the state to help flood victims.

The worst thing about that kind of news is, the minute you hang up the phone, you realize that, some way or other, you're gonna have to explain that shiner to the guys.

My heart is like a singing bird.
—Christina Rossetti
(Left by A. Bastrop, newly retired
from teaching middle school)

Chapter 17

Andrea Henderson

When I arrived at the office Tuesday morning, Bonnie was unusually giddy. She met me in the hallway before I was three steps in the door. Eyes wide, she laid a hand on my arm, her fingers tightening around my wrist. "He was just here. Did you see him out in the parking lot?"

"*Who* was here?"

She had the awed look and fiery blush of a teenager at a rock concert. I couldn't imagine what would spark that level of enthusiasm so early in the morning.

"I guess you just missed him." She let go of my arm and fanned her face. "Whoa, he's hot."

"Who?" There must have been a FedEx delivery this morning. Bonnie had a thing for the FedEx man. Actually, she had a thing for the UPS man, too, and the food-service truck driver who delivered supplies to the doughnut shop next door. "You know, if you don't stop ogling the

FedEx guy, we're going to end up with some kind of harassment complaint."

"Pfff! Not him. The *game warden.*" Her eyes widened, her mouth spreading into a smile. "Holy mackerel, you didn't tell me he was, like, hot to the third power."

I blinked dumbly, my mind racing to assimilate information. Mart had shown up? Here? How did he even know where my office was, and why would he come all this way? Had something happened to Birdie? "Mart McClendon? What did he want?"

Stretching onto her toes, Bonnie craned to one side and scanned the front door, as if she were hoping that Mart would show up again. I found myself checking behind me with the fleeting thought that I wished I'd arrived at work a few minutes earlier.

Bonnie settled back into her shoes. "He came by to try to catch you before you headed out to appointments this morning. But finally he couldn't wait any longer. He had leave town to rescue flood victims in southeast Texas." Bonnie breathed the words *rescue flood victims* with reverence and awe. "He had on a uniform, a gun belt, and a cowboy hat—the whole deal. And he was, like, so . . . so . . . ." She was momentarily at a loss for words, which must have meant the world was slightly off its axis. She finally finished with, ". . . rugged."

Rugged . . . I mused. I had the sudden urge to call Mart and tell him our administrative assistant thought he was *rugged*. He'd get a laugh out of that. "I hadn't noticed." That was completely untrue, of course, but it sounded convincing.

"You are so totally blind," she complained. "He's like, all man. He even had a teenie bit of a black eye. He probably got that while he was making an arrest—protecting little fuzzy animals or something."

"He had a black eye?" Where had Mart been this morning? I hoped the black eye didn't have anything to do with Birdie. Surely, it wasn't from Len. "He was fine last night."

Bonnie caught a breath. "So you *do* have a thing going with him." With a flash of carefully curled lashes, she snaked a hand out and swat-tapped me on the arm. "I thought so. I knew I saw him looking around your office while he was writing you that note."

"He wrote me a note?" Leave it to Bonnie to skip the important information in favor of ferreting out personal details. I started down the hall, and she followed, of course.

"And some papers in an envelope. He said he'd tried to call you a little while ago, but you didn't answer."

"My phone went dead last night. I forgot to turn it back on this morning." A flutter of excitement caused the corners of my lips to twitch upward, and I averted my face to hide it. The last thing I needed was Bonnie knowing that Mart had actually kissed me on the dock in the moonlight. She'd make more of it than it was, and pretty soon my personal . . . whatever would be fodder for office conversation. My professional image would be out the window.

Peeking around the edges of my all-important professional image was another, completely random thought. It flitted by in bright colors I couldn't ignore.

I was on his mind this morning. . . .

Bonnie caught him checking out my office. . . .

I thought of the kiss, and my cheeks flamed. As if she sensed what I was hiding, Bonnie followed me into my office, pushed the door partially closed, and stood with her hand on the knob, ready to shut it all the way if the dish was really good. "So what's the note say?" Her eyes brightened with anticipation.

I quickly unfolded the piece of printer paper and scanned it. It was an update on Len and Birdie. Mart had asked Reverend Hay to catch Len on the lake this morning and explain to him that some people would probably be coming by his place soon to talk about Birdie, and Len should be cooperative. Mart apologized for the fact that he was being sent out of town and wouldn't be available to help facilitate things. Reverend Hay had agreed to help make introductions, should a CPS investigator be sent out.

Inside the envelope, Mart had placed the information he'd gathered on Len and Birdie. There was also an e-mail containing some details on Len's history. The e-mail addresses had been torn from the top of the paper, to keep Mart's source confidential, I guessed.

"It's business," I said.

"What's business?" When I looked up, Taz was standing in the doorway. I supposed it was as good a time as any to bring his expertise into the situation with Len and Birdie. I hoped I hadn't crossed the line, getting involved without consulting Taz.

It was difficult to gauge his reaction as I shared the story. He listened patiently, stroking his chin, as I described our visit to Len's house, the facts of the situation as we knew them, my first contact with CPS, which so far had failed to generate action, and Mart's subsequent trips to Len's house.

I left out the part of the story in which the rugged game warden and I stood on the dock in the moonlight. The memory and the sensations woven into the fabric of that scene played in my mind, though, and I felt my body quicken. *The next time he asks me to go for a boat ride, I'll say yes.* The impulse in my head surprised me, but even as I discounted it, I was scanning Mart's note, trying to recall whether it said how long he'd be out of town. It didn't, unfortunately.

"Mind if I take a look at that stuff?" Taz smacked his lips, tasting the details of the case, contemplating the possible ingredients.

I handed over my materials. "No, not at all."

Muttering to himself, he scanned the puzzle pieces of information. "Your friend's got some connections. Any idea why he didn't just turn this over to the sheriff's department? This isn't the sort of thing a game warden would normally dabble in." A brow lifted in my direction, indicating more than a casual interest. I wondered if my boss thought I'd been playing vigilante.

"He hasn't had the best cooperation from the sheriff's department." A nervous sweat formed underneath my shirt and dripped down my spine. Maybe I'd really screwed up here. What if Mart had intended the contents of that envelope for my eyes only? What if I got him in trouble? What if I'd committed some major technical error by handling Birdie's situation the way I had?

"Hmmm . . ." Taz muttered.

The muscles in my neck went stiff. I felt the need to explain my way out of trouble—just in case I was in some. "The grandfather, Len, is something of a recluse, and with his mental limitations . . . well, he's leery of people he doesn't know. He seems well-intentioned enough, but apparently someone warned him not to talk to Social Services. When it was mentioned, he became agitated. A heavy-handed approach here could make a difficult situation worse."

"I see." My boss's expression neither softened, nor hardened. I couldn't tell if I was about to get the axe or just a mild reprimand. "Neither of you felt that this . . . grandfather might be a danger to the child?"

Here it comes, I thought. What in the world would I do if I lost my job? Maybe I could beg, and Taz would have mercy. "I don't think he would be, intentionally. He seems to care about her, and I think he is providing for her to the best of his ability. My hesitation is that I don't know how far that ability goes, and what happens when and if the mother shows up again. It's clear from even a short assessment that this child has experienced a significant trauma, and right now her sense of security appears to lie with the grandfather. I question what will happen if that's taken away from her, but at the same time, there's no denying that she needs further evaluation and undoubtedly counseling, and that the grandfather would require support services, caregiver training, probably assistance completing the forms to enroll her in school, and so forth. Then there's the issue of the biological mother and guardianship."

The phone rang on Bonnie's desk, and she turned sideways to slide through the portion of the doorway that wasn't filled by my boss.

"Complicated," Taz observed, scanning Mart's notes again.

"Yes, it is."

"What do you think should happen next?" Heavy folds of skin drooped beneath pale gray eyes, but the look in them was acute, measured. That question had the feel of a test about it. Without his overtly telling me so, I knew a lot was riding on my response.

"I'd like to secure a CPS referral and get back up there. The sooner we figure out where that little girl has been and what's happened to her, the sooner we can try to create a viable, developmentally healthy situation for her."

Still holding the information from Mart, my boss took a step backward into the hall. "Let me see what I can do with it. I know a few people at CPS." He grinned and winked in a way that said, *Hey, I own the place.*

"Oh . . . uhhh . . . all right." I felt my professional confidence tumbling Humpty-Dumpty style, shattering into a gooey mass of shell and yolk on the office floor. Apparently, I wasn't being fired, but Taz was taking over the case, which meant he didn't think I could be trusted with it. The amount of letdown I felt was startling. I'd never anticipated that I would have so quickly become invested in this job. I wanted to be good at it. I wanted the pain and upheaval of the past year to count for something, to lead to something. I wanted to believe that, despite my clumsy way of fumbling through this life change, there was a plan, and I was on the path to it. I wanted to believe that Birdie was part of the plan, that all the trial and betrayal and humiliation of the past year had taught me about people—given me a sixth sense, an understanding of the clients I was serving.

Years ago I heard a missionary say that, until you could feel the pain of the people you were serving, you were only an actor, acting a part. *Shame does not lie in suffering,* he'd asserted, *but in wasted suffering. Suffering must produce revelation.* I wanted to believe this past year had been a shaping process, turning me into something more than an actor.

Watching Taz walk away with my file made me feel like a farce.

Pausing in the hall, he glanced over his shoulder, as if he knew I was watching. "I think I can get you that referral without causing too much brouhaha," he said, then winked before shuffling away, leaving a final assessment floating in the air behind him. "Good work, Henderson. In this business, you either think on your feet or sink on your feet. You've got what it takes."

As his loafers squeaked out of earshot, I reveled in the very first triumph of my new life. I had what it took. And that opinion came from someone who knew this job inside and out.

With a tiny and properly controlled cheer, I sat down at my desk, clicked on my computer, and pulled up the morning schedule, eager to get on with the day. Suddenly the appointments ahead seemed like opportunities, a chance to affect lives. Maybe I wouldn't be able to make a difference in all of them, but I could make a difference in some.

A summer storm system blew through later that morning. For the rest of the week, water, wind, and random tornado warnings caused travel to be unpredictable at best and completely out of the question in some rural areas. On the far side of the lake, the roads became a boggy maze of flooded low-water crossings, with mudholes deep enough to sink a Humvee, washouts, and downed tree branches that made it almost impossible for me to navigate to some of my appointments. Travel to Len's place, either via land or water, quickly became out of the question. Even though Taz had successfully arranged for a low-key visit to Len's house by a CPS investigator, who could then arrange a referral for me, the weather had closed in before anything could take place. I could only hope that, whatever was happening at Len's farm, Birdie was safe. Now I was more determined than ever to push through Birdie's referral, so that I could begin working with her and, hopefully, coax clues to her past from her.

Interestingly, the mud and foul weather that would have discouraged me only a few days ago, now felt like a challenge to be met, a rite of passage, a chance to prove myself. When Taz called on Sunday to suggest that I borrow the jacked-up four-wheel-drive truck he kept for trips to his small weekend ranch, I took him up on it. I even went out with him on Sunday afternoon and took a four-wheeling lesson. While we were discussing fascinating things like self-locking hubs, rear differentials, and the laws of physics as they applied to mudholes and four-wheel-drive trucks, my boss asked about Dustin.

I spilled more than I meant to about our continuous head-butting sessions and Dustin's reluctance to participate in our new life in Moses Lake. No matter what I suggested, he refused. I was hoping against hope that the start of the water safety course might snap him out of his funk, but now I was worried about how I was going to transport him to the class. I hadn't heard from Mart. While buying gas at the Waterbird, I'd learned that he was still tied up doing flood duty in southeast Texas. No one had seen Len, either, but that wasn't too surprising, considering the weather.

"I'm just hoping Dustin doesn't go into total protest mode about the water safety course tomorrow," I told Taz glumly. "He's just so . . . oppositional these days. It's like he thinks if things get miserable enough here, we'll pick up and move back to Houston. He won't even give Moses Lake a chance." I knew, in a way, that I was the pot calling the kettle black. I'd arrived in town determined not to get too involved in the community—to make Moses Lake no more than a temporary stopping-off point in our journey to some sort of new life. But day by day, Moses Lake was drawing me in.

Taz nodded, seeming unsurprised by the revelations about Dustin. "Take the truck on home and give him a ride in it. I haven't met the teenage boy yet who couldn't relate to a hemi engine, a lift kit, and four knobby mud tires. You know, I've got some boxes to sort through at the office and some new shelves to put together. Once he's done with water safety, I can give him some work the first couple weeks of August, if you think he'd be interested."

"That would be great." Maybe setting Dustin up with his first paying job would distract him from the fact that he was supposed to be at his father's house. Dustin might actually enjoy working at the office. Taz would take him under his wing, Bonnie would spoil him, and the doughnut lady would feed him apple fritters. "Maybe a change of scenery will help." Among other small favors, I'd landed in a job with the world's nicest, most understanding boss.

On the way back to Taz's condo, we talked a little more about Dustin and the tasks he might be able to help with around the office. After dropping off Taz, I drove home, feeling foolish behind the wheel of the big blue truck. At stoplights, it seemed as if people were looking at me, surveying the truck, thinking that I didn't belong in it. I splashed through rain-swollen intersections and ran over a curb or two, but overall, I piloted the big rig pretty well for a girl who'd never driven anything larger than a minivan. Turning into Larkspur Estates, I envisioned Dustin running out of the house with his mouth agape when he heard the hemi engine roaring up the driveway. Oddly enough, though, the house was quiet. Maybe Dustin was asleep, or back in his room with his earphones on.

I parked the truck in the driveway, positioned for an evening junket to someplace muddy, then I dashed through the drizzle and slipped into the house via the carport door. Dustin was nowhere to be found, but the light was on in the boathouse. A mixture of suspicion and irritation stirred inside me, a pot working toward a boil. Why would Dustin be in the boathouse on a day like this? I doubted that Mrs. Blue would allow Sydney and Ansley out while storms were still passing over. What could Dustin possibly be doing down there? Unless . . .

Unless his friends had come back.

Irritation turned to panic. Surely they wouldn't go out on the lake in this weather. The water was choppy and dotted with whitecaps. I couldn't see a single boat out there.

Grabbing an umbrella from the stand on the back porch, I hurried down the hill, water sloshing into my tennis shoes and soaking the hems of my jeans, my brain whipping up worrisome scenarios as to what might draw a fourteen-year-old boy outside on a day like today. The answer to that question became perfectly apparent as I rounded the corner, bringing the interior of the boathouse into view. A bicycle was parked under the overhang on the front of the building, and along the edge of the empty boat stall, side by side, sat my son and a petite, dark-haired, olive-skinned girl I could only assume was Cassandra. So much for her being grounded. Dressed in a faded cami top, short shorts, and dime-store flip-flops, she looked like she was ready for a party.

I stopped halfway into the building, the water from the roof pelting my umbrella in large droplets. "Dustin, what do you think you're doing?" was out of my mouth before I even had time to consider how it would sound.

Dustin snapped upright, and the girl scrambled to her feet. Lashes flying wide, she darted a gaze around the room like she was looking for an escape hatch. *She'd better be,* I thought. Just the idea of her and Dustin alone in the boathouse, maybe even alone in the house, made me queasy. How often had they done this? What might have been going on during the week while I was at work?

Dustin flipped his hands into the air, then let them slap to his thighs. "Mom, we were just hanging out." He turned a red-cheeked look my way. The resentment, anger, and hurt there shocked me.

"You are grounded, Dustin. You didn't have permission to have a—" *girl in extremely short shorts and too much makeup*—"guest over here." The degree to which I sounded like my mother was staggering. The word *guest* even had the sharp edge of condescendence to it, a subliminal message to Cassandra, of sorts. She didn't belong here. *Her mother cleans cabins for a living,* ran through my mind, and I was ashamed of the thought. It sounded like something my parents would say.

Nostrils flaring, Dustin sucked in a breath and stood up. "Mom!" he gasped, mortified at my rudeness. Somewhere in the back of my mind, I was mortified myself. It was wrong to treat a child that way, and despite the attempt to look grown-up, Cassandra was a child.

She sidestepped toward the door, her neck retracting into her shoulders, as if she were afraid I might throw something at her. Her dark eyes rolled upward, soulful, puppy-like, with a wide, white rim underneath. "I . . . better go," she choked out, her voice barely a whisper.

"Mom!" Dustin repeated insistently, blocking Cassandra's exit. "We were just sitting here talking. Besides, you said I was grounded for two weeks. Tomorrow is Monday. That's two weeks." His eyes met mine, and in a strange instant of transference, I levitated across the boathouse and was standing in his shoes, young, confused, embarrassed by my mother's behavior. One minute I was having the time of my life, and the next I was being squashed under my mother's thumb. Nothing I ever did was right. She always assumed the worst, never trusted my judgment. I couldn't wait to grow up and get away from her house, out from under her control. But when I did get out on my own, I lacked confidence in my ability.

By not trusting Dustin, by not listening to him, would I teach him that he wasn't trustworthy, that his opinions weren't worth considering? Would I cause him to yearn for love and acceptance so badly that he would jump into the wrong relationships just to get it?

"I called Dad," Dustin said, and I felt the floor dropping out from under me, felt the cold splash of water as my head went under. "Dad said it was all right, as long as we stayed outside. He's gonna call me back about August in a couple days, too. He's been busy."

"You called . . . wh . . . Excu . . . excuse me?" The words choked the air from my throat. Karl had actually bothered to answer the phone? And how in the world would he know what was *all right?* He had incredible nerve, handing out his approval. Why would Dustin think Karl's permission counted for anything? The answer was obvious, of course. Dustin knew his dad would tell him what he wanted to hear.

"It's not your father's decision," I bit out. "You should have called me."

Dustin stretched taller, suddenly seeming more man than adolescent. "I couldn't get you on your phone, so I called Dad, and I got ahold of him this time. Cassie's finished being grounded. None of the other kids even got grounded."

Cassandra rolled a sympathetic look toward Dustin, uncertain whether she should jump into the argument or run for cover. Shifting from one foot to the other, she twisted her arms, pretzel-like.

I stood between her and the only available exit, feeling almost as insecure as she looked. Should I give in? Should I draw a hard line, revoke Dustin's parole, just to prove the point that his father didn't have a right to an opinion? My thoughts raced, my mind and heart struggling to weigh the consequences of every possible reaction. I didn't want to turn into my mother. I didn't want Dustin and me to have that kind of relationship. But there were so many dangers in this new life, so many things that could go wrong, and Dustin had so little experience. Until now, he'd been sheltered, protected, monitored. He'd never been in a situation where other kids might lead him astray.

He'd never been around girls who dressed like Cassandra. . . .

"Hello-o-o down there in the boathouse." A voice traveled through the mist, and my heart skipped, then fluttered. I knew who was coming down the hill before I turned and saw Mart approaching on the footpath, wearing a long oilskin slicker, like he was ready to round up some doggies in the outback. While he walked, he was whistling "Deep in the Heart of Texas," a cheery tune that seemed out of place amid the ongoing drama in the boathouse. He lifted a hand in greeting as he came closer.

Dustin and Cassandra leaned out over the water to see who was approaching. When they figured out who it was, Cassandra ducked back into the shadows, and Dustin groaned, "Oh, great. What does *he* want?"

"Dustin," I snapped. "Drop the attitude. You're in enough trouble already. Mr. McClendon is trying to do you a favor with the water safety class. You're lucky you didn't end up in juvenile court."

In a surprising show of bravado, undoubtedly for Cassandra's benefit, Dustin answered, "Whatever."

Cassandra seemed shocked, reacting with a soft gasp and a quick headshake that indicated even she thought he'd gone too far.

Mart stepped off the path onto the mottled, overgrown cement surface that had once been a boat ramp, and I felt the memory of the kiss speeding toward Dustin's issues like atoms in a supercollider. If Dustin suspected what was happening between Mart and me . . . I couldn't even begin to predict what the fallout would be.

Worry scampered through my mind, running breathlessly but going nowhere, a hamster on a wheel. What should I do now? Try to act cool and businesslike? Hope that Mart would get the hint? What if he didn't? I could send Dustin to the house, remove him from the situation completely. Once he was gone, Cassandra would probably gather up her bicycle and leave.

Mart and I would be alone then. A heady swirl of remembered sensations followed that thought, and I had the brief realization that Bonnie was right. He did look rugged.

A rush of self-recriminations pushed the observation aside, covered it over with wide strokes of emotion painted in dull gray—guilt, embarrassment, self-doubt. I was a thirty-eight-year-old woman with a child to raise. I needed to stop acting like I was Cassandra's age.

Mart, completely unaware of my mental dialog, smiled pleasantly, then turned his attention to the kids. He greeted Dustin first, receiving a muttered hello that notched up the temperature in my cheeks. Mart didn't seem to notice. He smiled at Cassandra who, at the moment, appeared to be considering diving into the water and swimming to freedom. "You finished being grounded, Cassandra?"

She blushed and nodded, digging a toe into the dock. "Yes, sir."

Mart's posture softened further. "And we'll be seeing you at the water safety course tomorrow?"

Tucking her chin, she rolled a remorseful look at him, her eyes large and dark and wounded, the kind of sad eyes a teenage girl uses to get what she wants. "Yes, sir. I'm sorry we got in trouble that day on the lake."

The hangdog face worked on Mart. He stepped under the roof and gave her an encouraging look. "Come on, now. The water safety course isn't that bad. You might even learn something."

"Yes, sir." Shifting her weight, she uncrossed her arms and pushed her hands into her pockets, one eye squeezing shut, as if she had something on her mind and couldn't decide whether to bring it up. "Ummm . . . Do you know when we'll be done? When the class will get out each day, I mean?"

In the corner, Dustin turned his attention to Mart. The conversation had suddenly become of interest to him, too.

Mart paused to scratch his chin, letting the suspense build. "Five, six o'clock, maybe."

Cassandra's mouth dropped open, and Dustin sucked in a breath. Considering that the class started at two in the afternoon, five or six o'clock was a little hard to imagine. I'd thought it was supposed to be about an hour each day.

The slightest hint of mirth twinkled in Mart's eyes. "Why, you got a hot date?"

Both kids turned three shades of red, and Cassandra rolled her toes inward, looking like a shy little girl at a spelling bee. "No, it's just that I've gotta . . . my . . . ummm . . . I'm supposed to . . . ummm . . . help my mom clean the rooms at the resort and . . ." She caught Mart's expression and stopped midsentence, studying his face, a look of awareness dawning. "You're, like, pulling my leg, aren't you?"

Mart chuckled. "You didn't read the water safety course brochure I sent home, did you?"

"No, sir. Guess I should've, huh?"

"Guess so."

"I think my mom read it." Cassandra smiled hopefully, and in spite of the fact that I'd been

319

determined not to, I found myself liking her. She seemed like a pretty nice kid, actually. Apparently, her mother expected her to work, which was more than could be said for most young people from this side of the lake.

Mart drummed his fingertips on his holster. "Your mom taking the class?"

"No, sir," Cassandra admitted, but she and Mart were smiling at each other when she said it. The implication was clear. He'd made his point without having to strong-arm anyone. It occurred to me to wonder why he didn't have a family of his own. He was good with kids—patient, firm, but with a sense of humor.

"The class'll go better if you'll read the brochure ahead of time, like you're supposed to. You'll know what to bring," he suggested. "You too, there, Dustin."

"I read it already." Dustin's declaration surprised me.

"Learn anything?" Mart addressed Dustin with the same good-natured yet authoritative tone he'd used on Cassandra. No doubt, his magic would fall flat this time.

"A little," Dustin admitted, and I watched with complete surprise as the snotty teenaged mask fractured slightly. "My mom told me to."

Mart's lips slowly parted into a smile. "You've got a good mom."

Right then, I could have thrown myself into

Mart's arms and kissed him. Dustin didn't agree or disagree with Mart's assertion, of course, and we drifted into an uncomfortable conversational lull, until finally Mart broke the stalemate. "So whose rig is that in the driveway? You trade the car in for a tricked-out four-by-four?"

Dustin perked up. "Four-by-four?" He craned toward the doorway.

Suddenly everyone was watching me with interest. "Borrowed it from my boss," I replied, as if it were the most natural thing in the world. "With all this rain, the roads are such a mess. I can't get to my appointments out in Chinquapin Peaks."

Mart quirked a brow. "You know how to drive that thing?"

"I took a lesson," I answered confidently. Didn't I look like a four-by-four driving kind of girl? Mart's eyes caught mine, and I knew he'd picked up on an undercurrent of challenge in those words—as in, *Want me to prove it?*

He touched his tongue to his lips, seeming to think about it. Fortunately, both Dustin and Cassandra were busy trying to catch a glimpse of my new ride.

"There's a four-by-four up there?" Dustin's voice cracked, and he swallowed and cleared his throat, then finished the sentence in his new man-voice. "Seriously?"

"There is," I confirmed, stepping out of the way. "Go check it out, if you want."

"Awesome!" Dustin's voice squeaked again, and Mart responded with a sympathy wince. Dustin bolted toward the yard, his footsteps echoing through the boathouse and causing the deck to rock on the water. A half-dozen steps outside the door, he screeched to a halt, remembering that he had company. "C'mon, Cassie."

Cassandra walked to the edge of the boathouse, stepped into the drizzle, then stopped. "Ummm . . . I better head back." Flicking a glance toward Mart and me, she hovered on the boat ramp, watching Dustin as if she were waiting for something. "I'll . . . ummm . . . see ya later, 'kay." She darted another glance my way, then added, "I mean, at the class Monday." I found myself watching her body language intently, wondering if she'd be sneaking back the minute I headed off to work. Maybe I should talk to Sydney and Ansley, try to discern whether they'd seen any visitors coming by the house.

"I'll text you," Dustin answered, torn between truck fancy and a cute girl. "You sure you don't want to hang around and see the truck?"

Cassandra's lips pouted, the bottom one jutting out a little. "I better not. I just got ungrounded, you know?"

"Okay, cool," Dustin said, and after another awkward moment, Cassandra waved good-bye with her thumbs still hooked in her pockets, then hurried to her bicycle and disappeared on a footpath that led to a public boat ramp down shore. Back in the day, a prominent *No Trespassing* sign had warned patrons of the public access area that the footpath was on Larkspur Estates property and was only for private use. Even then, kids from the public access area had often ignored the sign and ventured down the path to see how the other half lived. My sister and I liked to hang out at the boathouse and watch for cute boys strolling by. Who would have thought that a girl would now be biking that same path to visit my son?

Dustin jogged up the hill without looking back, leaving Mart and me alone at the boathouse. The situation suddenly felt intimate—a daylight re-creation of the night of the kiss.

"Guess we never did take that boat ride." Mart's mind seemed to be moving along the same channels as mine. He squinted toward the choppy water, his eyes a contemplative shade of green, almost the color of the water in this misty light.

The mention of the boat ride brushed a tingle of anticipation over my skin. I couldn't let him know that, of course. That kiss, that night, was so far away from anything I'd planned, it was still hard to believe I'd let it happen. "Well, there's no accounting for the weather."

He frowned at me, seeming disappointed that I

hadn't picked up on the unspoken invitation in his mention of a ride on the lake. "True enough. It's supposed to break tonight. I'm planning to try to get your CPS investigator up to Len's place via the water in the morning. It'll be another day or two before that last low-water crossing by his house is passable by truck. You're welcome to ride along tomorrow, if you want. I'm meeting the investigator and Reverend Hay over at the Waterbird, first thing."

Yes was on my lips before I'd even sifted through tomorrow's schedule in my mind. I had an early staff meeting, and then the day was packed with appointments, many of which had already been rescheduled, due to bad weather last week. On top of that, there was the issue of Dustin and Cassandra. Maybe I needed to make a surprise visit home for lunch. . . .

"I can't," I admitted. "The schedule is jammed tomorrow. Will you let me know what happens— not just with Birdie, but also with my other little client, Daniel? His grandmother is bringing him to the water safety course. I'm hoping it will be good for him. And could you maybe . . . keep an eye on Dustin while he's there . . . and Cassandra?" I winced, knowing I was asking too much, but I needed help, and there wasn't anyone else to rely on. "I'm sorry, I just . . . I'm worried, and . . ."

Mart stepped closer, and I felt my gaze being

drawn upward, into his. "It's fine," he said softly. "I don't mind."

For a moment, everything around me and everything inside me hushed—the sloshing of the waves against the dock, the soft *slap-slap* of wet leaves falling on the tin roof, the rhythmic croak of a frog somewhere down shore, the whirl of fear and worry in my head. There was nothing but the realization that I'd missed Mart while he was gone, and now he was finally back again.

Nature is always hinting at us.
—Robert Frost
(Left by an angler who didn't catch a thing,
but it didn't matter)

Chapter 18

Mart McClendon

Monday morning the weather finally broke. I was at the Waterbird early, waiting for the CPS investigator to show up. I'd sent Hay on ahead to see if he could catch Len on his way down to the lake and let him know that we'd be coming. I figured the more warning Len had, the more likely the meeting would go well. I wished Andrea could be there. Both Len and Birdie knew her, and she wasn't rushing to any judgment. My worry about bringing in an investigator was that the investigator might take one look and decide the easiest thing was to move that little girl to some kind of foster-care shelter.

At the Waterbird the docksiders were in rare form after days cooped up inside playing dominoes and drinking coffee, waiting for the storm to break. Pop Dorsey let me in on the fact that while they were hemmed in by the rain, Burt and Nester had sneaked into Sheila's coffee canister, dumped out all the decaf, and replaced it with the real stuff. Now they were buzzed on unlimited caffeine. They looked happy as horses on spring grass, sorting out their bait and tackle, getting ready to take to the lake.

"You need any help going up there to Len's place?" Burt asked, tying a little spinnerbait on the end of his line. "You got backup and all that, in case ol' Len goes off the handle?"

I shook my head. "I don't figure we'll need it. I was up there a couple times last week before the rain came in. Len didn't give me any trouble."

Nester cocked his head back, lowering a bushy eyebrow. "You probably don't know it, because you ain't from here, but when Len's mama went in the hospital for a stroke and ended up in the nursin' home, Len come down and stole her right out of the bed and took her back to that cabin. One of the attendants tried to stop him, and Len pointed a twenty-gauge shotgun at her. That man ain't normal."

"Odd duck," Pop Dorsey agreed, wheeling himself from behind the counter, since he didn't have any real customers in the store right then.

"Len's bait done swum the bucket a long time ago," Nester added. "If he really does have a daughter, she must be some kind of mess to leave a little kid up there. You know, maybe she didn't *want* to leave the little girl there. Maybe Len stole 'er. Maybe he threatened the mama or did somethin' to her, or . . ."

327

I held up a hand to get Nester to quit. A car had just pulled up outside, and I figured it was the CPS investigator. "Listen, all I'm doing is providing transportation across the lake. It's the investigator's job to get to the bottom of things. But it won't help any for you two to be filling his head with stories. So far I haven't had any trouble with Len—not over this situation with the little girl, anyway. I want to see he gets a fair shake. That's it."

"Be careful," Burt advised, and both Nester and Dorsey nodded, their faces real solemn. Then they started up a conversation about spinner-baits.

The door opened, and a kid, maybe in his midtwenties, stepped in. He was carrying a scuffed-up leather briefcase, so I figured he was my contact. I stepped up and introduced myself. Randy Alsup had the kind of soft, wimpy handshake other men don't respect, and he was geared up in loafers and dress pants. He looked like he'd stepped straight out of a college class somewhere and didn't have a clue that we were about to slog through the mud to a cabin in the middle of nowhere. If Len did give us trouble, this guy wouldn't be any help, but on the other hand, I had a feeling Randy was so out of his element, he could be talked into anything.

Maybe that was the way Andrea's boss had planned it. I'd already talked to her on the phone this morning, and she'd told me that her boss, Tazinski, *had it covered*. She figured that sometime in the next few days, she could have Birdie's referral in the bag—assuming Len made a decent showing in front of the investigator.

Nester and Burt slipped out of their seats, started gathering their gear, and waved their good-byes on the way to the back door. A couple of their buddies were already waiting down at the dock. I knew where they were all headed. They'd be in their boats, across the lake, and up the river channel before I could get there, then they'd hang around, dropping a line in the water and watching for me to come along with Randy in tow. One way or another, the docksiders were going to make sure that if something interesting happened, they were close by to see it.

Pop watched them go, his face long and forlorn. Back in the day, he would've turned the store over to his wife and been right there with them. I decided if everything went all right with Len, I'd cut off my workday when the water safety course was finished this afternoon. I could come back to the Waterbird and figure out what it would take to rig up the ramps to get Pop down to the dock. With some railings and gates down there, maybe Sheila wouldn't be so worried about Pop rolling off into the water.

If we worked at it, we might even be able to come up with a way to get Pop into a boat again—some kind of hoist and pulley. Right now, the man was a prisoner in his own store. The thing he liked the best was right outside his window, just a stone's throw away, but out of reach. It wasn't right for a good man like Dorsey to end up this way.

I pointed Randy toward the door and told him we'd better get going. He was agreeable enough, and we headed down the hill, talking about the weather. On the trip across the lake, he let me know that this investigation was just one of many. He'd only been in this job a few months, and he already had a list longer than his left arm. I had a feeling that the last thing he wanted to do was process more paperwork on Birdie than was absolutely necessary.

The farther we went across the lake, the more worried Randy looked. By the time we'd made it to the river channel, passed the bystanders in their boats, and started the trek through the woods, he'd asked me four times how much farther it would be. Guess he'd never gone to an appointment by boat and hike before. All the way up the hill, he kept checking the woods, still shadowy and quiet in the morning light. Some nocturnal critter scampered past in the brush, and I thought Randy was gonna jump out of his loafers. "What was that?"

"Probably just a bobcat or a coyote on the way to den up for the day."

"Holy smoke!" he whispered, his eyes tracking the sound.

"Don't worry. He won't come over this way." I started walking again, and Randy followed along, all the while watching the trees.

"People *live* up here?" he asked, about the time we were clearing the edge of the woods.

"Some people like it." We started through the tall grass toward the cedar break that hid Len's place. "They have their reasons."

Puppies scampered out from under the house when we cleared the Johnson grass and hit the broomweed patch that doubled as a farmyard. In back of the house, the big white pit bull woke and barked. A second later, another dog joined in, and Randy took out his pad, making notes while we slogged through the patchwork of mud and grass.

Hay was waiting on the porch with Len. The place looked freshly swept, and the raccoon skins that'd been hanging on the porch posts had been moved. Hay must've convinced Len to clean himself up, too, because he was wearing a plaid shirt that wasn't ripped, torn, or worn through, and he had on jeans that hung over his frame like a feed sack, but at least they were clean. I couldn't smell him from six feet away, either, so maybe he'd bathed, or maybe he'd just been out in the rain the last few days. His hair looked like it might've been combed, but it was hard to tell under the axle-grease-gray ball cap.

I stood off to the side while Hay made the introductions, and we took seats on a bent-up lawn chair, two overturned buckets, and a cooler with a crack in it. Randy explained why he was there, but it was hard to tell how much Len really understood. Andrea had warned Randy ahead of time not to mention Social Services or CPS. Len didn't react when Randy explained that he was from the Department of Family and Protective Services. That was more big words than Len could process all at once. For some reason, Len tried to get us to walk down the lane and look at his garden. Randy wanted to talk about the little girl, of course.

"Sh-sh-she slll-sleepin'," Len said, like that was explanation enough. He gave the screen door a worried look and touched a finger to his lips, letting us know we ought to be quiet.

"All right. Well, we'll talk to her in a few minutes, then." Randy checked his watch, then rubbed his forehead, frustrated already. He opened his notepad and started asking questions—how had Birdie ended up with Len, where was her mother, did Len have a phone number to contact her, had she indicated when she'd be coming back, did Len know where she lived? Len's answers were spotty. As was usual with Len, what was probably confusion and lack of understanding came off looking like stubbornness. Hay and I glanced at each other, knowing the interview

332

could have been going better. So far Len's story was that Birdie and her mother showed up a few weeks ago, in the middle of the night. They didn't have any suitcases with them—just some trash bags in the trunk of the car.

Len didn't know where his daughter lived, where his ex-wife lived, or whether the ex-wife was even still alive, but he had seen them from time to time in years past. After a little questioning, the pattern was clear enough. At some point, the ex-wife had figured out that between his military pension and what he earned trapping, fishing, and selling vegetables, Len usually had some spare cash stashed around. For years she visited when she needed money, bringing a little girl named Norma, who was supposedly Len's daughter.

Once Norma grew to be an adult, she knew the trick, too. It was even easier to pull off after Len's folks died. Len hadn't seen the ex-wife in a long time, but the daughter paid him visits every so often. If Len didn't have cash on hand, she sometimes stayed until his check came in. Then she took what she could get, and left. It sounded like she moved around a lot, because occasionally she stored stuff in the barn or the old school bus. She'd lived there a few times when she was out of a place to stay.

"Her ugg-gotta go back 'n work, all-time," Len said.

"Back to work?" Hay interpreted. "Do you know where she works, Len?"

Len shrugged his bony shoulders.

"Did she go back to work this last time?" I asked. I had a bad feeling about the kind of individual Birdie's mother probably was. A woman didn't show up in the middle of the night with her kid in pajamas and no suitcase unless she was running from something . . . or someone. Whatever had happened, Birdie had probably been through it right along with her.

Len shrugged again. "Uddd-dunno."

"And you don't have a contact number for her?" Randy pressed. "A phone number? A way to call her?"

"Unnn-no, sir."

"Maybe a check belonging to her, a piece of mail—something like that?"

Len rubbed his palms over his pants legs, fidgeting under the pressure of all those questions. "Unnn-nope. I uddd-dunno." He got out of his chair and told us he needed to go down to the lake to run his lines now. In his mind, the visit had gone on long enough.

"I'll need to talk to . . . uhhh . . ." Randy flipped through his papers, then finished his sentence. "Lillian now. I'll also need to see the inside of the house—her bedroom, the kitchen, and so forth."

Randy stood up and headed for the screen door, but Len beat him to it, then slapped a hand over the frame and held it closed. "Her s-s-sleepin'," he insisted, the word coming out in a hail of spit that made Randy glance at his notes. Tiny dots of moisture ran the ink.

"Do you leave her in the house alone when you go down to the lake?" Randy asked, and I had a feeling this meeting was about to slide off a cliff.

Hay must've been thinking the same thing, because he stepped in before Len could answer. "Now, Len, I explained to you that he was going to need to see the kitchen, and the house, and talk to Birdie. Remember? We discussed that, and you said it'd be okay."

Len squirmed like he had a nest of red ants in his shirt.

"Len," I said, but I didn't stand up. I didn't want Len to think we were putting the rush on him. "You know how the other day I told you there're rules about keeping wild animals—like that baby coon? Remember that? It's my job to look after wild animals and make sure they get the right kind of care from the right people, so that they can grow up and be safe and happy."

Len's gray eyebrows gathered low in his forehead, but he nodded, so I went on. "There're people who do that same job for little kids. They've got to make sure that when a little child stays somewhere, it's a proper place for a child. That's what Randy's here to do. He has to see inside the house to do his job. You understand?"

Len's look turned hard, and he squeezed a hand over his chin. "Y-y-you took my urrr-raccoon."

Right away, I realized I hadn't made the best comparison. The raccoon was a sore subject. "I know that, Len, but that was the law. When something's the law, you don't have any choice about it. The law says that Randy, here, has to see Birdie and see where she's living. As long as it's all right, you don't have anything to worry about."

Len stuck his hands in his pockets, a few coins jingling as his fingers dug around. He looked from me to Hay and back, his lips working back and forth over his teeth. "They ugg-got a ugg-game warden fer k-k-kids?" he asked, finally.

Hay nodded, and I said, "Yeah, Len, they do. They've got game wardens for kids."

Len's shoulders sank, and he took his hand off the door. If he didn't understand everything else, he did cotton that game wardens had authority, even when you were on your own property. He opened the door and went in without another word. Randy followed him, clipboard in hand, and Hay and I trailed after. Inside, the house smelled of mildew and fry grease. The corners of the living room and an entire front room that might've been a bedroom once were piled high with junk of all sorts—old clothes, magazines and newspapers, cardboard boxes filled with pecans Len must've collected last fall, empty milk jugs and laundry detergent bottles waiting to be used for jug lines, deflated inner tubes, beach towels, Styrofoam coolers, minnow buckets, shoes, flip-flops, flotation devices, and all manner of flotsam that'd probably been found around the lake.

In the center of the room, a threadbare sofa listed to one side, bulges of dirty foam rubber pushing through the green covering, like skin peeking through the gaps in a fat man's shirt. Across from the sofa sat a console television with rabbit ears that wouldn't pick anything up anymore. Not much chance Len had heard about the national conversion to digital signal. The screen and knobs were covered with a layer of dust—evidence that the set had been out of use for a while. Beside the sofa, a faded gold velvet recliner was draped with a quilt and pillow, like someone had been sleeping there regularly.

"Who sleeps here?" Randy asked, pointing with his pen.

"I ubbb-been," Len answered, and continued on through the living room, his hands nervously clenching and unclenching the front of his shirt. "I ugg-got food . . . for ubbb-Birdie." Without waiting for an answer, Len moved on through the doorway into the kitchen, which wasn't as bad as the living room. The sink was clear of dirty dishes, some mismatched china and a frying pan sat drying in a drain rack on the chipped green

Formica countertop, and above the counters, a bank of open shelves were packed with home-canned goods. It looked like Len's mother had taught him a few things. He knew how to wash dishes, make preserves, and keep a kitchen halfway functional. Watching Len in the tiny kitchen, his big ol' hands still worrying the front of his shirt, it was hard to picture him canning produce.

Hay and I stood in the doorway while Randy and Len moved around the crowded space. Len was talkative when it came to canned goods, and after a while it was clear that he wasn't working up sentence after sentence just because he was proud of his produce. After I mentioned the raccoon, he must've hit on the idea that he needed to show he could keep a little girl fed and watered, like a pet animal.

"I ugg-got 'maters, n' corn, n' pin-no bean. Ugg-got more in the ubb-barn." He started toward the back door, his eyebrows lifting hopefully, but Randy shook his head, standing in the gap to block Len's exit. The white dog in the backyard came to the screen and growled, and Randy sidestepped, putting the stove between the dog and his rear end. "I really need to see Birdie now." He pointed toward a closed door off the other end of the kitchen. "Is that her bedroom?"

"Ubb-bedroom?" Len asked, seeming confused by the question.

"Is that where Birdie sleeps?" Randy took a glance at his watch, blinked hard and frowned, like he couldn't believe how long this was taking. "Her bedroom. Is that Birdie's bedroom? Is that where she stays?"

" 'S my umm-mama's room." Len opened the back door and spit a plug into the yard. He gave the dog a pat before pushing it out of the way and shutting the door. "She don' like unn-nobody in 'er room. Mama udd-don't."

Hay slipped closer to the bedroom door. Other than a tiny bathroom and washroom off the side of the kitchen, and the junk-filled front bedroom, the area behind that closed door was the only other living space in the house. "I think it'll be all right if they go in, Len. It'd be okay with your mama, since that's where Birdie's been sleeping." Hay's voice was low and soft, patient. He laid a hand on Len's shoulder and guided him forward, and Len softened in his grip.

For a second I just stood there watching Hay's hand, wondering how long it'd been since anyone had shown that kind of tenderness toward Len. Most folks tolerated him at best and used him as the butt of their jokes at worst, but Hay treated him with the same care he would've given anyone—like all the talk about *Love thy neighbor as thyself* wasn't just talk with him.

Maybe the next time Hay came around my house in the evening, bringing vegetables he'd bought from Len or trying to talk me into helping with his latest production at the Tin Building, I'd be more welcoming. Maybe Hay wasn't trying to get nosy or push his way into my business. Maybe he saw in me a man who'd been raised going to church every Sunday, and gotten mad at God, and quit. Maybe he could tell that deep down inside of me, there was a part that'd started to face the fact that you're not always going to understand why God does things the way He does, but you don't do yourself any good by turning your back on your faith, either.

We found Birdie asleep in the bedroom, curled up next to the toy raccoon from the park gift shop. The place was surprisingly clean, except for a coating of dust that looked like it'd probably been collecting for years. The bedroom set was antique, but simple—an iron bedstead that was probably white once, a walnut dresser, a night table, and a washstand with a mirror. A blue-and-white enamel pitcher and basin still sat on the washstand, and next to it lay a woman's dresser set of brushes and mirrors like the ones my grandmother had when I was a kid. There was even a perfume bottle with a little billows bag on the back. The bottle was still half full, the perfume now thick and brown, the color of motor oil. Nothing in the room seemed to have been touched since Len's mother passed. Her shoes were still in the corner, her clothes in the closet, her Sunday hat hanging on the bedpost. Here and there, tiny fingerprints and wavy trails in the dust showed that Birdie had been investigating her surroundings. I wondered how Len felt about that, being as he'd kept his mama's room the same all these years.

I glanced over and caught Randy looking around, his forehead knotted up, like he couldn't figure out why the rest of the house was piled with junk, but this room was clean as a whistle, except for the dust. I realized that Len must've cared quite a lot about Birdie, to be letting her stay in a room he'd kept perfect all these years. Judging from the dishes and clothes in the old school bus, when Birdie's mother came here, either she bunked in the bus, or Len did. The only signs of activity in this room were Birdie's tiny fingerprints.

Randy moved around the interior, inspecting it from a distance, like he wasn't sure he should touch things, either. His toe hit the bedpost, and Birdie woke up, then rolled over and stretched, her blue eyes moving in a drowsy zigzag. She studied me for a minute, and I could tell she remembered me from before. Beside me, Hay leaned close and said, "Hi, Birdie. Did you have a good sleep?"

She answered by pulling the sheet up under her chin bashfully, then smiling a little, her eyes twinkling like she wanted his attention. Apparently, Hay's magic was still working on her. A cardinal jumped onto the windowsill, and Birdie smiled at Hay, sitting up and pointing at the bird. Pursing her lips, she did a pretty good imitation of the bird's call. It was the first time I'd ever heard her voice.

The cardinal flew off, and Birdie noticed Randy there in the corner. Her smile straightened, and she checked to make sure her grandpa was near. Scooting out from under the sheet, she moved across the bed and stood next to Len, her fingers fisted over his shirttail and the stuffed raccoon, her face partly hidden behind dark hair and partly behind Len's shirt, so that only one eye and a slice of frown showed.

She looked like a kid who knew that waking up with strangers in the room wasn't good. Len settled a big hand over her hair and patted her, his touch gentle.

Randy moved closer and sat on the edge of the bed, trying to get on her level and look friendly, I guessed.

His gaze hung for a minute on a group of dust-covered pictures on the wall behind Birdie— black-and-whites of a man holding a team of plowing mules, a crackled wedding picture of a woman, a photo of Len dressed in his army uniform. Next to it was a faded silk banner with a star on it—the kind parents hang in their windows to tell the world they've got a son serving in the military.

I looked into the eyes of the young man in the photo, wondered what thoughts were in this mind right before the photographer snapped the picture. It was tough to tell. Mostly, he seemed determined . . . and real young, just a kid playing dress-up, the hat oversized, the chin so clean he probably only had to shave every third or fourth day. Seeing him now, it was hard to imagine Len like that. It didn't seem like there was much of the bright-eyed young soldier inside the old man with the droopy mouth and the scarred-up ear, but he was there, I guessed. Len deserved more respect from folks than he got. Sometimes it was easy to look at where a man ended up in life and forget that he was once a boy, and he'd probably planned something better for himself.

I wondered if a guy as young as Randy could look at that picture on the wall and understand. Maybe he didn't want to. When you're young, you think you can go through the world like a steam locomotive on a straight track from here to there. You don't realize that sooner or later you'll run up against mountains you can't climb and canyons you can't get across. You'll make detours and stop to build bridges, gain passengers and lose passengers, experience things you couldn't have imagined. I doubted if Len had ever imagined that little girl who hung on his shirttail now.

Randy's interview with Birdie didn't take long, because Birdie didn't want to talk. Just like every other time I'd been there, she watched with eyes that showed understanding, but she never said a word. I knew it probably wasn't a point in Len's favor, but there was nothing to be done about it. Finally, Randy put his pen away, told Len he'd be getting back in touch and they'd be trying to contact Birdie's mother, and we left.

When we got back to the boat, the docksiders were still trolling around the river channel pretending to fish. They gave me the hawkeye as I loaded Randy and took him across the lake. When I looked back over my shoulder, I saw the docksiders catching up with Hay's boat, so they could do a shakedown for the latest news.

Randy and I didn't talk much on the way back to the Waterbird. Mostly, he seemed to be in a hurry, and at that point, so was I. The trip to Len's had eaten up more time than I'd planned, and if I didn't grab some lunch, take care of some things I had to do at my office, and hurry over to Andrea's to pick up Dustin, I'd be late for the water safety class. Considering that I was supposed to deliver the opening spiel about water safety and I'd contributed about half the population of the class on citation deals, that'd be pretty embarrassing.

When we got to the Waterbird, Randy grabbed his stuff, stepped out of the boat before I had it tied up, and just about ended up in the water. "Thanks," he said, after he got his feet under him. He stuck his hand out to shake mine. "And thanks for the assist today. This job sends me to some strange places, but that one takes the cake." It was hard to guess what he was thinking about Len or what he planned to do.

"Listen," I said. "It's not my business to tell you your job, but be fair with Len, all right? I know he's a different sort, and that place he lives in doesn't look like much, but Len's never given anybody any trouble. As far as I can see, he's a man trying to make the best of what he's got. I think he's trying to do what's best for that little girl, too."

Randy seemed to get my point—as well as someone who hadn't even hit thirty yet could, anyway. "I'll be looking at the case and trying to track down information about the mother, and then we'll see where we go from there." He thanked me again, then headed up the hill, taking the steps two at a time.

I went into the Waterbird for a sandwich, hoping it'd be just Dorsey behind the counter, but of course Sheila was there, and she wanted the rundown on what'd happened with Len. I let her know I was in a hurry for my sandwich, and that Hay would be along after a while. As much as

345

Hay liked to talk, he'd fill her in on the whole story.

Sheila wasn't happy about getting the brush-off. "Where are you headed in such a hurry?" she asked as she was putting my usual sandwich together.

"Corps of Engineers has the water safety class at the community center at two. I'm helping with it." I moved to the soda machine to fix myself a drink.

"Two?" Sheila glanced at the clock. "What's your hurry?"

"Got some things to do at the office, and then I need to head across the lake and pick up Andrea's son. She's putting him in water safety instead of letting him take the citation. Good choice."

"Andrea?"

"Henderson. Dustin's mom." I put a lid on my drink, then turned around and caught Sheila giving me the once-over. I realized about a half second too late that I should've kept my mouth shut.

"That's nice of you." She blinked with a one-sided grin as she handed me the sandwich.

"No big deal. She didn't have a way to get him there." I grabbed my stuff and headed for the door. "Put it on my tab, okay?"

"Sure, no problem." Bracing her palms on the counter, she leaned forward and smiled. "Tell *Andrea* hello for me, when you see her."

Every day is an open door to a new room.
—Anonymous tourist

Chapter 19

Andrea Henderson

Dustin arrived home from his first day of water safety class in a good mood. He and Mart had gone by the Tin Building Theater to talk to Reverend Hay about the Christmas play, and Dustin seemed to be considering it. "Sydney and Ansley probably won't leave me alone unless I do it, anyway. Their grandma goes to church up there, and they're gonna come and help paint sets or something." He rolled his eyes, but there was a hint of light in him this evening—a bit of the boy he'd been before the divorce. "Sydney and Ansley, like, bug me all the time. I can't even work in the yard without them following me around. Today their grandma made them go inside, and they pulled the screen off their window and dive-bombed me with water balloons." He huffed and tried to look disgusted. "There's probably a law against that. It's assault or something."

"They like you," I pointed out, trying not to smile since we were discussing a possible criminal offense.

"Whatever." His yawn took the shape of a smile, which he quickly covered with several fingers. "I had to come inside and change clothes after they got done throwing stuff at me. I was soaking wet. I think we should call the FBI. They're probably missing those two from juvie someplace."

"Dustin!" I squealed, laughing. It felt good. I couldn't remember the last time Dustin had cracked a joke.

"I'm serious," he added, then turned away and headed for the shower.

After showers, we shared a late dinner at the counter in the kitchen. Dustin noticed the light flashing on the answering machine, and I caught his hopeful look as he pushed the button. When the message wasn't from his father, his pleasant mood collapsed like a tower of dominoes. He didn't want to talk about it, of course, and as usual, he secluded himself in his room and cranked up his music.

I returned the answering machine message—a call from Megan. She was busy trying to get the twins in bed. She invited us to go to Oswaldo's company picnic in a couple weeks, and I jotted it on our calendar, trying to think positively about what the next few weeks might bring. Things were in such a state of flux right now, and two weeks was a long time in the life of a teenager. On the other hand, two weeks from now we'd be well into August, and there would be no denying that Dustin wouldn't be spending the month with his father. Maybe if I packed some fun activities into the schedule, it would soften the blow.

I turned on the television and tried to concentrate on something positive. As daylight waned and darkness fell, then deepened, I found myself watching points of light travel over the lake. I wondered if one of those boats was Mart's. I waited and hoped one would turn my way and drift up to the dock. The lights came, and passed, and came, and passed. Dustin fell asleep with his computer on and a movie playing. I went into his room and turned everything off, then covered him with a blanket.

My phone rang as I was closing his door and heading up the hall—Mart. The minute he flashed his lights by the dock, I was out the back door and running down the hill in the dark. I met him on the dock, and we sat talking. I revealed more than I'd meant to about my past history, and how I'd ended up divorced at thirty-eight and living in my parents' lake house. Mart didn't seem the least bit fazed by the load of baggage trailing behind me.

"Well, you know what they say," he commented as we sat side by side, gazing out at the moonlit water. "If you have one eye on yesterday, and one eye on tomorrow, you'll be cockeyed today."

I chuckled. "Well, now, there's a picture." Leaning back, I looked up at the moon. The here and now seemed pretty good at the moment. "I never noticed that advice at the Waterbird. They have so many quotes on that wall."

"Yep, it's there—on the Waterbird's wall of wisdom. There's another good one above the back door, but I can't think of it right now." I knew before even turning his way that he was smiling. "I remember reading the cockeyed one when I was a kid. My grandfather used to say it, too. We all just thought of it as an excuse to make cross-eyes at each other. We didn't really get the meaning, of course. Kids spend all their time looking forward—wanting to be older, waiting for birthdays, Christmases, the start of summer. You're either waiting for something to happen, or you're in the moment. You never hear a kid saying, 'I remember when I was seven-and-a-half. Man, those were good times.' That changes sometime after thirty, I think."

"Good point," I observed. Mart was something of a philosopher, when you got to know him. He pondered things. "I didn't realize that you lived here as a kid. I thought you'd just moved here." I couldn't remember why I had that impression—something he'd said in one of our conversations before, I supposed.

"It's a long story. Not all that interesting."

The tone of his voice, the intimacy of it, caused

me to turn his way, thinking, *I'm interested.* I wanted to delve further into the mystery of him, but he met my gaze, and I lost the thought. Something about him, this place, the night, was mesmerizing.

He kissed me then—a soft, tender kiss that reached into me and touched desires I'd never known were there. When I pulled back to look in Mart's eyes, there was a connection I couldn't explain. I felt as if I could show all the hidden parts of myself, even the little rebellious streak my mother swore would be my undoing. Mart didn't seem to expect anything of me, other than just to be myself, to sit talking about the day, or listen to a story about something that had happened to him at work, or analyze a quote from the Waterbird. The connection I felt with Mart was startling, exhilarating, and at the same time frightening. I wasn't ready for it. I wasn't ready for a relationship, and I didn't know if I'd ever be—yet here I was, on the dock with him again, the night and the moment sweeping me away.

He kissed me, and I let it happen. Again.

I didn't just let it happen. I gave myself over to it, to him, to the moment.

When the moment was over, after we said good-night and I went back to the house, reality crept over me, stealing away the comfortable, languid feeling. As I stepped in the back door, artificially chilled air encircling me, the dewy warmth of the night evaporated from my skin, and I just felt cold.

By the next afternoon, Birdie's referral was waiting for me in my inbox, an e-mail forwarded from Taz. "It's yours now," he said, standing in my doorway and smiling. "There's a service plan involved, too. Looks like it amounts to safety and cleanliness issues, mostly. If the grandfather wants to have a chance at temporary guardianship, he's going to have to remedy some deficiencies—do some work on his place, take care of issues with the dogs in the backyard, bring the girl in for a medical checkup, get her enrolled in school, and so forth. Once the school year starts, the school may want to do some testing, to see where she's at developmentally. Right now we don't even know how old she is for sure. Neither does the grandfather. The investigator asked him." Taz wagged a finger toward my computer screen, sighing and shaking his head. "Pretty strange case. You sure you want to take this on?"

I wondered, briefly, if I was getting in over my head, but the alternative to working things out with Len was an emergency foster care placement. Foster care in this county was incredibly overcrowded already. Every time I thought of moving Birdie, I saw her clinging to

Len's shirt, him leaning down so that she could whisper in his ear. If they were separated, would she close herself off completely?

"What—you don't think I can handle it?" The question came out sounding almost glib, which I knew Taz would appreciate. After two days of four-wheeling the back roads in Taz's pickup, I felt like a cross between Evel Knievel and Wonder Woman. There was something surprisingly empowering about four-wheel drive and a great big hemi engine.

"I think you can handle it." Taz gave me a sly smile.

I resisted the urge to put forth a gushing thank-you. "I might even be able to get through the low-water crossing tomorrow. I drove by there and checked it today."

"Don't get my truck washed off down a creek."

"I won't." I flipped a hand to let him know it was all under control. Everything seemed to be coming up roses the last two days, in spite of the general sogginess of the landscape. I'd made some progress toward convincing Lonnie that life with a man who beat her up in front of her kids, was cruel to animals, and threatened the school bus driver, wasn't healthy. My appointment with little Daniel's grandmother had yielded not only a good report about the water safety course, but the approval of more potentially healthy activities for a wannabe fifth-grade dropout.

Yesterday I'd even helped to find some support services for the mom whose husband was deployed with the military, and I'd talked a pregnant teenager into considering real drug rehab, instead of a do-it-yourself program that included hanging out with her old crowd.

Now having Birdie's referral safely in my hand felt like the icing on the cake. Mart was the first one I wanted to call. I was on top of the world and couldn't wait to share the victory with him.

"That truck's gone to your head," Taz observed, and a blush warmed my cheeks. It wasn't the truck that was in my head right now.

"I like the truck," I admitted. "Dustin and I think we need to trade in the car and buy one." Not that there would be a shiny new four-by-four appearing in my driveway anytime soon, but at breakfast Dustin and I had enjoyed doing a little fantasizing about buying a truck like Taz's. "When I make my first million."

Taz chuckled. "You need to move to LA and psychoanalyze reality-TV stars and potential plastic surgery patients to get the big bucks."

"Nah, I think I'm happy where I am." Taz and I smiled at each other, just as Bonnie wandered by.

She stopped and poked her head in the door, her gaze traveling from me to the big boss and back. "What's going on here? Everyone looks so . . . happy." In an office where the business was dealing with people's issues, the mood frequently ranged from vaguely preoccupied, to frustrated, to downright glum. At the moment, Taz was grinning like a dime-store Santa and rubbing his stomach with a look of satisfaction. "It's a good day when things work out. The old man still knows a few things, eh?"

"Nothing like learning from the best," I chirped, and held my hands in the air, bowing in homage over the desktop. I really was learning from the best. How I'd gotten so lucky, I couldn't imagine. This office was exactly where I was supposed to be, Taz exactly the kind of mentor I needed. My having landed here was practically a miracle. Practically . . . a gift? A gift from the God I had been certain had turned a blind eye my way?

With a belly laugh, the world's most supportive boss turned and left my office before things could grow too sentimental.

Bonnie gave me a quizzical look. "Wow, that's the happiest I've seen him in forever. He looks almost . . . relaxed. It's weird."

"He needs to relax a little." I swiveled back to my computer screen, because Bonnie had scooted a few more inches into my doorway and was starting to look comfortable there. I had reports to finish, and then I was ready to head home for the day. On the way I'd call Mart and let him know I'd gotten Birdie's referral and would need to set up an appointment time to meet with Len.

Since Len had no phone, I'd need Mart's help with that. . . .

I fought a giddy little smile, looking forward to the prospect. Unfortunately, Bonnie was still in my doorway. "You look happier than normal, too." The statement was open-ended, a question almost. "Seen the hunky game warden lately?"

"Huh?" I muttered, trying to appear too focused on work to be thinking about hunky game wardens. "Oh . . . ummm . . . not recently." I felt my cheeks sizzle. Spitting out a lie was incredibly wrong after two days loaded with undeserved blessings. Even so, I couldn't imagine letting Bonnie—or anyone else—in on my personal life, especially the part that included Mart. Which was exactly the problem. As much as I enjoyed spending time with Mart, as much as that time felt natural and right when we were together, I couldn't picture where this was going, or where it could. When I thought about other people finding out, about their reactions, about what my parents would say, what Meg would say, what old acquaintances from Houston would think, how Dustin might react . . .

My mind whirled and my stomach clenched at the idea. It had been over a year since my life with Karl fell apart, but still . . . What if people thought I was just out looking for a replacement, that I was jumping into a relationship because I couldn't make it on my own?

What if I was?

I swept away the mind storm before it could rain on my perfectly sunny day. *If you have one eye on yesterday, and one eye on tomorrow, you'll be cockeyed today.* Good advice from Mart and the Waterbird. For the time being, everything was fine. I just needed to concentrate on the present.

"Uh-huh . . ." Bonnie murmured doubtfully, and then she invited me to singles game night at her church again.

"I don't think singles night is for me, but thanks." I remained focused on the computer screen.

In the corner of my eye, I saw Bonnie take a step toward the door, giving up.

She turned to leave, then paused. "You know, there's lots of divorced people there. We've all got issues. God loves people with issues, too."

"I know." But the truth was that I didn't. Spreading your issues out on the table and having people love you anyway wasn't within my normal frame of reference. I suppose, in spite of all the times I'd heard *God loves you just the way you are* during Sunday school classes and women's retreats, or helped kids to write that phrase on construction-paper butterflies and keepsake bookmarks, I'd never really internalized it. I'd twisted the meaning to fit my perceptions. *God loves you when you're the way you're supposed to be, and so will other people.*

If you want to be loved, don't be impulsive, don't be careless, don't be flawed.

Yet, here was Bonnie, offering friendship when I'd rebuffed all her invitations, when I often made her job harder by bungling my own, when I was anything but perfect. I wasn't really even competent at my job yet. I hadn't done much to impress anybody, yet Taz was willing to support me, and Bonnie was inviting me to social engagements, showing me kindness I really hadn't earned.

"Maybe in a few weeks, when we're settled in," I said, and Bonnie backed a step into the hall, tossing a length of sleek blond hair over her shoulder, her eyes seeming too large and luminous in her thin face.

"Well, the invitation's always open."

I glanced up at her, and she smiled a private little smile.

"But in the meantime, you're crazy if you don't go after the hunky game warden."

I couldn't help it. I laughed. I didn't trust myself to answer.

"Just trying to be of assistance." Bonnie wandered off down the hall, and I went back to work with her suggestion buzzing around in my brain, making lazy circles like a dragonfly on a summer day.

You're crazy if you don't go after the hunky game warden. . . .

Bonnie's voice was still in my head two hours later, as I wrapped up my day and drove back to Moses Lake.

Topping the hill above the Waterbird, I spotted Mart's truck in the parking lot, and the gravitational pull was more than I could resist. I drifted in . . . to buy a soda and some sandwiches for supper . . . or . . . something.

When I stepped through the door, Mart was near the cash register, studying the doughnut case with serious interest. No one was behind the counter, and the usual crowd of coffee-drinking men had gathered on the back porch at the picnic tables. Sheila was busy cleaning the fryer in the kitchen area, so I let the door close silently, then tiptoed across the room to surprise Mart at the doughnut case.

For a half second, I was tempted to put a hand over his eyes and say, *Guess who?* Like an adolescent trying to flirt. Instead, I slipped in behind him and said, "Sir, I'm going to have to ask you to step away from the doughnuts." A giddy sensation fluttered through me as he started to turn around, and in an instant of wild abandon, I imagined stealing a kiss while Sheila's back was turned. How would he react, if I did?

I didn't have the guts, of course, and aside from that, I knew it would be the wrong thing to do. It would only further confuse an already muddled group of issues. Even so, the idea was like chocolate—tempting, hard to resist, a delight to all the senses.

Mart turned with a quick jerk, his face a mask of surprise that quickly changed to a guarded expression. It set me back on my heels. The welcome I'd expected wasn't there. My giddy flutter died, descending flightless. A random rush of thoughts compiled possible reasons for that look. Maybe he didn't want to be seen with me here. Maybe he was busy with work and didn't have time to talk. Maybe he had something else on his mind. Maybe he didn't like me after all.

Maybe he didn't think about those nights on the dock at least two dozen times a day. . . .

Maybe I was just something he did when he was bored in the evening. A way to pass time. . . .

Maybe he was he involved with someone else. Or more than one someone. . . .

Maybe he was here with someone else right now. . . .

The idea that Robin Hood might have other Maid Marians stashed here and there around the lake stung in a way I hadn't expected. I surveyed the room again, mentally preparing myself to see a woman there, to find him on a date with someone. The thought was humiliatingly awkward.

A head popped up from behind the candy counter, and I stood staring with my mouth open.

Cassandra? She glanced at Mart, and I knew they were here together. Her dark eyes widened at the sight of me, and her lips hung open a fraction, as if she didn't know what to say.

She ducked behind the counter, and my mind did a Bambi-on-ice scramble. What was going on?

Cassandra reappeared, and this time someone else was with her. Dustin?

A flash of trepidation crossed his face, but he quickly masked it. "Hey, Mom. I was just gonna call you. I mean, I woulda called earlier, but I knew you were working."

"What are you doing here?" I groped mentally, trying to piece together an explanation. How had Dustin gotten here? Had Mart come in just before me and caught Cassandra and Dustin in the store together? That would explain the weird look when Mart saw me. Maybe he was afraid World War III was about to erupt.

Dustin glanced sideways at Mart, and Mart rolled a stern look in Dustin's direction. "I thought you said you called your mom, Dustin."

My son squirmed, his shoulders wriggling as if his T-shirt were made of steel wool. "I was gonna . . . as soon as she . . . got off work." Clearly, he was making the sentence up at he went along, searching for something that would smooth the waters. He lifted both eyebrows in a beseeching look that said, *Please don't make me look like a stupid little kid right now.* "I knew you'd be in counseling sessions and stuff, and then we got busy and . . . well, I forgot. That's all."

"Dustin . . ." After fourteen years as a mother, you know that *I forgot* really means *I was afraid you'd say no, and I wanted to do what I wanted to do.* It's easier to ask for forgiveness than permission.

"My fault, totally," Mart stepped in. "I should've made sure he called before we headed out." All of a sudden, I felt like they were ganging up on me—conspiring the way Megan and I used to when we were trying to get around my parents' razor-wire fence of rules.

Conspiring the way Megan and I used to . . . Was I jumping to conclusions, thinking the worst when I should have been keeping an open mind? Dustin was with Mart, after all. Didn't I spend my days teaching parents how *not* to escalate conflicts with their kids—how to be fair, nonjudgmental, and open-minded until they'd gotten all the facts and considered them rationally?

I took a deep breath, pulling the lid off the boiling pot and letting the steam dissipate. "Well, so what's going on? What did I miss?"

Dustin and Cassandra were momentarily shocked, and then Dustin stepped from behind the candy shelf, looking newly confident that shrapnel wasn't headed his way. "The projector and sound system in the community center blew a cog before water safety class, so the dude from the church, Reverend Hay, brought over his projector and sound system so we could have class. But then his equipment wouldn't work either, so the COE dude just, like, talked to us, and we were out early. I told them I knew about sound systems because Dad and I used to run ours at church, and I could probably fix it, so we took it over to our house. Then Mr. McClendon had to go check some boats for these zebra mussel clam-looking things that are an invasive species. They're bad for the lake. He asked if I wanted to go along and help, so I did. Then we came by here to grab a coke and a candy bar, and Cassandra was next door helping her mom clean cabins, so she came over. Mr. McClendon's about to go to the dock and do some measuring to build ramps and a guardrail so Pop Dorsey can get down there in his wheelchair, and I told him if he needed help, I didn't have anything big going on right now."

The sentence finished on a hopeful high note that pleaded with me to leave him at the Waterbird, where he could do man projects in view of the cute girl. "Beats the heck out of sitting at home," he finished, as if he'd just remembered that acting too enthusiastic might affect his coolness rating.

"It's easier to do that job with a couple extra

hands," Mart added and cast a sideways glance at me, his eyes a warm camo green. It looked like Dustin wasn't the only one enjoying the day.

I vacillated between making some excuse that Dustin was needed at home, and letting him go. Having Mart give my son rides to water safety class was one thing, but seeing them acting like friends was another. The idea of letting Dustin develop a connection with a man I'd met just a couple weeks ago felt like a risk, a tiny crack in the security fence. When it came right down to it, I knew very little about Mart. I had no real idea what his intentions were. I knew very little about his past, or how he'd ended up in Moses Lake, or his plans for the future. Most of our conversations had been about his job, Birdie, or about me. Even if I was willing to dangle myself over what might turn out to be an emotional cliff, I couldn't afford to take chances with Dustin. Beyond that, there was a deeper question—what if Mart was only interested in Dustin because Mart was interested in me? If . . . when I finally had to come down to earth and admit to Mart that I wasn't ready for a relationship and didn't know when I'd ever be, would he toss Dustin aside like yesterday's news? Dustin couldn't take one more rejection in his life.

On the flip side of the coin, there was my son, bright-eyed, smiling, enthusiastic for the first time in months. Even Taz's four-by-four hadn't lit him up like this. He had the gleam of looking forward to something, of enjoying the moment and not worrying about what lay ahead or behind, or the fact that August was less than a week away.

Above the doorway to the back porch, a plaque caught my eye. The bit of backwoods wisdom Mart had mentioned last night but couldn't call to mind at the time.

Stop looking ahead. Stop looking back. Stop. Look around.

I took in my son's buoyant smile. How long since I'd seen him this happy? How long since he'd had a moment like this? I couldn't even say.

"Sure," I answered. "Sure. That sounds like fun. I'll see you at home when you're finished, all right?" My heart caught in my chest, as if I were blindly feeling my way through a dark house, knowing that something dangerous could be hiding around any corner. By the time I saw it coming, it would be too late.

"Thanks, Mom." Dustin grinned ear to ear, then quickly toned down the boyish enthusiasm. "Cool. I'll see ya later, then." Clearly, that was my cue to get out of the way and let the evening's adventure continue.

For an instant, I was jealous. I wanted to be in on the fun, rather than heading home to cook supper and pay this month's bills.

"Do you need some money for a snack?" I asked Dustin, reaching into my purse.

"I got it." Mart opened the doughnut case and made a selection, then waved Dustin to the counter. "I owe Dustin for the help this afternoon."

Nodding, Dustin whispered something to Cassandra, then headed to the cash register with his candy bar in hand. I left Mart and Dustin standing side by side at the counter, looking out the window and talking about guardrails.

When Dustin came home later, he was as happy as a boy with summer reading and half an English workbook to complete could be. While telling me about his day, he ate the sandwich I'd left for him. An old Robert Redford movie, *Jeremiah Johnson*, came on TV, and we sat watching it together.

After finishing his supper, Dustin stood behind the sofa, as if he couldn't quite decide whether to stay with me or go to his room.

"Stay and watch awhile," I said. "You can work on your English homework in the morning."

" 'Kay." He shrugged and sat down. "Ummm, by the way . . . Is it okay if I go help next week down at the Tin Building Theater? They're working on some sound and lighting stuff. The Rev asked if maybe I could work with them on it. I told him about the huge sound booth that Dad . . . at our old church."

"The Rev?"

Dustin nodded hopefully. "Reverend Hay.

Cassandra calls him the Rev. She goes there to church . . . at Lakeshore Community, I mean."

"That sounds fine," I said.

His eyes lit, just as they had when I'd given the green light earlier that afternoon. "Thanks, Mom."

He watched a few more minutes of the movie, then brought up another subject without looking away from the screen. "We're starting the ramps and the guardrail on the dock tomorrow afternoon, so Pop Dorsey can get down to the lake in his wheelchair. I can go, right?" His level of interest was surprising. A motherly sixth sense told me that a good deal of that interest was related to Cassandra. Part of me wanted to say no, to keep Dustin safely at home in his little cocoon. On the other hand, he needed to know that I trusted him, that I believed in him. He needed to be allowed to begin navigating the path through teenagerhood, with all the rights, privileges, and stumbling blocks that involved.

"All right, but make sure you're paying attention to the power tools and not just looking at girls, okay."

Dustin blushed and swallowed hard, nodded, and focused on the movie. Watching him, I vacillated between being grateful for the newfound enthusiasm and worrying about it. As nice as Mart seemed to be, as much as Mart had assured me that Cassandra was a sweet girl, all of this felt like a risk, a potential train wreck in the making. I'd just let Dustin step onto the train.

Even as those cautionary notes played in my head, I found myself watching the lake with one eye and the movie with the other. Somewhere between Robert Redford being a greenhorn and learning to survive in the mountains, Dustin fell sound asleep on the sofa. After that, I watched the lake with both eyes, looking for lights in the cove.

Outside the window, Larkspur Cove remained dark, and as the clock ticked past eleven, I felt a heavy sense of disappointment. Mart wasn't coming tonight.

Just as I was finally facing that fact and getting ready to wake Dustin so he could move to his bed, the phone rang. I grabbed it and headed for the porch, answering with anticipation pinwheeling in my windpipe, making my voice higher than usual and syrupy sweet. "Hey." I searched the lake, looking for Mart's boat. "What's up?"

He yawned before answering. "Aw, stuck out here in my truck. Had a complaint called in about some yay-hoos night-shooting coyotes off a county road. There's a state park campground a couple hundred yards through the trees. Idiots." He yawned again, and I pictured thick, dark lashes brushing his cheeks.

"You sound tired." The words seemed intimate, like pillow talk.

He laughed softly, and I felt it deep in my chest. "Some long nights catching up with me."

I blushed, even though no one was there to see it. I was responsible for at least the last few of those long nights. Once Mart and I started talking, it seemed as if we could go on forever—not about anything vital, just silly things. Stories from the lake, the quirky people he ran into on the job, my work, his work.

Last night we'd talked about the water safety class, and how Dustin, Cassandra, and my ten-year-old client, Daniel, were doing. Once, I'd even found myself laughing about Meg and me, and how we'd spent our teenage years tangled in a tooth-and-nail battle of sibling rivalry.

I can't imagine what you'd have to be jealous about, Mart had said. *But then again, I haven't met your sister.* He'd given me a flirty look that was evident even in the dim light. I'd swatted him and told him Meg was married. He'd grinned and said, *Just my luck,* and then he'd kissed me.

Remembering that kiss now brought a surprisingly potent sense of disappointment. He wouldn't be motoring up the cove tonight. This cell call was it. Some logical part of me said that was probably for the best. Things were happening way too fast. Still, I cradled the phone on my shoulder, hugging my knees. "You should turn in earlier."

"Had better things to do."

My skin went hot and prickly all over. It was probably a good thing he wasn't here in person tonight. "So, I want to move forward on Birdie's referral as soon as possible." Sliding into work talk was what my boss would have referred to as a *defense mechanism*—a way to maintain distance when things got too close. Probably a smart move, all issues considered.

Mart didn't seem conscious of the switch. "Yeah, I got your text message. When're you heading up there?"

"I have a slot at eleven a.m. tomorrow, and I think I can get through the low-water crossing, but I don't have any way of knowing if Len will be home. It's not like I can ring his cell. I hate to ask, but is it possible for you to let him know I'm coming?"

"Len is usually hunkered down at the house in the heat of the day, but I'll catch him out on the lake in the morning and let him know your plans. If he has a problem with the time, I'll call you." He paused, and I heard a radio call in the background. He turned down the sound before coming back on the phone. "How about lunch after?"

Air bounced like a basketball behind my ribs. "If you'll set up things with Len for me, I'll even bring the chow."

Mart laughed. "Well, that's an offer I can't refuse. I was gonna suggest lunch at one of the bakeries in Gnadenfeld or at the artist colony, though."

Even though I undoubtedly wouldn't see anyone I knew at either place, the idea of our going out in public together tightened the muscles in my spine and tamped down the fluffy air ball in my stomach. "I'd rather listen to the mockingbird, I think."

"Sounds perfect."

We arranged a time, and then the conversation ended abruptly when he saw a spotlight through the trees.

"Be careful," I told him.

"Always," he answered, and hung up.

I said a little prayer for his safety, without even realizing it at first. From that thought I drifted, somewhat unconsciously, into a vague contemplation of what it would feel like to be with someone who put himself in harm's way for a living. Before the thought process could go too far, I cut it short, covered Dustin with a quilt, and went to bed.

I fell asleep thinking about the trip to Len's house and wondering how the visit would go. I'd never been there alone before, but sooner or later, I had to start. It wasn't right to ask Mart to hold my hand when I went to Len's this time. The man did have a job of his own to do, after all.

In the morning, I started the day with a murky sense of trepidation, as if something had happened overnight and I wasn't aware of it yet. The feeling stayed with me through a staff meeting at the office and my first client session of the day, during which both Daniel and his grandmother gave glowing reports about the first two sessions of water safety class. Now Daniel wanted to be a game warden or work for the Corps of Engineers when he grew up.

After I left the Crandall house, I sat in the car for a few moments, trying to gather my thoughts and analyze the knots in my stomach. Birdie's case wasn't so different from others I'd taken on in this job. Why did it seem different? Why, when I imagined her, did I see the image from my dream—the one in which she was balancing on the bridge railing, innocent, vulnerable, unaware that she was in danger?

Perhaps it was the mystery surrounding her that concerned me most, or perhaps it was Birdie herself. What secrets were hiding behind her soft blue eyes, and how could I unearth them? What had happened to silence her voice? What was she afraid of now? Where had she been before she came to Moses Lake?

The questions swirled randomly as I drove the road to Len's house, fording mudholes and bouncing over furrows cut into the roadbeds by runoff from the weekend storms. The low-water crossing was touch-and-go, but I made it and crawled up the other side with all four tires grinding through the wet caliche, showering the truck with dirt, pebbles, and mud. If my boss saw all the mud, he'd probably make some joke about my abusing his truck, and then he'd pat me on the back and call me *cowgirl*. If he had any doubt that I could handle Birdie's case, he hadn't shown it. *Just go with your gut,* he'd advised. *When you get there, you'll know what to do.*

I hoped he was right, because as the truck idled quietly up the lane to Len's farm, my gut wasn't doing anything but churning.

Turning the corner, I peeked through a gap in the wall of scrappy cedar trees and spotted activity in the tomato patch down the hill. Len was slogging through the garden mire, tying up tomato plants that the storm had beaten down. He'd obviously been at it for a while, because his boots and threadbare jeans were caked with mud. Behind him, Birdie was similarly attired—mud-caked jeans and a T-shirt that had probably come from the emergency stash at Lakeshore Community Church. Her oversized red boots had been cinched onto her feet with twine again, but the heavy mud sucked her down with each step, forcing her to hold the boot tops with her hands, so that she duck-walked along after Len. Over one arm she had a plastic bucket that appeared to be for collecting tomatoes knocked from the vine during the storm. Every step or two she stopped, let go of the boots long enough to gather fallen produce off the ground, then hooked her bucket over her arm and resumed the duck walk. Len waited patiently for her to catch up before moving to the next plant.

Near the middle of the row, Len lifted a fallen tomato vine, took something from underneath, held it flat in his hand, and leaned down to show Birdie. Their heads bent close over his palm, and I could tell that they were talking. A moment later he pointed to the trees in the old fence line at the edge of the garden. Setting down her bucket, Birdie stood with her hands braced on her hips, studying the branches with obvious curiosity. Finally, she pointed, jittering excitedly in place. Steadying her hand, Len pulled something from his shirt pocket and laid it in her palm. She asked a question, and he answered. But for the mud and Len's torn, grease-stained clothing, they could have been the postcard picture of grandfather and grandchild, enjoying a sunny day in the garden.

I watched, feeling like a voyeur as they continued on to the next plant, where Len plucked something from the wire tomato cage and placed it on Birdie's arm. Cocking her head to one side, she held the arm stiff in front of herself. I leaned out the window, my curiosity piqued. Pointing a stubby finger, Birdie gently touched whatever Len had given her. A caterpillar, I decided, even though I wasn't close enough to see the details. I knew how it would feel against her skin—a soft, brushy tickle, almost as if it wasn't really there.

My mind rushed back in time, and I remembered my grandmother doing the same to me when I was small and Megan too young to compete for my space. Back then, I felt like the apple of everyone's eye—the one who was big enough to point out redbirds and bluebirds, and help my mother and grandmother plant flowers in the garden. Before Meg had learned to talk, walk, run, dance, cheerlead, and be good at everything, I was the one everybody admired. My mother and I actually had a little bit in common before I grew a chip on my shoulder and became determined to resent anything she liked. Why had I let go of the good memories, in favor of recalling all the years Mother and I butted heads and Meg and I had tangled like sumo wrestlers in the ring of sibling rivalry?

Birdie threw her head back, laughing, and I heard the voices of my own childhood—high, light, filled with joy. Joy, I realized, isn't so much a circumstance you find yourself in but a choice you make. There was Birdie, in what most people would have considered to be bleak circumstances, yet her face was alight with happiness over something as small as a caterpillar and a moment of her grandfather's undivided attention.

There was a lesson in that for me. Most of my life, I'd been focused on all the things I thought should be different, better, easier, less painful, or all the ways I thought I needed to be different. But when you're busy worrying about what should be, you miss what is. I'd let moments like Birdie's with the caterpillar slip by unnoticed, unenjoyed. A moment unappreciated is a moment lost. I'd wasted far too many moments in my life.

Letting off the brake, I rolled past the line of cedars and down the hill, the sloshing and rattling of the vehicle causing Len to notice me and stand up, squinting toward the road. I lowered the side window, so that he would know who I was. Birdie turned and saw me, and her smile faded into a suspicious frown. Slipping behind Len, she brushed the caterpillar into her tomato bucket and added whatever she'd been holding in her hands.

They met me at the edge of the driveway, neither seeming pleased that I was there. I put on a friendly face and tried to make things as nonthreatening as possible. Establishing a good rapport was critical to long-term success. I introduced myself and asked if they remembered me from my visit here with Mart, and then I explained why I had come this time.

Len only stood frowning at me, and Birdie

slipped farther behind his leg, muddy denim clutched in her fists.

"I guess Mart McClendon told you I'd be coming by to see you?" I said, finally.

Len nodded. "Yyyy-yes'm." He paused to stomp the mud off his boots. "Y-y-you a ugg-game uww-warden fer uhhh-kids, too?"

"A what?" I killed the engine and opened the door. This was as good a place to park as any. I doubted I'd be blocking traffic in Len's driveway.

"A ugg-game uww-warden fer uhhh-kids." Len's leathery skin reddened, the saggy side of his mouth struggling over the production of each word. I felt guilty for forcing him to repeat himself, but I had no idea what he was talking about. "Y-y-you ugg-gotta see ubb-Birdie's urr-room, where s-s-she uhhh-sleepin'."

It occurred to me then that Len was equating my visit with that of the CPS investigator, and that somehow he'd decided that the investigator was similar to a game warden. He turned, as if to lead me to the house, but just from looking at the place, I wasn't in a hurry to go in. Aside from that, it was a clear summer day, and I had a feeling that both Birdie and Len would be more relaxed outside.

"I don't need to see Birdie's room right now. I just come to do counseling sessions. . . . To talk," I said quickly. "Your caseworker will probably

377

want to look around the house when he comes, but that might not be for a week or more."

With the current backlog, there was no telling when Birdie's CPS caseworker would pay a visit. In general, caseworkers in this county were doing well to check in once a month. Typically, those were short visits. Because my counseling sessions with client families were weekly, and an hour long each time, I was the one with regular contact. "If you like, we can talk more about what your CPS caseworker will be looking for, what things they'll need you to do for Birdie. If there are issues you're worried about, we can talk about those, too."

Len's shoulders lifted in an uncomfortable shrug, and he slipped his hands into his pockets. He swallowed hard, his lip hanging in a lopsided arc afterward.

"Is there a place we could sit down?" I asked. Here at the edge of the tomato patch, the sun was beating down, so that it felt like a blast furnace. A channel of nervous perspiration had started dripping down my back, wetting my T-shirt. "Over there in the shade, maybe?" I pointed to some hunks of cut-up tree trunk underneath the scrubby elms in the fence line.

Len acquiesced with another shrug, and we walked through the soggy grass to the shade— Len leading the way, with Birdie clinging to his pants, and me following. The logs were wet, the humidity thick even in the shade, but I imagined that this was still a more comfortable location than the house. There was an old portable air-conditioner hanging in one of the side windows, but it didn't appear to be running at the moment. I could only guess what it felt like and smelled like inside the house after several days of rain.

I selected an upturned tree slab, looked for spiders and other crawly things, then sat down. Len used a muddy boot to roll a three-foot section of trunk and check underneath, then he sat down across from me. Birdie stood a short distance away, silent and suspicious as I did my best to explain things to Len and tell him what would happen next. It was painfully slow going. With Len, there were no reference points for terms like *permanency plan, advisory hearing, alternative family placement,* and *parental rights.* "The caseworker probably mentioned that CPS can seek a conservatorship, if Birdie's mother isn't able to take care of her properly. Did you understand what he was talking about there? Did the caseworker explain?"

Len pulled a dirty bandana from his pocket, shook his head, and wiped his brow. "Unnn-nope. I udd-don't think . . ." He scratched his forehead, seemingly trying to remember. Finally, he folded a fist and tapped it against his forehead. "My umm-mind udd-don't know things ugg-good."

I felt a rush of sympathy for him. How

frustrating would it be to live with a mind that had been normal but was now struggling along, sluggish and uncooperative? "That means that the caseworker—the game warden for kids—would keep looking after her while she's staying here with you. They'll give you lists of the things that have to be done to make sure Birdie is healthy and the house is a safe place for her to be. Those will be things like we just discussed when I talked about the service plan—getting her signed up for school, cleaning the inside of the house, perhaps doing some repairs, making sure the dogs are safely fenced away from her, keeping guns locked up, seeing that she isn't left by herself in the house, or allowed near the water without someone watching her, and so on. If Birdie is going to stay here, you'll have to do that whole list of things, and you'll have to keep doing them as long as she's here. We could probably find people to help you with some of it. Does that make sense?"

Len's lips trembled, and he looked at the ground, shaking his head. "I udd-don't . . . udd-don't . . ." Flustered, he mopped his neck with the bandana again. He was sweating even more than the heat called for. He looked up at me, his eyes red-rimmed and moist. "My umm-mind udd-don't think ugg-good unn-no more." His voice hitched on the last word, and Birdie left her bucket and came to stand behind him. Sliding her tiny arms around his shoulders, she rested her chin there, as if she were trying to comfort him. He had the look of a defeated man, and my heart tugged. Clearly, he loved his granddaughter and wanted to take care of her. How much was that love worth? Was it worth living in a ramshackle house in the middle of nowhere, with a caretaker who had cognitive limitations?

Birdie's wide, blue eyes studied me, her expression soulful, bleak, silently pleading for me to leave things alone. They didn't teach you how to deal with situations like this in psychology class.

"Listen." I reached across the space between us and laid my hand on Len's arm. "I'll do everything I can to help you. I promise." My mind spun ahead. I didn't even know how well, or if, Len could read the list of items on the DFPS Service Plan. If Birdie's medical checkup showed signs of former abuse or neglect, things would become even more complicated. Either way, there would be court proceedings. Someone would have to help Len understand the schedule of appointments— where to take Birdie and when. I could see about arranging a Court Appointed Special Advocate, CASA, volunteer to assist. Then there was the house. Len wouldn't know how to get it into some sort of acceptable condition. Habitat for Humanity wouldn't consider coming all the way out here. Perhaps some volunteers from Moses Lake, or a church, or charity? Len didn't like visitors. Would he cooperate?

What if Birdie's mother came waltzing back in the same way she'd left?

Maybe a CPS conservatorship and a foster home would be best. It's the simplest way, the easiest. . . .

But I'd made that promise to Len for a reason. There was nothing easy or simple about the look in Birdie's eyes. She clung to her grandfather the way a flood victim clings to a tree—as if he were the last solid thing in the world. Somehow I had to make sure that in trying to help her, we didn't do harm.

"I'd like to talk to Birdie for a while now, if that's all right." Our appointment time was ticking away, and I hadn't even attempted to make meaningful contact with Birdie. "Maybe she and I could take a little walk, and she could show me her room, or some things she likes to play with."

Len's lips worked back and forth over his teeth, and he shifted uncomfortably, touching the circle of Birdie's arms.

"We won't go far." I tried to appear reassuring, accessible, safe. "Just to the house." Birdie flicked a glance toward the yard. "So she can show me what things she likes to do." Typically, kids were more willing to talk about pets and favorite toys than anything else.

Rubbing the stubble on his chin, his lips pleating and smoothing, Len nodded, finally. "She ugg-got a c-c-coon." Saliva sprayed over my arm, and I fought the urge to wipe it on my jeans. "A p-play c-c-coon. Ugg-go show 'er, Birrrdie."

Birdie unlaced her arms and disconnected herself from Len, then stood with her hands balled into fists and her head tucked.

"It'sss all urr-right." Len patted her on the head as he might a favorite dog. "Ugg-go on." He rose from his seat as Birdie moved a few steps onto the driveway. Birdie cast an uncertain look at him, digging a toe in the gravel. "Uggg-go on," Len said again, picking up the buckets.

I walked to the driveway, stood beside Birdie, and extended a hand to see if she'd take it. "Birdie, can you show me some of your favorite things? Things you really, really like?"

Her response was a bemused frown, and rather than taking my hand, she spun around, dashed back to Len, and tried to grab the tomato bucket. Len resisted the pull at first, but then she whispered something, and he lowered the bucket to let her reach inside. She slipped in one hand, pulled something out and held it in her fist, then slipped in the other and repeated the process before clomping through the ditch to stand with me again. Apparently, the first things she wanted to show me were rescued tomatoes.

"What do you have there?" I asked, bending close to her and tapping the back of her hand. "Did you find something interesting in the bucket? Did you bring something for me to see?"

Her eyes brightened, her cupid's-bow lips quirking sideways, as if she were trying to hide a smile.

"Is it a surprise?"

Tucking her chin and hiking her shoulders, she offered a barely audible snicker.

"Can I see? I love surprises." I held out my hand, palm up, and she rested one fist inside it, then slowly revealed the contents. In her palm lay a tiny eggshell, soft blue and paper-thin, in jagged halves, like two pieces of a puzzle. "Oh," I said, touching it with a fingertip. "That's beautiful. Look how small it is. I guess there must be a nest near your garden." Turning the shell gently, I studied it, realizing that while they were working in the garden, Len had been taking her on a treasure hunt of sorts—showing her caterpillars and hatchling eggs blown from a nest in the storm. Things most people would walk by without noticing. That kind of attention was rare and valuable for a child like Birdie. For any child. "I wonder what sort of baby bird came out of this egg?"

Grinning, Birdie brought up her other hand, opened it beside the eggshell, and revealed a tiny feather no larger than my thumbnail. The sun reflected against it, causing it to glow iridescent blue.

"Oh, that's so pretty," I whispered.

Bending close to my hand, Birdie rolled the eggshell and the feather carefully into my palm, then stroked the feather. "Pretty bird." Her voice was little more than a breath, but I heard it. The words were clear and intentional.

"Yes, a very pretty bird." Emotion choked my throat, and for a moment our situation felt anything but clinical. "A bluebird, I think."

"Blue," she whispered. The breeze lifted her hair, so that I could see her face, her eyes the deep hue of the feather, as fragile as the eggshell. "Blue pretty bird," she whispered, and smiled.

"Yes," I agreed, and then she stepped away, turning toward the house. I closed my fingers over her tiny treasures, and as we walked up the driveway, she slipped her hand over mine, as if she were protecting them, too.

When we reached the house, we deposited the eggshell and the feather safely in an empty butter tub from her soggy sand pile, and then proceeded with a tour of Birdie's favorite things—her plush toy raccoon, a used baby doll that must have come from the church, pink Barbie pajamas that had been carefully laid on her bed.

A pair of tennis shoes in her size and some clothing sat piled partially in a used grocery bag in the back bedroom, as if it hadn't occurred to anyone to put the things away after Reverend Hay brought them. Considering the rest of the house, that was no surprise. The edges of the rooms were filled with accumulation of all sorts, allowing living space only in the centers. No telling what might be lurking in all those piles.

In the old school bus beside the house, Birdie showed me a partial set of plastic dishes and a generic Barbie. Apparently she'd been using the bus for a playhouse—dirty clothes, puppy droppings, and all. My stomach wrenched as we finished the tour and returned to the fresh air. Near the barn, Birdie captured a scrappy-looking calico cat and carried it as we walked back to the garden to find her grandfather. On the way, I asked questions about her mother and where Birdie had been before coming to Grandpa's house. All of a sudden, she didn't have anything to say.

I left the appointment uncertain of what should happen next, but also firm in the conclusion that, after several days at home alone with Len during the storm, Birdie seemed to be happier and more communicative than she was the first time I'd seen her. She was getting better, not worse.

At lunch, Mart and I discussed the visit while the Wailing Woman sang her soft, moaning song, and the mockingbirds responded in kind. A call came in on Mart's radio, and lunch ended abruptly, with Mart apologetically grabbing his barely touched sandwich and heading for his boat, and me checking out the park restroom, then finishing lunch in the car with my computer while a group of canoers stopped on the shore below to picnic.

That evening Dustin came home dirty and tired from helping with the dock project at the Waterbird, but he was in an upbeat mood. Mart had been called away again, so Reverend Hay had dropped Dustin at our dock. Before heading for the shower, Dustin filled me in on the afternoon's dock building and the plans to create some sort of hoist system that would allow Pop Dorsey to get out of his wheelchair and into a boat. Tomorrow one of the Waterbird regulars planned to bring a portable welder, and Dustin was going to learn to weld. I was obliged, of course, to offer a few cautionary mom notes like, "Be sure to wear safety glasses, okay? You know those things are dangerous."

Dustin responded with an eye roll and a reminder that he was *fourteen,* after all. Not a baby anymore.

"You're *my* baby," I said, and he answered with the boyish grin that had always melted my heart, then he continued on to the shower.

Over dinner we discussed Dustin's day and Mart's boat in even greater detail. I learned about the differences between the loaner boat that Mart was driving and his regular patrol boat, which was in for repairs. Dustin couldn't wait to see the real patrol boat when it came back. He was looking forward to riding in it, and Cassandra had assured him that the patrol boat was *seriously prime.*

I hid my concern about Dustin spending time with Mart and Cassandra and tried not to overanalyze things too much. After dinner Dustin and I walked down to the dock, and I ended up chatting with Mrs. Blue while Sydney and Ansley lured Dustin in for a swim.

"They're so glad he's next door this summer," Mrs. Blue offered, laughing as the three of them tried to climb onto a giant inner tube. "I hope they're not driving him crazy."

"I think he enjoys it." Right now, Dustin seemed to be having a ball. He was a rock star being showered with adoration, albeit between dunkings. It was two on one, and Sydney and Ansley could definitely hold their own. "It's lonely out here for him."

Mrs. Blue nodded sympathetically. "Normally, we wouldn't stay here at the lake all summer. It was just a fluke that a broken water main flooded our house just as the girls were coming for their usual visit. So here we are. Who knew the girls would have someone so charming to pester right next door?"

"Thanks for looking out for him." We turned our attention to Dustin and the girls as they descended into a particularly raucous bout of inner-tube war. *A fluke,* I thought. *Just a fluke that they're even here this summer. . . .*

But it didn't feel like a fluke. It seemed that this place, Moses Lake and the people here, had been prepared for us, designed ahead of time as a nurturing nest, a soft place from which to grow new wings.

When we went into the house, Dustin headed for his room to work on English, and I put on my sweats and snuggled in with a book and a cup of decaf. I was drowsily reading just one more chapter when lights drifted up the cove. My eyes popped open like roller shades. I sat up and checked the hallway. No glow under Dustin's door. After class and working and swimming, he was probably more exhausted than usual. In a heartbeat I was at the back door slipping my feet into flip-flops, then hurrying down the hill in the darkness. I met Mart on the other side of the boathouse.

"Thought you might be asleep," he said, standing with one foot on the dock and one in the boat, in the Robin Hood pose.

"Couldn't sleep." The words surprised me. The meaning was clear by the tone. *I couldn't sleep because I was watching for you.*

Mart smiled, as if he understood the silent message. "Nice night to sit out."

"Yes, it is."

"Nice night for a boat ride, too." He extended a hand, the palm open, waiting for me to place my fingers inside it, to be bold enough to accept the invitation.

"Yes, it is," I agreed and slipped my hand into his, felt his fingers close over mine. The boat shifted as I stepped off the dock, and Mart caught me in the strong circle of an arm. For a moment I was suspended above the water, feeling the steam rising from it, and then the warmth of his body. His lips touched mine, not with a careful unfamiliarity this time, but as if he knew me, as if he'd been waiting for this for hours.

I realized that I had been, too. I'd lived it a dozen times since the abrupt end to our lunch. Now I abandoned myself to it, left behind every hesitation, every shred of worry, let him sweep me away into the night like a thief.

The bird of paradise alights only
on the hand that does not grasp.
—John Berry
(Left by John and Ann from Dallas,
on their 50th anniversary trip)

Chapter 20

Mart McClendon

The lake was quiet and dark, the surface so glassy-smooth the stars glittered in it. The water rolled out in a reflection of the night sky, uneven at the edges where it touched the shore, weaving into cliffs and crevices, hiding pitch-black under the shadows of overhanging trees. On nights like this, with the lake calm and not another human in sight, it was hard to believe there could be anything wrong in the world.

As we left Larkspur Cove, I looked at Andrea, said, "Hang on there, shotgun," and pushed the throttle. The boat dragged down in the water, then jumped like a frog off a lily pad. Andrea slid a little in her seat, catching the side rail with one hand. Laughing, she tossed back her head, shook her hair into the breeze, then let her hands fly into the air, roller-coaster style. For a moment I forgot that I was piloting the boat across a ribbon of captured sky, speeding toward the moon.

I finally looked away, got my bearings, tugged my brain back into my head, and snugged it down with a ratchet strap. For the first time, I understood how one watercraft could run into another when there were miles of open space in all directions. Maybe the guy driving was looking at the pretty girl in the passenger seat. . . .

We crossed the lake, and I throttled down and let the boat idle along while we wandered past Eagle Eye Bridge, where the long, twisted branches of live oaks and sycamores shook hands over the water. Somewhere in the cliffs a mountain lion called, the sound high and sharp like a woman screaming. Andrea jerked upright in her seat.

"Just a mountain lion. He's a long way off," I said, and turned the boat around, cruised along the shoreline. The hull rode soft and quiet as we ducked up a cove into Nightingale Canyon. The low rumble of the motor bounced off the limestone cliffs, and far away, I heard music from one of the campgrounds at Seven Springs, where cold water from underground fed into the lake, creating favorite swimming spots like the Ice Hole and the Blue Moon.

"I'd forgotten how amazing this place is." Leaning back, Andrea rested against the seat, watching the cliffs draw a jagged line between the sky and its reflection.

"Not a bad place to work," I agreed.

"Completely different from southwest Texas, that's for sure. Down there, the job's all about driving dry-dirt roads, looking for hikers and rock climbers who end up in a bind, counting a few black bear up in the mountains, nabbing poachers after mule deer or snakes, and helping Immigration watch for border jumpers and drug traffickers. There's some water work on the river. Had a population of stray alligators show up down from Presidio a few years ago. That generated some excitement around town."

"So that's where you grew up—Presidio?" She was still leaning back in the seat, taking in the view.

"Thereabouts—Alpine, mostly. My daddy worked in the oil patch, did construction, and cowboyed on ranches until I was fourteen, so we moved around a lot. Seemed like every year we started school in a new place—sometimes moved two or three times in a year."

She turned toward me. "That sounds rough."

"You know, the thing is, we were pretty happy, the way I remember it," I said. "Kids don't need a perfect life. Lord knows, we never had one. Our family was crazy from one end to the other, always changing, always moving. Mama and Daddy fighting over money and him never being happy with a job, or a place. Sometimes we were living high on the hog; sometimes we ate dollar-a-pack hot dogs and boxed macaroni and cheese.

But no matter where we were, we always knew that Mama would be solid as a rock. Even after they split up and Daddy took off for some ranch job in Wyoming, Mama held us four boys together."

Andrea studied me a minute, like she was thinking about something. Then she shook her head. "I admire your mom. You know, it's so easy to get wrapped up in thinking your kids need to have everything all the other kids have—that they won't grow up okay if they're not top of the heap."

I let the boat drift into a turn, then idled, soft and quiet, back up the canyon. "Kids don't need all the junk people buy—the video games, and the high-dollar sports stuff. Get 'em a pole and send them out to fish. It's healthier. Look at that lawyer's kid who was driving the boat at the Scissortail—a blank check isn't doing him any good. Kids need somebody to love 'em and look after 'em, and give time instead of dollar bills.

"I see youngsters out here on the lake, and they've got everything. But when I pick them up for driving without a license or nab them with alcohol and I call the parents to let them know what happened, they don't even have time to wonder how the kid got into the mess or why. All some of these parents care about is how they can sweep it under the rug, so nobody'll know and it won't interrupt their plans. They don't want the kid to get kicked off the football team, or the baseball team, or to miss some vacation, or have to do community service, picking up trash on the side of the road." Every time I dealt with parents like those, I couldn't help being mad all over again that my brother was taken from his kids too early.

We motored out of the canyon, and I noticed that Andrea had straightened in the seat. "You thought that about me when you caught Dustin, didn't you?" Her voice had a hint of a laugh, so that I could tell she thought it was funny—now.

I pretended to be busy steering around the rocks at the canyon's mouth. "Can't recall," I answered.

"Pppfff ! Yes you can. You thought I was horrible."

"I thought you were cute."

I pictured the first day we met, her marching down the hill in her suit and high heels, me covered in swamp slime and gator scat. What a postcard.

"I'll bet."

"A little uptight, maybe."

She slapped a hand over her eyes, her laughter jingling into the night air. "I'm remembering the look on your face that morning. That look didn't say *cute but a little uptight.*"

"It'd been a long day." We moved out onto the open water, the boat just lolling along, back toward the Scissortail and her place. I wasn't in any hurry to finish the trip.

Overhead, a nighthawk darted in a jagged line, hunting insects. Both of us watched it, and the conversation lulled. Andrea threaded her fingers into her hair, bracing her elbow on the backrest and leaning on her hand. "So do you still have family down there, in Alpine?"

"Some." It crossed my mind that the conversation tonight was more about me than usual. The better everything got here in Moses Lake, the more I wanted to leave the past a few hundred miles down the road, shake it off like west Texas dust. "A brother and sister-in-law and their three girls, another sister-in-law and her three boys. Some aunts, uncles, cousins on my mama's side of the family—that sort of thing. We generate a pretty decent crowd at holidays."

But the truth was that those holidays had always centered around my mother. Now that she was gone and the old house had been sold off, nobody seemed to know what to do. Get-togethers reminded everyone that Shawn, Aaron, little Mica, and now Mama were missing. There were too many holes in the fabric for it to hold together anymore.

"Sounds nice." Andrea's comment fell like a ball in left field, dropping a long way from the glove. "I always wanted to come from a big family. Growing up, we just had my mom, my dad, Megan, and me . . . and my grandmother and grandfather, and one uncle sometimes, but my mother and her brother never liked each other much. My dad was an only child, and his parents were gone by the time I could remember."

"Be careful what you wish for. Growing up as part of a passel isn't any picnic, either. Nothing's ever your own, but you learn not to be late to the table—that's for sure. You show up late when you're one of four boys, you'll starve." My mind was so far back in the past, I didn't even realize where I'd gone until I'd opened the door.

"That must be something, being one of four boys," Andrea clicked her tongue against her teeth, like she was trying to picture it as we came into Larkspur Cove. "What was that like?"

"Wild. Car trips were always fun. Mama didn't even bother to figure out who'd started the fight. She just reached in the back and started smacking." I could've told her stories, but we were closing in on the dock, and I knew time was about up. Like it or not, pretty soon I'd be saying good-bye and heading home to the raccoon. My wildlife rehabber was recovering from a post-surgical infection, so the little bandito was still with me. I'd thought I was rid of him when I'd dropped him at the vet clinic on my way to do flood duty, but no such luck. The minute I was home, the vet wanted me to take the little troublemaker off his hands.

"Seemed like my mama spent half her time patching skinned knees and the other half out at the willow tree, cutting a switch. She grabbed me by the ear and tanned my hide many a time, that's for sure. But I've gotta say, I had it coming. She was a good God-fearing woman, and she was bound and determined to make sure that none of us went the wrong way."

We were within a few feet of the dock now, and I turned the wheel, pulling the boat alongside and tossing a line on. When I looked back, Andrea was still in her seat, her face turned toward me. "So one of your brothers lives in Alpine. Where do the rest live?"

It hit me like a right cross, then—that feeling of being backed up against the cold stone wall of stuff I didn't want to talk about. I could either slide out of there in a hurry, try to change the subject, or crack open old wounds right in front of her. On the other hand, if you want to get to someplace new, sooner or later you've got to take a step in a different direction. "There's just my middle brother, Jay, and me, anymore. My oldest brother was killed in Afghanistan, and my baby brother passed a few years ago. It's one of those stories that's tough to go into. I'll tell you about it sometime, but not right now, all right?"

She nodded, her shoulders tucking in, like she was embarrassed to have brought up something painful. "I'm sorry. I didn't mean to . . ."

"It's okay," I said, and I felt her hand slip into mine, small and warm. Her face turned upward, her eyes dark in the moonglow, like liquid. Slipping a thumb under her chin, I tilted it upward, looked into her in a way I never had in all the years of hits and misses, and girls I'd dated but never got too attached to. I'd always been satisfied to keep my issues to myself and let other people keep theirs. With Andrea, things were different in some way I didn't even understand yet.

I leaned over and kissed her, because we'd talked long enough.

When the kiss was over, we stood on the dock and talked some more—longer than we probably should've. She asked about how I felt when my daddy left, and so I told her. "For a while, Mama just kept telling us he was gone working, but then she finally sat us down and let us know they were splitting up. There she was with teenagers to raise, and she must've been worried about whether she could handle everything, but she didn't let it show. She just told us we were still a family, and it'd be okay, and we believed her. She made it all right, even though she had to earn a living, and she never knew for sure when my daddy would drop by or whether he'd bring money. Mama just told us that what he decided to do didn't have anything to do with us or with her—it was him that was broken, and he'd have to work it out.

"But I think the best thing my mama did was not take any excuses. She let us know that everyone's got struggles, and she still expected us to say *yes, ma'am* and *no, sir,* and keep up in school, and do our best not to embarrass the family name—which wasn't to say we were always successful at that. We were boys, after all."

I left off before adding that sometimes what Mama had to say wasn't what we wanted to hear, but you could count on her to give you her opinion anyway. The last thing she'd said to me, when she was thin and pale as a ghost in her hospital bed, was *It's time to quit hiding under the blanket, Martin.* At first I thought she was cold and that she wanted a blanket, but then I got the message. She was telling me I needed to quit holing up in the grief over Aaron and Mica. It was time to shuck off the blanket, get out of bed, and get busy with the hard work ahead.

Those were tough words to hear, but she was right. I wasn't hanging on for Aaron and Mica; I was doing it for me. Now it was time to move on—not just a little, but all the way out from under the blanket.

I walked Andrea to the edge of the dock and kissed her good-night, then watched as she headed up the hill to the house. I waited until she was inside before I got in the boat and went home.

For once, my cabin was in one piece—the little bandito hadn't found a way out of the cage. To make things even better, there was a message on my answering machine from the rehabber. He was in shape to take in animals, and he'd be coming by to pick up Bandito tomorrow, which meant I'd be a single guy without a roommate again.

I went to bed, thinking I was actually gonna miss Bandito a little bit. But just a little bit.

By the next day, I was ready to throw him in the lake. He'd chattered and carried on most of the night, upset that he couldn't get the cage open. One thing about raccoons—when you make them mad, they stay mad. I hadn't gotten a nickel's worth of sleep.

I showed up at the Waterbird for morning coffee looking rough enough that even the docksiders noticed. Sheila gave me the hawkeye while I was paying for a doughnut. She tried to pawn off a breakfast burrito on me, but I'd learned to stay away from those things. With Sheila in charge, there was no telling what you'd find hidden in there—healthy stuff that might shock a meat-eating man's system and cause him to do something weird, like listen to opera or watch figure skating when there was a perfectly good football game on.

"You look awful," she pointed out, like I didn't know that for myself. "Long night?"

"Not so bad."

"You work on the lake after you left here?" For some reason, Sheila was on me like a tick on a back-porch hound. I wasn't in the mood for it, really. I had a headache, and I was kicking myself for not asking Andrea on a real date when we were together last night and the mood was right. It was time to quit sneaking around in the dark, like there was something wrong with us seeing each other. Time to move on with life. I was even thinking of telling Reverend Hay I'd take that little part in his next theater production. There wasn't much reason for me to avoid Hay anymore, since sometime in the wee hours of the night I'd promised God that, if He'd just make that raccoon shut up, I'd go to church. God could probably get through to a lot of wayward folks if He'd just send a raccoon to keep them up thinking all night long.

"Quiet evening out on the water after it got dark. Not much to do," I said, and waited while Sheila dragged her feet about getting napkins and gave my doughnut dirty looks. She was wishing she could talk me out of that thing and into one of her tofu burritos. Fat chance.

"I noticed there wasn't much traffic." Finally she found the napkins, then took the time to put some in the basket on the counter before delivering a couple my way. "You catching anyone fishing without a license up in Larkspur Cove?"

In the docksiders' booth, Nester choked on a swallow of coffee. I checked over my shoulder and caught Nester, Burt, and Pop Dorsey watching me. They had a couple of the regulars with them this morning, too—Charley from Catfish Charley's and his brother, Herbert. I got the idea that I'd been the hub of conversation before I walked in. Leave it to Sheila to be watching the lake at night.

"Saw your lights headin' across-water in a hurry when I put the dogs out." Nester tossed in his two cents. "Figured you was after somebody. You apprehend any dangerous felons when you left Larkspur, did'ja?"

Burt snickered again, and Dorsey joined him. It didn't take a genius or a fully awake man to know what they were getting at. I felt my ears going hot. "It's way too early for this," I said. "Hand me my thermos. I'll go fill it someplace where the clientele's not so windy."

Nester belly laughed. "Whew, listen at Romeo, there! He's breakin' out the five-dollar words now. *Clientele.* Been hangin' around in Larkspur, gettin' all high-tone."

"Y'all . . ." Sheila jumped in like a schoolmarm hushing a couple troublemakers, but the word came out in a laugh, like *ya-ha-hall.* She grabbed my thermos and headed to the coffeepot to fill it up.

"All right, that's it. I'm heading out," I said, then

moved down the counter so I'd be ready to hit the door with my breakfast. Not that I minded the ribbing so much, really. It was probably the push I needed to get on with asking Andrea for a real date. Looked like everybody knew about us anyway. It was so obvious that even the docksiders had figured it out. If I didn't do something in public with her now, the boys would have me pegged as some kind of waterborne Casanova, sneaking around under the cover of darkness.

I pointed a finger at their table while I was waiting on Sheila to cap my thermos and hand it over. "Next time I catch one of you yay-hoos over limit on fat bass in your live wells, I'm gonna throw the book at you."

Nester, Burt, and the others roared, but Dorsey's smile faded a little. "Guess I'm safe on that one," he said when the noise quieted down. "Since Sheila won't let me get near the water." He scowled toward the counter, like a prisoner looking at his jailor.

Quick as a flock of sparrows, the laughs were gone. Sheila huffed and set my thermos on the counter. I grabbed it and my doughnut. "You give us a few more days, Pop. We'll get that dock fixed up to where even Sheila can't find a reason to worry."

"We're gonna use my welder and some scrap iron this evening to get Pop's boat hoist in shipshape," Burt added.

Sheila rolled her eyes, huffed, and disappeared into the kitchen.

"Guess we got rid'a her." Nester chuckled.

Pop gave me a grateful look. The docksiders started talking about the hoist, and I headed out while the conversation was on something other than Andrea and me. Before I started down the hill, I called to see whether Andrea would be up in Chinquapin Peaks around lunchtime. I suggested lunch at the park—my turn to bring the food—and she took me up on it.

"I'll grab something at Catfish Charley's so we don't have to eat alfalfa sprouts and goat cheese," I told her. "Sheila's on a nutrition push again."

Andrea laughed and said, "I don't mind alfalfa sprouts."

Lunch in the park wasn't really the date I had in mind, but I figured I still had a couple days before the weekend—enough time to come up with something good to do this Saturday.

We went on like that for the rest of the week—I called her in the morning, found out where she was going to be around lunchtime, and we met for lunch. The only thing that bothered me about it was that, whenever I cycled the subject around to her plans for the weekend, she found some way to change to another subject—any other subject. We talked about life and movies, and favorite TV shows when we were growing up, where we'd gone to school, the fact that we'd both spent time around Moses Lake.

I told her why I'd wanted to come back, and while we sat listening to the Wailing Woman and the mockingbirds, I told her about losing Aaron and Mica in the boat accident.

"That must be hard," she said, slipping her hand over mine. "I can't imagine."

"It is hard," I said. "It really is hard."

"If you ever want to talk about it, I'm a good listener."

"I know." I squeezed her fingers, but I didn't say any more. I wasn't ready to, and she seemed all right with that. She didn't push for more details. We just sat together listening to the river pass.

Friday night, while we were sitting out by her boathouse, we talked about her first couple visits with Birdie—two in three days, which was more than normal. She'd made the extra visit because the case had her stewing. I knew she wasn't supposed to discuss the details of what went on in a session, but Reverend Hay had told me about all the things CPS wanted Len to do, so it wasn't really any secret. CPS had a long list, and for someone like Len, it was way beyond what he would be able to do or pay for. Len didn't understand it all, but he knew enough to be worried.

I was only halfway focused on the conversation. After a whole week of lunches in the woods and nights at the boathouse, it was clear enough to me that Andrea still didn't want Dustin to know about us. I'd taken him to class all week, and he'd helped me with a few projects on the lake and with Pop Dorsey's guardrails and hoist. Somehow, even the docksiders had figured out not to bring it up about Andrea and me when the kid was around. So far, Dustin didn't seem to have a clue. I didn't think I ought to be the one to tell him, so I just didn't say anything.

It was getting to me, though. Sitting here behind the boathouse in the dark, I felt like we were still hiding from everyone and lying to her boy. I was worried about what he'd think when he found out. To my mind, it was better to make things public, to be honest about it—to just go ahead and have a real date. I started thinking through the possibilities, trying to come up with something good. We had a few waterfront restaurants on the lake—greasy spoons and Catfish Charley's. There was a little movie theater down the road a piece in Cleburne, where folks from the lake did their real grocery shopping and went for hardware, paint, plumbing supplies, and that sort of thing. Back in the day, there'd been a drive-in movie theater in Moses Lake, but it'd been closed for years. The Eagle's Nest Resort had a nice restaurant overlooking the water. I'd have to make reservations ahead for that. I could grill something over at my place, but the cabin wasn't much to look at. . . .

"We'll have to find some assistance for Len," Andrea said, but my mind wasn't in Chinquapin Peaks. It was closer to home. "But I'm still not sure the caseworker sees him as a decent long-term caretaker solution."

"I think Len could be, if he had help fixing up his house, and someone to explain things, like how and when to get Birdie to the school bus once school starts, and why he has to. I think he'd try, and once it's a routine, he's pretty much a creature of habit. But he'll be slow to understand it all at first. A guy like Len takes patience, more than anything," I told her, and then we both sat looking at the lake for a minute, thinking.

"We're about done with building Pop's boat hoist at the Waterbird," I said, finally. "While everyone's got their tools out, I thought I'd get some of the docksiders together next week and head on up to Len's to see if we can help shape up the place—just make a couple big days of it. Like one of those work frolics the Mennonites do, or a barn raising, only kind of the opposite." I stared out at the lake, thinking about how to steer the conversation to another track. It was Friday night. Time to leave work behind. Time to talk about doing something tomorrow. Something out in public.

Andrea sighed, her fingers slowly shredding a dead leaf that'd blown onto the dock. She was dropping little pieces into the water and watching them float away. "Well, I think I've figured out how to help with the clothes and school supplies, at least. Sheila told me there's a thing called Community Closet going on tomorrow afternoon at the Moses Lake gym. Several area churches and organizations hand out school supplies, and kids can shop through donated clothing and shoes. I offered to take Birdie there, and surprisingly enough, Len agreed. From what I could gather, they'll be out at the Crossroads selling vegetables, and I can stop by and get her anytime after lunch. I hope he doesn't change his mind."

"I doubt he will. Len's mind is pretty one-track." Right then, my mind was, too. But it wasn't on Len. "If it's Saturday, you can figure he'll be out by the state park entrance all day, catching the weekend crowd. That's got to be pretty boring for a little girl. He's probably happy you offered to take her off his hands for a while."

"I guess." Andrea watched the bits of dead leaf float toward shore on the moonlit water. "Birdie still has such a long way to go before school starts, though. She's barely communicative."

"Give it a little time." I tossed a pebble from the dock and sank one of her little leaf-boats. "You can plow a field in a day, but you can't make the crop grow."

She dropped the rest of the leaf and nudged me with her shoulder. "You're right." She turned my way, and I would've kissed her, but that was where all our conversations ended. This time I wanted to get some things said. Now was probably as good a time as any.

"So how about we hit the lake tomorrow morning for a while—you, me, and Dustin? He's been after me to take him on up the river channel and show him the caves with the mammoth fossils. My partner's covering the lake this weekend. I'm off work. Free as a bird."

Where I'd been hoping for another smile and something like, *That sounds good,* instead, she pulled away and looked at me like a squirrel caught in the middle of a six-lane highway.

"I can't." The answer was quick, like she didn't even have to think about it.

I hoped she meant she was tied up working tomorrow morning—behind on those reports she was always plugging away on in her living room late at night.

"Well, Hay's got a dinner on the grounds planned at Lakeshore Church on Sunday after service—horseshoes, swimming, homemade pie, that kind of thing." Not my favorite sort of shindig, but it was sure enough public. "Dustin has it in his mind to go, by the way—don't know if he talked to you about it yet. Cassandra and her folks will be there, if that explains anything. You know, maybe we could even talk Len into bringing Birdie down. You said she needs to be around people."

"Oh . . . I don't . . ." It was pretty obvious that Dustin hadn't mentioned the Sunday dinner to his mom yet. Hopefully he wouldn't mind that I'd let the cat out of the bag.

Andrea's shoulder shifted away from mine. She pushed her palms together and tucked her hands between her knees, her head bowed forward, so that her profile was a shadow against the moonlight. "Mart . . . I . . ." She didn't have to finish the rest of the sentence for me to know I wasn't going to like what was coming next. "I can't. I'm sorry. I don't think . . . Dustin isn't ready for something like that. He's finally finding his feet here, healing a little bit, even. I can't take the risk of . . . derailing him."

"Risk?" Maybe I was just worn out after a long week, or maybe this game of cat and mouse with Andrea was finally getting to me, but aggravation buzzed around me like a mosquito looking for a place to land. "I'm not sure I see how a day on the lake or dinner on the church grounds is a risk."

She stiffened, her back straightening, her chin coming up. "I can't have him getting his hopes up."

"Getting his hopes up for what, exactly?" Wherever her train of thought was, I'd just been left behind in the dust.

She took a breath, held it a minute before letting it out, looked down at her hands. "I know I should have said something earlier, Mart. I'm sorry . . . I just . . . I haven't been thinking . . . the way I should. I'm a mom. I have to consider Dustin first. It's my job to protect him."

"Protect him from *what?*" The words came out sharper than I meant them to, but by now, I was irritated. All this hiding behind the bushes was ridiculous. We were both adults, after all.

"From being disappointed again. From having his heart broken. From having false hopes. He's already been through so much. He's had someone he idolized, someone he loved and needed, who was supposed to love him and protect him, just toss him out like yesterday's toy. He's vulnerable, fragile." She flipped a hand through the air, then tucked it between her knees again. "He doesn't need anything else to think about. He needs stability, safety. He can't handle anyone else coming and going from his life."

Coming and going. Those words painted an ugly picture. It stung, and I was offended. "So you're saying you think I'm the kind of guy who'd spend time with your boy just to impress you? That if you and I called it off at some point, I'd just drop him like a hot potato?"

She huffed a breath, like I'd misunderstood her. "I'm not *saying* anything. I just can't take the chance. He can't handle another heartbreak."

"He can't, or you can't?"

"I have to think of Dustin. . . ."

The muscles pulled tight in the corners of my jaw. This was like talking to Laurie about Levi's birthday. No logic, all emotion. "So it's better to just lie to him? Sneak around in the dark?" One thing I'd never been was a diplomat. It wasn't like me to tiptoe past a situation.

"I'm not . . ."

I didn't wait for her to finish. "So what happens when he hears about it from someone else? People around here aren't stupid, you know. They've figured it out."

She pulled further away, looked at me. I read the shock in her voice even though I couldn't see her face—just the outline of her hair, moonlit around the edges. "*Who* has? What are you talking about?"

"People know, Andrea. They're not blind."

She scooted back and stood up, and I did, too. "*Who* knows? Did someone say . . ."

A sudden glow flushed across the yard, and she jerked toward it, catching a breath when she saw that the back-porch lights had come on, and a floodlamp was flickering to life, illuminating the upper part of the yard. Someone was moving around in the house, turning on switches.

"I can't do this, Mart," she said, then hovered there a second. Finally, she added, "I have to go."

Before I could say anything else, she was gone.

What we seek, we shall find;
what we flee from, flees from us.
—Ralph Waldo Emerson
(Left by Danny G., walking coast-to-coast
on one good leg, after cancer)

Chapter 21

Andrea Henderson

Panic crashed through my mind like waves at high tide, my emotions a brackish mixture of embarrassment, confusion, self-reproach, guilt, fear. I'd created this moment—built it one phone call, one moonlit conversation, one kiss at a time, and now I was terrified of it. The idea of going public, of involving Dustin . . .

The screen door slammed behind me, shutting out the night as I rushed onto the porch. Instead of being in bed, Dustin was in the utility room on the lower half of the split-level. I saw him through the French doors as I crossed the back porch, wiped my eyes, and slipped inside. The mother in me instantly became suspicious. What was Dustin doing down there this time of night? Sneaking out? Hiding something? My heart sank. This past week things had finally seemed to be getting better. He had the old bounce in his step. Surely it wasn't all an act, a smokescreen.

Part of me didn't want to know. I couldn't handle one more unexpected collision right now. I couldn't. I felt like I was cracking in half—half Dustin's mom, half . . . someone else. A person I didn't recognize. Part of me liked that other someone, the girl who ran through the dark to the lakeshore at night and made a difference on the job during the day. Part of me felt the need to go back to what was safe and comfortable—the old Andrea Henderson, who kept everything under control and did what was expected.

I startled Dustin on his way across the living room. "Mom! Where'd you come from?" he asked, jerking back, wide-eyed. He looked nervous, out of sorts, his hair sticking up in all directions.

"I've been here," I answered, and instantly tasted guilt. Which one of us was lying now? Who was sneaking around, hiding things?

Dustin's nose wrinkled in confusion. "I looked all over the place. I couldn't find you anywhere."

"I was outside." The half-truth pressed my chest, emptying it like a billows, holding it closed, so that catching another breath was difficult. Everything about this was wrong. Doing things I had to hide from my son was wrong. Mart was right—I was lying to Dustin. I was lying to both of them. Letting Mart believe I could be what he needed was wrong. I wasn't what anyone needed. I didn't even know where my own life was going.

Even if Dustin was unaware of the details, he could tell that something wasn't kosher. "In the dark? The porch light wasn't even on." He blinked, as if trying to get a better view of me, to figure out who I was and what I'd done with his mother. How many times had he heard me repeat the diatribes I'd inherited from my mother. *A gated community isn't gated along the shore. You never know who might be on the lake. Watch out for snakes. Mosquitoes carry diseases. Don't forget to spray . . .*

"It's nice out this time of year." The answer was intentionally vague. "Is something wrong? You look upset."

"Dad called. Didn't you hear the phone?"

"Dad?" The word caught in my chest. "Your dad called?" *Now he decides to call? At eleven thirty on a Friday night?* "What did he want?" Clearly, Dustin was upset. What had Karl said to him?

Dustin moved closer to the phone, as if he thought it might ring again, and it was urgent that he not miss the call. "He wanted to talk to you. He was really . . . He was crying and stuff, and he needed to tell you that . . . that . . . He just kept asking for you. I was looking around the house, and then I went downstairs, and . . . and I couldn't find you, and then he said . . . he said . . . And then the phone went dead, and he didn't call back."

Tears welled in my son's brown eyes, and for

an instant he looked so much like his father that it could have been Karl standing there, years ago. When Karl was a young associate pastor, he was so passionate about his work that his cheeks were sometimes wet with tears as he spoke in front of the youth group. After the past year, it was hard to believe that any of those emotions were real. How could a man who really took the Bible to heart, who wanted to serve God, develop a sense of entitlement that allowed him to steal from the college, lie to his family, maintain a secret life, disappoint scores of people who were counting on him, leave his own son behind?

Maybe Karl was calling because something had happened between him and Delayne—a breakup, a fight. Maybe she'd left him. Maybe he'd lost his new job. Maybe he was on the skids, and calling me was some sort of reflex reaction.

The idea was appealing in a way I wasn't prepared for. I found myself savoring the thought of Karl's pain like something delicious. *He deserves it. He has it coming. He has at least that much coming. Let him see how it feels to have everything cave in on you, to be rejected, to have everything you've planned fall apart.*

On the other side of the coin, the one I didn't want to examine, was Dustin, teary eyed, red-faced, filled with worry, filled with love for his father, even after everything that had happened. Anything that hurt Karl would hurt him.

"All right, calm down." I reached out and held Dustin's upper arms, rubbed my hands up and down the cold skin there. "I'm sure it'll be okay. What, exactly, did your dad say?"

Dustin sniffled, swiping a hand across his nose. "He said that Grandpa died."

"Grandpa . . . what?" My father's face flashed through my mind, but then I realized that, if something had happened to my father, Meg or my mom would be calling.

"Grandpa Henderson?" Karl and his dad had been on the outs since his father sold the North Dakota ranch that had been in the family forever and used the money to help Karl's younger sister out of a financial crisis. Karl felt that he'd been cheated out of his inheritance. For a while, I'd tried to heal the breach, but then I'd given up, let time go by. I'd prayed that they would reconcile but never stepped up and done anything to help those prayers along. Dustin hadn't seen Karl's father in six years. Karl's father probably didn't even know we were divorced. Now Dustin would never see his grandfather again.

I pulled Dustin into a hug, and he melted against me, sobbing. Before the inheritance spat, he'd been crazy about his grandpa. He was Joe's only grandchild. I shouldn't have let anything come between Dustin and Grandpa Joe. I should have insisted that Karl be the bigger man, for our son's sake. I should have taken Dustin to

North Dakota myself. "I'm sorry. Sweetheart, I'm so sorry."

"I should've gone to see him." The words came out in a sob, almost unintelligible. "I should've gone to . . . gone to . . ."

"Ssshhh." I stroked his hair, rocking him back and forth as if he were a little boy. "None of this is your fault. Honey, none of it's your fault." It didn't matter whether it was Dustin's fault or not; he was the one hurting over it. "Grandpa knew you loved him. He loved you so much. Oh, he loved you so much." Tears filled my eyes, and my mind was awash with grief, with so many years of shared history—Karl's, mine, Dustin's. Over time, countless intricate threads had come to bind our families together, our marriage growing outward like a spider's web, silken ties taking in friends, acquaintances, church members, family. It was so hard now to know which should be severed, which should be preserved, which could never be repaired.

I led Dustin to the sofa, sat down with him, pulled a blanket over the two of us, and held on until he'd cried himself out. Finally, I walked back to his bedroom with him, sat on the edge of the bed as I would have in the past. Some nights we'd spent forever talking about his day before saying good-night prayers. Then I'd watched him drift off to sleep, safe, secure, in good hands. God's hands.

Tonight it seemed as if he were all alone. I'd robbed him the same way Karl had robbed him of his relationship with Grandpa Joe. Because of my own pain, because of my anger at Karl, at former friends and acquaintances who'd spread hurtful rumors and turned their backs on me, because of my disappointment with my life, I'd shoved God not only out of my world, but out of Dustin's. I'd been so certain that a perfectly smooth, perfectly predictable, perfectly blessed life was my rightful inheritance for having been a regular churchgoer, a volunteer, a devoted mother, and a good and faithful servant. When the road turned rocky, I was angry that I'd been robbed of what I deserved. What I was owed. I was like one of those spoiled kids Mart talked about—the ones who had everything and took it all for granted.

It wasn't fair for me to let my resentments spill into Dustin's life, to cause him to wander alone through the toughest time he'd ever known. I was cheating him. I was cheating myself.

"We should have night prayers, huh?" I whispered, my voice shaking with emotion.

He nodded, his eyes still closed, his dark lashes matted against his cheeks. When he spoke, his voice was barely a whisper. "Can we go to church this Sunday?"

Church. Mart had mentioned Sunday at Lakeshore Community Church. If we went there, we'd undoubtedly run into him. I wasn't sure what to say or how to handle the situation between us now. "Maybe we'll go in Cleburne. Bonnie at the office has been trying to get me to visit there. She says they have a lot of activities for young people."

Dustin shook his head, turned his face sideways into the pillow to wipe fresh tears from the corner of his eye. "I want to go here at Lakeshore. I want to go with Reverend Hay and Mart." At some point during the week, Dustin and Mart had come to be on a first-name basis.

"We'll work something out," I whispered. "Let's just say a prayer about Grandpa Joe now and . . ." I swallowed hard, dug down in search of some measure of grace, and finished the sentence. ". . . and for your dad."

Dustin opened his eyes, studied me as if he were trying to decide whether I meant it. If he could find the answer to that question, he could let me know it, because I wasn't certain myself. I only knew that I wanted to ease my son's pain and that I didn't want him to someday end up in Karl's position—regretting the fact that he'd severed a relationship and finding that it was too late to do anything about it.

Dustin and I said good-night prayers, and then I left him to rest. It was after twelve, but he could sleep in tomorrow. Maybe we both could. Maybe I could go to bed, wake up in the morning, and find that today was only a dream—that everything was as it had been before. Maybe tomorrow night I would watch the cove, and Mart's boat would come drifting up to the dock, the same as always. The fantasy was tantalizing, but dangerous. In reality, what Mart and I had was just a risky game of let's pretend—stolen moments that had always been destined to collide with real life. What did I think was going to happen? How in the world did I think it would end?

It was just a fantasy, a dream. It was never real.

I wasn't the woman who ran through the grass in the moonlight. I didn't have the courage.

Even so, I went to bed, closed my eyes, and slipped into the fantasy. I imagined Mart stepping onto the dock, taking me into his arms, his eyes smiling at me in the moonlight. He didn't speak. He only leaned down and kissed me, no complicated questions between us. . . .

A noise outside the house woke me with a start. I jerked upright, the leaden feeling in my body letting me know I'd been asleep for a while. I was cold. Outside the bedroom window, the night had turned foggy, a dusting of high clouds blotting out the stars.

I heard the noise again—the muffled sound of a radio playing and a car engine idling in the driveway. I glanced at the clock. Who would be outside our house at three in the morning?

A pulse fluttered softly in my neck, and I

clutched a hand over my throat as I stood up. Anyone trying to rob the place wouldn't drive up with the radio playing. Maybe someone was lost—coming home from a wild night at some local watering hole and confused about which house this was.

As the song ended, I recognized the last verse. I knew the voice that rose to a crescendo on the final note. It was my son's. Dustin and his father had recorded that CD with the church youth group just a few months before Karl's secrets came to light. The kids sold the CD in the foyer, raising money for a mission trip to build houses in Mexico. Since it was Dustin's first year to travel with the youth, Karl and I were planning to go along as chaperones. I was hoping that the quiet time away from all the demands of the college would give us a chance to talk. There had been so much distance between us. While I was going about the business of our normal lives— charity work, PTA meetings, flower beds in the spring, fall carnival in October—Karl seemed to be pulling further and further into himself, excusing himself from more family events. I was glad when he and Dustin worked on producing the youth group CD together.

By spring break the truth had come out, the reason for the distance between us became clear, and our lives were in shambles. We'd fallen from grace with no soft place to land.

Why would Dustin be out in the driveway playing that CD in the middle of the night? Had he awakened, thinking about his father? Maybe he didn't want to upset me, so he'd gone out there?

Pushing my hair out of my face, I got up and went to the living room, thinking vaguely that I should have put my hair in a ponytail. It would be hard to comb through in the morning. The wind had whipped it into wild tangles while I was on the lake with Mart.

Mart . . . The way I'd ended things steamrollered through my mind, compressing one set of thoughts indiscriminately into another. Mart deserved better than a few babbled, cryptic excuses and a quick fleeing of the scene. He hadn't done anything wrong. I'd more than led him to believe that I was ready to . . . get involved with someone. With him. He'd only taken the natural next step.

Perhaps that was one of the things that bothered me. It was so easy to lean on Mart, to slip into his arms, to bring him into our lives and allow him to fill the empty space. But Dustin and I needed to learn to stand on our own, to become a family unto ourselves, to be healthy and complete, and then someday, maybe it would be time to expand that picture. Right now we were too needy, too vulnerable, too confused, too fragile. I couldn't risk another failure, another heartbreak—

Dustin's or my own. We were still broken in too many ways.

Another song started on the CD as I opened the front door and peeked out. The cab of Taz's truck was dark, the windows covered with nighttime condensation. I couldn't tell if anyone was inside.

I'd reached the end of the front walkway before I realized there was a car behind the truck. Karl's car. The secondhand one he'd bought after we'd sold almost everything of value to cover legal bills and the lump sum of cash he'd agreed to pay the college in order to avoid prosecution. I moved toward the car, the music pressing my ears, loud enough to disturb the neighbors, even though the houses were far apart. The dome light was on, the engine still running. Karl was slouched over the wheel, his hands clasped atop it, his thick hair, longer than I remembered, falling over his fingers in disarray.

The moment was surreal, unbelievable, like it was part of a dream. Any minute now I would wake and reprimand myself for allowing him to invade my subconscious mind. I felt as if I were watching from above—seeing a dark-haired woman move around the car, lean close, knock on the window.

Karl jerked upright, looked at me through the glare of streetlamps on the glass. His eyes were puffy and bloodshot, his cheeks wet. He seemed gaunt and pale, his skin translucent in the dim light. A vein was pulsating in his temple. I flashed back, thinking of the times I'd sat in the corner of his classroom, watched the vein pulse when he covered the finer points of theology. I could picture him now, his forehead red with vigor, his eyes filled with passion and indignation, with faith and devotion.

Now his eyes were hollow. Nothing larger seemed to occupy them. There was only emptiness strewn with shattered pieces of self. Part of me gloried in it. Finally he was as wounded as I. Finally he knew what it was to be broken, lost, alone in the middle of the night. Why had he come here? What did he want?

I motioned for him to roll down the window, and he reached for the switch, pinching his free hand over his eyes.

"From the Inside Out" spilled into the darkness, a little girl's voice singing in the foreground, the youth choir behind her. The girl was McKenna, Delayne's eldest daughter. Karl's stepdaughter now.

Venom coursed through me like bile, burned in my throat. "Turn that off. It's the middle of the night," I hissed. "What are you doing here?"

He drew back, seeming confused about the source of the music, as if he'd forgotten it was playing. Fumbling with the buttons, he managed to still the sound, then sank against the seat, as if even that small action had exhausted him.

"Why are you here?" I wrapped my arms around myself, the damp night seeping quickly through my pajamas. The words echoed down the silent street, louder than I'd meant them to be.

He drew a breath that seemed to come in jagged pieces. "I couldn't . . . think of where else to go. I was headed to North Dakota for the . . ." His eyes closed tightly, his face compressing in pain, his lips drawing back in a grimace over clenched teeth.

"I'm sorry about Joe. I know it must be hard." The words were without emotion. In truth, I wasn't sorry—not for Karl, anyway. Not for his pain. *You deserve this. It's your own fault that you haven't seen him in all these years. It's your own fault for being such a jerk.*

He nodded, mistaking the words for genuine sympathy. "I thought there'd be . . . time."

He looked at me, and for just an instant, I felt his anguish, even though I wanted to be numb to it. I imagined myself in his shoes. What if it had been my parents? Wouldn't I have the same regrets? Wouldn't I be right where Karl was, wishing there were more time, wishing we'd had a better relationship? I'd been so busy resenting the things my parents weren't, that I'd never tried to appreciate them for what they were. I'd been so offended by their advice and their criticism that I'd never even thanked them for standing by me after the divorce, for showing up in Houston with a moving van, for having the lake house cleaned and ready for Dustin and me.

What if suddenly all my chances to say *thank you* or *I love you* were taken away?

Clenching a hand over his face, Karl sobbed softly. He slumped forward, and his elbow hit the horn, causing it to shriek out a loud complaint. I jerked away. Next door, a light turned on in Sydney and Ansley's room, and across the street, a dog barked. I needed to get Karl out of the driveway. Now.

"Come inside," I whispered, without taking time to think about what might happen after. If I didn't do something, one of the neighbors was likely to call the police.

Stepping back as he opened the car door, I tried to find a measure of grace. The man had just lost his father, after all. Joe was gone. In my mind, I could picture Joe sitting on the porch of the old ranch house, his jeans dusty from a day's work on the family land, his gnarled fingers clasped over the handle of a coffee cup.

Before things went so wrong, we'd spent some wonderful vacations at the ranch, first visiting Karl's grandparents there, and then his parents after they took over the place and moved back to North Dakota. I still remembered those visits as if they'd happened yesterday. There was *that* bond between Karl and me, if nothing else.

I watched as he pulled the keys from the

ignition and exited the car. He was dressed in a golf shirt and shorts, as if he'd come straight from the course. His arms were tan below the sleeves. Obviously, he'd been on the course a lot. *He has money for golf. He has time and money for golf, but he can't come to see his own son and send the child-support checks on time.*

I turned toward the house, trying to leave the baggage in the driveway and see Karl only as a man who was grieving. He wasn't in any shape to be driving right now. Walking slowly past Taz's truck, I kept my arms wrapped around myself, moving ahead of Karl on the path to the front door, so that our shoulders wouldn't touch.

Inside the house, we stood in the entryway, uncertain what to do with each other. I couldn't remember the last civil conversation between us.

"You look like you could use a cup of coffee," I said quietly.

"Thanks." He followed me to the kitchen, his feet shuffling over the tile as if he were already burdened by the weight of his father's casket.

I occupied myself with preparing the coffeepot, while he slid onto a stool. My mind was spinning toward morning, trying to decide if it would be better for Dustin to see Karl and share memories of Grandpa Joe, or if I should make Karl leave before then. "How is your sister?" I asked as he leaned on the counter, waiting for the coffee to brew.

He watched the rich, brown liquid drip into the pot. "Not doing very well, I think. I need to get up there to take care of the funeral arrangements."

"It's good that you're going." Perhaps, at this point, he could at least salvage the bond with his sister. I couldn't imagine being estranged from Meg that way. "She loves you, you know."

He nodded, seeming reluctant to confirm or deny it. We waited in silence for the coffee to brew. Finally I sneaked a cup and handed it to him. "Here, go on into the living room and sit down. I'll be there in a minute." I needed a second to clear my head, to decide what to do next, where the conversation should go. Did I ask about Delayne and her girls? Did I act like they didn't exist? Why wasn't she with him? Why was he driving across the country by himself in such a state? I nodded at the cup. "Black, right?"

He started toward the living room, tipping his head over the steaming liquid. "Same as always."

I stood alone in the kitchen after he was gone, watching the mist rise over the boathouse, outlining it in silver. The lights of a houseboat shone in the cove, and I thought of Mart. Where was he now? What was he thinking? Would he ever speak to me again after I'd handled things so badly?

For now, there was Karl's problem to deal with. At the very least, he should know that Dustin was upset. Karl shouldn't have blurted out the news of Joe's death without preparing Dustin. If Karl was here with the intention of talking to Dustin about Grandpa Joe, I wanted to make sure he didn't say anything negative about Joe or rehash old family wounds as a way of explaining his own stubborn behavior. I wanted Karl to be willing to admit that even if he didn't agree with his father's choices, he should have risen above it, that now it was too late and he was sorry. Maybe somewhere during the conversation Karl would realize that if he didn't start nurturing the bond with his own son, history would repeat itself.

I poured another cup of coffee, added cream and sugar, and proceeded to the living room. When I got there, Karl was sound asleep on the sofa. I stood above him, wondered if I'd ever really known who he was. He seemed such a stranger, his thoughts, his actions, his choices a mystery to me, even yet. How was it possible to have known someone most of your life, to have lived in the same house, and still be strangers?

I considered waking him but finally decided that perhaps it was better that he'd fallen asleep. He wasn't in any shape to drive, and if we sat there together, I didn't know what we'd talk about. Everything would be clearer in the morning, and Karl would be in a more rational frame of mind. Dustin always slept in until nine or ten on the weekends unless I woke him, so there would be plenty of time to talk to Karl before Dustin came out of his room.

Throwing an afghan over the man who had been my husband, I stood looking at him again, trying to remember how things used to be between us. Mostly it was the externals of our life that came to mind—the goals we had together, the things we did, the life we built, the house we decorated, the vacations we took, the achievements we coveted, the son we raised. It was as if we had been playing roles with no real emotional investment, never really feeling it. I could count on one hand the times we'd ever had a conversation that went below the surface. We'd been roommates and acquaintances, rather than helpmeets, soul mates, and lovers.

I finally left him there and went to bed, letting sleep soothe my wondering.

In the morning the sun was well up before I awoke. I heard voices in the living room, a woman talking in a loud, angry hiss.

My mother?

Then my father's voice, then Karl's.

I was fully awake before my next breath. Throwing on sweats, I rushed up the hall, checking Dustin's door on the way. So far, whatever was going on, at least he hadn't become caught up in it.

In the living room I found Karl on the sofa,

twisted into an unnatural sitting position, his hair askew, his eyes blinking rapidly, as if he'd just been rudely awakened and was trying to determine if my parents were really there or he was having a nightmare.

Mother whirled toward me when I came into the room, her hand snaking out, a rigid finger pointing toward Karl. "What is *he* doing in *my* house?" Her nostrils flared, indicating that his very presence had polluted the air. Beside her, my father was angry red from the neck up, his lips clamped into a fierce line.

"Mother," I placated, keeping my voice low. "Ssshhh. Calm down, please. Dustin's still asleep." So much for having a rational conversation with Karl. Suddenly everything was a mess. What were my parents doing here?

"I want to know *what is* the meaning of this?" Mother clicked the volume down a notch. "How long has *this* been going on?" She waved a hand from Karl to me in an appalling indication that we were sneaking around in some intimate way. My father nodded, seconding the horrifying insinuation.

"Shhh!" My own forcefulness surprised me. Mother blinked and drew back, offended. "Let's go out on the porch, all right? There's nothing to be upset about."

Karl stood up, and we marched single file through the living room, my father swinging his arms at the front of the line in a territorial gesture reminiscent of King Kong.

On the porch, Mother quickly repeated her demand for information. I explained that Joe had passed away suddenly, and Karl was headed to North Dakota to make funeral arrangements. I left out the part about his arriving here at three in the morning, an emotional wreck.

Mother stood with her mouth hanging open, torn between offering proper condolences and starting a spitting match.

"Dustin is very upset, of course," I pointed out, attempting to soften her resolve. Joe wouldn't have liked all the fighting. He had been a gentle, even-tempered man with a big heart, which was how he'd ended up getting dragged into his daughter's financial mess.

Mother opened her mouth, as if she were about to say something unpleasant, then she clamped it shut again, rethinking. "Well, I suppose it was *decent* of you to come tell Dustin in *person*." She bit off the end of the sentence.

As much as I hated for them to think the best of Karl, I didn't contradict her version of the story. Karl cast a grateful, slightly surprised glance my way. Now fully awake, in the bright light of morning, he looked more like himself. Cooler, more aloof, more in control. At this point, he was probably embarrassed about last night.

"Mother, why are you and Daddy here?" I

posed the obvious question. Mother's chin went up immediately, so I quickly added, "Did you need something?"

"We just came to fill the feeders." She flashed a look that said, *And it's a good thing we did!* As if she and Dad needed to defend me. "And we're going to Dallas for the day, shopping. We thought Dustin might want to come along and pick out some things for *his new school.*" She aimed the last words at Karl, no doubt to point out that not only did Dustin have to adjust to a new school, but *they* had to buy school clothes for him. It was all Karl's fault for being a fraud, a philanderer, an embezzler, and now an inconsistent check writer when it came to child support. Thank goodness Mother hadn't noticed the golf tan yet.

"I really appreciate that." My gratitude was genuine. A grandma and grandpa shopping trip for school clothes would definitely help out. "But I think Dustin had better stay here this morning, so he can have a few minutes with his dad before Karl leaves for North Dakota."

Mother huffed softly. She and Dad exchanged glances, indicating that it wasn't safe to leave Dustin and me alone here with the monster who had broken their daughter's heart and ruined her life. "We need to fill the feeders, at least."

"Just leave the seed, and I'll do it." I caught my mother's gaze, then my father's, pleading with them to trust me for once, to believe that I could handle the crisis on my own.

They vacillated for what seemed an impossibly long time, caught between repeating old patterns and taking a leap of faith. Thirty-eight years old, and my parents were still deciding whether I was ready to do grown-up things.

"I'm fine," I said. "Everything's fine. Really."

My father swallowed, his lips trembling. Slipping an arm over my mother's shoulders, he attempted to turn her toward the door.

Mother stiffened, then emitted a sigh of acquiescence. "Well, at least walk us out, Andrea."

"Sure," I said. We exited the porch and crossed the living room, leaving Karl standing on the porch alone, gaping bleary-eyed into the morning mist, like a man who'd just dodged a speeding bus.

On the front walk Mother leaned close, whispering, "Are you certain you're okay? We can stay. Don't you let *that man* take advantage of your sympathies. You don't owe him *one thing*. He doesn't deserve anything from you."

She was right, of course. A part of me wanted to bless Karl with the truth of whose fault his situation with his dad really was, and then kick him to the curb. Another part said that if I could dig down deep and extend a measure of grace, even to Karl, I'd be healing myself in some way—proving that his actions didn't have to dictate my responses. I'd be taking back control.

I stood at the car with my mother and my father, thinking that there was no way I could possibly explain that oddly circular bit of logic. "I'm fine. I really am. I feel sorry for him, having things end up this way with his father. That's all."

Mother spat a puff of air as Dad unloaded the birdseed. Rather than just leaving the bag, they made a production of filling the front feeders, and I waited uncomfortably on the walk, anxious for them to depart.

Mother glared toward the house when they'd run out of excuses to stay. "I'd like to tell him what I think of him," she muttered. Dad nodded in agreement as he shut the trunk and rounded the car to stand with us.

"You already have, Mom. Several times."

"Well, it wouldn't hurt him to hear it again. Maybe it will sink in through that thick skull of his. Maybe he'll finally realize what a horrible, horrible man he's become. Maybe he'll decide to repent and ask forgiveness."

I sighed, thinking of Karl's face last night. What had possessed him to come to me, of all people, for comfort? Was it habit? Desperation? Nostalgia? "I think that's going to have to be up to him."

"You be careful." Moisture gathered in the corners of Mother's eyes. In spite of her sometimes bullish way of showing it, all she wanted was to keep me safe. "I just can't stand to see you setting yourself up for a fall."

"I'm a big girl," I said softly, and Mother's lips trembled. I'd hurt her feelings, made her think I was saying that I didn't need her. "But thank you for looking after me. I know I haven't really said it, but without you two and Meg, Dustin and I wouldn't have survived this last year. Thanks for being there for us."

I reached out and slipped my arms around my mother, hugged her and really meant it for the first time since I was a little girl. She was stiff initially, shocked, then she softened and held me close, smoothing a hand over my hair and rocking me back and forth.

"We're here anytime you girls need us." The answer was her way of saying that we *would* need her and Dad, of course. Meg and I would never completely be allowed to fly the nest, but there were worse problems to have.

"And sometimes when you don't," my father added, as if he'd read my mind. I hugged him, and he cleared his throat, patting my shoulder awkwardly. My father had never known quite what to do with girls, other than hand them money and occasionally admire someone's church dress on Sunday morning.

As I waved my parents off, I felt like I was turning a corner. Maybe I just needed to accept my parents for who they were and get over myself. Maybe I was finally at a place in life where I could. After watching them drive away, I turned and walked back into the house, feeling like it was a good day, in spite of the fact that Karl was still holed up on my porch.

Voices in the living room told me that Dustin was up. I found Karl sitting on the sofa, looking strangely relaxed, and Dustin digging through the cubby in the end table. "Here it is," he said, coming out with a dust-covered atlas. Apparently Karl needed a road map to get from Texas to North Dakota.

"You guys all right?"

Dustin seemed calm enough. Clearly, finding his father here hadn't upset him. He sat down beside Karl, as if it were the most natural thing in the world, and turned a look of bright anticipation my way. "Dad's taking me to North Dakota. After the funeral, we're gonna drive by the old ranch and then, like, come home the long way, spend a few days seeing the West."

Dad's taking me to North Dakota. I stopped halfway across the room, stunned, then panicked, then angry. Karl didn't look at me. He knew what I was thinking. He knew what he'd done. He'd wormed his way into my house, and as soon as my back was turned, he'd taken advantage of the moment to fill Dustin with fantasies about going on some trip. Karl was feeling needy, and since

Delayne and her kids couldn't fill this need, he was back in our lives, dangling a carrot in front of my son. How dare he do this without asking me! If I said no, I would be the ogre, the ridiculously mean mother, the bitter one who couldn't let bygones be bygones, even in the hour of Joe's death.

Karl had offered Dustin exactly the thing Dustin couldn't refuse—time with his dad, a promise of a renewed relationship. My head was spinning, possible reactions whirling by so fast I couldn't get a grip on any of them. "I'm not sure that's the best thing. . . ."

Karl turned a pleasant look my way, blinking and drawing back slightly, as if he couldn't imagine why I would say that. The broken man from the night before was gone, and the cool, calculating, blameless one had returned. "We'll be back long before it's time for him to start school."

Anger swelled inside me, a hot, murderous rage that made me want to throw something and hit him with it, to wipe the patronizing smile off his face. I wished I'd left him in the driveway last night. "That's not my point, Karl. I don't think Dustin needs to be taking a trip right now— especially not that far." *With you.*

"Mom, please!" Dustin interjected, and I held up a hand.

"Honey, I'm not mad at you. Your father should

have asked me before he said anything about this." I glared at Karl, hated him all over again. The grace I'd felt just moments ago was completely gone.

Karl saw the change. He reacted by hooking one leg over the other and laying a hand on his shin, leaning comfortably back on my sofa. "Well, technically August is my time anyway. Tomorrow is the first of August."

"*Your* time?" I coughed in disbelief. Was it possible that he could have the nerve to bring up the visitation arrangements after all these weeks? "Since when have you *ever* cared whether it was *your* time, Karl? Since *when* have you ever shown up? Now you want to just breeze in here because you're feeling down, because you need someone, and take my son on a cross-country trip?"

"Mom, please!" Dustin's volume rose to meet mine. "I want—"

"Dustin!" I snapped. Even though I knew we shouldn't be doing this in front of him, I couldn't stop myself. "This is between your father and me." It wasn't really. The war was between Karl and me, but we were firing shots right over our son.

"I don't see what the problem is." Karl lifted his hands, free to play the victim.

"Yes, you do. Yes, you do, Karl. That's why you didn't ask last night, or this morning. You knew I wouldn't want him going with you."

"What about what Dustin wants?" Karl shifted forward, his body drawing a more aggressive line. "Who says everything has to be your—"

"Stop it!" Dustin's outcry reverberated through the room as he stood up. "I don't want any more fighting!" He turned to me. His eyes, only a moment before glittering with excitement, were now brimming with tears. "I just want to say good-bye to Grandpa Joe, all right? I just want to go there, and see the ranch again, and say good-bye. Mom . . . please. I know what I'm doing. It's okay. I just want to go, all right?" His plea ended in a sob as he swiped a hand across his eyes. I felt myself breaking, as if my heart were being torn from my body, as if someone were asking me to hang it on a string and send it to North Dakota . . . with Karl, of all people.

I just want to say good-bye to Grandpa Joe. Dustin deserved that chance. If I stole it away from him, he would resent that forever. It wasn't like he wouldn't be safe, in the physical sense, anyway. Karl and Dustin had traveled together any number of times in past years on church mission trips, or when Dustin went along to one of Karl's conferences. They'd enjoyed hotel pools and quirky local tourist attractions together. Dustin read the maps, Karl did the driving, and they ate at every hole-in-the-wall diner they could find. Maybe this trip would remind them of those good times, make Karl

442

realize that Dustin's love was something too precious to throw away.

But there was also Dustin's well-being to consider. What if this trip raised his hopes, only to have Karl crash them again when life went back to normal?

What if it didn't? What if this trip helped to rebuild the bond between them? What if this was the beginning of something new—the genesis of our learning to function in a way that, if not friendly, at least didn't hurt our son? If that was possible, I owed it to Dustin to take the chance.

"All right." It hurt to give in, even though everything inside me was telling me it was the right thing to do. "Go pack your things. You have some clean laundry in the utility room, if you need it."

Dustin's eyes widened in surprise, then amazement, then anticipation. He spun around, ran in place several steps like a cartoon character on ice, then took off across room. At the start of the hallway, he slid to a stop, smiled at me, and said, "Thanks, Mom!" and then careened down the corridor toward his bedroom, his footsteps shaking the house.

"I'll go grab his laundry for him." Karl stood up and sidestepped toward the utility room. No doubt he was afraid to be alone with me. He could probably read on my face all the things that were going through my mind. None of them were fit for polite conversation.

"You'd better take good care of him," I bit out, because I didn't trust myself to say anything else.

Karl glanced back over his shoulder. "I will." His body language added, *What? Did you think I was going to dump him at a gas station alongside the interstate somewhere?*

I clenched my teeth, wishing again that I'd never let him in the door.

Before disappearing down the stairs, he paused, his shoulders softening. "Thanks for letting him come."

"Just make it a good trip for him, all right? You can't take him to North Dakota, and then bring him back here and just ditch him again. He needs you to be consistent in his life. He needs to know he still has a dad who loves him and cares about him and can't wait to spend time with him. Be the dad you used to be to him. Don't end up with him where you've ended up with your father, Karl. That's all I'm asking."

"I know." Karl didn't turn around, but this time the words seemed to come from a deeper place, a place that was real. "That's the reason I came here." He drew a breath, his shoulders rising and sinking as if he would say something more, but then he just continued across the room and disappeared down the stairs.

Tears pressed my eyes, and I walked onto the

back porch to try to clear my head. It wouldn't do Dustin any good to see me crying. He'd only feel guilty—as if he were being forced to make a choice between his father and me. I wished I could just fly to North Dakota with Dustin myself, but that wouldn't do anything to help Karl and Dustin rebuild their relationship. Aside from that, there was no way I could get time off from my job to travel up there. Taz wouldn't be able to handle the load, even for a little while. I had so many ongoing cases, and there was the tenuous situation with Birdie. I'd planned today's school-supply run partly as a way of spending more time with her, encouraging her to communicate more freely. Next week, she had appointments with the school psychologist and the caseworker. I wanted those assessments to go well.

I tried to put the rest of the day and the rest of the week out of my mind as I helped Dustin get his things together for the trip. Within twenty minutes, he was ready to leave. A lump clogged my throat as I kissed him good-bye, then stood in the driveway, watching the road long after Karl's car had disappeared.

I sent a prayer along in their wake. *Please make this trip what it needs to be for Dustin. Please make this the first step on a new path.*

When I went back inside, the house felt too quiet and too empty.

I stood gazing out the back windows, unaware at first what I was looking for, and then, of course, I knew. I was watching for Mart, wishing I could talk to him about Karl and Dustin, and get Mart's opinion. Wishing that last night hadn't ended the way it did. Wishing that last night hadn't ended. Living within the fantasy was so much better than dealing with reality.

On impulse, I picked up my cell phone and checked for missed calls. There were none, of course. Why would he call, after the way I'd left things? No doubt he'd decided that I was a complete basket case—warm one minute, cold the next. He probably thought I was playing some sort of neurotic game—enjoying the thrill of our clandestine meetings, with no real intention of taking things any further. How could I explain to him that I had no idea what my real intentions were? If I were one of my clients, I would have told myself that the inconsistent behavior was a sign that I wasn't ready for a relationship. I needed to move beyond past pain and resentments before I could expect to be successful in the present. It was only logical. There were so many layers of defensive insulation wrapped around my heart and soul right now.

But another part of me, somewhere beyond logic, begged the question, How could something that seemed so much like it was meant to be, be a mistake? When Mart and I were together, we were perfect, as if we were made for each other. We fit together like two oddly shaped pieces of a puzzle. What if I never found that again?

I dialed his number, then disconnected the call before it could go through. Setting down the phone, I went to the bedroom to shower and get dressed. I rummaged through my clothes, unsatisfied with everything. It really didn't matter what I wore today. I was only planning to hang around the house for the morning and then go to the Crossroads this afternoon to pick up Birdie and take her to the Community Closet. Shorts and a T-shirt would be fine for that. The day was already shaping up to be a hot one. A great day for being on the lake.

A great day for being on the lake with Mart. . . .

After last night, why in the world would he want to be on the lake with me?

The question drummed in my head as I wandered around the house, looking for things to do. I finished the laundry, cleaned the kitchen, scrubbed the bathroom, went outside and filled the rest of the bird feeders, then swept the back deck. Next I hosed down the screened porch, helped Sydney and Ansley cut some old-fashioned roses for their grandma, gathered fallen twigs and branches, and finally weeded a flower bed, watching the lake glisten below, teeming with ski boats and sailboats, paddleboats and water bikes from the resort. Filled with tourists enjoying the last few weekends before the start of school.

Empty of the one thing I was looking for. Where was he today?

Finally I drifted back inside, fixed a late lunch, and checked my phone. No calls.

I watched a rerun of *Little House on the Prairie*, then took another shower and got ready to head for the Crossroads. It was late enough. After one o'clock. By the time I made it to Len's selling spot, picked up Birdie, and drove to the Community Closet, the people who'd preregistered would have gone through the line. Since Birdie wasn't on the list, she had to wait for the leftovers, but leftovers would be better than nothing. At this point, I was actually hopeful about making the trip with her. Some coloring and writing supplies might be useful in bringing out more details about her past. Perhaps when we were finished at the Closet, I'd follow Len back to his farm and have an unofficial session with Birdie. Anything would be better than sitting around home, watching the phone and the lake.

I couldn't keep myself from looking for Mart one more time as I gathered my materials and left the house. When I passed by the Waterbird, his truck wasn't in the parking area. Still, I looped around at the end of the lot, turning in while entertaining the random thought that Mart usually came to the Waterbird by boat, so he could be there. I exited my car and walked into the store with no idea of what I was going to say if he was inside. Part of me wanted to just make pleasant conversation, as if the dramatic parting scene last night had never happened.

Part of me knew that would be incredibly juvenile and completely unfair. Mart would think I really was a schizophrenic loony tune. I owed him an explanation and some sort of indication of how I felt about the future.

As my eyes adjusted to the interior, I looked around, hoping to see him, nervous about what to say, wondering what he would say. What was there to say? *The company's right, but the timing's wrong. Maybe we could slow down, just be friends for now and see what happens—* something like that?

I quickly concluded that the store was deserted, except for Pop Dorsey, who was putting straws in a dispenser behind the counter. I bought a drink, so it would look like I was there for a reason.

"Everythin' all right?" he asked, perhaps sensing my disappointment as I paid for the drink and prepared to leave. Normally, I would have been looking forward to helping a child shop for school supplies and clothes. I'd been doing that since long before getting my counseling degree. Volunteering at the free supply extravaganza was one of the activities I'd truly enjoyed back in

Houston. There was nothing like seeing a child's eyes light up over backpacks, colored pencils, crayons, and free coloring books from places like the National Safety Council. Today, even that had lost its luster.

"Everything's fine," I lied to Pop, and he frowned, as if he could tell it. "Kind of quiet around here today, isn't it?" I really didn't care why the store was deserted. I was angling for information about Mart. Stretching upward, I looked out the back window. Some of the fishermen were working on a welding project below—the infamous handicapped hoist, undoubtedly. It looked to be almost complete. Mart wasn't down there.

Pop Dorsey nodded. "Yeah. Sheila had to make a run to Wal-Mart, and the fellas are pluggin' along on the dock project. We're gonna give 'er a test run in a bit, if Sheila'll stay gone long enough."

And where's Mart? I waited, but Pop didn't divulge any more information. "That's good."

Pop shrugged, casting a glum look toward the lake. He probably wanted to be down there with the guys. "You and your boy headed out to enjoy this fine weather today?"

"Not today, I'm afraid." I sounded as unenthusiastic as Pop did. "Dustin left on a trip with his dad to attend his grandfather's funeral in North Dakota, and I'm driving out to the

Crossroads to pick up Birdie and take her to the Community Closet for clothes and school supplies."

Pop nodded his approval. "Sorry to hear about the funeral, but that's a real good thing about Birdie. After we get done with the dock project this weekend, we're gonna rummage around and see what we can gather together to help out at Len's place. I got some old chain-link fence and a little lumber and whatnot stored behind my shed. Got some leftover paint around, too. It's all just goin' to rot. I can't do much anymore, but I can fill a trash bag and run a paintbrush. From what Reverend Hay said, Len's place needs a lot of that. I tried talkin' to Len about it when he was by here with tomatoes yesterday. He didn't say much, but then again, he never does."

"I think that's a great idea," I agreed. "Len needs the help." Thank goodness for Reverend Hay. Not just anyone could convince people to care about someone like Len.

"That Birdie sure is a sweet little gal." Pop smiled. "Cute as a bug's ear. Len brung her in here yesterday. She likes penny candy, so me and her are friends now."

In the farthest reaches of my memory, I recalled coming into the Waterbird and leaving with free penny candy. Pop Dorsey was younger then but just as friendly. When my mother found out, she let us know that we should beware of strangers offering free gifts.

"I'm glad he's taking her out around people more." I'd been trying to communicate to Len that Birdie needed to interact with people, that he didn't have to keep her hidden in the woods anymore. "I'll try to talk to him about the house projects when I see him today. He might need a little time to process an idea like that."

"Well, there's a lot of us not as quick as we used to be," Pop observed. "But that don't mean we haven't got somethin' to offer. You know, Sheila and I talked the other day, and we'd be willing to watch after Birdie anytime. If Len can't get ready to keep her right away, we could move her in with us. My wife, God rest her soul, and I raised four kids of our own and seven foster kids in the back of this ol' store through the years. I bet you didn't know that."

"No, I didn't." My spirits lifted a little. A supportive community could make all the difference to Birdie. "Thanks for offering. I really think that with the right amount of pitching in, we can make this work. It's just going to take some time."

"Most worthwhile things do," Pop remarked, closing the cash register. "I think Len will come around to seeing that folks want to help. Sydney and Ansley were here when he came by yesterday, and they took little Birdie in like she was a brand-new baby doll they just got. Mrs. Blue told Len to bring Birdie over anytime the girls are out swimming or playing in the yard. I think he might actually do it. And say, speakin' of Len—if you get a chance while you're at the Crossroads, would you mind pickin' me up another gallon bucket of his tomatoes? Tell him they're for the Waterbird, and I'll put money on his account, here at the store."

"Sure."

A customer came in the door, and I stepped back from the counter. Pop smiled and waved me off. "Pretty drive out to the Crossroads—lots of views of the lake. Water looks like someone sprinkled it with diamonds today. Take yer time and look around." He pointed to the motto above the door.

Stop looking ahead. Stop looking back. Stop. Look around. For today, that would be my theme song. I was going to stop worrying and obsessing and just enjoy what the afternoon had to offer. "I'll do that, thanks." I stepped out the door into the sunlight, feeling the questions in my head dissipate a little. Pop was right. It was a beautiful afternoon. Not the kind of day for walking around under a cloud.

On the way to the Crossroads, I tried not to mull things over too much. I took my aggressions toward Karl out on a few mudholes and laughed a little, thinking that Karl would probably have a heart attack if he could see me now. He didn't know I was capable of powering through the mud in a monster truck.

The trip around the eastern corner of the lake left the truck covered in sludge. I was a little proud of it, actually. Len, in his strange, shy way, would probably say something like, *Ooo-eee! Uuuh-you ugg-got some umm-mud.* When I was leaving after my last visit with Birdie, Len had admired the state of the truck—as if the coating of mud were a badge of honor, proof that I really belonged in the hills.

When I rounded the corner and came within sight of the Crossroads, I didn't see any sign of Len. Under a tree on the side of the road, an elderly couple was selling watermelons. I pulled over and asked them if they'd see a man and a little girl selling vegetables from a gray truck, and they told me they'd been alone all day.

"That's strange," I muttered, and checked my watch. It was after two o'clock. Where could they be?

Pulling under the shade of a tree, I rolled down the windows and turned off the engine. It was worth waiting at least awhile. Surely Len wouldn't miss an entire Saturday of tomato-hungry tourists. Maybe he'd had trouble with his truck—a flat tire or something. He knew I was planning to meet him. So far, Len had been reliable. Between Mart, the caseworker, and me, we seemed to have convinced him that missing appointments could get him into trouble.

I checked my cell phone, hoping deep down that there would be a message from Mart but telling myself that if there was reception, I'd call Dustin and see how the trip was going. I was almost afraid to check. If Dustin didn't sound happy, I wasn't sure what I'd do. By now, he was hundreds of miles away.

The phone showed a one-bar signal, so I dialed Dustin's number and achieved a patchy connection long enough to hear his voice and ask if he was doing all right.

"Yeah, I can hardly hear you, though. Where're you at, Mom?"

"I'm out at the Crossroads waiting to meet up with Len. I'm taking Birdie for school supplies, remember?"

It was hard to tell whether Dustin really heard me or not. A hiss of static answered, and then ". . . kay. I better go. Don't worry about me, all right?"

Don't worry about me. Easier said than done. "I love you, sweetie." Shutting the phone, I laid my head back against the seat, watching a family with a pull-behind camper select watermelons across the street.

The lack of sleep was starting to weigh on me. I let my eyes fall closed, thinking, *Maybe just a little nap. Ten minutes.* If Len and Birdie didn't show up by three, I'd go to the Community Closet event by myself and see if they'd let me pick up school supplies and select some clothes for her. Since Sheila was working, and she knew about Birdie's situation, I could probably pull it off. It wouldn't be as much fun as actually watching Birdie select things for herself, but it would be better than completely missing the opportunity. When a child has nothing and needs everything, you can't afford to pass up a chance.

The breeze combed my hair as I drifted off. Considering the heat of the day, it wasn't bad, sitting here in the shade. Comfortable, actually. Relaxing, after a really rough night and a strange day. Maybe all of it really was a dream. I'd wake up any minute now and find Dustin asleep in his bed. Mart would call while I was on my way to work . . .

"Y-y-y-you uuh-takin' ubb-Birdie?"

I jerked upright and opened my eyes, my head light and logy. I was . . . Where was I?

In the truck?

"Yy-you takin' ubb-Birdie?"

I turned toward the open window, my neck protesting the movement. Len was outside. He had his hand on Birdie's shoulder.

Fog glazed my eyes as I checked the clock. It was almost four. If Birdie and I didn't get going we'd miss the school supply event completely. "Oh, um, I . . . yes . . . I guess I fell asleep while

I was waiting. I thought you'd be here earlier, selling tomatoes."

"Him uggg-got c-c-colic. Umm-my umm-mule," Len answered. "I ubb-been w-w-walkin 'im. Ugg-gotta go ubb-back, too."

For a man of few words, Len did a surprisingly good job of filling me in on the events of the day. I quickly recalculated the rest of the afternoon, while realizing that Len had left what he was doing and driven all the way here, either because he didn't want to miss our appointment or because he didn't want to deprive Birdie of the shopping trip. Not every parent I dealt with would go to that extent. "Tell you what. You go ahead and do what you need to do. I'll take Birdie to pick up her school supplies and clothes, and then we'll get some supper, and I'll bring her back later this evening. Would that be all right?"

Len seemed momentarily confused, then he shrugged and said, "All urr-right, I ugg-guess."

Len walked Birdie to the passenger side of the truck and let her in. I buckled her into the seat, noting that among the other things we needed to accomplish was the procurement of a booster seat. In Texas, kids weren't legal without one until seven years old.

She sat like a little statue as I turned on the ignition. Her eyes tracked the disappearance of Len's truck, her head remaining face-forward, as if she were afraid to move.

"We're going to have some fun today, Birdie," I said. "We'll get crayons and some paper and other good things for school, and some clothes and maybe even a toy, if we can find one." She flashed a look my way at the word *toy,* and I knew I'd hit on a temptation. Maybe we'd make a quick stop at the dollar store.

As we circumvented the lake, Birdie and I began getting along famously. She and I even shared some conversation—mostly observing birds and flowers on the roadsides and spotting cars and signs that were red, like her boots. After that we sang "Jingle Bells," because Birdie had spotted a trailer house with leftover Christmas decorations wilting in the sun.

When we reached the Community Closet event in the Moses Lake High School gym, Sheila was at the registration table, and much to my surprise, so was Bonnie, from work. Her church outreach group had helped gather boxes of clothing and school items for Community Closet. Birdie seemed happy to see Sheila, and in short order, Sheila and Birdie were shopping the goods while I stood talking with Bonnie, since the crowds were pretty well gone by then.

"She's so cute. I wish I had one," Bonnie remarked wistfully as she watched Birdie fill her new backpack with donated supplies, then shop through what was left of the gently-used clothing. Sheila had tucked away some things in

Birdie's size, so the pickings were pretty good.

"You will, one of these days," I said, but I understood Bonnie's longing. I missed Dustin's little-boy years.

"I'm so tired of waiting." Bonnie peeled her name tag off her shirt, folded it, and dropped it in the trash, seeming uncharacteristically blue. "Guess in the meantime handing out school supplies to cute kids is better than nothing."

"And taking care of Taz," I added. "He's like a big kid."

Bonnie chuckled, leaning over the counter to peek out the gym door. "He really likes you, you know. The office is a whole lot more relaxed since you started taking care of the fieldwork."

"It's been a great learning experience," I said. "Sort of baptism by fire, but great."

Bonnie frowned at the words *learning experience* and *baptism by fire*. "Please tell me you're not going to get tired of us and, like, move on. Taz tried to hire two different people before you, and once they got a good look at the job, they ran away screaming." Straightening some Post-it Notes on the desk, she glanced at me. "I wasn't supposed to tell you that, by the way."

I blinked, surprised that two people had tanked in my job before me and that Bonnie had kept it a secret. "I'm not going anywhere." I started to add that I felt as if this job and I were meant for each other, but a customer came to the counter, and Bonnie was obliged to stock her sacks with various free pencils, advertising pins, and a fish-shaped paper fan from the Moses Lake Chamber of Commerce.

I excused myself and walked to the other end of the room to help Birdie and Sheila look through the clothing. After some searching and trying on, Birdie ended up with two pairs of shoes, three dresses, three shorts, and a pair of jeans (red, she observed), as well as various T-shirts sporting everything from Mickey Mouse to Texas Rangers baseball. Sheila put the things into Wal-Mart sacks while Birdie changed into one of her new outfits in a makeshift dressing room. When she came out, she took a Wal-Mart sack from Sheila and clutched it against herself as Bonnie filled a goodie bag at the checkout counter. Birdie smiled when Bonnie admired her new dress and shoes. She had the glow of a happy little girl. Bonnie even offered to procure a free booster seat through her car insurance company and promised to bring it to the office early next week.

After leaving the gym, Birdie and I meandered along the main street of Moses Lake—a strip of turn-of-the-century limestone buildings that were the remains of what had been a farming community before the lake was formed. I stopped off at the dollar store to let Birdie pick out a toy, and the process took longer than I'd planned. She wandered up and down the toy aisle, carefully investigating toys and packaging, as if she'd never before seen such wonderful things. We talked a bit about sandbox toys, and Barbies, and a set of plastic dishes, but in the end, she selected a stuffed rabbit from a bin of leftover Easter goodies.

"You got you a bunny?" the teenager at the cash register asked, and Birdie ducked her head, nodding shyly.

"Tell her what color the bunny is, Birdie," I prompted, wondering if Birdie would come out of her shell a bit.

"Hmmm," the cashier said playfully. "Well, I dunno. I think it's yellow."

Birdie giggled, sneaking a glance at her with one eyebrow lowered. "Blue." The word was barely audible, but at least she answered. She smiled afterward, as if she was pleased with herself. After leaving the dollar store, we walked down Main Street, past the old-fashioned hardware store, and the small row of quilt and antique shops that catered to summer tourists, to Moses Lake's combination gas station, Chinese food hut, and pizzeria across from Lakeshore Community Church. There, Birdie curiously watched the children of the Thai family who ran the place, as they played in a back corner that was stocked with toys and a television set. I encouraged Birdie to join them. Initially, she only shook her head and ate her pizza, but by the time we were ready to leave, she was checking out their toys and showing them her blue bunny.

After making friends in the pizza place, we headed back to Len's house with the radio pumping out seventies tunes and Birdie bobbing along to the music in the passenger seat. In spite of the day's upside-down beginnings, and the disaster with Mart last night, I had a sense of accomplishment as we sloshed along the muddy roads, weaving our way into the hills. I was on a volunteer high—the kind you get when something you planned turns out really, really well.

Birdie fell asleep before we made it to the low-water crossing, and her head lolled against the seat, bouncing at the chuckholes. I finally felt sorry for her and laid a hand over her hair, holding her head in place as we traveled the last few miles of rutted road to Len's place.

The hills were a dusky gray in the distance as we topped the rise and rattled through Len's garden. In spite of the beauty of the evening, an uncomfortable feeling pricked my happiness bubble. I hadn't meant to return Birdie quite this late. I would need to drop her off in a hurry and head home to get out of Chinquapin Peaks before nightfall. The last thing I wanted was to be stuck up on these roads after dark—honkin' big four-by-four truck or no.

I woke Birdie and helped her gather her bags as

we idled toward the house. Apparently Len had been driving in the yard today, because the area in front of the house was a muddy mess of churned-up earth and tire tracks. Rather than parking in the mire, I rolled into the grassy space behind the old school bus and led Birdie around the back of the bus to the house. She had new shoes on, after all.

Len didn't answer when we knocked on the front door, and the place was strangely quiet. The lights were on in the barn, so I sent Birdie into the house with her packages and I moved to the edge of the porch, studying the quagmire below and trying to decide how I could traverse the yard without ruining a perfectly good pair of tennis shoes. Just as I prepared to step off the porch, something caught my eye in the fading light behind the barn. There were three vehicles out there—Len's truck, an old brown pickup, and a white SUV dotted with rust-colored primer. Who was here?

As fish are caught in a cruel net,
or birds are taken in a snare,
so men are trapped by evil times
that fall unexpectedly upon them.
—Ecclesiastes 9:12
(Left by Bob, who's out of a job.
Got fishhooks and faith. Life's OK.)

Chapter 22

Mart McClendon

Some days you don't get far before you find out you would've been better off staying in bed. Before I'd even opened my eyes to Saturday morning, someplace on the other end of the county, the day was taking on a life of its own. Not long after sunup, a sheriff's deputy patrolling on the far side of the lake had stopped a Ford Bronco, a late-model Malibu, and a brown pickup out on County Road 1556. The three vehicles were traveling together, all running over speed, and the inspection sticker was out of date on the pickup. When the deputy tried to run the tags, Dispatch had a problem with the computers, and they couldn't pull up the information right away. The deputy, being young and impatient to go home at the end of his shift, decided he'd just hand out a couple warnings and let it go at that.

The group looked harmless enough—low-rent types packed for a camping trip at the lake, their vehicle windows bulging with boxes, stuff in trash bags, and what looked like bedrolls.

When the deputy walked back to the cars to write out the warnings, he decided he'd give the drivers a little scare, so they'd slow it down in the future. He asked all three drivers to step out of their cars, so he could read them the riot act before letting them off with the warning. About that time, he noticed the lady in the passenger seat of the Malibu scrambling like she was trying to hold something down on the floorboard. It let out a sound that was somewhere between a cat squall and a baby's cry, and the lady tossed a lit cigarette out the window so she could use both hands to control whatever she had underfoot.

The deputy hollered to her that she'd better put out the cigarette before the dry grass caught fire—it was summer, and even with the recent rains, we were under a burn ban. She yelled back that the car door didn't open on her side, and if the deputy wanted the cigarette put out, he'd have to do it himself. Meantime, a little trail of smoke was rising out of the ditch. The officer also noticed that none of the drivers had exited their vehicles, and the front driver was arguing with his passenger.

Right about then, the deputy knew he was in trouble. He got ready to pull his pistol, and all of a sudden, something in the car screamed like a banshee, there was a commotion, and an animal the size of a small collie dog jumped out the window and darted off into the brush. Even with the dim morning light, the deputy got a look at it. He swore it ran like a cat and was striped like a tiger.

The lady in the car screamed, "It bit me. I'm bleedin'!" The cigarette lit the grass like tinder, and the mystery animal climbed a tree in the right-of-way. The officer didn't know whether to draw his gun, put out the fire, or go after whatever was up the tree. A moment of hesitation is all it takes for a situation to go from strange to dangerous, and before the deputy knew what was happening, the driver in front hit the gas, tossed gravel, and took off. The second driver followed, and the Malibu bumped the deputy as it spun out after the other two. He ended up flat on his back with a pretty good goose egg on his head, a grass fire the size of a trash-can lid and spreading, and the mystery critter growling in the tree. By the time backup made it to the scene, he was fighting the fire and the critter had escaped. He swore it was a baby tiger.

The deputy, of course, got a lot of jokes about the bump on his head, the tiger sighting, and whether he'd been drinking on duty. I got a morning wake-up call about the vehicles and the possibility of an escaped exotic cat somewhere along 1556. I didn't have too hard a time buying the story. Both here and in the Bend area, trafficking contraband exotic animals went right along with the drug trade. I figured if we found those vehicles, they'd be packed for something other than a campout.

When the computers at dispatch finally came back up, they ran the tags, and word came back that the Malibu was registered to a woman who had no prior history of arrest, but recently the car had been reported in two separate pump-and-run thefts at local gas stations. In both cases, a man was driving. No doubt the woman who owned the car had herself a new boyfriend of the unsavory variety. Those types usually traveled in their girlfriends' cars, since having one of your own requires a steady job. The brown pickup was stolen from one of the Mennonite farms up in Jake's area, and the Bronco belonged to the sister of a registered sex offender who had warrants out for his arrest on a drug charge and a parole violation. He was a bad customer. It was a lucky thing he'd decided to take off instead of shoot. The deputy could've ended up with a lot worse than a bump on the head and a story to tell.

I spent the day involved in the manhunt with the state police, sheriff's department, and agents from the Drug Enforcement Agency. While driving back roads and ranch roads along 1556, I kept one eye out for the suspect vehicles and one eye out for the mystery animal, which, after I found a couple tracks in the moss near the grassfire area, I concluded probably was an exotic cat of some variety, most likely a juvenile. Being domestic, the poor thing was probably scared out of its mind. It wouldn't survive too long in the woods. If coyotes, a mountain lion, or a redneck with a gun didn't get it, it'd probably starve to death soon enough.

Late in the afternoon, I got a call that some picnickers in the park near Eagle Eye Bridge had seen what looked like a small exotic cat watering along the shore. It'd run into the bathroom building, and they'd trapped it in there. I went to the park, and in pretty short order had myself a thirty-pound tiger cub. I wish I could've said the capture was dramatic, since I had an audience and all, but the truth was that the little fella was mighty glad to see me. After a day in the woods, he was looking for someone who might feed him and put him in a nice, quiet cage. He was tame, all right. The rednecks had probably been keeping him as a house pet, because he was still little enough to be cute. The picnic crowd took pictures with him in the back of my truck.

It wasn't until I was leaving the park that I thought about the fact that this was *our* park— Andrea's and mine. This was the place where I first looked at Andrea and saw something more than just a pretty girl with an attitude. Now, considering what'd happened last night, I felt a lot like that wannabe Robin Hood, sitting on the back steps of the school auditorium. Only this time, there wasn't anyone to come along and patch up the wounds with an ice cream cone. I was glad it'd been a busy day. Not a lot of time to think.

After I'd made it back to Moses Lake and dropped the tiger cub at the vet clinic, I got the call that the state police and sheriff's department had given up the manhunt. That put me officially off duty. All at once the day that'd seemed full to the brim felt empty. I didn't have anywhere to go or anyone to share the tiger-hunt story with, unless I wanted to hang out at the Waterbird with the docksiders. Pretty pathetic Saturday evening for a single man under forty.

I decided that maybe I'd go out on the lake for a while, drift up Larkspur Cove, and see if Andrea was out. Maybe I'd just not mention last night—act like it never happened. Could be, I'd been pushing too hard. That was, after all, why Melanie and I hadn't worked out, back in Alpine. She couldn't stop pushing for things to happen on her timetable, especially after Aaron died. To her, the accident was proof that we didn't have any more time to waste *just dating*. Before that, she'd been pretty content to stay wrapped up in separate lives—her traveling as a sales rep, and me working the Bend area. Then suddenly she wanted a house and a family. To me, the fact that I'd let my job come before Aaron and Mica was proof that I wasn't good for anybody. Finally, Melanie couldn't take it anymore—the grief over the accident, or how I used it as an excuse to keep dragging my feet.

Over time, things could work themselves out at Andrea's pace, couldn't they? I knew what it was like to be pushed for something I didn't have to offer right then, and I didn't like it when I was on the receiving end. If we needed to keep it cool until she thought Dustin could adjust to the idea, a decent guy would respect that. He'd wait. Wouldn't he?

It was a risky plan, I knew. I'd taken a pretty good blow last night, and I was still smarting from it. If a girl could knock the wind out of me like that after only a few weeks, how much worse would it be after another week, or two, or ten? In the meantime, I'd feel like I was lying to her boy. What would he think when he found out?

Maybe the right thing was to do what she asked and leave her alone. Sometimes, even when something seems good, the timing's just not right. My mama would've said that a gentleman respects a lady's wishes. Always.

That student teacher who got me to wear the green tights and the Robin Hood outfit would've said that Robin Hood wouldn't let the rules stand in the way of love.

Love?

That idea came out of nowhere, like a dust devil rushing around the edge of a barn, carrying all sorts of debris in it. Was it possible to start to feel that way about someone you'd only just met? I'd really let myself get blindsided, and if I didn't watch out, I'd end up flat out on the turf, off my feet. And for what? A woman I'd known less than a month? A woman who came with a whole lot of baggage I had no control over? Did that really make any sense? She'd made her position pretty clear last night. The smart thing to do was just back off and let her be. . . .

I tried to talk myself into the *back off and let it be* approach as I drove home from the vet's office, but no sooner had I made it to my cabin than I was out on the lake, telling myself I needed to tool by the Waterbird to see how Pop's hoist was coming along. I was curious, since I hadn't been able to help today. Yep, I was curious about the hoist. And while I was out, I should probably take a loop around the lake and make sure the run of bass hadn't tempted some fellas into going over the keeper limit. Heard they'd been biting out past the Scissortail . . . up around Larkspur Cove.

I knew where I was going, of course. Before dusk had settled, I'd circled the Scissortail three times and wandered up Larkspur Cove twice, looking at registration stickers on fishing boats trolling along the shore. By the time night fell, it was obvious there was no one at Andrea's house. Not a light on in the place. Maybe she and Dustin had gone somewhere.

It crossed my mind that I ought to call Dustin's cell phone—let him know that, since today'd gotten gummed up with work, I planned to put in some time on the dock project tomorrow after the dinner-on-the-grounds at Lakeshore Church. That'd tell me whether Dustin had talked his mom into coming to the Sunday picnic. . . .

It was a lame excuse, but I dialed the number anyway. Dustin's voice was faint when he answered. I finally put it together that his grandpa had died and he was headed to the funeral in North Dakota with his dad. His mom wasn't with him. He told me he was sorry he couldn't help with rest of the dock-and-hoist project, and then we hung up.

I cruised around the lake awhile longer, then went back by Andrea's house. Nobody there. She'd probably gone out to dinner or shopping somewhere, since that was what women did when they were on their own.

Thinking about dinner reminded me that I was hungry, so I headed to the Waterbird to get a sandwich before they closed up for the night. Sheila was working the counter when I got there, and Pop was over at the tables with a couple of the docksiders, playing dominoes. They were discussing the hoist in whispers, so as not to bring Sheila into the conversation. I decided I'd hang around awhile. There wasn't anyplace I needed to be, and I figured I'd cruise through Larkspur on the way home.

"Heard y'all had a pretty good adventure today, over in the Chinquapin Peaks area," Sheila said, nodding toward the police scanner. When things got dull at the Waterbird, the police scanner served as backup entertainment.

"You catch them drug pushers, Mart?" Burt asked. He and Pop were playing dominoes with a couple docksiders and Hay. Nester was AWOL tonight. His wife must've made him stay home.

"Not yet," I admitted, getting my sandwich and moving to the table next to theirs. I opened the sandwich and checked for soybeans and alfalfa sprouts. It looked safe enough. Just meat and normal vegetables. Some good homegrown tomatoes from Len's place. "If you fellas see any vehicles matching those descriptions holed up on the park roads or down along the shore, don't mess with them, just call it in."

"We will," Burt promised. "We been passin' the word along."

"I'm sure y'all have," I said and took a bite of the sandwich. That was one good tomato. Len sure knew how to raise fine produce.

"Heard Dustin's grandpa died," Hay

commented, and the rest of them flicked stray glances my way to see if I was already in on the news.

"Yeah, I heard that," I said, trying to keep it cool. I didn't need the whole crew nosing into my business.

Burt studied the dominoes to make a play. "Seems like you'd be down to Larkspur Cove tonight, bein' as somebody's all alone this evening. She might need help with something."

They yucked it up among themselves, and I went on and ate my sandwich. Maybe stopping by the Waterbird wasn't such a good idea.

"Yep, I figured they were out on a hot date somewhere tonight," Pop put in. "When Dustin's mom came by here earlier, I asked her to get me some more tomatoes from Len while she was out at the Crossroads. She said she would, but she never did stop back with my produce. Figured she was with you."

"She told you she'd come back by here and she didn't?" I asked. "You sure?"

Pop frowned and slid a poised domino back into his hand. "I been here all day."

A warning light flickered in the back of my mind—like a radio call trying to come through out of range. The Crossroads was on the way out to Chinquapin Peaks. That side of the lake wasn't the safest place to be today, with the manhunt going on. . . .

The odds that Andrea would've run into the group we'd been chasing were a million to one . . .

No sense jumping to conclusions. . . .

It *was* possible, though. . . .

I pulled out my phone and dialed Andrea's number—the house first, then her cell. She didn't answer either one, which left me wondering whether something was wrong, or she just didn't want to talk to me. I called a second time and left messages both places, asked her to call me or call the Waterbird, just to let us know everything was all right.

I ate a few bites of my sandwich, telling myself I was jumping to conclusions. She could've gone any number of places after she finished taking Birdie for school supplies. She could be over at her parents' house, visiting her sister, or at a movie with her phone on silent. . . .

"Seems like she'd be listening for her phone, being as her boy's traveling," Burt commented, like he'd read my mind. "You know how mamas worry when their kids are out of pocket."

I thought about my mother. Whenever any of us kids were away from home, she stayed near the phone, especially after dark. It was past nine o'clock now.

"I agree." Sheila finished counting the change in the cash register and went to the front door to lock it. With her fingers still wrapped around the bolt, she turned a worried look toward the lake.

"I've got a general bad feeling about this. I think you'd better go check her house—see if she's out in the yard or something."

Any other time, I would've poked fun at Sheila for being such a mother hen, but right now, I had a bad feeling, too. "I think I will," I said, grabbing my leftovers and heading for the back door. Good sense stopped me before I stepped out. "Listen, if there's still no sign of her there, I'll radio my partner, the sheriff's department, and the park ranger's office—have them keep a lookout for her truck on the roads. Could be she broke down or got stuck somewhere out around the Crossroads. If I don't find her at her house, I'll head on up the river channel toward Len's place—see when she dropped Birdie back with Len."

"Be careful." Sheila folded her hands prayer-style and pressed them against her lips, and for once I didn't feel like she was making a mountain out of a molehill. "Let us know." She reached over and turned the scanner up.

"You need any help?" Burt asked. "I can grab my old thirty-thirty and follow you up the river channel, just in case you run into the guys y'all were manhunting earlier."

"Burt was in the army before he was a school principal," Pop Dorsey added, like that ought to be credentials enough for me to take Burt along as backup.

I shook my head. The last thing I needed was Burt Lacey trailing me in his boat with a loaded thirty-thirty. "I'm sure it'll amount to nothing. Andrea's probably at her house—just not answering the phone."

But she wasn't, and I knew it even before I docked at her place and walked around, looking in the windows and banging on doors. Little Sydney and Ansley were out in the yard next door, catching fireflies. They told me they hadn't seen Andrea since early that afternoon. They pointed out that the clumps of mud from tire treads were dry and hard as rocks in the driveway, which meant that Andrea hadn't been back all afternoon. Smart girls.

I put a description of the truck out to my partner, the park ranger's office, the sheriff's department, and the highway patrol, and asked them to keep an eye out. No one was near Len's place. My partner, Jake, was almost an hour away, but he said he'd check the Crossroads and then head toward Len's house, keeping an eye out for Andrea's truck as he went. I headed for Len's place by way of the lake because I could get there faster by boat.

The water was quiet under Eagle Eye Bridge and up the river channel where Len usually put his rig in, but a storm had started gathering off in the hills. Len had tied his boat up to a tree near the shore instead of dragging it up into the brush for the night, which was strange, especially considering the weather. That johnboat was of value to Len, and normally he brought it up and hid it in the brush after he finished in the evenings. Today it was rocking at the edge of the water, hooked to a cedar branch, like he'd meant to get back to it before dark.

I idled to the shore, secured my boat, and stepped off, breaking my gun forward in the holster on the way. I wasn't so worried about what might be in the woods as I was worried about Len's dogs. It wouldn't have surprised me if he let them out at night to keep varmints away from his place, and one thing was for sure— neither the dogs nor Len were used to visitors showing up after dark. I'd have to make sure he knew it was me before I got close to that cabin.

About halfway up the hill, I heard something— voices. Two men. Not by the cabin, but downhill between the river and me. They hadn't come off a boat—I would've heard it. Hunters, maybe, out night-shooting varmints . . . or a couple fellas harvesting a marijuana patch they'd tucked back in the woods somewhere. Nobody else would be out walking around in the trees at night, especially with a storm starting to gather.

My belt radio hissed, and I jerked my hand up to silence it. Not quick enough, though. The fellas by the water stopped walking. They knew they weren't alone.

"Who's over there?" one of them called out. "That you, B.B.? You come sneakin' up on us, you're like to get your sorry self shot clean through. Whoever that is, you better come outta there right now."

I ducked behind a tree, doused my flashlight, and waited while they moved my way. My mind sprinted ahead, analyzing the logical next step and how the situation might develop, based on what I decided to do now. If I called for backup, I'd give away my position. If I didn't, I was on my own until whenever Jake made it to Len's house. There'd been more than one game warden who got waylaid in the woods and was never heard from again.

I slid my pistol out of the holster and waited while they walked past. They were taking their time, looking around, shining a flashlight into the dark, sending long shadows slinking across the forest carpet in shifting, crooked shapes.

"That you, girl?" The voice was nearer this time, and the good-ol'-boy tone was gone. "That you, you better come on out now. You don't, somebody gonna tan your hide. We ain't gonna hurt ya. C'mere, girl. C'mere. You better quit hidin'." They were getting closer, their movements cautious, telling me they knew someone was nearby. I heard the click of a rifle going off safety. It'd only be a matter of time before they stumbled right over me.

One thing I'd learned from experience is that you're better off finding a perpetrator than being found by one. At least then you've got the element of surprise in your favor.

I waited a minute longer, listened, tried to gauge their exact positions from the footsteps. Twelve, maybe fifteen feet, the two of them together. A beam of light strafed my tree. There was a man's shadow in it, one arm longer than the other, dangling a rifle.

I gripped my flashlight with one hand and tightened my fingers on my pistol, ready to identify myself and hit them with the beam. They'd be blinded for a moment when I did. Hopefully, that'd be long enough.

I took in air, got my mind still and focused, ready.

An owl called somewhere overhead, then took flight, and in the brush a few feet away, a small animal—rabbit or coon, maybe—made a run for it.

"There she is!" one of the men hollered. "She's over that way!" They turned and headed for the lakeshore, crashing through the brush, their flashlight beams bobbing.

I leaned against the tree and caught my breath, taking advantage of the opportunity to call for backup. If the situation turned out to be nothing more than a couple poachers whose hunting dog had run off in the woods, and Len was up there in his cabin, and Andrea had left hours ago, I'd come out looking like an idiot, but that was a chance I was willing to take. There was an uneasiness up my spine that told me something more was going on.

I moved up the hill, staying off the path and working my way through the woods to the edge of Len's field. Before stepping into the clearing, I stopped, listened, looked around. The lights were on in the cabin, but the rest of the place was dark. It seemed quiet enough. Peaceful, but something didn't feel right. The place was too quiet. No puppies scuffling and yipping. No dogs barking.

There wasn't any way those dogs would let me come up after dark without raising a full-out ruckus. What were the chances that Len had packed up all the dogs *and* Birdie and gone somewhere? Not too likely.

Something was way south of normal.

I slipped from the tall grass and rounded the yard from behind, staying in the shadow of the barn, thinking it'd be just my luck that any minute now, I'd find out the dogs weren't gone; they were just dozing. But the eerie quiet thickened, the only sign of movement coming from Len's milk cow stomping and calling out long, low complaints, her bag in need of an evening milking. Len wouldn't have gone off and just left her in that condition.

Moving closer to the house, I turned on the flashlight and shined the beam around, called out Len's name. The back door was hanging open, the bottom section of screen flapping loose. No one who'd experienced the Texas-sized mosquitoes around the lake would go to bed and leave a door open at night.

The makeshift gate to the backyard was hanging loose on its bailing-wire hinges, which explained why the dogs weren't barking. They were out . . . somewhere. Stepping through the gate, I called Len's name again, moved into the yard. A long, low whine answered from inside— a dog whimpering. The grunting and whining of puppies followed. I slid my gun out, shined my flashlight beam on the door, then downward to the rock steps. A sticky red trail glistened against the light. Blood.

My pulse sped up and my stomach squeezed tight. I had a vision of Len and Birdie dead inside, the dogs making a meal of them. It wouldn't be the first time dogs had turned on their owners. What if Andrea had walked in on it, and the dogs came after her, too? In a heartbeat, the past was there with me, burning like a scalding pot. I was at the coast, watching the boat pull in with Mica's small body wrapped in a plastic sheet. They'd find Aaron a couple hours later.

Not again. Please, not again.

I ran the last few steps, took the stairs in one jump, kicked the door out of the way and braced myself behind one side of the frame, called Len's name and Birdie's, shined the flashlight and pointed the gun inside.

There was a dog on the floor, panting in a pool of blood, a gunshot wound in her hip. The puppies were clustered around her, some curled up sleeping, some whimpering and licking her fur.

I called out again, waited, listened. No answer. No sound except from the pups, which scampered to my feet, looking for help or food, or both. Stepping in the door, I hit the light switch with my elbow, radioed my backup, then moved into the kitchen. The place looked like a tornado had passed by, shattered glass and bits of dishes everywhere. A chair lay splintered to pieces on the far end of the room, a kitchen cabinet hanging off-kilter, Len's home-canned goods splattered on the floor like finger paints. The door to the bedroom was partway open. Drops of blood led through it.

I followed the trail, stood aside at the entrance, stretched out an arm and pushed the door. The hinges yawned as the opening widened, fanning light into the room. With a quick sweep, I took in the details. The white dog was on the floor in pretty bad shape, shot or beaten—I couldn't tell. The window was open on the other side of the room. A half-dozen loose sheets of paper lay strung across the floor, fluttering in the breeze. The bed was in oddly perfect shape—not a wrinkle in the faded quilt. The picture of Len in his army uniform had been knocked off its nail and now rested against the baseboard, the glass broken. Something beside it caught my eye. A wallet. I crossed the room, skirting anything that might be evidence, slid a pen from my pocket, opened the wallet, looked at the driver's license. The picture landed in the pit of my stomach. Andrea. A lipstick had rolled under the edge of the bed, a set of keys lay nearby. Was her truck here? Having come in from the back, I wouldn't have seen it. But if her vehicle was here, where was she?

Leaning through the open window, I spotted a couple of grocery store receipts and a plastic comb clinging in a scrappy cedar bush below. The grass was mashed and muddy. No distinguishable footprints, but someone had gone out this way. Apparently Andrea. What'd happened here tonight? Where were Andrea, Birdie, and Len?

A radio call let me know that Jake Moskaluk was coming up Len's road. He'd gotten an ETA on the sheriff's deputies. Another ten minutes yet.

"We need them now," I said. "We need them ten minutes ago." My mind was working in fast circles, trying to figure out where Andrea and Birdie might be and whether they were all right.

They had to be all right.

Jake's truck lights bobbed over the uneven ground on the far side of the cedar break as I walked through the front room of the house. "Mart, there's someone out here in a vehicle." His voice was low over the radio. I turned down my volume and pressed the unit to my ear. "They're headed your way, and . . . Yeah, they've made me out and turned for the woods." Outside, Jake's engine revved. He flipped on the floods and lit up the field, then sped through the high grass and over the slab wood fence. Whoever he was chasing wheeled around at the end of the field and took a run at the driveway. I got a make on the vehicle. Bronco. White. We'd been looking for these guys all day. Jake cut them off again, and they started my way, the headlights blinding. I squatted down behind the corner of the porch, pulled my side arm, hollered, "State game warden. Stop where you are!"

A shot rang out, struck the cabin wall a couple feet away. I hit the deck. Another shot struck, closer this time. I returned fire, even though all I could see were headlights. Their next shot splintered wood and tar paper on the corner of the cabin right above my head. Flattening myself to the floor, I belly-crawled backward to a better position, saw Jake's truck whip around, heard him return fire. A siren sounded across the cornfield near the front gate. The sheriff's boys had arrived a little ahead of schedule, right where we needed them to be, for once.

Another bullet flew over my head and grazed a porch post; then the driver in the Bronco saw the posse at the front gate and spun his truck around, heading for the woods. We had him now. There wasn't anyplace for him to go over there. Whoever he was, he wasn't messing around. We were onto something big. With that idea came another. Andrea and Birdie and Len were mixed up in this, too.

They're all right, I told myself. *They're all right.* But self-assurances weren't what I wanted. What I wanted was to find them, get Birdie someplace safe, then take Andrea in my arms. If we all made it out of this, I wasn't wasting one more minute worrying about how things ought to happen between us, or how long it might take for her to be ready to tell Dustin about it. I was just going to enjoy the moments for what they were and figure the Big Man Upstairs had the game plan under control.

One thing I finally understood, pinned down on the porch with shotgun pellets peppering the cabin walls, Jake's truck slinging mud in the pasture, and the sheriff's boys charging up the lane— you've got to take your chances as they are. God gives what He gives, and only He knows why. If you're smart, you open the gift while it's on the table. Enjoy it. Be thankful for it. Live every minute of it while it's happening. Aaron and Mica and what had happened to them was in the past. I couldn't change it. They ran out of time before they should have, but I was still here, and there had to be a reason for that. Maybe this was the reason.

If I got the chance to take Andrea in my arms again, I wasn't letting go.

The birds of the air nest by the waters;
they sing among the branches.
—Psalm 104:12
(Anonymous senior citizen,
the Bus Birders tour group)

Chapter 23

Andrea Henderson

I heard shots echo somewhere in the distance, the sound reverberating against the trees, bouncing off the hills, skimming the carpet of last year's leaves, seeming to come from everywhere at once. I pushed into the cedars, the branches raking my arms as I dragged Birdie with me. *Please, God,* I thought. *Don't let it be Len they're shooting at.*

There had been shots once already—how long ago? Maybe an hour? Longer? There were three shots just after we'd slipped out the window of Birdie's bedroom. I'd heard dishes breaking in the house, Len yelling, the dogs going wild, a man screaming in a way that curdled my blood, then three shots, and the dogs went silent. I hadn't turned around. I'd just grabbed Birdie's hand and bolted to the woods. There was no other choice.

Now there were more shots—several in rapid

succession, but faint and far away. Had we traveled that far from the cabin, or were they on the road somewhere, or in the woods, trying to find us? What would happen if they did?

If they found us, would they shoot me to get Birdie? After what had taken place in the cabin, I knew the answer to that question, even though my mind couldn't process it. The last hour seemed like a scene from a movie, something horrific enough that you were glad it wasn't really happening.

I'd seen them coming across the field with Len just a moment after I'd noticed the extra vehicles behind the barn. They were jostling him around, demanding something. Birdie had already trotted back to her bedroom with her sack of new clothes. She was singing to herself. Then she stopped, listened. Ducking against the wall, I slid soundlessly into the house, rushed across the living room. Birdie was wide-eyed in the bedroom doorway. She grabbed my hand and pulled me into the bedroom, pushed the door closed behind us. They were coming. Several men, three at least, and a woman. When Birdie heard the voices, she crouched behind the bed, tugged my hand and pulled me with her.

As they entered the house, Birdie's bedroom door fell open slightly. Through the narrow crack, I heard the ongoing argument, saw figures moving in the living room like shadows. They wanted to know if Len had any money stashed away.

"I bet he's got a bunch," a man's voice asserted. "Prob'ly been cashin' them big ol' government checks all the time and buryin' it in the backyard. You been buryin' money in the backyard, old man? Huh? You got a million bucks out there?" He laughed, a razor-edged vindictive sound.

Len stuttered, attempting an answer.

A second man laughed, then did something that wrenched a gasp from Len. Afterward, he demanded that Len produce the *bags* Norma had left in the old school bus.

Norma . . . Len's daughter? She was with them—ordering Len to give her the bags one minute, defending him the next, pleading with the men not to hurt him, saying in a sticky-sweet slur, "C'mon, C.J., give 'im a minute. You know he's dumb as roadkill. Give 'im a minute to think. What'd you do with the bags I left in the school bus, Pops? The black plastic trash bags with stuff in 'em. That's C.J.'s stuff. I shouldn'ta took it, and he wants it back. You gotta tell us where it's at now." Her voice rose on the last note, quivering, fearful, desperate, conveying that she was far from in control.

Len's answer was slow and slurred. I couldn't make out all the words—something about having burned the bags when he burned the trash.

"You better not've!" C.J. exploded. "You better

come up with my bags, old man. Where'd you put 'em? You and Norma hide 'em somewhere? You holdin' out on me, Norma? You been dealin' my stuff while I'm stuck in the stinkin' county jail?"

I heard the *thwack* of a fist on flesh. Len moaned. Something metal crashed to the floor and rolled across the room.

C.J. roared, spitting out a string of expletives. "You gimme my stuff or I'm gonna find that little snot-nosed kid, wherever you got her hid, and you ain't never gonna see her again."

Birdie shrank against me, her body quivering, her hands pressing over her ears, her eyes widening in silent anticipation of what was coming next. She'd been through this before.

"You hear that, you little brat?" C.J. roared. "It don't matter where you're hidin'. You know I'll find you out."

My heart seized in my throat, stopping the flow of air. What now? What should I do? Confront them? Hide? Make a run for the back door? The dogs were in a frenzy out there. I could hear them growling and clawing at the screen. They knew Len was in trouble.

A breeze touched my cheek like the back of a hand, slid under my hair, stilling my thoughts, causing me to look up. *The window . . .* If I could pop the screen out without making too much noise, we could slip through, sneak around to my vehicle on the other side of the old school bus, get in, and go for help. I had to get Birdie to safety. We couldn't stay in the bedroom. Even if we hid, sooner or later, they'd see my vehicle and know someone was here. They'd find us.

Thank goodness the mud had caused me to park on the other side of the school bus. Otherwise, they would have discovered us already. If we were lucky, we might be able to get to the truck, start it, and drive away before anyone could stop us. . . .

Pressing a finger to my lips, I looked Birdie in the eye, shook my head. I rose to my knees, checked over my shoulder, heard someone or something slam against the wall in the living room. The house shook, and behind me the bedroom door creaked open another inch. Stilling the trembling in my hands, I pressed a palm against the screen, pushed gently, then harder, with both hands.

The screen, encrusted with paint and dirt and riddled with holes, tore like old fabric, the mesh dry and rotten around the edges. Dust fell in a cloud, and bits of rotten wood landed silently in the growth of weeds outside. Checking over my shoulder, I motioned for Birdie, lifted her onto the windowsill, then leaned through, lowering her down. She stepped away from the house, her blue eyes skittering about helplessly.

"Wait," I whispered, then drew back so that I

could go through feet first. Chaos broke loose in the living room. I heard the fight moving into the kitchen, saw the bedroom door swing open, saw Len and another man fall across the doorway in a twisted heap, heard Norma scream.

A hammer thumped in my chest. I tried to scramble through the window. Something was holding me back. My purse. The strap was hung up and still wound around my shoulder. I threw my weight against it, felt the strap tear, heard my wallet and car keys spill onto the floor.

The jagged window frame sliced my back as I tumbled toward the ground.

Norma screamed. "C.J., look!"

"Hey! What're you doin?" one of the men yelled. I didn't know if they were yelling at us— if they'd seen us or not. Shedding the last shreds of my purse in the tall grass, I grabbed Birdie and ran, crashing through weeds and cedar bushes. Tripping and rolling into a drainage ditch, Birdie and I tumbling in a painful tangle. I heard the struggle, and the dogs, and the shots. I didn't look back, just grabbed Birdie and started running again. If we could make it to the road, maybe we could find help—a passing car, another house. Anything.

But when we reached the road, they were there—a white SUV roaring up Len's driveway, then along the road, the headlights illuminating the dusky gray in the ditches, Norma was calling

Birdie's name, the tone falsely enticing. Birdie grabbed my hand, pulled me back into the cedars.

She shook her head, her eyes wide.

"Ssshhh," I whispered against her ear.

The other men were crashing through the brush somewhere downhill, calling Birdie's name, telling her she'd better stop hiding before her mother got mad.

Pulling her close against me, I pressed deeper into the cedars, the limbs grabbing my T-shirt, clawing my skin. If we tried to walk out via the road, we wouldn't get far before they saw us. In the woods, in the dark with no flashlight, I'd be completely lost. I didn't have any idea which way to go to find help.

"It's all right," I whispered against Birdie's ear. "I won't let anything happen. We'll just wait. We'll just wait for someone to come." But nobody knew where I was. How long before anyone might come looking for me? How many times might Dustin call before he figured out something was wrong? I thought of him, far away on a trip with his father, with no idea that I wasn't safely home. Would he even call to check in tonight? If I didn't answer, would he bother to call back?

It could be hours. It could be all night. What condition was Len in now? Where was he? He might not have all night. We probably didn't, either.

If we stayed this close to the house, sooner or later C.J., Norma, or the other men would discover us. I had to find a way out. It was getting darker by the minute, the night settling in moonless and damp. I had no way to see, no keys, no cell phone, no means of protecting Birdie or myself. How much chance was there of getting to safety on foot, in the dark, with a six-year-old?

But I had to do something.

Think, Andrea. Think.

The road wasn't an option. My vehicle wasn't an option. If I took Birdie into the woods now, anything could happen. We could end up wandering in circles . . . or worse. How many times had Dustin come home filled with Mart's war stories about campers and hikers lost in the state park? Word of a hiker attacked by a mountain lion a few months ago was still the talk of the community. It didn't happen often, but it did happen.

If you're ever lost, head for the water, Mart's voice was in my head now. *In the summer, there's plenty of traffic on the lake. . . .*

The path to the river was back by the cabin, but if we went that way, we'd be circling right into C.J.'s men.

Every place in the woods has its own sound, if you stop and listen, Mart had told me as we picnicked near Eagle Eye, listening to the mockingbirds and the Wailing Woman. *The river has a sound, and the hills have a sound, and the rocky draws have a sound, and the cliffs have a sound. Folks wouldn't get themselves so lost in these hills if they'd stop and listen.*

He was probably on the water tonight. Why did I feel as if he were close by?

"Birdie, do you know how to get down to the river?" I whispered. "Do you know how to get there from here?"

Birdie nodded, her eyes round and earnest in the fading light.

I hesitated a moment longer, wondering at the wisdom of depending on a traumatized child. But what other choice did I have? I took Birdie's hand, and we crawled through the cornfield to the forest, then started walking.

Finding our way in the dark was harder than I'd thought it would be. I had a feeling we'd been wandering in circles, but in the dark it was impossible to tell. The distant shots pushed Birdie closer to me. If those shots were coming from somewhere near Len's cabin, we'd traveled a long way. Birdie had stopped trying to lead. Now she was following, as lost as I was. The blind leading the blind.

The night air was surprisingly cool, and Birdie's fingers had turned icy inside mine, clinging mechanically as she stumbled along. I didn't dare pick her up. I'd tripped over roots, twigs, and rocks at least a dozen times and fallen hard. My left ankle was swollen from our hasty escape out the window, and a sticky film of blood had pasted my T-shirt to my back.

Maybe we should stop until morning, I thought. *Curl up in the driest spot we can find and try to sleep.* Maybe we were far enough away from the cabin to be safe. . . .

But what if they were still following us, still searching for us? What if we fell asleep, and they found us? I couldn't take that chance. And what about Len? I had to get help.

I thought again of Dustin. Had he called my phone? Was he worried?

Birdie sniffled, a small, wavering, vulnerable sound that touched the deepest part of me. I stopped beside a tree, picked her up, and she wrapped herself around me, her legs bare and thin and cold. "It's all right," I whispered. "It'll be all right."

I realized that she knew this kind of fear all the time. Possibly, she'd known it all her life. Perhaps Len's house was the first safe place she'd ever been. I couldn't fail her now. I couldn't fail myself. As much as I'd tried to tell myself that my ending up in this job was a random act of nature, I'd known for a while that it wasn't. This job was my calling, something I was meant to do. I hadn't just ended up here. I'd been brought here. Even a weary, tattered faith like mine knew that we're never given a calling without being given the resources to accomplish it. I still believed that.

I still believed.

Birdie shifted in my arms, tightened her fists over my shirt, holding it in handfuls. "Shhh," I whispered. Leaning against the cool bark of the tree, I closed my eyes, let the forest, the darkness, the mist fade away, heard only the whisper of my own thoughts, of a prayer. *Show me which way. Give me a sign. Find me.*

The night grew impossibly quiet, seeming to close in around us. Through the silence, I heard a song, the notes far away but clear, no two measures the same.

"Bird," Birdie whispered.

"I hear it, too," I said.

"Her a mockin' bird."

"Yes, a mockingbird." My mind traveled back to the picnic grounds along the river, to the mockingbirds. Could we be close by? What were the chances that we'd somehow circled back toward the river? I listened to the bird's repertoire, waiting for the Wailing Woman's telltale moan.

"Her cryin'," Birdie whispered, as if she'd read my mind. I felt Birdie's breath against my neck as she let out a long, low whistle that sounded like the Wailing Woman. I listened, but all I could hear was the bird. So far, it hadn't mocked the Wailing Woman's cry. Was it possible that Birdie was so in tune with the sounds of the lake that she could hear the Wailing Woman cliffs in the distance when I could not?

"Which way?" I asked. "Where do you hear the crying?"

Birdie pointed in the direction of the birdsong.

Setting her down, I caught a breath, felt hope flow through me. "You lead the way. Go toward the crying lady, all right?"

She didn't reply—just listened a moment, then started forward. I walked beside her, flailing my free arm ahead of me to protect us from branches. The moon was making a low loop over the horizon now, casting a dim light across the canopy, but on the forest floor, it was still impossibly black. Birdie seemed unbothered by the blackness, moving through it with an ease that seemed unnatural. As we followed the mockingbird's song, I heard the faint, far-off call of the Wailing Woman. An almost euphoric joy overtook me at the sense of finally knowing where I was. No one would be at the day-use picnic grounds this time of night. Birdie and I could go in the restroom building, lock the door, and we'd be safe and dry until I could figure out what to do next.

I sped up the pace, pushing branches out of the way, lifting Birdie over clumps of brambles and underbrush, scrambling up hills and tripping down hills, thinking that we must be close. But after an hour of wandering, we were still lost. In the woods at night, sounds traveled. The voices of the mockingbird and the Wailing Woman had been closer and farther away, closer and farther away, so that it seemed as if they were moving, tantalizing us, playing a game of cat and mouse. The truth, undoubtedly, was that we were walking in circles, following sounds that were bouncing off cliffs, and rocks and hills. Nothing was as it seemed, and in the dark, there were no landmarks. Birdie hung back now, once again uncertain of which way to go.

"Okay, honey, we have to stop. We have to stop for a while." I couldn't walk any farther, and neither could Birdie. What was the point, anyway? "We'll find a spot under one of these trees and wait until morning. Then we'll be able to see where we are." Would seeing make any difference? The state park covered thousands of acres. We hadn't come across a single sign of civilization in all this time. By now, we could be miles from anything recognizable.

I could feel Birdie watching me, confused, uncertain, afraid. If her mother and C.J. were any example of what she was accustomed to, she hadn't been able to rely on many people in her life.

Squinting into the darkened woods, I turned in a circle, trying to find a place that seemed safe. A breeze slid through the trees, and Birdie shivered, her teeth clattering. She pressed close to my leg, as if she were afraid I might leave her there in the dark. Overhead, the canopy rustled, swaying wildly. Thunder rumbled in the distance. I slipped my hands over Birdie's shoulders, holding her, looking up into the trees, thinking, *Please, no. Not a storm. Not now . . .*

Branches shivered apart atop the hill, and I saw something. A light. Not natural light from the moon, but something else. Something more intense. Headlights? Was there a road up there?

Birdie spotted it, too. She pointed, taking a step toward the glow as the branches closed again, and the light disappeared.

I grabbed her hand and said, "Let's go." My body, weary only a moment earlier, came to life. Swinging Birdie onto my hip, I struggled up the hill, my feet sinking into thick piles of dried leaves. As we drew closer, the headlights circled, strafing the trees, illuminating shapes beyond the underbrush—a stone barbecue grill, a table. The picnic grounds! The mockingbird and the Wailing Woman had led us to the park, after all.

The lights turned the other way, leaving only the dim glow of security lamps as we pressed through the last of the underbrush. I squinted through the darkness, trying to make out the vehicle . . . a Tahoe or a Suburban . . . brown or green . . . with some sort of official decal on the back. A park ranger, maybe? The truck was moving away, preparing to turn onto the county road.

"Wait!" I hollered, but my voice was hoarse after the night outdoors. "Wait!" The vehicle continued past the last picnic tables and left the park just as I made it to the edge of the pavement. Birdie swiveled in my arms, trying to see the vehicle as it roared away. Finally she slid to the ground, and we stood like shipwreck victims watching a boat disappear on the horizon.

"It's okay," I whispered, but having come so close to finding help, I felt more alone than ever, more helpless. A teary lump rose in my throat, and I swallowed hard. At least we'd made it to the park. We'd found shelter. The men's restroom door was closed, but the women's was hanging ajar. "Let's go inside." But even as I led Birdie into the tiny restroom building, closed the dry-rotted wooden door and locked it behind us, a cold blanket of fear settled over me, turning my skin clammy. As easily as the park ranger's vehicle could cruise through this place, Birdie's mother, C.J., and their accomplices could, too. The park was only a couple miles from Len's across country—farther via the road, but not that far. Perhaps they'd be watching to see if we showed up here. Maybe they were watching now.

I turned back to the door, held the latch hesitantly. Perhaps we were better off in the woods. . . .

Somewhere along the riverbank, a mountain lion cried out, the scream causing hair to rise on the back of my neck. I turned the lock and pulled my hand from the door, the decision made. The source of that call was way too close. Hugging Birdie to my chest, I slid to the floor, let my head rest against the door. "It's okay. We're safe here," I whispered. We had to be safe here. There was no other option.

Exhaustion washed over me, pulling my eyes closed, setting my mind adrift, pushing away the images from the night until they felt strange and unreal again. In the murky fog, my thoughts swam homeward, told me that in the morning I'd awaken on the sofa and none of this would be real.

The sounds of the forest faded, and Birdie's breaths grew long and even against my chest. I drifted and drifted, floating toward sleep, small shivers pulling me back, reminding me of where I was, vague apprehensions warning me not to let go, to stay awake and listen. Slowly, my skin warmed, the remnants of the daytime heat seeping from the thick stone wall and into my body. Sleep chipped away at my awareness, taking it a piece at a time. I felt myself sinking, then jerking awake as my head fell forward, then sinking again, deeper each time.

The screams on the hillside and the song of the mockingbird dimmed, and I was home. Safe. The night was clear and silent, warm inside the lake house. Outside the windows, a panorama of stars twinkled. In the distance, a motor hummed, slowly growing closer. Leaving the sofa, I hurried to the window, looked out across the water. Mart was coming. I opened the back door, ran down the hill, the grass damp and dewy beneath my feet. Overhead, a mourning dove cooed softly, the sound soft, hypnotic.

Mart was waiting on the dock. He gave a crooked grin beneath his cowboy hat and spread his hands. I crossed the dock, slipped into his arms. He lifted me and twirled me in a circle as I threw my head back, laughing, giddy like a young girl in love.

"You're here," I whispered against his skin. "You came."

"Did you think I wouldn't?" Setting me on my feet, he looked into my eyes, and I wondered how I could have ever thought about telling him good-bye.

He'd left the boat motor running. . . .

The sound was loud, growing louder, causing the ground to tremble under my legs. I turned away, trying to block out the noise, felt my head bob forward until I gathered an awareness of my surroundings again. I wasn't home. I wasn't with Mart.

The rumble of the engine remained. I jerked upright, adrenaline rushing through my body, pushing away the fog of sleep. A car door opened and closed.

Someone was outside the building.

I shifted, and Birdie squirmed drowsily in my lap, a soft gasp escaping her. "Shhh," I whispered against her ear.

Footsteps crunched on the gravel, came closer. I turned my ear toward the sound, straining to gather information.

The park ranger, maybe? Had he come back? Or someone else. The truck was running rough, a set of what Dustin called *glass packs* giving it a loud rumble that vibrated the ground. A state truck wouldn't have glass packs on it. . . .

Maybe the truck belonged to teenagers, out for a good time on Saturday night, or someone who'd been fishing or camping on the lake. Someone who could help us.

Maybe it belonged to C.J. and Norma. Their vehicle was loud.

Birdie twisted in my arms, swiveling toward the noise.

"Shhh," I whispered again. Someone was right outside the building. I heard him try the door on the men's restroom, twist it back and forth and rattle it hard against the frame, trying to gain entry. Apparently it wasn't just closed, but locked. Through the scalloped bricks near the ceiling, I could hear a man's breathing, the sound labored and impatient, angry. Pulling Birdie closer, I huddled in the shadow of the wall, scooting silently away from the stream of light that pressed through the tiny window overhead. A string of muttered curses followed as he smacked the men's room door, sending a thundering echo through the building.

Birdie jumped, then burrowed against me, whimpering at the noise, her body trembling. Clasping a hand over her mouth, I pulled her close and held her so as to smother any sound.

The footsteps moved across the gravel until they were right outside our door. I slid a hand silently upward, clasped the doorknob, grabbed tight, hoped the lock would hold. It jiggled and twisted in my hand as he tried to turn it in both directions, then he shook the door, so that it vibrated against my back.

Someone tapped the vehicle's horn, and Birdie let out a soft, fearful whine. I held my breath.

"Cud-it-out!" the man roared, his words thick and slurred. I tried to decide whether I recognized the voice.

A woman answered from the vehicle, only bits and pieces audible. ". . . ocked up . . . et's go!" Was that Norma? Or was it someone else?

I clung to the doorknob as the man answered with another string of obscenities, then slammed a fist against the door so hard that the frame splintered around the lock, the door bumping forward. I rolled onto my knees, depositing Birdie on the floor. Bits of wood plinked against the cement. *Please,* I cried out in my mind, bracing my shoulder against the door. *Please.*

Birdie scrambled into a restroom stall, her breath coming in ragged gasps. If he stopped cursing long enough, he'd hear her.

Be quiet. Be quiet now.

Thunder rumbled, and as if in answer, a long, eerie scream split the night, the sound bloodcurdling, so close it was deafening. Echoes pressed through the small screened window above, sending a primal chill over my skin, raising gooseflesh.

The intruder moved away from the door at the sound, muttering.

The woman's voice called out insistently, "Let's go! That thing's right there by the Dumpsters! I can see its eyes!"

Breath gushed into my lungs, then out, as I heard footsteps move away from the building. Moments later the truck door slammed, the engine roared, and they drove away.

I pressed myself against the door and didn't move. Birdie scrambled across the room, into my lap, and I hung on to her, rocking her until she quieted. Together we listened to the mountain lion prowling around the park, rifling through trash cans, looking for an easy meal. Finally the cat ate its fill and moved off into the woods.

Exhaustion slowed my heartbeat, seeped into my arms and legs, tugged my eyelids closed.

My mind came and went from the small stone building, until I couldn't keep it there any longer. I let go, let myself drift away again. No dreams tempted me this time. There was only darkness, only weariness.

When I awoke again, the soft gray light of dawn was pressing into the building. A sudden elation swirled through me at the realization that it was morning. We had made it through the night. I said a prayer of pure, heartfelt thanksgiving for the new day and realized it had been far too long since I'd done that—since I'd been grateful for simply being healthy and safe and greeting the sunrise. For the past year, I'd been so busy focusing on all the things that had gone wrong in my life, that I hadn't seen how truly blessed I was. But this morning I was thankful for all that I'd been taking for granted— my home, my family, my son, Moses Lake, my life . . .

In my lap, Birdie shifted. I looked at her and realized she had opened her eyes, fixed her gaze on the door handle. Someone was turning the lock—not attempting to force it, but opening it with the key. I slid away, tried to get up, but my legs were numb. The door creaked open. A flashlight beam came through along with the dawn. It settled on us.

"We've been looking for you," a voice said as my eyes adjusted to the sudden influx of light that made a silhouette of the man in the doorway. He was wearing a uniform of some sort. A park ranger? "State game warden," he said, but the voice wasn't Mart's. "You're safe now, ma'am."

Relief spiraled through me, tears pressing my eyes as he entered the room and set his flashlight on the sink. "Jake Moskaluk." He introduced himself while helping both of us to our feet, trying to ascertain whether we needed medical assistance.

"We're fine," I told him, clasping my hands together and pressing my thumbs hard against the base of my nose to keep from breaking down. "We're really all right."

When I looked up, he was thumbing over his shoulder toward his truck. "Guess I'd better radio that in. There's been a lot of folks worried about you two."

"Wait." I caught his arm before he could go. "Len . . . He was at his house. They were beating him . . ."

Jake's gaze slid to Birdie, and she watched him silently, waiting.

"The sheriff's deputies found him in the barn. Guess he'd crawled in there and hid himself in the hay. He'd been roughed up pretty good, but we got him to the hospital right away. Those dogs of his probably saved his life. Looked like somehow he'd gotten the back door of the house open while he was being knocked around, and the dogs had held that mob off just long enough for Len to get away."

"Oh, thank God." I realized that the dogs had probably saved our lives, too. They'd slowed C.J. and the others long enough for Birdie and me to reach the brush.

Bracing his hands on his knees, Jake leaned close to Birdie. "Your granddad's gonna be okay. He's got to have some surgery, but he's a tough old bird. The doctors are taking real good care of him, all right?"

Birdie nodded, her hand sliding to the hem of my T-shirt uncertainly.

Jake stood up. "I better go make the call before I get myself in trouble." As he walked to his truck, I turned on the water and stood looking at myself while Birdie cupped her hands and took a drink. I barely recognized the woman in the mirror. She was covered with tiny scratches from briars and brambles, her face smudged with dirt and mascara trails. Her hair hung in dark tangles encrusted with dirt and leaves. No one who knew me in my old life would have known her. No one would have believed Mrs. Karl Henderson capable of surviving such a night, of finding her way in the wilderness. But this woman in the mirror, Andrea, had done just that. Looking at her, I saw a little of Aunt Lucy, a bit of the woman I'd always wanted to be. The woman God created me to be.

Wetting a paper towel, I did my best to wash Birdie and myself while Jake made calls on his radio. When we walked out, he was waiting with blankets, a couple of Snickers bars, and bottled water from his cooler.

"Figured y'all had to be hungry, thirsty, and cold after last night," he said, laying a blanket on the tailgate, then lifting Birdie into it and bundling her up before giving her the candy bar and drink. I took a blanket and wrapped it around my shoulders. The day would be warm soon enough, but at the moment it was still foggy and dim, and I was chilled to the bone. All I wanted to do was go home, curl up on the sofa, and sleep.

"I just got the report that they caught the couple in the white Bronco. State police had been hunting them since the shootout at the cabin last night."

"Shootout?" Acid gurgled into my throat. Suddenly the idea of food seemed unappealing. "Is everyone all right? Was anyone hurt?"

Hooking a leg over the edge of the tailgate, Jake shook his head. "Oh, you know, we Fish and Game boys are bulletproof. To hear McClendon tell it, anyway. You can ask him about it yourself." He motioned toward the river, and I heard the whir of a motor somewhere in the thick, milky fog that eclipsed the Wailing Woman's cliffs and Eagle Eye Bridge. "Sounds like your ride's just about here."

Jake's voice seemed far away. My mind had slipped into the dream from last night—the one in which Mart sailed across the water and took me in his arms while the mourning doves cooed overhead. Somewhere nearby, a dove was cooing now. On the horizon, the sun inched above the hills, working its way toward the river channel to burn off the moisture and clear the day.

Holding the blanket around my shoulders, I took a few steps toward the river, squinted into the fog, tried to see who was coming. Even though the ranger had just assured me that C.J. and Norma were safely in custody, I couldn't shake the feeling that they were here, hiding in the fog, waiting.

The whir of the motor grew louder, fanned out and traveled on the fog, then separated. More than one boat was coming. I moved closer to the drop-off, stood high on the edge of the bank. Below, a little flock of mallards pulled their heads from under their wings and turned toward the noise, and in the trees, the mourning doves stopped cooing, as if even they were waiting in breathless anticipation.

Lights melted slowly out of the fog, drawing small circles in the mist, first one set, then two, then three, then four. The lead boat materialized, the bow first, then the windshield, then the man behind it, standing over the steering wheel with one foot braced on a cooler. Even in the morning shadows, I recognized him. I would have recognized him anywhere. Robin Hood.

An armada of merry men trailed behind him in a ragtag fleet of fishing vessels and aluminum boats. I recognized the people inside. Everyone I knew must have gotten involved last night when Mart was trying to find me—Burt and Nester, my parents, Meg and Oswaldo, Bonnie and Taz, Reverend Hay, Sheila, and even Pop Dorsey, wrapped in a neon-green life vest. When he saw me, he let out a yell and waved his hat over his head, like a cowboy swinging a lasso. Laughing, I waved back at him.

Mart pushed his boat up to full throttle, outdistancing the rest of them and reaching the park first. Swinging into the shore, he jumped from the boat and looped a line over a tree branch without even looking to see where it landed. Throwing off the blanket, I half ran, half slid down the rocky slope, bolted toward him with no thought as to how he would feel about it or who might be watching. He opened his arms and caught me, the impact driving him back a step and pushing a puff of air from him.

"Whoa, there," he said, pulling me close, his arms tightening around me, a strong, safe circle it seemed nothing could break. "Easy, now." He tucked my head beneath his chin, cradling me against his chest. I took in the feel of him, heard his heart beating beneath my ear. This was finally real. He was here.

Dimly, I heard the other boats pulling in—Jake talking, Sheila taking charge of Birdie, my mother worrying about how to get out of the boat, Meg crying and thanking God, Taz saying, "Good work, Henderson. I knew you were top shelf all along!" Nester asked how we'd been found, Pop Dorsey promised Birdie her pick of the penny candy, Jake related details about having discovered us in the restroom.

Mart pulled away from me, held my face in his hands and looked down, his eyes a warm, earthy green in the morning light. "You're all right." It was a question, a statement, a sigh of relief.

"We're fine." Tears pressed into my eyes, but I blinked them away. This wasn't a time for tears, even happy ones.

He slid a thumb across my cheek, catching a stray droplet of moisture. "Pretty good trick, finding your way through the woods in the dark."

I shrugged in a way that I hoped seemed cavalier. "Piece of cake. What do I look like, some kind of city slicker?"

"Not a bit." His gaze took me in, and I knew he didn't see the old me. He saw the woman who had stared back at me from the mirror this morning. Just Andrea. The one who'd finally found out what she was capable of, who she was meant to be. A rebel with a cause, a woman with a purpose.

"Besides," I said, "a guy once told me that all you had to do was listen, and you'd find your way to the water."

"Smart guy." He grinned that stupid, playful, crooked grin that I could have looked at forever. The idea sent a warm flush through my body, a sense that everything that had happened had been leading us here.

"Yeah, he is," I agreed, and then I kissed him. I was uphill, so I didn't even have to rise onto my tiptoes to do it. For once, my feet were firmly planted on the ground, firmly in my own life, and Mart was there, too, and I knew that was as it should be. I'd finally found my way—to him, to the future, beyond all that was unplanned and painful. Beyond fear, and regret, and shame, and bitterness, to a place in which I could let it all go and just be.

In the stillness was a voice, soft like the mourning dove, yet persistent like the endless refrains of the mockingbird. It beckoned me with its sweetness, warmed my soul, comforted my heart, promised that even when I'd been the loneliest, in the deepest despair, even when I thought I was lost in the darkness, I was never really alone. God had been there, even when I could not see Him, even when I could not hear His call, even when I denied His presence. He had been there in the wilderness, as He is in all places. I had only to be still, and listen, and let Him lead me home.

God prepares a banquet
in the lakes and the rivers and the forests.
Then He waits for us
to come to His table.
—Anonymous
(Left by a visitor who came and went unseen)

Chapter 24

Mart McClendon

There's something about Moses Lake that changes people. It's anybody's guess as to why that is, but I think that's what my mama was hoping for when we came here all those years ago. She was hoping my daddy would change. He might've, but he packed us up and left before the place could work on him. Before the Good Lord could use it that way.

For folks who stay a little longer, the hills, and the draws, and the water, and the people piece together like an old quilt, wrapping around, comfortable and warm. Safe. There's no mystery to it after a while. You just know you're in the right place. You feel it deep in your soul.

Even little Birdie could sense it—that assurance that everything would be all right. You could see it in her face when she ran out the doors of that old stone church, the ribbon streamers of

517

a little kite she'd decorated in Sunday school twirling behind her. Bolting downhill toward the water, she followed Sydney and Ansley's lead, all three of them laughing, holding their kites overhead, letting out the string a little, so that the streamers wobbled and dove.

Len hollered after her, "Ubb-Birdie, uww-watch out fer the uww-water!"

Beside him, Sheila glanced up and added, "Not too close now, girls!" With Sheila in his business, Len sure wouldn't have much chance to disappoint Social Services. She'd make sure all the I's were dotted and the T's were crossed, and she'd elected herself construction foreman for the volunteer work at Len's house, too. She had Len and the docksiders working so hard it was cutting into their fishing time, but so far nobody'd had the guts to complain. Today she'd even gotten Len all cleaned up and into a suit jacket with his old jeans. He glanced over his shoulder and shucked the jacket off on his way down the hill to the picnic tables, where the ladies were putting out dinner on the grounds. Normally, Sheila would've been in the middle of that, too, but at the moment, she was busy talking tofu, bean sprouts, and weight loss with Andrea's boss, Mr. Tazinski, and their office secretary, Bonnie. That wasn't much of a way to treat visitors, but Tazinski didn't seem to mind. Bonnie looked like she had her mind on sneaking peeks at Reverend Hay. I had a feeling he'd had more than just a friendly interest when he'd told Andrea to invite her co-workers to the dinner on the grounds that'd been postponed two weeks ago after the wild night in the woods. It felt good to have everyone here together—like all was right with the world.

From down by the tables, Andrea smiled at me and held up a chocolate pie she was pretending she'd baked. I knew that pie came out of the case at Catfish Charley's, because I'd driven her over there last night to meet her family for supper. But the secret about the pie was safe enough with me. Dustin was another story, though. He was still looking for a way to talk his mama into letting him take Cassandra out on a date, and that little bit of information about the pie might be just the leverage he needed. He was with us when that pie was bought, too. That dinner with the family had been a big step, but it was a good step. A good night for all of us. Nothing says getting-to-know-you like eating with a hundred-pound catfish looking over your shoulder.

It looked like Dustin hadn't gone completely teenage Romeo, though. When he caught sight of the girls trying to fly their kites, he left Cassandra behind and loped off down the hill to get in on the action. Before long, he had Sydney and Ansley's kites in the air and was trying to convince Birdie to give hers over, so he could launch it for her. Birdie shook her head and hung on tight while Len did his best to explain how the kite was supposed to function. Birdie didn't look like she believed him. She'd worked hard on that kite, and she didn't want to let it go.

Watching them reminded me of something my grandfather had said a long time ago when he took four little boys out to the hayfield with four new dime-store kites. He caught me keeping mine low—just letting it float up a few feet and then pulling it back, so it wouldn't get loose or tangle in a tree. He came across the field and knelt down next to me and said something I'd carried with me all my life but never taken to heart until I stood there watching Birdie, her blue eyes wide as she finally let go of her kite.

"A kite is like a man's life," my granddad had said as I weighed the choice between letting that kite soar and holding it down. "No matter how much he tries, he can't make it more than a piece of paper and a ball of twine, on his own. He's got to give it over to something bigger, let the Good Lord breathe into it. After that, he just has to do two things—turn his eyes toward heaven and keep hold of the string."

Acknowledgments

As the little town of Moses Lake, Texas, opens its doors for visitors, I'd like to thank a few people who joined this beach party early. As with every book, *Larkspur Cove* would never have come into being without the help of old friends, new friends, and kind strangers. Thank you first of all to Mike for tirelessly answering questions about all things related to the fascinating careers of state game wardens and for lending expertise to Mart's career. Thank you to Vickie for answering questions pertaining to Andrea's work as an LPC. Thanks to my favorite Wingate fisher-boys for answering fishing questions and lending funny fishing phrases to the wall of wisdom at the Waterbird Bait and Grocery. The docksiders wouldn't have had nearly as much fun without you.

My gratitude goes out to my family for tireless support. Thank you to my mother for editing, talking over stories, and for being a wonderful traveling companion. Thank you to my sweet mother-in-law for helping with address lists and feeding my boys on deadline days, when there's nothing at home that's nearly as exciting as

Nanny's cooking. Thanks also to relatives and friends far and near for encouraging, supporting, hosting us on book trips, sharing stories, and deciding that books make perfect Christmas gifts. I'm incredibly grateful to Teresa Loman for heading up the Facebook reader's group and being an incredibly fun gal pal, and to Ed Stevens for constant encouragement and help with all things technical. How blessed I am to have such wonderful friends! Thanks also to my friends and fellow Southern gal bloggers at www.Southern BelleView.com: authors Marybeth Whalen, Rachel Hauck, Jenny B. Jones, and Beth Webb Hart. What a hoot to be sharing a cyber-porch with you and blogging about all things Southern!

On the publishing end, my undying gratitude and heartfelt high-fives go to the incredible group at Bethany House Publishers. To Dave Long and Julie Klassen, thank you for being everything a writer could hope for in editors. Thanks for your guidance, astute suggestions, and encouragement, and for helping Moses Lake come to life. To the crew in marketing, publicity, and art—I so admire the awesome job you do in bringing the books to the shelves. To my agent, Claudia Cross at Sterling Lord Literistic, thanks again for all you do.

Last, but not least, gratitude beyond measure goes out to reader friends far and near, without whom I'd just be . . . well . . . some crazy lady tapping away on a computer and talking to myself. Thank you for sharing the books with friends, recommending them to book clubs, and taking time to send little notes of encouragement my way via e-mail and Facebook. Imaginary friends are great, but the real kind are ever so much better. They come with stories of their own, for one thing. Thank you, all of you, for being a blessing, a joy, and a treasure.

I hope you find a few treasures of your own in Moses Lake, and that this story returns the joy and the blessings in some small measure.

Discussion Questions

1. Moses Lake is a favorite vacation spot for many. Do you have a favorite vacation spot? A favorite vacation memory?

2. In the beginning of the story, Andrea feels hopeless about the turn her life has taken. Have you ever felt as if a closed door in your life was the end of everything good, only to find out that something new and amazing was right around the corner?

3. Andrea worries that because her life and her marriage have fallen apart, her son might never again be happy and healthy. How do traumatic family events in our childhoods shape us, strengthen us, or change the way we look at the world?

4. Mart has moved to the lake in an effort to leave behind the pain of his brother's death. Have you ever returned to a treasured childhood place in a moment of personal tragedy? In what ways do the places that harbor happy memories comfort us?

5. Andrea feels that because she has lost faith in God, God has lost faith in her. What is your opinion on this? What would you tell her?

6. Even though Birdie has clearly experienced trauma, and Len is in many ways unprepared to take care of her, Andrea and Mart elect to leave her with Len and try to improve Len's ability to parent her. What are the benefits of their plan? Risks? Do you agree with the plan or not?

7. In order for Len to succeed, the help of the community will clearly be needed. How can strong communities help members struggling through difficult situations? Has your community ever helped you in a time of need?

8. Even as adults, Andrea and Megan struggle with the aftereffects of strong sibling rivalry. How do old rivalries affect our adult relationships with siblings? Can we ever leave the past behind and be as gracious with siblings as we are with friends and acquaintances? How can we accomplish this?

9. Though both of their children are grown and are raising children of their own, Andrea's parents have a difficult time letting go and

allowing their girls to be independent adults. Have you ever struggled with an interloping parent? Have you ever been tempted to interlope? Are we always parents to our children, no matter how old they are? How do we set boundaries?

10. Andrea realizes her bitterness toward her ex-husband and members of her former church has helped to separate her son from his faith, causing him to be even more alone in the world. How do our parents' beliefs affect us? Have you seen or experienced situations in which a parent's lack of faith affects a child?

11. In her new job, Andrea finally feels a sense of purpose and of finding herself. Have you ever found yourself blooming in an unexpected time or place? In what way? Do you have a dream that hasn't yet been realized? What it is?

About the Author

Lisa Wingate is a popular inspirational speaker, magazine columnist, and national bestselling author of several books, including *Tending Roses*, *Talk of the Town*, *Good Hope Road*, *Drenched in Light*, and *A Thousand Voices*. Her work was recently honored by the Americans for More Civility for promoting greater kindness and civility in American life. Lisa and her family live in Clifton, Texas.

Visit Lisa at her Web site, *www.lisawingate.com*.

Center Point Publishing
600 Brooks Road ● PO Box 1
Thorndike ME 04986-0001 USA

(207) 568-3717

**US & Canada:
1 800 929-9108**
www.centerpointlargeprint.com